Book IV
Gamadin: GAZZ

Book IV

GAMADIN™

GAZZ

Tom Kirkbride

WIGTON

Publishing

Published by Wigton Publishing Company
1611 S. Melrose Drive, Suite A214
Vista, CA 92081-5471

For ordering information or special discounts for bulk purchases, please contact:

Wigton Publishing Company, 1611 S. Melrose Drive, Suite A214
Vista, CA 92081-5471, (760) 630-2181

Design and composition by Silvercat.

Publisher's Cataloging-In-Publication Data
(Prepared by The Donohue Group, Inc.)

Kirkbride, Tom (Thomas K.)
    Gamadin. Book 4, GAZZ / Tom Kirkbride. -- 1st ed.

    p. : ill., maps; cm.

    ISBN: 978-0-9840643-6-6

1. Extraterrestrial beings--Fiction. 2. Space warfare--Fiction. 3. Surfers--California--Fiction. 4. Science fiction. 5. Fantasy fiction. I. Title.

PS3611.I75 G264 2011
813 / .6

Printed in China

10 09 08 10 9 8 7 6 5 4 3 2 1
First Edition

For my Aunt Millie

The *Millie*

1. Mowgi's Perch (Bowsprit)
2. Spinnaker Sail **
3. Fore Sail
4. Main Sail & Main Mast
5. Mizzen Sail
6. Gamadin Pennant
7. Crow's Nest
8. Ratlines
9. Forecastle
10. Main Deck
11. Quarterdeck & Ship's Wheel
12. Poop Deck
13. Captain's Quarters
14. Bow
15. Gun Deck & Gun Ports
16. Turbo Propeller & Hatch **
17. Stern
18. Rudder
19. 54th Century Keel **
20. Port Side (Left)
21. Starboard Side (Right)
22. Hanging Black Knife Talisman

** Modern devices not found on 16th century-type galleons

Illustrations by Author

And all I ask is a tall ship and star to steer by,
And the wheel's kick and the winds song and the white sails shaking
And the gray mist on the sea's face and a gray dawn breaking."

John Masefield (1878-1967)
Sea Fever (1902), st.1

When I came here, I gave an oath to God,
I didn't give an oath to be God.

Assoc. Justice Clarence Thomas,
U.S. Supreme Court
October 1, 2007

Who were the Gamadin?

Many, many thousands of years ago, when Hitt and Gibb were the cultural elite centers of the Omni quadrant, the Gamadin ruled the cosmos -- not in an authoritarian way, but as a protective force against the spreading Death of evil empires and their acts of conquest and domination. A wise and very ancient group of planets from the galactic core formed an alliance to create the most powerful police force the galaxy had ever seen. This force would be independent of any one state or planet. They were called "Gamadin."

Translated from the ancient scrolls of Amerloi, Gamadin means: "From the center, for all that is good." The sole mission of the Gamadin was to defend the freedom and happiness of peaceful planets everywhere, regardless of origin or wealth. It was said that a single Gamadin ship was so powerful, it could destroy an empire.

Unfortunately, after many centuries of peace, the Gamadin had performed their job too well. Few saw reason for such a powerful presence in their own backyard when the Death of war and the aggressive empire building were remnants of an ancient past. So what was left of the brave Gamadin simply withered away and was lost, never to be heard from again.

However, the ancient scrolls of Amerloi foretold of its resurrection:

"For it is written that one day the coming Death will lift its evil head and awaken the fearsome Gamadin of the galactic core. And the wrath of the Gamadin will be felt again throughout the stars, and lo, while some people trembled in despair, still more rejoiced; for the wrath of the Gamadin will cleanse the stars for all; and return peace to the heavens . . . ."

1

And the Winner is...

"The envelope please!" Ms. Marleigh requested.

It was Oscar night in Hollywood. The Dorothy Chandler Pavilion in Los Angeles, with its grand crystalline chandeliers, wide curving stairways, golden rich décor complimented the three thousand-plus glamorous Academy attendees decked out in black-tie and high fashion attire.

At the top of this star-studded heap was Phoebe Marleigh, the hottest starlet in Tinseltown, who would be announcing the winner for Best Actor. To leave no doubt in anyone's mind that she deserved every penny of her eight-figure-per-picture stardom—plus residuals— she showed up in a sheer, beige vest over a long, sequined, black, hand-made Dolce and Gabanna column dress, open clear up to the thigh. The audience gawked in awe at every inch of her five-foot-eleven, statuesque form as she twirled around in killer black heels. A beautiful courier appeared on stage and handed her the envelope.

Phoebe Marleigh leaned into the mike as she opened the envelope. "And the winner for Best Actor in a Leading Role of a Major Motion Picture goes to..."

Adding drama to the moment, she took her time removing the card from the large white envelope. When she saw the name of the winner, her bright blue eyes turned as round as twin saucers. She coughed, her red lips forcing a strained look of disbelief as she stuttered the winner's name. The surprise was genuine. "Si... Simon Bolt?"

She looked up at an auditorium of open mouths and stunned silence. The audience seemed as bewildered as Ms. Marleigh. Then someone in the back began to clap, and as the crescendo slowly rose across the theatre, she went on with her announcement: "For his leading role in the science fiction blockbuster of the decade... *Distant Suns!*"

*   *   *

A half-world away, it was sunny and hot, and the deep blue waves were cranking off an unknown atoll in the South Pacific. In the sweet spot of a perfect tube, Harlowe Pylott was getting it on, cutting across the glassy face of a twelve-foot wave with his brother Dodger, when quite unexpectedly, an unworldly winged predator swooped down from the sun and snatched Harlowe off his board. The dragon rose in the air before it fell back toward the beach and dropped the fuming teenager on the white sandy beach.

Harlowe jumped to his feet, dusting sand from his body as he glared at the shrinking beast transforming back to his normal dog-like self. "Mowgi, you toad! I was having the ride of the day!"

When the transformation was complete, the undog jumped into Harlowe's arms as if he hadn't seen him for a month. Truth was, Mowgi had been with Harlowe yesterday at 42nd Street in Newport Beach, California. Parked not too far away was the rover that the Gamadin crew endearingly called the "grannywagon." The sleek, wheelless 54th-century vehicle reminded Riverstone of his grandmother's 1957 red and white Buick Century Estate Wagon with big chrome bumpers, big steering wheel and thick cushy seats his grandmother still drove at age 91!

In the back of the grannywagon was an assortment of surfboards and baseball supplies Harlowe and Dodger had brought with them across the Pacific at Mach 2 on their short surf escape before the start of the school year.

The atoll was uninhabited and had no name because it was barely a pixel of ink on any sea chart. Covering about the same area as Lu's Place on Mars, its small grove of coconut trees was surrounded by a wide, sandy beach and an ocean of clear blue-green water. As high, fluffy clouds floated above in a deep blue sky and glistening waves broke flawlessly just beyond the reef, the tiny islet was a perfect example of paradise found.

Harlowe scratched Mowgi behind a large parabolic ear. "How did you find me, Mowg? I didn't tell anyone I was coming here, not even that beautiful green-eyed girlfriend of mine." Harlowe knew from experience, however, that wherever the undog was, Leucadia Mars was close by.

He looked high into the deep blue tropical sky and saw nothing except gulls and clouds. "So where is she, Mowg?"

Mowgi yipped twice, his normal reply for "yes."

The wait was short. As Dodger stepped out of the surf carrying both his surfboard and Harlowe's, a Mars Corporate helicopter thundered over the tops of the tall coconut palms behind them. The chopper banked once over the surf, swung around, and gracefully touched down near the grannywagon. Leucadia stepped out onto the sand, and the tall, leggy goddess strutted toward Harlowe like a Vogue model with long blonde hair flowing in waves behind her. Her step appeared so light Harlowe wondered if she left footprints in the sand. As usual she was dressed to impress. She wore a stylish, white linen blouse from Paris over a flowing white sundress from Milan. Once away from the whirling blades, she turned to the pilot and signaled for him to take off.

Harlowe watched as if she had been sent from the heavens. *Man, she's hot!*

* * *

Simon lifted the Oscar proudly above his head as he stood at the podium in front of the crowd of reporters. Never letting an opportunity for publicity go to waste, Phoebe Marleigh was all smiles standing next to him, basking in the digital flashes of hundreds of photos of the two Hollywood superstars.

"How does it feel to be the first science fiction actor ever to be awarded the top prize, Mr. Bolt?" a reporter asked.

"Humbling," Simon replied with no hesitation.

Ex-pro football star Michael Stenkman didn't bother raising his hand for Simon to call on him. His six-feet-five, two-hundred-sixty-pound frame was all the credentials he needed to put himself at the head of the line. "You seem much more confident and self-assured than when you destroyed the furniture at the Beverly Hilton two years ago, Simon," Stenkman began arrogantly. "What caused the transformation, dude?"

"A long journey."

"Rehab?" Stenkman questioned, displaying a crafty smile.

"You might say that."

"Whoa, tell us more!"

"I already have," Simon replied. "You saw the movie. That was my story."

"But that was science fiction," Stenkman retorted with a distrusting snicker.

Simon eyed the reporter, deadly serious. "For you maybe, but not for me."

"You lived it, huh?"

"Every day."

The crowd of reporters laughed at the absurdity.

Stenkman wasn't about to let this opportunity for a headline go to waste. The other reporters, eager to hear more, urged him on. "Really, Mr. Bolt, how does a B-actor become an Oscar winner overnight?"

Simon's face turned somber. "By becoming part of something no one in this room could imagine."

"Did you find God, Mr. Bolt?" a woman reporter asked thoughtfully. She was serious and her tone considerate. She wasn't trying to be flip, like the others.

"Yes, in a way I did, Miss," Simon replied. Again his answers were concise and filled with conviction. If the subject matter had been anything other than off-worldly, many might have believed him.

Another reporter asked, "Phoebe, can you shed some light on what happened to Mr. Bolt?"

The starlet took the solid arm of the six-foot-six, physically fit movie star and replied, "No. I can't. But who cares? What a hunk he's become, huh, ladies?"

The women reporters giggled like starstruck teenagers at the thought of having a date with Hollywood's newest Oscar winner.

"Will you and Ms. Marleigh be going to the post-*Vanity Fair* Oscar party together?" a lady reporter asked Simon.

Phoebe's ruby red lips smiled at the audience, knowing the answer was obvious. Of course they would!

Simon answered her politely, "I'm afraid I must decline. But if a friend of mine was here, he would swim through sharks to be Phoebe's date tonight!"

Phoebe released Simon's arm, stunned that he had jilted her in front of billions around the globe.

Stenkman asked skeptically, "Where is this friend, Mr. Bolt?"

"On a planet far, far away," Simon joked.

"A journey all his own, huh?" a reporter asked.

"Yes, a journey, and a very important one at that."

Stenkman snickered, "Doing God's work, hey Simon?"

"Doing work for all us," Simon replied soberly.

Stenkman looked over the crowd, smiling arrogantly. "Like Captain Starr, your friend is saving the galaxy. Isn't that right, Simon?"

The room laughed again.

"If you only knew, Stenkman," Simon replied.

Stenkman turned back to Simon. "When can I get an interview with the galaxy's savior, Mr. Bolt?"

Before Simon could answer, someone in the crowd cried out, "So you can destroy him like you did General McRubie?"

Stenkman turned to the direction of the accuser. "I didn't destroy McRubie. He destroyed himself. The General's comments were about the President. The world had to know."

"You sandbagged him," another voice said.

Stenkman squinted, trying to find the voice in the bright lights. Before he could locate the testy reporter, a bookish-looking girl with glasses warned him, "Be careful, Michael, you may find yourself on a planet far, far away if you pursue Mr. Bolt's friend."

Stenkman sneered. He didn't believe in aliens, abductions, or anything remotely related to off-world mumbo-jumbo. He didn't believe in God, country, or apple pie, for that matter, and made fun of those who did. He was famous for brown-nosing his way into someone's life, then doing a hatchet job later in his Internet news blog. He was proud of having destroyed more careers than he created. He scoffed at her, dismissing her caution with a small, disdainful chuckle. "I would find that fascinating, wouldn't you?"

"Very."

"Maybe someday I'll get the opportunity."

"The sooner the better," another voice cracked. "Can we move on, please?"

The crowd clearly had enough of Stenkman and returned to the man of the hour. "So you'll be going alone to the Vanity Fair party, Mr. Bolt?"

Simon extended his hand out to a six-foot three-inch vision sauntering toward him from the sidelines with long platinum hair and dark glasses. "No, I already have a date."

Phoebe Marleigh's mouth dropped open as she quickly went from the Oscar night's Number One hottest babe down to Number Two.

"Ladies and gentlemen, may I introduce my very special girl?" He took her hand and announced. "This is Sizzle, the future Mrs. Bolt."

2

GRB

Leucadia and Harlowe embraced and kissed as if they had been away from each other for weeks instead of a day.

"Oh, yuckeeeee," Dodger cried out, his face contorting in twenty different directions at the sight of their greeting. It was another one of the most embarrassing moments of his life.

Harlowe and Leucadia broke their clinch, chuckling. "It's just Lu, pard," Harlowe said.

Dodger turned away. "Yucky, yucky, yucky!" He had seen enough.

Leucadia watched Dodger walk away in disgust. "You think he's damaged?"

Harlowe nodded with a smirk. "I'll call Rerun's shrink when we get back."

They smiled at the thought while still in each other's arms. Harlowe wanted to finish what they started, but Leucadia felt that displaying any more affection in front of an eleven-year old who still thought girls had cooties was inappropriate. They parted as Leucadia turned her attention to the waves of perfect glass. "How's the surf, Captain?" she asked.

Harlowe pointed at the undog. "Fun until Big Ears plucked me off my board. What's up with that?"

Leucadia defended the chinneroth. "You went surfing without telling anyone where you were going."

"That was the plan."

"Bad boy."

"Even Gamadin captains get a day off, Lu."

She kissed him on the cheek, then made an observation. "When you command the most powerful war bird in the galaxy, you don't get days off, Captain Pylott."

Harlowe lifted her sunglasses over her forehead so her bright green eyes were unobstructed. "So why are you here? You didn't fly here because you miss me."

Leucadia forced a smile as her eyes confronted his intense blue stare. "True. Matthew will fill you in."

Harlowe was surprised. "Riverstone? He's still on Tomar."

"He's been trying to reach you since yesterday."

Harlowe and Leucadia walked toward the grannywagon, where Dodger was laying the surfboards on the sand.

"Can I go on the next mission with you and Captain Starr, Harlowe?" Dodger asked.

"Who said anything about a mission? Even if there was one, you're going nowhere. You've got school, pard."

Harlowe's words fell on deaf ears. "I've never been on a spaceship before!"

"I said no."

"There's no school for two weeks."

"*Nada*, end of discussion."

"Aw, geez! I never get to go anywhere in outer space."

Harlowe turned Dodger's shoulders around toward the surfboards still lying on the beach where he had dropped them. "Stow those boards before I pull a Mom on you."

Dodger's head slumped. He went away kicking sand and mumbling lines like "It's not fair," and "Why can't I go to other worlds, too?"

As they watched Dodger dragging his feet toward the boards, Leucadia commented, "He will make a good Gamadin one day."

Harlowe locked eyes with Leucadia. "Don't tell Tinker that. One Gamadin in the family is enough for her."

Leucadia looked at Harlowe thoughtfully. "Do you miss being a boy, Harlowe?"

Harlowe's focus went back to the waves. "Does it matter?"

"Just wondering."

"It's done, Lu. My boyhood was lost when Simon's boat went belly up and I plucked you out of the water," he said.

"Would you do it again?"

"Knowing what I know now?"

"Knowing everything?" Leucadia replied.

Harlowe let her stew as he thought about where Fate took him that day when he rescued her from the sinking boat. Would he have changed his mind?

Leucadia's frown intensified. "Harlowe, you're taking too long."

"I'm thinking."

"You would do it all over again, wouldn't you?"

"Maybe. Maybe not."

She grabbed his arm and twisted it behind his back. "Tell me the truth, or I'll break your arm."

In one quick motion, he was out of her hold, tossing her high into the air. He flipped her around and was about to slam her down hard. Then he abruptly stopped her fall an inch off the sand. "Pluck me off a wave again like that and I'll make you walk the plank."

Their noses touching, she purred, "Sounds like a threat."

They kissed again.

Harlowe's steel blue eyes didn't waver. "It is."

In the distance a voice cried out, "Yucky, yucky!"

Ignoring the audience of one, they kissed again.

"Arrrdy Arr Arr," Leucadia said, imitating the tone of a medieval pirate.

"I'll shackle you in a dark, rat-infested bilge for being disrespectful to your captain," Harlowe added.

Leucadia smiled defensively, believing Harlowe was teasing her. "You wouldn't."

Harlowe's brow knotted. Maybe he would, maybe he wouldn't. "Don't test me, Ms. Mars, or you might find furry rodents as your new roommates."

She laughed as Harlowe lifted her to her feet. Hand in hand they returned to the grannywagon. Harlowe reached into the back seat and picked up the com that had been lying untouched for the past two days. He switched it on and an instant later a holographic image of Riverstone materialized at eye level in front of them.

"Hey, Toadface, what's so urgent? Can't find a date for Friday night on Tomar?" Harlowe joked.

Riverstone faced the screen the instant he heard his voice. It didn't take Rerun's shrink to see that Riverstone's mood was serious. This was an "on-the-clock" business call. "Dog, where have you been?" His gaze focused on the surf behind Harlowe. "You've been surfing?"

Harlowe's reply was testy. "Yeah, I've been surfing. Why does everyone have a problem with that?"

"Because a GRB is about to strike Gazz, Dog!"

Harlowe glanced at Leucadia. "What's a GRB?"

Leucadia and Riverstone answered together. "A gamma-ray burst!"

Harlowe glared at Leucadia briefly before he asked Riverstone, "So, what is it?

Riverstone searched for an answer. "I'm not sure what it is. That's what Lu and Wiz called it."

Leucadia took her cue and replied, "It's an intense beam of electromagnetic radiation released when a star goes supernova. It's serious, Harlowe. It kills most life forms in its path."

"That's right, Dog. Sharlon says if we don't stop it from hitting Gazz, the planet's toast."

"Many scientists believe a GRB may have killed the dinosaurs on Earth," Leucadia added.

"I thought it was a meteor," Harlowe said.

"My calculations show it was a GRB," Leucadia stated, as if her conclusion was the correct one.

Unlike Riverstone, Harlowe never doubted her conclusions. When it came to science, Leucadia knew far more than the brightest minds on Earth. "Gazz is a planet?" he asked.

Riverstone cut in. "Yeah, here in the Omini Quadrant, Dog. We're the only ones who can stop it."

Harlowe wondered aloud, "Why can't Gazz handle the burst?"

It was Leucadia's turn again. "Because they don't have the technology. Gazz is a medieval planet. It's like being back on Earth 600 years ago. They sail wind-driven galleons, fight pirates, and fire cannonballs and muskets with black powder."

Riverstone added impatiently. "Sharlon has been there. It's a backward place, Dog. No In-N-Outs, no shakes, no Internet."

Leucadia's eyes turned grave. "Millie is the only hope for the planet, Harlowe."

Harlowe wanted Ian in on the conversation. He adjusted his com again and a second screen materialized next to Riverstone. Ian was sitting in his center command chair onboard *Millawanda's* bridge.

Ian spoke right away. "We've been trying to find you for two days, Dog. Where have you been?" Like Riverstone, Ian saw the waves breaking in the background. "You've been surfing?"

Harlowe's eyes rolled skyward. "What's your take on this gamma thing, Wiz?" Harlowe asked.

"It's narly, Captain."

"I got that. Where'd the burst come from?"

On yet a third screen, Ian displayed interstellar graphics to illustrate the problem. "Fifty years ago this star went supernova. When it exploded, it emitted a burst of electromagnetic radiation right at Gazz like a rifle shot." In slow motion the graphic showed how the intense beam would strike the earth-like planet with its deep blue oceans and green vegetation, turning its surface into lifeless cinders.

"How do we stop it?" Harlowe asked. "This isn't a bad guy we can just shoot and call it a day, is it?"

"Lu has a plan," Ian and Riverstone said together, as if they knew their lines beforehand.

"So I'm the last one to hear of this?" Harlowe asked.

"You were surfing," Leucadia, Ian and Riverstone said, like a well-rehearsed trio.

Harlowe ignored the dig and faced Leucadia. "You have a plan, huh?"

As Leucadia explained the details, Ian placed a holographic image of Gazz with *Millawanda* in high orbit above the planet so they could all follow along. "By modifying Millie's force field we can extend her shields like a protective umbrella over the planet's stratosphere. The lethal rays will bounce off of her field and Gazz will live happily ever after."

Harlowe's faced turned pensive. "Millie can do that?"

"Lu says it's a slam-dunk," Riverstone added.

"Well, not exactly a slam-dunk. There are some risks," Leucadia cautioned.

Harlowe stated the obvious. "There usually are. What are they?"

Ian was comfortable with the plan. "I've run the simulations. It's nothing Millie can't handle, Captain."

Harlowe pressed his lips together. Did he have a choice? With all the life forms of an entire planet on the line, was there a risk too great? "How much time do we have?"

Ian glanced up at the overhead control screen. "10 days, 3 hours, 22 minutes and counting."

"Travel time?"

"At top cruising speed…a week, Captain," Ian replied. "We should get there in plenty of time to set up before the GRB fries everything."

Harlowe had the problem clear in his head now and the urgency to move. It appeared this his surf holiday was being cut short. "Is Millie's force field ready, Wiz? I need an answer, not a guess," Harlowe stated straight out.

"Aye, Captain. She's ready. By the time we reach Gazz, Lu and I will have worked out all the kinks."

Harlowe's thoughts were always on the safety of the ship and his crew. Whenever he heard the word, "slam-dunk," his stomach lurched. Leaving Earth in *Millawanda* was never trouble-free. He trusted his crew to give him all the minuses along with the pluses. The problem was always, *always*, the hidden glitches that no one ever anticipated.

Harlowe sighed, looking at Leucadia with a face full of doubt. "A slam-dunk, huh?"

She took his hand. "Don't worry, Captain. Everything will be all right. We have time. That's important. Millie will be ready."

Harlowe glared at Leucadia. "You hurt my ship and you will walk the plank. That's a promise!" Without allowing her to say anything more, he turned back to the com screen and said to Ian, "You and Prigg had better wrap it up. Where are you?"

"At the bottom of the Marianas Trench," Ian replied. He and Prigg had taken *Millawanda* to the lowest point on Earth to pick up a few rock samples and tiny sea life for Professor Farnducky's science class.

"We're packing up now, Captain. We'll see you in a couple of hours," Ian replied.

Harlowe signed off with Ian, then tilted his face toward the sun, feeling its hot soothing rays all over his body. After a moment of harmony with heaven and earth, he said to Leucadia. "Thanks for helping out with Prigg's family."

"A little more than you expected, huh?"

"A little."

What had started out as a Good Samaritan trip back to Prigg's home planet, Naruck, got a little carried away. For weeks upon his return to Earth, Harlowe fretted about leaving Prigg behind with his wife and eight little Priggs on a radioactive planet. It broke his heart, thinking about his little crewman surrounded by radioactive waste and toxins. He'd be unable to look at himself in the mirror if he didn't do something to save his friend, so Harlowe returned to Naruck and brought Prigg and his *whole* family back to Earth to live. And by "whole" family, Harlowe learned that Prigg couldn't leave unless *all* of his relatives, three generations back, went with him.

"My wife will be so lonely without them, Your Majesty," Prigg said to Harlowe.

Harlowe felt like Moses leading his people out of Egypt as he loaded all 322 Priggs and Prigglets up *Millawanda's* rampway that day!

"Thank the President. He found the abandoned military complex in Nevada a hundred miles from the nearest human."

"Perfect."

Leucadia turned concerned. "You think the desert will be all right for them?"

"Naruckians aren't water people. Trust me, it's like Rodeo Drive compared to where they came from. They'll be happy as a *chee* in heat there."

"I hope it's not too much work for Mrs. Prigg while Prigg is away."

"I gave Prigg a couple of clickers to help with the clean up and the kids. You should have seen his three eyes light up."

Leucadia giggled at the thought as Harlow's re-focused on the surf. To his disappointment, the waves had lost their form. The wind had shifted, turning the glassy pipes to lumpy white chop. He had hoped for a full day of riding perfect tubes, but now he had to save a planet. "Baseball, anyone?" was the only choice left.

The look of disappointment on Dodger's face quickly changed. "Can I bat first?"

Harlowe reached in the back of the grannywagon and pulled out a bat and ball.

"Baseball?" Leucadia asked suspiciously as she looked over the tiny island for any place to play. "Here on a deserted beach?"

"Yes, on the beach. Wanna play?"

"I don't play baseball."

"Try it. It's fun."

"Just the three of us?"

"Don't be a dweeb." Harlowe pointed down the beach. "Our *Field of Dreams*, Gamadin style, is right out there."

To Leucadia's astonishment, standing out on the wide-open white sandy beach were robobs, where a second ago there was only sand. The clickers were all decked out in blue Dodger baseball caps, jerseys with numbers and real leather mitts.

Dodger took the bat from Harlowe and introduced the players. "That's Pitch on the mound, Lu," he said, stepping over to home plate. "Twobagger's on second. Shortstop is over there between second and third. Homerun in left field, Moneyball is center, and the one over there in right field is Zinger. Watch out for him. He a charmer, Lu." Zinger politely removed his cap and bowed to Leucadia.

Leucadia giggled at Zinger's advance and blew the robob a kiss, followed by a seductive wink. "He's a handsome dude."

Harlowe placed the baseball in the robob's mitt behind the plate. "And this is Catch."

Catch took the ball and rifled it to Pitch on the mound, who caught the ball easily.

"You're missing two," Leucadia pointed out. "Who's on first and third?"

Pitch brought his mitt and ball together and waited for Dodger to step into the batter's box.

"No one," Harlowe replied. "Trust me, after you see them on defense, you'll wish there was just Pitch out there."

Dodger tapped the holographic home plate on the sand and took a couple of practice swings before nodding he was ready for the first pitch. Pitch wound up and tossed a BB down the middle. Dodger nailed it, smacking a line drive that looked like a Major League double. Not so! Twobagger dove, stabbing the liner out of the air, robbing Dodger of a hit.

One out!

Dodger slammed the bat down in disgust as Leucadia stared in disbelief at the robob's skill. "I see what you mean."

Harlowe smiled. "Narly team, aren't they?"

* * *

The rules for beach baseball were slightly different than normal baseball rules. Each player stayed at bat until three outs were recorded. No one ran bases in beach baseball. Base runners were imaginary. To get a base runner, the batter had to hit a ball on the fly over an imaginary line drawn between first and second, or third and second. A hit was one on, two hits, two on and so forth. To score a run, a batter had to get at least four hits before the third out. Five hits scored two runs, unless the batter hit a home run over an outfielder's head, after which the batter needed four more hits to score another run. Three strikes was an out. A ground ball was also an out, as was a foul ball. No one ever walked in beach baseball because Pitch never threw anything that wasn't a strike. After three outs, it was the next batter's turn. When everyone had a turn at bat, the inning was over. Like regular baseball, a complete game was nine innings.

A game never lasted more than an hour because the clickers were so good on defense. But after two hours this afternoon, two innings still remained. The score was Dodger-2, Harlowe-5 and Leucadia- 21. Not since Quay had Harlowe ever seen anyone hit the ball as hard and as far as Leucadia. It was yet another side of her he had never seen before. She had just cleared the bases with her second grand slam of the inning.

Suddenly the air became still as if all life had stopped. Leucadia and Dodger turned to Harlowe, looking for answers. Should they be worried?

Harlowe wasn't worried. He nodded toward the water, at the waves that had become flat and the ocean that had turned as still as the air. Had the entire ocean suddenly morphed into a peaceful lake? About a mile out from the shoreline, a pale blue light spread across the surface.

Leucadia again turned to Harlowe, looking for his reaction. Even in the middle of the Pacific Ocean, the owner of the world's most powerful corporation still had enemies. Her security forces were hundreds of leagues away. If by some chance her security had been breached, the chances of anyone helping the three of them were slim. They were on their own.

Harlowe remained unfazed. There was nothing to fear. He put a comforting arm around her and brought her closer. "It's only Millie," he said calmly while they watched the golden dome of the mighty ship break the surface and rise slowly out of the sea.

Dodger forgot about the game, the waves, and everything else they had come to the island for. The sight of something as large as six nuclear aircraft carriers rising from the ocean was enough to blow any ten-year-old's mind. "Wow, Harlowe, that's your ship?"

Harlowe stared with boundless pride at his sleek gold ship drifting toward them as if it were the first time he had ever laid eyes upon her. "Yeah, that's her, Dodger."

"Why is she rising out of the water?" Dodger wondered. "Shouldn't she be coming from outer space?"

"Wiz and Prigg have been doing a little underwater exploring," Harlowe explained.

"Your spaceship can do that?"

"As easily as she flies in the air."

"WOW!"

Leucadia saw Harlowe's devotion to his Gamadin ship. She put her arms around him. "My mother would be so proud."

Harlowe watched as the massive ship overhead dwarfed the atoll. "Dodger, say hello to *Millawanda,* the hottest babe in the galaxy."

Dodger jumped up and down with excitement. "She's so cool!"

Harlowe turned back to Leucadia and said, "I'll see ya in a couple of weeks."

There was a hint of *not-so-fast* in her reaction. "I'm coming, too," Leucadia said.

Harlowe was having none of that noise. "Not a chance."

"Ian can't handle the calculations alone," she stated.

Harlowe leaned into her face before he picked up the surfboard Dodger had left beside the grannywagon. "You show him what to do." He put the surfboard in the back and then tapped an activator on the dash that sent the grannywagon racing toward the mothership by itself.

"You're meeting up with Matthew and Sharlon," Leucadia said.

"So?"

"Sharlon is Neejian. I want to meet her."

"It's not happening, Lu. It's never that easy. You're staying here."

"She's from my mother's home world."

Mowgi yipped twice.

Harlowe pointed a finger at the undog's snout. "You keep your green tongue out of this!"

"I insist!"

Harlowe pounded his chest. "I'm the Captain." He pointed at *Millawanda* next. "That's my ship. What I say goes. You're not going."

"That's not fair!"

"Life's not fair."

"Harlowe..."

"You have enough to do here. Don't you have a couple of acquisitions to make or congressmen to elect?"

"The election is over and Tinker and Digger, I mean our new president, are busy redecorating the White House. I'm as free as a bird," Leucadia said, taking his muscular tanned arm as she charmed him with her feminine logic. She was hard to resist. "Sizzle wants to go, too."

"Sizzle?"

Leucadia looked sad. "She wants to see her mother."

"Is Rerun down with that?"

"It's not his decision, Harlowe. It's Sizzle's."

Harlowe had seen the disappointment in Sizzle since coming to Earth. He wondered if their relationship was suffering, seeing the way she appeared less and less excited by the future plans Simon had for them, especially marriage, being so young. From the private conversations they had when Simon was away filming *Distant Galaxy*, she wanted to do more with her life, like Quay, she told him. Not even Leucadia was aware that she wanted to be a part of the Gamadin mission, not a spectator. She wanted to follow her sister and maybe even find her one day.

In any case, it was Simon's problem, not his. When his crew was off the clock, he made it a rule not to interfere with their personal lives unless it affected the smooth running of his ship. He had enough problems of his own. He stared at Leucadia's bright green eyes thinking of an old Star Trek movie: *Resistance is futile.* "I'm not winning this one, am I?" he asked.

"Just say, 'yes dear' and get it over with."

Harlowe was about to give it one last shot when Dodger yelled back, pleading, "Can I go, too, Harlowe?" The kid had ears like the undog. "Pleeeeease? I won't be any trouble. Honest!"

There was no wiggle room for compromise on this one. "You have school, pard. You're going nowhere but back to Lakewood."

"I don't have school for two whole weeks, Harlowe!"

"With Ian and I working on the GRB, there will be little danger, Harlowe," Leucadia added, siding with Dodger.

"There's always danger, Lu." He turned back to Dodger. "Nothing doing."

"Mom's going to be in Washington. I'd rather be with you," Dodger whined.

Harlowe looked around for support. Even the seagulls on the beach had turned away.

Harlowe sighed in defeat as he lined them both up, sticking a finger in his little brother's chest. "Listen up, little bro. *Millawanda* is my ship. While onboard, I am the Captain. You do exactly as I tell you. You jump when I say jump, or this will be the last trip for both of you!"

Leucadia and Dodger came to stick-straight attention and saluted. "Aye, aye, Captain!"

When a blinker materialized on the sand, Harlowe instructed Dodger to go to the disk and step on it. The disk would transport him into the ship. Without the least bit of hesitation, Dodger ran over to the disk, jumped into the center, and blinked away in an instant. Hand in hand, Harlowe and Leucadia made their way across the sand toward the same blinker.

"How did Simon do?" Harlowe asked.

"He won the Oscar."

Harlowe nodded, enjoying the news as if he had known the outcome beforehand.

"Harlowe, you didn't! You fixed the winner?"

"Tweaked it a little," Harlowe said in his defense. "Simon is the actual winner, but Ian discovered that the balloting had been rigged to name somebody else. So Ian changed it back."

Harlowe then asked about Monday Platter, or "Squid," his head of security who had been away from the ship the past week on a special assignment. "Is Squid back yet from doing the President's favor?"

Before taking the last step onto the blinker, Leucadia replied, "No, he's still in Africa."

3

More Questions

There was a reason for Simon Bolt's career turnaround and Michael Stenkman wanted to know why. "Who is this captain you owe so much to, Mr. Bolt? I'm sure the world would like to know more about this fearless dude. Is he as heroic as Captain Starr?"

"You have no idea, bro," Simon replied. Stenkman was testing his patience. In the old days, before becoming a 54th-century soldier, he would have jumped off the stage and smashed the reporter's face in. The brawl would be in the next morning's tabloids around the world. But now he was a changed man. He was disciplined and controlled, a good soldier.

"Enlighten us then, Mr. Bolt. Tell us why your career turned a one-eighty?"

"You wouldn't believe it."

"Another sci-fi yarn?"

"I've said enough."

As Simon ignored Stenkman, a woman reporter asked from the back of the room, "Would you die for him?"

Simon found her in the lights and replied, "Yes, as he would for me."

Sizzle spoke in Simon's ear. "Now?" Simon asked. Sizzle pulled on his arm. It was important.

"May we have a word from your fiancée?" Stenkman asked.

Simon's reply was short. "No."

Someone in the audience added, "She doesn't speak English?"

"How do you communicate? I know for a fact that you don't speak anything but English, Mr. Bolt," Stenkman challenged.

Simon gritted his teeth. Stenkman was testing his limits. If Simon told him he had a 54th-century implant behind his ear that translated every language in the galaxy, would Stenkman—or anyone—believe him?

Not!

Stenkman kept up the pressure. "Is she like all the rest of your bimbos, Mr. Bolt? An airhead?"

That was it! Simon kicked the podium aside and dove out into the crowd for Stenkman.

*   *   *

Security officer Joe Martin waved his nightstick at the long black limousine to move along. The limo driver was taking advantage of his patience. For security reasons, no one, not even the big stars, were allowed to linger in the drop-off zone for more than a minute. If the driver failed to move the vehicle after a final warning, he had it towed.

Officer Martin knocked on the driver's side window and said, "I've told you twice now that this is a restricted security area, pal. You can't park here."

The limo remained parked with the engine running.

So far Oscar night had been trouble-free. Officer Martin hoped it would stay that way. He tapped on the window again. "I said, move it, pal. You can't park here!"

The limo remained parked.

"All right, stupid, have it your way." Officer Martin removed his radio from his belt and clicked in the call button. "Hey, Jesse, I've got a problem here. There's a limo in the drop-off zone that won't move."

"Roger that, Joe, I'll have City Towing over in a couple of minutes," Jesse replied.

Officer Martin tapped on the window a third time. "Show me your license, pal."

A tense moment passed before the window cracked open an inch and the driver's license was slipped to the security guard. Officer Martin switched on his penlight and stared at the license like someone was pulling a prank on him. The card was perfectly legal, however, complete with a holographic California state seal. What was peculiar was the photo of a mechanical man with a blue band around its circular, triangular-shaped head.

"Is this a joke?" Officer Martin asked, feeling like he was being played for an idiot. Officer Martin raised his black baton as though he would smash the window, when the low growl of a beast stopped him. He turned to the snarl as a great white tiger, twice as large as he had ever seen in his life, lumbered around the back of the limo.

Before Officer Martin lost his water, the stage exit door of the Dorothy Chandler Pavilion swung open with a crash. Emerging from the doorway was a young couple making a mad dash for the limo. The tall, handsome man's tuxedo was disheveled and torn. His hair was messed up like he had been in a brawl. The giant cat didn't startle him. In fact, the tiger was happy to see the couple.

The man quickly opened the door to the limo and asked, "What are you doing out here, Rhud? Get back in there before you freak out the neighborhood!"

The young lady gave the big cat a quick hug and guided the tiger into the limo. The couple was in a hurry. Officer Martin had never seen such a gorgeous movie star in the ten years he had been working the Oscars. He forgot about the driver's license and illegally parked limo the instant he caught a glimpse of her eyes glowing in the dark like bright green emeralds.

"I hope he didn't scare you, officer," the young man said to Joe Martin. "He's really a lovable little puddy-tat."

Officer Martin remained speechless. He didn't know what to say.

"We're in a hurry, Officer. Is there something wrong?" the young man asked.

Officer Martin blinked himself back from the vision he saw entering the limo. "You're parked in a security zone."

The young man understood the problem. "Of course. We're leaving now. Is that okay?"

Officer Martin was a large man. He was six-foot-three and two hundred and fifty pounds, but when the young man came toward him, he made him look small. "Who is she?" he asked, nodding toward the tall blonde that had entered the rear door of the limo.

"My fiancée."

It suddenly dawned on Officer Martin who he was talking to. "You're Simon Bolt, aren't you? You won the Best Actor tonight."

Simon Bolt held out his hand. The actor's grip was like a vise. "Nice to meet you, uh…"

Joe Martin shook his hand in shock. "Joe…"

"Nice to meet you, Joe." Simon Bolt jumped into the backseat and said to the driver. "Step on it, Jewels!"

The driver's window lowered, revealing the spindly-fingered mechanical man with a bright bow tie attached below a blue-lighted triangular-shaped head. Its mechanical fingers reached out and snatched the driver's license from Joe Martin's hand as the limo burned rubber, speeding off from the security zone as if they were making a getaway. At that moment, a dozen cars came screeching around the corner, racing after Simon Bolt's limousine.

* * *

It was a mad race down U.S. Interstate 10 for the reporters pursuing the Oscar winner's limo. The mechanical driver cut through traffic, picking up highway patrol and police cars, breaking every law on the books as it sped to the end of the freeway where the four-lane highway turned into Pacific Coast Highway in Santa Monica.

Overhead, police helicopters joined in the pursuit as the limousine broke away from the highway and continued across the sandy beach straight toward the ocean. Police and reporters tried to follow the limo, but all were stopped dead in their tracks the instant their wheels touched the soft beach sand.

The helicopters, however, stayed with the chase. At the edge of the ocean, the limo transformed into a bullet-shaped vehicle and blasted across the open water, racing too fast for the police helicopters to follow toward the full moon hanging like a giant golden disk on the horizon. Finally, the unidentified object lifted gently into the starry night and disappeared in a blink.

4

Flying High

08:42 hours
Thirty-five thousand feet
Interior Aftcabin of President Babagú's private 737 jetliner

"How dare you enter my quarters!" President Babagú shouted at the tall soldier who stood before him. The man was big and built like a block of black granite. Dressed like one of his elite guards in a jungle camouflage uniform, the soldier had exploded through his high security door and into President Babagú's private quarters at the back of the jet with ease. The seemingly unarmed intruder stepped forward to confront the President.

Babagú stared past the intruder, looking for his guards. What he saw from his heavily cushioned leather chair were his guards lying face down in the aisles on the other side of the doorway. None of them moved. "What is the meaning of this?" Babagú asked.

"We need to chat," the man replied.

A general and two other high-ranking officers with Babagú pulled their weapons on the intruder, but with two powerful slaps from the intruder, both officers fell cold to the floor. A forearm to the chest sent the general back to his chair, gasping for breath.

"I will have you shot," Babagú threatened.

"I doubt it," replied the man.

29

Babagú removed a chrome-plated .38 revolver from a hidden side pocket on his chair, but before Babagú could aim his weapon, the intruder had disarmed him and pointed the weapon at the president's face.

"What do you want?" Babagú asked again.

The man grabbed the general by the front of his uniform and tossed him aside like he weighed nothing at all. He then sat casually in the general's chair and replied, "Like I said, I came to chat."

Babagú reached for a decanter of liquor. "May I?" he asked, before removing the crystalline lid.

The man nodded, allowing him his drink.

Babagú began pouring. "Will you join me?"

"I don't drink."

"And with whom am I having this chat?" Babagú asked.

"It's not a friendly chat."

"Are you going to kill me?"

"If you don't cooperate."

Babagú kept his cool as he sipped his rare, twenty-five-hundred-dollar bottle of Glenfiddich. "How may I help you then?"

"The President of the United States sent me to warn you that if you continue with your nuclear program, there will be consequences."

Babagú smiled. "We have no nuclear program. The President knows this."

The man reached into his uniform and removed a file folder containing evidence of Babagú's secret underground nuclear facility a hundred and twenty miles inland, deep inside a desert mountain range.

"We're under new management now. This President will not look the other way. No more money for oil when you are trading your people's prosperity for your own personal gain."

Babagú picked up the documents and scanned them superficially. "Impressive. This new President is very thorough. How did you get these?"

"It doesn't matter."

Babagú tossed the folder on the table and asked, "Why has he sent you? Why not go through normal diplomatic channels?"

"He tried those in the past. They don't work."

"So he sent you?"

"That's right. This is not a social call, sir. He is saying in no uncertain terms that your oil profits will no longer pay for your extravagant lifestyle or your grand ideas of building a nuclear arsenal. The money will go to free your people of poverty and your dictatorship, or there will be consequences."

Babagú laughed. "How noble. Your new President is a dreamer." He leaned toward the man, losing his smile. "You can tell your new President that President Babagú does not scare so easily. If he wishes to play with my oil, let us see how your country will like it when I begin selling at market prices instead of the preferred rates your country has been enjoying in the past. I will double the price."

"So your answer is no, then? You will not join the President with a new spirit of freedom for your people?"

"Yes! The answer is no! You can also tell your President that my nation will continue with its peaceful nuclear program." Smiling evilly, he added, "for the betterment of our people."

The man raised the pistol toward Babagú.

Babagú was not frightened. "Put that away. You will not kill me. That would be very bad for our country's relations with your new President. No, our business will continue as before—"

Babagú's jet suddenly lurched forward and shook as though it had hit an air pocket. The intruder seemed as surprised as Babagú. The shuddering continued for a full minute before it stopped and the whine of the engines tapered to a stop. After that, there was dead silence. The intruder rose from his chair, looking confused as a bright blue-tinted light replaced the starry night in the portholes.

Both men went to the nearest windows and looked out at the two young individuals standing outside the aircraft. "Captain?" the intruder uttered in disbelief.

"They're kids," Babagú observed.

"Don't tell the Captain that to his face," the man warned.

Babagú's eyes broadened his view from the small window. "What is this place?"

The intruder motioned Babagú toward the forward hatchway. "You'll find out."

*   *   *

The hatch door opened and a rampway materialized out of the blue-carpeted floor and attached itself to the plane. It was made of a thin golden metal that looked like it would collapse under the slightest weight. However, as the intruder led the president down the walkway, it was as solid as a flight of stairs made of structural steel.

At the bottom of the rampway, Harlowe greeted the intruder with a casual high five. "Surprised to see you, Captain," the huge man said.

Standing beside Harlowe was Ian. They were both dressed in dark blue Gamadin uniforms of the day, every bit as tailored and fine as the president's extravagant garb. "Change of plans, Mr. Platter," Harlowe said. "Introduce me to your guest."

The president had not made eye contact with anyone. He was awestruck when he saw his entire jet aircraft resting entirely inside the vast foyer of the Gamadin ship. A short distance away was a wide gap in the floor. Looking down, he watched as the ship passed over a dark blue ocean and moved toward the clear, cloudless morning sky over a great desert miles below.

"President Babagú, Captain," Monday replied.

"Have you wrapped things up?" Harlowe asked.

Monday pressed his lips together in frustration. "Not yet, sir. He seems to believe President Delmonte isn't a man of his word."

Harlowe eyed Babagú with a slight smirk. "A non-believer, huh?"

Monday looked at Babagú when he said, "He says he's going through with his nuclear program regardless."

Babagú came out of his stupor and gave Harlowe a disdainful glance. "I demand—"

"Shut up, Toad," Harlowe ordered, cutting off Babagú in mid-sentence. "You're president of nothing here. On this ship, I am the law, and I ask the questions."

Babagú tried to speak again, but Harlowe was in no mood for conversation. He lifted Babagú by his clean white shirt and tie, and marched him over to the edge of the open hatch.

"Is that your country down there?" Harlowe asked.

Babagú's eyes were watery from the stinging pain that Harlowe's grip had on his neck. "Yes..."

"Yes, sir," Harlowe corrected.

"How dare—"

Harlowe's grip tightened harder, making it difficult for Babagú to breathe. "Yes, sir..."

Satisfied they were speaking the same language, Harlowe lowered Babagú to the floor but kept a firm grip on his suit collar so he wouldn't accidently fall overboard. "Mr. Prigg," Harlowe called aloud to his control room.

"*Yes, Your Majesty,*" Prigg's voice answered.

Babagú glanced at Harlowe as if what he had heard was a joke.

"Don't say a word, Toad, or I'll let go of your suit," Harlowe warned.

Babagú nodded that he understood as Monday went back inside the aircraft and brought the general and two other officers he had disciplined earlier down the stairway to join the party.

"Locate the Toad's nuclear facility, Mr. Prigg," Harlowe ordered.

"I have it located, Your Majesty."

"Nuke it, Mr. Bolt!" Harlowe ordered.

"*Aye, Skipper!*" Simon's voice replied crisply.

As Monday and the three officers looked on from the edge of the opening, a narrow beam of blue light from the saucer struck the base of the mountain range. A massive explosion followed, sending clouds of black smoke and fire billowing from the detonation.

"Now the military bases," Harlowe added.

"All of them, Skipper?"

"All of them, Mr. Bolt."

"Aye, Skipper."

A short moment later, dozens of narrow beams struck the surface miles below with pinpoint accuracy.

Then, quite unexpectedly, the general and two officers standing near the edge of the opening tripped and fell through the gap in the blue-carpeted floor. Babagú watched in horror as his screaming officers became tiny specks. Their voices faded quickly and then disappeared from view.

Harlowe seemed unconcerned at Babagú's loss. "Mr. Platter was giving you some friendly advice and you treated him like a doormat."

"I'm sorry," Babagú whimpered.

Harlowe was in no mood for sob stories. "Too late."

"No, no, please, I will do whatever you ask."

"Do the right thing for your people then."

"I will, I will. I promise!"

Harlowe stood Babagú up straight, fixed his tie and straightened his fine tailor-made coat and white shirt. "You know, Bagoo," the mispronouncing of his name intentional, "I believe you. Now Mr. Platter, I and Mr. Wizzixs over there," he said, glancing at Ian near the stairway, "will be gone for a couple of weeks on a little errand, but we'll be back. While we're gone, I want to see some progress down there."

"Whatever you want...Sir."

"I want you to set the example of the new change that other countries in the world will follow."

"Yes, sir."

"Your country will be the first true free enterprise society. Your first decree will be to allow your people to live with no regulations, no taxes and no government toads telling them how to live and breathe without looking over their shoulders. You will release all political prisoners and turn your palaces into schools and hospitals. We'll get Disney to build a new theme park on the beach using the money you stashed away in your offshore accounts." Harlowe turned to Ian. "Think President Delmonte can do a little arm twisting to get that one done, Wiz?"

"I know he can, Captain," Ian replied.

"That would be sweet," Harlowe went on. "And free surf lessons for the kids. Oh yes, and new elections. Tell your people you've seen the light. You're turning over all your power to the newly "elected" president, who will be chosen by a fair and honest vote."

"I, I don't know, sir," Babagú replied, frightened. "My country is corrupt. If I try to change it, I will be the first to be killed before I can make the changes you ask."

Ian walked over and handed Harlowe three golden cylinders. "These will help guide you and protect your family from harm."

Harlowe then handed the cylinders to Babagú.

"This is powerful magic?" Babagú asked.

Harlowe grinned, guiding Babagú back toward the rampway to his jet. "You could say that, Bagoo."

"Yes, sir, I will make the changes you ask."

"I have faith in you, Bagoo." Before Babagú stepped onto the stairway to his aircraft, Harlowe had one last warning to make. "But Bagoo?"

"Yes, sir?"

"If you don't follow my requests, the great Mowg will pay you a visit and swallow you whole."

Harlowe pointed up at the top of Babagú's jet. Perched on top of the fuselage, looking down on the small group with terrifying yellow eyes, was a winged dragon flapping its black, thirty-foot wings over the jet, its long, green tongue flickering between its long knife-like teeth as it let out a heart-stopping scream that turned Babagú white with fear. If Babagú had ever imagined that Harlowe's warning was an idle exaggeration, he now knew what a Gamadin reality check felt like.

5

Black Mountain

Gazz's beautiful and wide oceans were as vast as Earth's, and perhaps slightly greener. Three major continents divided the water, each having a variety of mountain ranges, sandy deserts, flat plains, and long meandering rivers. Riverstone sighed as he looked down from the observation deck aboard the Tomarian flagship in a stationary orbit a thousand miles above the planet's surface. Thoughts of his own blue world three hundred light-years away struck a heartfelt longing for home. "That's so sick, Sharlon! Gazz looks so much like Earth!"

For the past two months, Riverstone and Sharlon had worked together supervising the mining planet Erati's liberation and reconstruction. Tens of thousands of slave laborers were given their freedom and allowed to return to their homes or move anywhere else in the quadrant. Many, knowing little else, decided to stay and work for wages that would make them richer than they had ever thought possible, not in a putrid, disease-infested environment, but in the new Erati that was being rebuilt to be safe and clean. Whether they stayed or not, all were given sufficient compensation to enjoy a life of peace without hunger for the rest of their lives. The transformation of Erati was absolute. It would take many cycles and passings to complete, but with the wealth of the Tomarian Corporation backing the enterprise, the mining planet would one day shine as an example of what business could do for its employees. That was the least Riverstone could do for Ela, the girl he had fallen in love with deep inside the slave mines of Erati. She had been his soulmate, his friend, his love, who had saved his life during his darkest moments when he was a slave of Erati himself.

"Gazz is like your home, Matthew?" Sharlon asked, standing close to the window with him.

Although Riverstone had worked beside Sharlon nearly every hour of the day, their relationship never ventured beyond friendship. It had remained proper and respectful at all times. Before he found Ela, Sharlon would have been a dream for him. On his pre-Gamadin days on Earth, he would not have hesitated to sweep her up in his arms like some brave knight and ride off to some gorgeous planet like the one he saw below to live happily ever after, even though she was a hundred and twenty-eight years old, Earth time!

But now he couldn't think about girls and relationships. It was too soon when the pain and the loss of his beautiful Ela was still vividly fresh in his mind.

He sighed. At night he still dreamed of Ela, smelling the mine dust around them mixing with her sweet breath as she spoke to him. She would be so in awe of the view he saw below him. Ela had slaved all her life in the Erati mines. It wasn't until Harlowe rescued them that she saw for the first time a cloud drift freely in the sky with the stars, the birds, and the ocean, all the things he showed her in her final, brief moments before she went to sleep forever in his arms.

"Yes, big oceans like this," Riverstone replied, returning his head to Sharlon. "When school let out, Harlowe, Wiz, and I would be down at the beach every day, checking out the waves and the babes," he said fondly, remembering all those times when their only responsibilites were mowing the yard, taking out the trash, and being home in time for dinner.

"Babes?" Sharlon wondered. "Is that another delicious food like your double-doubles?"

Riverstone laughed, feeling a little foolish. "No, not food. Girls. We liked to look at girls. For Harlowe and me it was a full-time occupation from the day we discovered that they didn't bite."

Sharlon smiled politely. "Oh yes, I understand. That is one of the pleasures the young men and women of Tomar also enjoy."

Riverstone eyes widened.

"You seemed surprised by that, Matthew," Sharlon said. "Do you believe we are so different than you?"

He looked at her, still in disbelief of her age. He saw so much of Quay in her that a few times he caught himself saying her name by mistake. "I guess I thought—"

"Tomarians are no different, Matthew," said Sharlon. "The galaxy may be vast but its people are much like you. They also yearn to live and love freely, without fear of oppressive rulers taking what is rightfully theirs." She turned fondly to the planet below. "Anor and I often came to Gazz to enjoy its simple life."

"I thought Gazz was a primitive planet."

"It is. Their vessels are wind-powered. That is what we loved most, its unspoiled beauty. We would come here for many days and leave the business of the quadrant far behind." She exhaled softly and closed her large green eyes, lost in thought. "I long for those days again, Matthew."

"Have you heard from Anor?" Riverstone asked, wondering if Sharlon's husband and head of the Tomarian Corporation had survived the Gamadin destruction of the combined Fhaal, Consortium, and Tomarian fleets.

Since the battle of Og, no one had seen or heard from Anor Ran. It was as if he was a magician and he left the quadrant in a puff of smoke. His ship was not among the starships that were destroyed. Knowing how resourceful the Tomarian businessman was, Harlowe believed he escaped in a hidden ship. Riverstone hoped he was gone for good. Harlowe was more realistic. "Give him time. When the smoke clears, he'll be back."

"To take his revenge," Riverstone said.

"Maybe," Harlowe had countered, "But I'd like to think it will be to rebuild. He wasn't an evil dude like Sar. He was protecting his property. No, he'll be back to pick up the pieces. You can count on that. Will we help him out? If he wants to make a buck, sure. If he wants to exploit the quadrant again, he'll have some problems."

* * *

"I'm sure Anor and Quay are both alive, Sharlon," Riverstone said.

"Let us hope, Matthew." She nodded toward the planet. "Will Harlowe arrive in time?" she asked.

Riverstone returned a reassuring smile. "He won't let you down, Sharlon. You can take that to the bank."

Her beautiful eyes glowed bright green. "Bank?"

"If anyone can save Gazz, it's Harlowe. Millie will be here within the hour. Lu is also coming. She's the smartest person I know. With her and Wiz working together, saving Gazz is a slam-dunk."

"Slam-dunk?"

"Yeah, easy. No problems."

A girl robob with long dark hair clickity-clacked over to them with two shakes and tall white straws in its pincers. Riverstone gratefully took the two drinks and said, "Thanks, Alice." Her task complete, the she-bob then turned and clickity-clacked away.

Riverstone stuck in the long white straws and handed a shake to Sharlon. "This will help the worries."

"What is it?" Sharlon asked.

"A chocolate shake. My mom always had one when she was tweaked."

Sharlon laughed. "A medical prescription?"

"You got it."

"You have the oddest sayings, Matthew." She took her first sip and her eyes lit up.

He wished his mom had a prescription for an ailing heart, but she didn't. Time was the only cure for that, he reckoned.

From the Tomarian flagship orbiting high above Gazz, Sharlon pointed at a long continental land mass that extended from the North Polar Region all the way down past the equator. The top third of the continent was white, indicating a polar cap much like Earth's.

"If you follow the land mass next to the great ocean, you can see the large dark mountain in the middle of the plain." Riverstone saw the mountain clearly. It stuck out like a big black eye against the white glaciers that carved their way down the side of its wide valleys. Surrounding them all were wide-open plains the color of wheat. The massive, dark mountain was nowhere near as large as Olympus Mons on Mars. No mountain was that big. By Earth standards, though, it made Mt. Everest, Earth's largest mountain, seem tiny.

"If you follow the line from the black mountain to the other side of the continent, you can see a long mountain range. Sharlon continued, " Anor discovered a deposit of thermo-grym there many passings ago. His geologists say it was the most concentrated form of thermo-grym they had ever found."

"Even better than Erati's?" Riverstone asked.

"Yes, many times more pure," Sharlon stated.

"Wow, he must have made a mint from that!"

"You mean his rewards were sizable?"

"That's exactly what I mean."

"Anor Ran did not profit from his find. On a planet of sailing ships, the people of Gazz are not ready for Tomarian machinery. It would disturb their way of life."

The Tomarian captain of the flagship entered and excused himself for interrupting.

Sharlon greeted him with a warm smile and motioned him to enter. "Please, Commander Lass, join us."

"Thank you, Lady Ran. The Gamadin ship has arrived."

Riverstone held up his shake. "See, what did I tell ya? Harlowe's da man. He's even a little early."

6

The Sea, The Sea

Everyone except Ian was at their stations when Harlowe emerged from his quarters, stretching and yawning the morning kinks out of his body with a blue towel draped over his shoulder. "Are we there yet, Mr. Platter?"

On his way to his usual morning workout with Quincy, Harlowe wasn't dressed for duty. He wore dark blue workout shorts, and a red-and-white Lakewood football jersey with Pylott and the number "7" stenciled on the back. Keeping in top shape was the duty of every crewman. Harlowe stressed that by setting the example.

"We entered the Gazzian system thirty minutes ago, Captain," Monday replied.

"Everything cool, Prigg?"

Prigg's center eye remained on Harlowe as the other two scanned the overhead holo-screen from the Captain's chair where he was sitting. "All is as it should be, Your Majesty."

"Any contact with Mr. Riverstone?" Harlowe asked Simon.

"They're waiting for us at the rendezvous coordinates, Captain. Jester says Sharlon is extremely happy that Lu came with us. She is honored that the daughter of the Triadian soldier Sook has traveled so far to meet her."

43

"Tell Mr. Riverstone we'll see him in a couple of hours, Mr. Platter. Let's enjoy the countryside for a while," he added, watching a giant blue world drift by the starboard observation window as *Millawanda* headed toward the inner planets of the star system.

"Aye, Captain."

Stepping toward the blinker, Harlowe chuckled when he saw Rhud lying legs-up against the observation couch, fast asleep at the far end of the bridge. This was way too early in the morning for the big cat. His day started at noon, when his stomach started growling.

He searched the bridge for the other animals and wondered where Molly and Mowgi were since they weren't in their usual spots. Molly was usually primping herself on the portside couch while the undog's big ears stuck out over the top of an unoccupied chair. At times, when they were all together, the bridge looked more like a zoo than the most powerful war bird in the galaxy.

"Dodger is showing Lu, Sizzle, and the pets the jungle walk he found," Simon replied.

Harlowe traded confused glances with Monday. Monday shrugged. He didn't know what Simon meant either. "Jungle walk?" Harlowe asked.

"That's what he called it," Simon said. "The way he described it sounded like a pool with a waterfall in the middle of trees and hanging vines."

Harlowe shook his head in disbelief. "I swear, that kid has been on this ship for over a week and he knows more about Millie's decks than I do, and I'm the Captain."

"Dodger wanted you to see it, too, but you were still sleeping."

"Not sleeping, Mate. Reading, and into the wee hours, I might add."

"*Master and Commander*, no doubt, Captain," Simon quipped.

"That's my favorite. But this one's called *The Far Side of the World* by the same author."

"Sounds cool."

"It is. I'll lend it to you when I'm done."

Prigg overheard their conversation and asked, "What is the book about, Your Majesty?"

"Sailing, Prigg, when the wind was the only power ships used to travel by." Harlowe smiled brightly, staring out at the large oceans of Gazz. "Aye, matey, those were the days."

"Would you rather captain a sailing ship, Skipper, than a ship of the stars?" Simon asked.

Harlowe smiled. "I would never trade Millie, Mr. Bolt, but to captain a tall ship would be cool."

Simon stood and raised his hand high like an actor playing his part. "*Let fall! Sheets home, sheets home! Hoist away there, mates! Cheerily there, in the foretop, look alive! The sea, the sea, the beautiful sea, the gray mist on the face, the kick of the wheel and the white sails shaking! Hands to the braces! Belay! Belay! Give them a broadside, Mr. Dillon! Aye, aye, Captain Aubrey, a broadside it is! Baaluuwy! Boom, boom, boom, the cannons roared. Make tight that fore topsail, if you please, Mr. Queeney. Sail ho! Two points, three points on the beam! All I ask is a tall ship and star to steer by . . .*" Simon bowed, ending his nautical recital to jovial applause from Harlowe, Monday, and Prigg.

"Bravo, Mr. Bolt. No one could have said it better," Harlowe said, still clapping.

Simon bowed several more times and then returned to his chair. "Thank you, Skipper."

Harlowe turned to the bridge blinker and spoke like a ship's captain he had seen in a movie once. "Carry on, Mates, if you please.

The bridge is yours, my able seamen. I wish you joy this wonderful morning."

Harlowe then stepped on the blinker and was gone.

7

Dodger's Jungle

Leucadia and Sizzle stood speechless, mouths agape, in the doorway of Dodger's jungle room. "Isn't this killer, Lu?" Dodger cried out upon entering the vast room of jungle trees, hanging vines, lush green ferns, bushes, and colorful tropical flowers. Some were familiar, like the feathery ferns, coconut palms, and the bright blue flowers Leucadia grew along her childhood yellow brick pathway. Others, though, like the red-stemmed pink flowers and the broad, yellow-leafed bushes with green fruit were quite alien to Earth. Through the lush foliage, they could see a nearby waterfall rushing from the top of a mossy green cliff and splashing down into a pool of clear blue water.

Molly ran on ahead, following a path to the pool as if she had played there a thousand times before. Mowgi took flight right behind her, feeling the freedom of the wide-open space. Once in the air he glided to the rocky pinnacle just above the waterfall, where his view was unobstructed of the entire forest, the pool, and anyone who entered the vast room. A small, pink sun appeared to rise at the east end of the room, corresponding with the ship's time clock. If it was morning in Lakewood, it was morning in the jungle room, too. As the day progressed, the small pale sun rose higher and brighter on its journey to the top of the dome. It then drifted down toward the opposite horizon, dimming again like any other sunset as a heaven full of twinkling stars appeared.

Leucadia watched the cawing, brightly colored birds flutter between the high branches of the trees. "This is incredible, Dodger! How did you ever find such a paradise?"

"Molly and Rhud brought me here."

"Does Harlowe know about this?"

Dodger shrugged. "I don't know. He's never said anything about it to me."

"Or me," Leucadia added. "He always said Millie is so big it would take him a hundred years to search every room. Maybe this is one of those places he's never been to. I'll have to show him."

Sizzle tilted her head up at the artificial sky. "Are there any moons, Dodger?" she asked.

Through his newly implanted universal translator, Dodger understood Sizzle as if she was speaking English. "I've seen three so far."

"Are they as wonderful as our moon, Dodger?" Leucadia asked, feeling romantic.

Dodger was too young to understand her question. "I don't know, Lu. They were moons. Big and bright like our moon. No biggie." He then tossed away his shirt and ran for the pool, leaving the girls behind. "Come on, the water is clean! It's salty like the ocean, but no seaweed."

Running along the path Molly had taken, Dodger dove headfirst into the pool and started swimming toward the opposite end where the waterfall emptied into it.

Seeing how much fun Dodger was having, Sizzle started taking off her clothes. Leucadia, however, quickly stopped her before Sizzle removed *all* of her clothes. "No, Sizzle. We need to wear swimsuits." She glanced at Dodger.

"I don't understand. He is human like us."

"I know, but he is a young boy. We should not swim without suits in his presence."

Sizzle was confused. "This is custom?"

"Yes, it is custom among Earthlings to wear a swimming garment while in the presence of others."

Leucadia spoke out to an unseen entity and requested the appropriate swimming attire. Within moments, Jewels, Harlowe's very punctual robob servant, came clickity-clacking into the room with swimsuits and towels for the girls.

8

The Power Room

Harlowe was still dripping sweat and his face was puffy and bruised as he entered the power room after his workout with Quincy. The power room was the place Ian and Leucadia had spent most of their time preparing *Millawanda's* powerful shields during the week-long hyperlight journey to Gazz. Once the shield calculations were ready, the ship would have the power to protect the planet Gazz from the advancing gamma ray burst. Next to the power room was the place where Simon had discovered the giant blue crystal that powered the ship. It made the hairs on his forearms tingle with tiny sparks whenever he entered the chamber.

"Making progress?" Harlowe asked, as he gazed at the bright, multi-colored graphs along the back wall.

"I'll need another day at least," Ian replied, red-eyed and tired from all the hours he was putting into the project. "How much longer to the rendezvous with Riverstone?"

"We're already here," Harlowe replied, noticing the frustration on Ian's face. "Not such a slam-dunk, huh?"

"Not so much."

"You'll make it in time, right?"

Ian looked hesitant. "Sure."

Harlowe bent down and locked eyes with Ian. "That's not the slam-dunk answer I was looking for. I'll get Lu down here, pronto."

Ian replied with an edge. "I'll have it ready, Captain. Lu wants to visit with Sharlon. Let her."

"She'll have plenty of time to girlie bond after the burst," Harlowe shot back.

"Let me do it, Dog! I need to learn."

Harlowe wiped his face with his towel. "All right, let me help, then. What do you want me to do?" he asked, trying his best to keep his cool without being a nag.

Ian's thoughtful blue eyes gazed over the wall readouts. "Well, if you could connect the expanders here," he said pointing to a lower graph on the wall, "then link to the overrides over here," another graph, "without blowing the multipliers inside the force field resonators next to the expanders, you could help a great deal."

Harlowe's eyes crossed. "All right, all right! It's complicated. I get it. I'll leave you alone." Before leaving the power room, he told Ian, "Not that I don't think you can handle it... but... I'm cutting Lu's visit short. We need her here."

"Let her go. She's traveled 300 light-years to see Sharlon. A few hours won't make a difference. According to the figures sent over from the Tomarian flagship, we still have two more days before the GRB gets here. That's plenty of time to get Millie ready, Dog."

It was against his better judgement, but Harlowe caved. "Okay, I'll tell her when she comes back from the pool Dodger found."

Ian casually replied, "Oh yeah, his jungle room?"

Harlowe was taken aback. "You know about the jungle room?"

"Yeah, he told me about it the second day. It's on the lower level, past the main foyer. You take the sunrise corridor, go another hundred yards, hang a right and it's the first double door on the left." (Since *Millawanda* was a perfect circle, there was no north or south, east or west. When they were living on Mars, the sun rose in the morning on one side of the ship. That corridor became known as the "sunrise side." The opposite end of the ship then became the "sunset side" to the crew. These reference points remained regarding the ship, wherever they landed.) "I thought you knew," Ian added.

Harlowe was bent. "No, I never knew it existed."

Ian smiled briefly. "You should get out more often. It's a cool place."

Harlowe headed out the door in a huff. "I will!"

9.

Pretty Necklace

Leucadia stood beside the bridge blinker with Harlowe. She was dressed to the nines. Harlowe wondered if something a little more conservative than her gold jumpsuit would be more appropriate for her first meeting with the Tomarian matriarch. Then a loud alarm went off in his head, recalling what his dad, Buster, had told him more than once about commenting on a woman's attire. *"If you want peace, son, whatever a woman wears is always perfect, even if she's wearing a gunny sack."*

Buster's wise advice had always served Harlowe well. Besides, compared to the green body glove number Sharlon had worn when he last saw her at the Ran Palace on Tomar, Leucadia would look like she was wearing his mother's pajamas. So he kept his mouth shut. He chose peace.

"Come with me, Harlowe," Leucadia pleaded with her alluring green eyes as she tried to steal a kiss on the bridge.

Harlowe held her at bay while he slipped the SIBA medallion over her head. "We've discussed this already. Until the GRB passes, I'm staying here."

Leucadia could see Harlowe was uneasy about her departure. "You want me to stay?"

"No guilt trips. Just go and get back here before Wiz has a cow."

"I'll stay if you order me."

Harlowe took the challenge. "I order you to stay."

She smiled. "But I'm not one of your crew."

"When you're on my ship, I'm Captain."

"Would you make me walk the plank if I disobeyed you?"

"I told you before, don't test me. You won't like it."

Leucadia was unafraid. She tried to sneak in another kiss while he made sure the chain around her neck was secure. At any other place on the ship Harlowe would be up to a proper goodbye, but not on the bridge. To him, the bridge was sacred ground, not to be profaned by pleasures of the heart. "Cool it, Lu," he said softly, but firm so only she could hear. "Not on the bridge, I said."

Her bright green eyes told him his words would soon be forgotten. She would try again to catch him off guard. "A girl can always try," she said, admiring the small gold disk attached to the beautiful chain. "Kinda outdoing yourself, Pylott. What's the occasion? Our anniversary?"

"A precaution."

"What's it called again?"

"A Self-contained, Individual Body-armor Array."

"You called it something else the other day."

"A SIBA."

She twirled it around with her fingers. "This one's much prettier."

" Wiz said you were more likely to wear it if it looked like a piece of jewelry."

"Smart boy. Does Sizzle get one?"

"She has one already and knows how to use it."

Leucadia turned serious. "Expecting trouble?"

"Always. A lesson I learned from a hard-nosed teacher. Don't lose it."

"I'll keep it close to my heart, always."

"Do that."

She then asked, "Is it like the one we've been training with?"

"Yep, the same. There's a couple of things the SIBA does we didn't cover."

"Such as?"

"Flying."

Luecadia flapped her arms playfully. "I know. I can fly like Supergirl when I spread them out," she joked.

"Hardly. Glide is more like it. That will be your next lesson when we get back to Earth."

She tried to snuggle closer. "You're a good teacher."

Harlowe glanced toward the forward windows. Gazz was barely visible, but three of its five moons were in clear view. He touched her nose playfully. "I want you back here in an hour."

"You'll miss Riverstone and Sharlon."

Harlowe nodded. "We'll have plenty of time to party after this is over."

"The Tomarian commander says his science officers have calculated the GRB wouldn't arrive for another two days."

"I'm not taking any chances. Nothing ever goes smoothly. You're the best I have. Remember, one hour max or I'm sending the cavalry after you."

Leucadia's mouth went sour. "Harlowe, that's not fair! Sharlon has planned a celebration for us."

"One hour."

"Is it because you'll miss me?"

"Go have your yuk-yuks and come right back. That's an order."

Leucadia snapped to attention and saluted. "Aye, aye, Captain."

"Where are Simon and Sizzle?" Harlowe asked.

"In the foyer saying their good-byes... properly," she said, trying make Harlowe feel bad for not doing the same with her.

"Tell Rerun to cut it short."

"You don't sound happy."

"I'm not."

"Anything I can do?"

"Yeah, be back in one hour and I'll be happy as a clam."

Lu tapped the communicator on the side of her suit. "I'll stay in contact."

"One more thing," Harlowe said. Before Leucadia stepped on the blinker, the door of Harlowe's quarters slid open. Jewels clickity-clacked over and handed her a large covered platter.

Leucadia took the handle and asked, "What is it?" as she turned the platter around, trying to guess what was inside.

Harlowe guided her toward the blinker. "A surprise for Riverstone. Don't let him hog it."

Leucadia blew Harlowe a kiss and stepped on the blinker. Without a sound or a spark, she was gone. Harlowe continued to stare at her empty space for a moment before he took a deep breath and returned to his command chair, where Jewels was waiting with a chocolate shake. Harlowe took the shake and sat there, nibbling on his straw without tasting the chocolate. His face portrayed the size of the pit in his gut.

10

Dear Friends

It was a short journey in the Tomarian shuttle from *Millawanda* to Sharlon's flagship, the *Jo-li Ran*. Leucadia had visions of Riverstone smiling from ear to ear, yelling "Let's party!" the moment she stepped onto the flight deck. It would be just like the good old days before Harlowe, Riverstone, and Ian first left Earth so many months ago. Was he the same Matthew? How had becoming a Gamadin changed him? How would he look? Would he be like Harlowe, taller, stronger and mature, a soldier's soldier, more handsome and dashing in his blue Gamadin uniform? Harlowe had told her of their exploits, their travels, and the many times Death had nearly taken them all. His accounts sounded more like tall, seafaring adventures than reality. She could hardly wait to engulf Matthew in her arms and hear his sarcastic voice heckle her about her clothes or the distance she had traveled to see him.

The moment the airlock door opened and she saw the tall, chiselled soldier waiting for just her to step out of the shuttle bay, her vision vanished. As Sizzle ran to her mother's arms, holding her like they would never part again, Leucadia and Riverstone remained frozen, unable to move. This was not at all what she expected.

Instead of sharing hugs and high-fives, they remained silent as each sought the proper words to say to the other. Riverstone had almost forgotten how beautiful Leucadia was. When she came into view, his heart throbbed, not from lust or desire, but from his joy at seeing his long-lost friend. The last time he had seen her was on the golf course in Las Vegas. He and Monday were about to be shot by a Dak blaster when Leucadia arrived in the nick of time to save them.

Riverstone began quietly, "Hello, Lu." His eyes became glassy with emotion.

Leucadia couldn't believe the transformation. This young man was hardly the same suntanned surfer with spiked bleached hair and pink cheeks she had last seen in the back of the rover that night over a year ago. She gazed up, short of breath, at the six-foot-seven soldier standing stick-straight before her. What had happened to him? Harlowe's stories were short on detail. He had left out the account of this alteration she saw before her. Riverstone was a boy no longer. He was a tall, handsome, young soldier. In his dark blue Gamadin uniform with gold trim, he was enough to make any girl swoon.

"You are so hot, Matthew Riverstone!" she exclaimed. He was much taller than she remembered. Now he was a head above her, with deep blue eyes that stared down into hers. Slowly they fell into a heartfelt embrace. Trembling, they continued holding on to each other as Sharlon's entourage left the area, leaving them alone to catch up.

Riverstone peered down. "Does he know how lucky he is to have you?"

Leucadia forced a smile. "Millie is a jealous mistress."

Riverstone looked past her at the empty shuttle air lock. "Why didn't he come?"

"He was worried about Wiz and being ready for the GRB."

Riverstone understood Harlowe's need to prepare. He would have done the same. "Wiz will handle it. Gazz will survive. Harlowe will see to that."

Leucadia turned toward a small portal where *Millawanda* was floating in a synchronized orbit with the *Jo-li Ran*. Suddenly worried, she wondered if she should have stayed with the Gamadin ship until the danger had passed. The burst was still days away, yet the concern she had seen in Harlowe was foreboding. Was she only thinking of herself, over the mission? Yes, she was, she admitted. *I won't be long*, she promised him across the void. She would return within the hour as promised.

Staying positive, she turned to Riverstone. "I can't believe it's you, Matthew! You have grown like Harlowe. You're a man."

Watching Riverstone wipe his eyes, she saw there was more behind them than his joy at seeing her. She saw a lifetime of pain and suffering that could never be erased. It was one thing to hear Harlowe's stories of their months on Mars, the General, the Omini Quadrant, the Fhaal destruction, Riverstone's captivity on Erati, and his lost love, Ela. To see the shocking change in Riverstone was another. How had he survived, she wondered? A thousand lifetimes could not give him the poise and strength she saw in him at this moment.

Riverstone touched the medallion around her neck. "I see he's playing mother Tinker."

"And you?" she asked.

Riverstone reached inside his shirt and displayed his medallion, only his was not as bright and jewel-like as hers. It was rather plain and dull like old gold. "I never leave Millie without it."

After one more hug, they locked arms. Riverstone led her from the portal down the hallway to the reception. "Come. Tell me all about Lakewood and my family."

"Wait!" Leucadia ran into the air lock and returned with the platter Jewels had given her.

"What is it?"

Leucadia shrugged an *I-don't-know*. "It's from Harlowe. He said 'don't let Riverstone hog it'."

* * *

Sharlon had prepared a feast for her guests. On large banquet tables in the middle of the hall were piles of Neejian junals, vats of rasali and mandos, along with generous slices of Tomarian brot, canella, and endless quantities of chontol, a rare Neejian wine. Sizzle stayed busy, enjoying the food from her home world. Riverstone and Leucadia sat by themselves at a small table near an observation window. Gazz and her magnificent moons took up the entire window. The platter Harlowe had given Riverstone filled the table in much the same way.

"Gazz is beautiful," Leucadia said, staring out at the breathtaking view of the watery world.

"It's hard to imagine a force of nature so powerful it could snuff out all life in an instant," Riverstone said. He turned toward her, worried. "Millie can pull it off, can't she, Lu?"

Leucadia's reply was confident and poised. She took him by the hand and assured him, "She will, Matthew, she will."

She closed her eyes briefly. They had so much to talk about and so little time. Together they stared at the platter on the table.

"Any idea what that is?" Riverstone asked.

"You know Harlowe. It could be anything." She motioned curiously. "Go ahead. Open it. It is your gift."

Leucadia held the platter while Riverstone unlatched the clamps. The heavenly odor hit them the instant he removed the lid. What they saw underneath made both their faces glow.

"Harlowe's da man!" Riverstone exclaimed as his eyes were filled with stacks of double-double In-N-Out burgers, surrounded with stacks of tacos, fries, guacamole, Tinker's homemade salsa, and five large shakes, all different flavors, plus two tall bottles of Blue Stuff. Riverstone could think of no better present than food from the old hometown.

He offered Leucadia a cheeseburger and was downing a Blue Stuff shake. She declined, marveling at the tables of Tomarian delicacies. Riverstone couldn't wait to bite into his first juicy cheeseburger in months, when the emergency alarm on Leucadia's com went off.

11

Problemos

It felt like the longest hour of Harlow's life. In five more minutes, Leucadia and Sizzle were supposed to board the Tomarian shuttle on their way back to *Millawanda* and safety. As an added precaution, he thought about sending a squad of clickers to escort the girls back to the saucer in case they forgot about the time.

"Are they on the shuttle yet?" Harlowe asked Monday anxiously.

"Not yet, Captain. The Tomarians say the party is winding down," Monday replied.

Winding down? Harlowe wanted it over. "Very well, Mr. Platter. Keep an eye on their progress. I don't want any snags."

He tapped the arm of his command chair, scolding himself for allowing her to go in the first place. He should have been man up enough and ordered her to stay. Against his better judgment, he had given in to her request. He swallowed hard, wondering what the penalty would be for his weakness.

"This is so amazing, Harlowe," Dodger beamed from Riverstone's seat to his right. Harlowe's little brother never thought outer space could be this cool. It was far beyond his already vivid imagination. From a thousand-mile-high orbit, the continents on Gazz were a riot of earth tones—reds, browns, and beiges, with deep purples and greens along the coasts and river valleys. Dark mountain ranges ran from north to south. Far above the equator, a huge black mountain stood all alone, sticking out of a great plain as if it had been placed there by mistake. The ice sheets of the white glaciers that flanked the black, majestic cone on all sides gave the mountain an evil look. Surrounding all the continents were vast blue and green oceans with swirling white weather fronts with powerful bolts of bright lightening flickering within the dark clouds. Floating above it all were bright moons that seemed so close and clear. Dodger felt as if he could pluck them out of the star-filled heavens and toss them through a hoop. "Have you been to a lot of planets like this, Harlowe?"

"A few," Harlowe replied, thinking of one in particular. Tomar would always be the other blue world that remained close to his heart. He wondered briefly how *she* was doing, if *she* was okay, and if Fate was treating *her* kindly.

Dodger may have been the Captain's little brother, but he had no special privileges. While on the bridge, he had to be well-mannered and appropriately dressed at all times, no exceptions. "If you want to be on the bridge, Dodger," Harlowe warned him the first day, "you will appear at all times as if you're on your way to church with Mom." Which meant his hair was combed, his face washed, and he wore a clean shirt and clean pants. No bare feet. No swim trunks. No attitude.

During the voyage from Earth, Harlowe allowed Dodger the run of the ship, except for the utility rooms. An unsupervised, curious, eleven-year-old kid exploring any of *Millawanda's* equipment rooms could mean a lot of trouble .

Harlowe kept one eye on the holo-screen while he focused the rest of his attention on the dull gray Tomarian shuttle. Through the portside window, he could see it still attached to the side of the *Jo-li Ran.*

Three minutes, twenty-seconds, but who's counting?

"It looks like Earth," Dodger commented, straining with curiosity to see everything at once.

"It has more water than Earth," Monday said from his station. He then compared Gazz and Earth side-by-side on the overhead, being careful not to disturb the Captain's view. "Gazz is only a few miles smaller in diameter. Except for its five moons and smaller land masses, Gazz could be her twin sister."

All Dodger wanted to know was, "Do they have surf?"

Monday pointed to the moons that were visible through the forward observation windows around the planet. "I've never seen the beaches, but with so many moons, I'm sure the tidal forces will have a big effect. The waves should get very big, Dodger."

Dodger's face lit up. "Wow, Harlowe, can we surf some?"

Harlowe didn't want to be bothered. "This isn't a surf trip, Dodger."

"Why not?"

Harlowe eyed the timer at the corner of the holo screen as it inched past the three-minute mark at a snail's pace. "Because the people on the planet don't know we're here. If we go down in a ship like Millie, it wouldn't be good."

Dodger was confused. "I don't understand, Harlowe. Millie wouldn't hurt anybody."

Harlowe made a hard glance at Monday to take over the Q & A. Explaining the concept of non-interference to an eleven-year-old was more than he wanted to deal with at the moment.

Monday took his cue with ease. "No, she wouldn't, not intentionally. But the Gazzians don't have airplanes or cell phones or cars. If they saw Millie, they might think she was something unfriendly and might hurt themselves. We can't take that chance."

Dodger's face was even more confused.

"Would you give a loaded gun to a baby?" Monday asked Dodger.

"No way. That would be dumb, Mr. Platter," Dodger replied.

"That's right, Dodger. Why?" Monday asked.

"Because a baby doesn't know how to handle a gun and he might shoot himself."

"Right again. Now think of Millie as a gun and the Gazzians as babies. The people there don't know about flying ships. They don't even know they exist. If we showed them the gun of the future, what do you think they might do?"

Like a light going off in his head, Dodger finally got the idea. As much as technology can assist a civilization, it can also become its destroyer. "They might hurt themselves?"

It was Harlowe's turn next. "We don't know, Dodger. That's why it's important to keep the Gazzians from seeing Millie. We can't take the chance of her being that loaded gun that might kill them."

Simon stepped off the blinker and headed for his weapons station. "Are the girls in the shuttle yet, Skipper?"

Harlowe checked the timer. "Two minutes, Mr. Bolt." He then added, "Check your weapons." It wasn't a request.

Simon swiveled his chair around as he peered over his readouts. "Aye."

Harlowe was about to contact Leucadia to hurry it up when Ian blinked onto the bridge, appearing in a state of panic. "Captain! We have problems."

Harlowe twisted around in his chair and looked at Ian's troubled face.

"A good news, bad news thing?" Simon asked, trying to keep the mood light.

Ian's hard glare at Simon sucked the good mood from the bridge. "All bad, Captain." Harlowe waited in silence. When Ian spoke in short sentences, he always listened. He wanted to know what Ian knew and didn't want to prolong the wait by asking questions. "We have company?"

Harlowe turned to Monday for confirmation. "I have them, Captain." Monday said, looking down in disbelief. He didn't know where they came from. "Nothing was there a second ago, Captain."

"The ships came in from behind the sun, Captain," Ian explained in Monday's defense. "If I hadn't been tweaking the sensors, I would have missed them myself."

"To drop in from behind the sun, they had to know we were here," Harlowe concluded.

Ian agreed. "That's how I see it."

"Good spot, Wiz. How many?"

"Five attack ships so far."

Dodger thought they were gearing up for a game of *Starship Trooper*. "Five! That's killer, Ian! Are we going to be in a battle?" he asked, eager for a fight.

Harlowe confronted his little brother, his eyes hot. "Dodger," he began, coolly, "go to the couch with Mowgi and Rhud and stay there until I tell you to move." Dodger tried to speak but Harlowe cut him off. This was no time for explanations. "That's an order! Do it!"

Dodger recognized the intensity in Harlowe's eyes that he had learned from a pro... their mom. When Tinker gave an order with that same look in her eyes, you did exactly as you were told. Dodger suddenly realized that an actual space battle was not a computer game. The thrill quickly drained from his face. Everyone had a job to do, even Dodger. Without protest, he went to his assigned place on the couch next to Mowgi and Rhud.

Without apology, Harlowe returned to Ian. "Does Riverstone know?"

"Not yet. I can't reach him. They must be disrupting communications."

Harlowe twisted around to Monday. "Use the Gama coms, Mr. Platter. They can't jam those. Tell Lu to get on the shuttle now!"

Ian held up his hand. "Belay that order, Mr. Platter."

Harlowe balked. "I want her and Sizzle back onboard Millie when things go south."

"I'll second that, Captain!" Simon urged.

Harlowe didn't need any help. "Stay on those weapons, Mr. Bolt. I'll handle this."

"Aye, Skipper!"

Harlowe felt the second problemo coming toward him at light speed. "Talk to me, Wiz."

"She doesn't have time. The GRB will be here in less than ten minutes. Even if she was in the shuttle and halfway here, she couldn't make it in time. If the *Jo-li Ran* doesn't go to light speed in the next few minutes, they're all dead, Harlowe."

12

Another Problemo

Monday looked up from his com station. "I have Lu, Captain."

Harlowe broke away from Ian and looked up at Leucadia's concerned face on the overheard. "What's wrong, Harlowe?"

"Bad guys are coming down our throats and that GRB the Tomarian brainiacs said was coming in two days, well, it will be here in less than eight minutes."

"Eight minutes?"

"That's right."

Leucadia already understood she was going nowhere. "We don't have time for the shuttle."

"Commander Lass has to break orbit and go to light speed immediately or you're all fried."

Leucadia wasn't as concerned about staying on the flagship as she was about the shields. "Harlowe, Ian can't make the calculations without me."

"No choice, Lu, get outta here."

"Harlowe, you don't understand. He needs to make a hundred adjustments every thirty seconds."

"He's the only pitcher I have left in the bullpen," Harlowe countered.

Ian stared up at the screen, terrified. Two minutes of indecision had already passed.

"Wiz," Harlowe called to him calmly, "what do you need?"

"I already transferred all shield controls to the bridge before I blinked."

"Can you do it?"

Ian jumped to his station at the console. "I have to."

With only a few minutes to go, Harlowe tried to keep everyone together. There was no time for emotion. He moved around to the giant window, with the planet Gazz taking up nearly every square inch of dura-glass.

Harlowe walked to Ian's side and gave him a confident pat on the shoulder as Prigg's eyes suddenly went haywire. "Attack ships are firing on the *Jo-li Ran*, Your Majesty."

Harlowe calmly faced Monday. "Inform Riverstone we're covering their escape, Mr. Platter." Then to Simon he ordered, "Take them out, Mr. Bolt."

If anyone thought the situation couldn't have deteriorated more, it just did. Ian turned back to Harlowe. "We don't have weapons, Captain."

Simon checked his readouts and threw up his hands. "Wiz is right, Skipper. They're dead! The weapon's array is offline!"

"That was the trade-off, Captain," Ian explained. "Weapons for shields."

Harlowe's teeth clenched. "We have nothing to defend ourselves or the *Jo-li Ran*?"

"We have shields. Their weapons can't hurt us, not even a little bit."

Dodger was about to get up to lend a hand. As if Harlowe had vision in the back of his head, he pointed to his little brother, freezing him in place. Harlowe didn't need to utter a word. Dodger figured it out on his own and stayed put.

"Two more attack ships dropped out of hyperlight, Your Majesty," Prigg announced.

"Course?" Harlowe asked.

The attack ship's plas-round struck *Millawanda*, jarring the bridge, before Prigg could respond.

"Understood, Prigg, message delivered," Harlowe replied.

Two more rounds struck Millawanda before Harlowe could ask Ian, "How is Millie holding up?"

"Doing fine, Captain. No damage," Ian replied.

Harlowe stared up at the holo-screen, sweating bullets. The *Jo-li Ran* was defending itself with everything she had, but she wasn't going to hyperlight. "Why aren't they moving?" To Ian he asked, "Time to GRB, Wiz?"

"Five minutes, seventeen seconds, Captain."

"Wow!" Dodger cried out in awe. "Look at that!" An incredible cloud of white light was expanding, coming their way. "What is it, Wiz?"

"The GRB," Ian replied in awe.

At that moment, Riverstone's face popped up inside the bridge. Before his Second-in-Command could say a word, Harlowe ordered, "Go to lightspeed, Matt!"

Behind Riverstone's image, the ship was ablaze with smoke and fire.

"We can't! The first shots took out the hyper-drive, Dog!"

Harlowe knew if they didn't think of something fast, the Flagship was history. "What do you have left?"

"She's dead in the water, Captain. We're putting everyone we can into the shuttle. Can you cover us?"

"Our weapons are down, Matt," Harlowe replied.

"Weapons down? What's up with that?"

"It gets worse. The GRB will be here in less than five minutes!"

During this entire exchange, Harlowe's mind had been racing through alternatives. There had to be a way. Like the General always told him, think like a Gamadin. Stay cool. Stay in control at all costs, even if you're about to fry!

Riverstone bolted for the shuttle, shouting into his com as he ran. "The GRB? It won't be here for days!"

"The Tomarian calcs were messed up," Harlowe countered. "Head for the Millie!"

"We're too far away!"

"Steer the shuttle toward the planet," Harlowe directed as he glanced at Ian for approval. "Millie will protect you once you're under her shields."

"It should work, Captain," Ian confirmed.

"Understood!" Riverstone confirmed. "Riverstone out!"

Harlowe shouted out a final boost. "Go, go, go!"

The last image they saw before the image winked out was Riverstone diving through the closing airlock shuttle door.

13

Going Down

"Release shuttle clamps!" Riverstone commanded as he rolled forward, bounced to his feet, and charged toward the shuttle bridge. Commander Lass was already working the left side of the command console when Riverstone jumped into the copilot chair next to him. "No countdown, Commander. Full throttle! Dive for the planet!"

Commander Lass stared at Riverstone like he was nuts. "We are surrendering, First Officer."

Riverstone wasn't waiting for permission. He jammed the throttle forward and told him straight out, "Oh no, we're not!"

Commander Lass reached down and pulled out a sidearm, pointing it at Riverstone's face. "Back away from the controls, First Officer."

"The burst is about to hit us, Commander," Riverstone warned. "If we don't get under *Millawanda's* shields, we're fried!"

The Commander jerked the steering column hard to starboard, heading away from the planet toward the advancing attack ships. "The burst is not due for another two days."

"Your scientists were wrong. It will be here in moments. Look!" Riverstone said, pointing at the bright cloud through the forward window. It was growing brighter before their eyes. "It's already here. Now do as I say!"

Behind them, two more officers backed Commander Lass with weapons pointed at Riverstone. From the way things were playing out, the assault on the *Jo-li Ran* had been planned from the beginning. Three more Tomarians had their weapons pointed aft, guarding the entry to the shuttle bridge.

"Sharlon is our prisoner," Commander Lass confessed. "With a Gamadin and her daughter, the reward will be even greater."

Riverstone rose from his seat. "Reward? That's stupid, Toad. You won't live to spend a dime if you don't head the shuttle back to the planet."

Commander Lass waved his weapon at his officers. "Disable him."

Believing his five Tomarians had the Gamadin well-guarded, Commander Lass returned to the shuttle's controls. An officer reached out to pull Riverstone away from the console when a hard fist twisted his neck sideways. Before the second officer could react, another fist slammed his head against the bulkhead. Riverstone then grabbed the fallen officer's weapon and cracked it against Commander Lass's head. The three remaining officers aft of the bridge were caught off guard by the Gamadin ferocity. Three shots to three heads and they, too, were out of the way.

Leucadia entered through the door the same moment Riverstone was tossing Commander Lass's body aft like a bag of trash. "Trouble?" she asked, appearing cool as she stepped over the bodies lying in the doorway.

"They ratted us out," Riverstone replied, jumping back into the pilot's seat.

Leucadia wasted no time filling the vacant copilot seat. "How can I help?"

Guiding the shuttle back toward Gazz, Riverstone nodded toward her side of the controls. "Redirect all shield power aft. They're not going to like us turning around."

"Roger that!"

No sooner had Leucadia diverted power to the aft shields than the first orange blast of plasma whizzed past the front windshield.

14

Out of Time

As the Gamadin watched with relief the shuttle turning back toward the planet, Prigg reported that the *Jo-li Ran* had exhausted its power. He counted eleven attack ships before Harlowe ordered him to stop counting and go to the empty science station and assist Ian.

Now that the *Jo-li Ran* was history, the Gamadin could concentrate on the mission: saving Gazz.

Dodger found it all fascinating. His eyes remained riveted to the forward windows, watching from his seat on the observation couch as if he was watching a video game on his computer.

Wow, look at all those lights! As much as he wanted to cheer his brother on—*Kill the toads, Harlowe! Beat their heads to a pulp!*—he wanted to help even more, even if was to wipe the sweat from Ian's brow. At least it was something!

Dodger kept his mouth shut and remained in place on the long couch next to Mowgi and Rhud until he finally got his call.

"Dodger!" Harlowe called out. "Come here!"

Dodger bolted to Harlowe's side. "What can I do, Harlowe?"

Harlowe grabbed his arm and put him into Riverstone's empty seat. This was not the help he was expecting.

"Stay there," Harlowe ordered. Harlowe flipped an activator and clamps snapped around Dodger's waist, legs, and chest, holding him fast to the chair. He was going nowhere. He wanted to protest but

Harlowe cupped his hand over his brother's mouth. "Not a word. Things are going to get rough. Everyone else on the bridge will be doing the same thing."

Dodger relaxed somewhat when Harlowe sat back in his chair and activated his own chair clamps. Around the room, everyone else was clamping down.

Riverstone and Leucadia appeared on the holo-screen. "We had some trouble, Captain. Lass was attempting to kidnap Sharlon."

"Two bad guys are hot on your tail, Matt," Harlowe said.

On the screen the shuttle was showing obvious hits as Riverstone and Leucadia bounced around in their pilot seats. The last words the Gamadin crew heard from the shuttle were Leucadia's.

"Uh, oh!" she said.

*　*　*

A bright ball of white light exploded behind the shuttlecraft. From out of the flaming debris field, the shuttlecraft tumbled out of control toward the planet. They were still miles from *Millawanda's* protective shield. Ian began deploying the *Millawanda's* shields like slices of a pie across the entire planet's surface.

The attack ships were gaining on them. "Hurry Wiz!" Harlowe cried out, watching Riverstone's shuttle plunge down on the overhead screen. Directly behind the shuttle, both attack ships fired more salvos, unaware that the luminous GRB was about to turn them to subatomic dust.

"I can't bring the shields to full power yet," Ian warned. "If I do, Millie will run out of energy before the GRB hits."

"Can you cover them now?"

"Yes!"

"Then do it!" Harlowe ordered. "They can't take another hit."

"But if I do—"

Harlowe nodded calmly. There was no other choice. "I know. Do it!"

Harlowe wished he had one shot left to blast the lead attack ship, but all he could do was sit and watch the Tomarian shuttle rush to get to the barrier line before the attackers hit them with a fatal shot or the GRB struck. Either way, they were toast if they failed to slide under the barrier in time.

Harlowe turned to Prigg. "Who are they, Prigg?"

Prigg's misaligned fingers touched the console. His fingers were crooked and malformed because he was born on Naruck, a planet that suffered a nuclear holocaust. Harlowe had wanted Prigg to have surgery to correct the defects, but Prigg protested. His defects were his and that was how he wanted it to stay.

When Prigg's three eyes went straight, Harlowe knew he had an answer. "They are Tock-hyban, Your Majesty."

Harlowe remembered the name of the planet from before. It was the one where Quay was traveling to at the time her transport was shot down by a Consortium battle cruiser.

"The shuttle's through the barrier line, Captain," Ian announced. "Buttoning up shields around the planet…" Ian ran his fingers over a dozen or more activators, "now!"

Gazz was locked tight, but before the barrier closed, a Tock-hyban attacker passed one last shot through the energy wall, blowing away the aft end of the shuttle. The crew watched helplessly as the shuttle began to break up just as the GRB slammed into the planet.

* * *

Leucadia helped Riverstone back into his seat. They both fought to control the shuttle. "What hit us?"

Leucadia stared at her gauges in front of her. "We're losing atmosphere, Matthew."

The cabin was losing life support and smoke was filling the cockpit. Riverstone slapped his SIBA medallion before he passed out. Leucadia was fading fast. She fought against the suffocating fumes but was losing control of her arms and legs. Struggling to keep control of the shuttle, Riverstone pulled Leucadia over to his side and activated her SIBA. Leucadia had begun breathing herself back to consciousness when Riverstone glanced through the bridge doorway and saw Sizzle, already in her SIBA, helping Sharlon and the others into the three escape pods.

Riverstone turned Leucadia around and pointed her toward the back. "Go help Sizzle!"

Through the top observation porthole, bright planet-wide flashes and bolts of searing gamma rays were pummeling the moons around the planet. It was like no planetary war Riverstone had ever witnessed. He knew Harlowe and the Gamadin crew was doing whatever they could to save themselves and the planet from total destruction.

This was no slam-dunk. Riverstone could see the GRB was far more deadly than anyone had figured. His spirits sank when he thought of *Millawanda* and his fellow Gamadin. How could they withstand such a massive surge of galactic energy?

Riverstone heard the first pod arm itself and blast away from the side of the shuttle. A second later, the next pod engine ignited and blew away from the burning shuttle. "Hurry, Matthew!" Leucadia called to him through his SIBA's com.

Riverstone looked outside and spotted a land mass on the horizon. They had to make it there, he figured, or fall into the ocean. "Wait, Lu! I see land."

The crackling sound of high-energy explosions came from the rear. Just as Riverstone looked up, the observation porthole exploded, sucking out the remaining air. The shuttle was moments from exploding.

"Hurry, Matthew!" Leucadia yelled again. She was holding the door open for him. The shuttle itself wouldn't last until it got to land. The last pod had to blow free or it wouldn't make it either.

Through the windows, the green ocean was coming too fast. Riverstone had no time to make it into the third pod. He had only enough time to run back to the pod and shut the door, forcing Leucadia back into the pod against her will. "NO, MATTHEW!" she screamed.

Leucadia tried to keep the door open, but Riverstone was stronger. He shoved the hatch closed and threw the locking lever over. At first, it wouldn't latch all the way. He reached around and grabbed his robob cylinder. Using it as a club, he applied three hard blows. The latch clanked into place and locked.

Riverstone kissed the cylinder, "Thanks Alice." With one hand, he reattached the gold-colored cylinder to his Gama-belt and struck the activating mechanism with his other. The pod blew away from the shuttle just as the hull began to disintegrate around him.

15

Like a Skipping Stone

Millawanda shook so hard it felt like she was going to bust apart at the seams. One could almost hear the ship screaming in pain from the forces that were against her. To communicate with his crew, Harlowe had to shout out his orders above the noise. "How much longer, Wiz?"

"It's not over, Captain!" Ian replied.

Harlowe was caught between turning down *Millawanda's* power enough to save her or keeping the max output up long enough to save Gazz. If the choice was to save the planet, Millie could die, her energy sucked out from her.

"What's happening to Millie, Harlowe?" Dodger asked.

"Not now, Dodger."

Harlowe turned to Ian as the turbulence increased, but before he could call out another command, Simon became the first to report the damage. "Skipper, my console's out!"

Monday turned to Harlowe. "Mine too, Captain. Everything's dark."

Ian knew why. "Millie's shut down, Harlowe."

Suddenly the shaking stopped. Harlowe looked out the windows and discovered the brilliant white light was gone. The stars had miraculously returned. "What happened?"

Ian nearly fell out of his chair from exhaustion. Harlowe caught him before he fell and lifted him up in his chair. After a brief visual, Ian had the only answer that made sense. "It passed."

Simon glanced up at the overhead to confirm. There was nothing there. The holograph had disappeared. Finding it gone, he searched the heavens from one edge of the windows to the other. "Where's the *Jo-li Ran*, Skipper?"

Prigg's head twisted around while his eyes seemed to go in the opposite direction. One had to wonder how the little Naruckian saw anything at all, yet according to Harlowe, Prigg's eyes were as sharp as theirs. "The Tock-hyban attack ships have disappeared, Your Majesty," Prigg stated in astonishment.

Monday had the logical explanation. "They were outside the force field, Captain."

Simon rose from his chair and went to the portside observation window to search the section of the planet where he had last seen the shuttle go down. "Nothing here, Skipper. Nothing but ocean."

Dodger pointed out the starboard observation window, away from where the others were looking. "There! I see something moving over there."

Releasing their chair restraints, Harlowe went to the window to see what Dodger saw. Along the way, Harlowe tapped his SIBA medallion, engulfing himself in his armored suit. With the overhead screen out, the powerful optics in his SIBA was the best way to see distances.

"It's the shuttle," Harlowe announced, as they were joined by Monday and Simon. Simon activated his SIBA, too. He had to see it for himself.

"Oh my God, it's breaking up!" Simon exclaimed.

*   *   *

Fresh out of extra escape pods in the disintegrating shuttle, Riverstone had only one choice. He dove out of the open hatchway and into the stratosphere with his SIBA fully deployed. Fifty miles above the planet's surface, he would have frozen in seconds without his SIBA to protect him.

At first, Riverstone felt no sensation at all of falling toward the planet, but the readouts inside his bugeyes said otherwise. There was no wind at this altitude. The air was so thin that there were no outside sounds of resistance. He was racing toward the planet like a human missile and picking up speed. Not far away, Leucadia's escape pod was drifting silently like he was. Soon they would feel the air buffeting around them as they descended into the denser atmosphere of the planet. The escape pod was designed to enter the atmosphere of a planet without burning up. Riverstone wasn't, however. He knew his SIBA's outer shell could deflect micro meteors and extreme heat and cold. Whether it could withstand the plunge into the Gazzian atmosphere was another question. The SIBA was not designed as a reentry device!

A sudden bright light from behind turned his attention back toward where he had come. It was the shuttle exploding into oblivion.

"MATTHEW! MATTHEW!" Leucadia shouted in his ear.

"I'm here, Lu," Riverstone replied calmly. What else could he be but a Gamadin, cool under pressure the way he'd been taught those many months on Mars. *"If you can survive here,"* General Gunn had told them, referring to the subzero lifeless planet with no waves and no In-N-Out hamburgers, *"you will survive anywhere."* Riverstone learned the lesson when General Gunn marooned them on one of the remotest areas of Mars with only minimal supplies in their SIBA utility belts. They had to depend on their own resources to cross the thousand miles of desolation and return to *Millawanda*, or die. And they did it. Harlowe saved them that time. This time, however, Harlowe was busy saving Gazz. There would be no ship coming to pluck him out of the sky before he burned up. As Riverstone looked out over the curvature of the planet, he knew that this time his survival depended on no one but himself.

* * *

"Wow, Harlowe, it just went blewy!" Dodger exclaimed as he stared at where the shuttlecraft had just exploded. It was like one of the *Warcraft* simulation games he played at home on his computer, only this was real.

With his three eyes moving constantly in different directions, Prigg discovered something no one else had picked up on in the confusion of the shuttlecraft's destruction. "We're losing altitude, Your Majesty."

Harlowe confirmed the downward drift of the ship. "Return Millie to a stationary orbit, Mr. Platter."

Monday stared down at his console. "Helm is dead, Captain. She's not responding."

Simon pointed to the back wall. "What happened to the lights, Skipper?"

Ian jumped out of his chair and checked the line of screens across the console. "She's sucked dry. There's not enough power to keep her from falling into the planet, Captain."

"What controls do we have, Wiz?" Harlowe asked.

Ian went back to his station and checked the readouts. "It's all out, Captain. No thrusters, no gravity assist." He searched the console for anything active. "Only a small amount of inertia dampeners, that's it."

Outside, they watched as the bow of the saucer turned downward. Ahead of them lay a massive ocean.

"Any suggestions?" Harlowe asked the bridge.

Ian looked at Harlowe. "No, sir. She's headed down."

"Check her shields. Anything left there?" Harlowe asked.

Ian returned to his station. "Some, but they're fading. They won't keep us from breaking apart when we hit the water, Captain."

Harlowe repositioned himself in his chair. "Divert what's left to me, Wiz."

"Aye, Captain."

"What are you going to do, Harlowe?" Dodger asked.

"Land her." Then to Monday, he said, "Mr. Platter, secure the animals to the middle of the floor."

"Aye, Captain."

Two robobs blinked onto the bridge with webbing to strap the cats to the floor. Mowgi didn't need to be strapped, nor would he let them. If he was going down, he was going down his way.

"Harlowe, are we going to crash?" Dodger asked, watching the planet growing fast.

Harlowe flashed him a confident grin. "Not if I can help it, Dodger."

"Millie will be all right, won't she?"

"Yeah, she'll be fine. Make sure your straps are tight."

With the determination of a young Gamadin, Dodger sat up straight in his chair and checked his straps. "I'm in, Harlowe!"

Harlowe gave him a wink as he returned to the window and the dark green ocean.

"Thirty seconds to impact," Ian called out.

Monday pointed to a spit of land on the horizon. "Maybe we can make that, Captain." Monday was right. The closer they could get to land, the better. If they landed too far out, they'd slip miles below the surface. The ocean pressure at that depth would crush them without shields.

With no thrusters and no maneuverability, *Millawanda* had to cross hundreds miles of ocean to reach the nearest land mass. Harlowe had his work cut out for him if they were to survive.

"Fifteen seconds," Ian called out.

"We're going to fall short, aren't we?" Simon asked.

Harlowe said nothing. He had his mind on the problem and falling short wasn't one he cared to discuss.

Only seconds before striking the water, Harlowe engaged the forward thrusters, lifting the nose of the giant saucer just enough to hit the water at an angle.

"Three, two, one..." Ian said, counting down.

WHAM!

Skipping like a flat stone, *Millawanda* bounced 50 miles across the water on her first leap. Her second skip was 30 miles. Heads snapped forward and back with each bounce, as if they were riding some wild bronco. After that it was fifteen miles, ten, five, one, until the giant saucer came to a big swooshing stop, creating a giant tidal wave that mushroomed out from her hull.

They finally settled, miraculously floating on top of the water. Harlowe looked around. "Everybody sound off."

"Yo, Skipper." Simon replied, reaching for his chair to stand.

Monday had to manually pry his straps loose from his body. "Aye, Captain."

"Okay here, Harlowe!" Dodger responded, energized. For him it was like a video game. He wanted another ride!

Ian turned around in his chair with thumbs up.

Prigg didn't respond. The little Naruckian was still strapped at his position, his head tilted and hanging to one side.

Harlowe unbuckled his straps and went to Prigg, shaking him back to consciousness. "Prigg! Wake up! Come out of it, little buddy." He shook him some more before he finally came around.

"I think he's more scared than hurt, Skipper," Simon said.

Once Harlowe was convinced that Prigg was in no danger, he looked for the pets. The cats were okay, snarling with attitudes, ready to be released from their restraining net. Mowgi was on top of the couch as if nothing had disturbed him at all. Harlowe wondered if a ten-megaton bomb could affect his composure.

16

Bugeyed Meteor

Turbulence surprised Riverstone, twisting him briefly out of control. By making small adjustments with his legs and hands, he kept himself aligned with Leucadia's escape pod. For the last ten thousand feet, the air around him had been glowing hot from the friction caused by the denser air around him. His SIBA skin read one thousand degrees. A few seconds later it was fifteen hundred and rising fast. He caught a quick glimpse of the escape pod and saw that it was experiencing the same reentry friction as he was. Because of its mass, the radiance around its hull was more intense. The escape pod's shields were keeping Leucadia and the others from burning up. On the other hand, he was unsure just how long his SIBA would hold up against the searing temperatures.

Two thousand degrees!

He checked the readouts. The numbers were climbing at an alarming rate. The temperature inside his suit was a comfortable eighty degrees, but his breathing and heart rate were elevated. That was expected, he figured. "So far, so good," he mumbled to himself.

Worried about how far he could push his suit before it would rip apart, he thought about releasing the gossamer wings from under his arms to slow his descent. But his airspeed was still supersonic. If he dropped his wings now, his arms would rip out of their sockets. No, he had to stay patient and ride it out. His SIBA was tough, he reminded himself. *It's 54th-century stuff, right? Stay the course.* He would be okay. When he hit the denser air at the lower altitudes, he would slow down. Besides, he needed to keep the escape pod in sight. To do that he had to keep pace.

Two thousand five hundred!

His SIBA was getting warm, like Las Vegas in summer. If he looked anything like the escape pod, he was glowing like a bugeyed firefly.

Peering through the brightness of his SIBA, he observed that the geography of the planet was growing steadily larger and more defined. Where before he saw only solid earthtones, deep sea greens, and blues of vast oceans, he now made out white swirling clouds, forests, deserts, and the tall peaks of long mountain ranges. Directly below him was the enigmatic black mountain Sharlon had pointed out from the *Jo-li Ran* observation deck. The ancient volcano was so high and majestic in the middle of the surrounding plains, he felt like he could reach down and touch the six-mile-high peak with his claw. Nothing grew above the tree line on its slopes. Inside its great rock valleys were wide rivers of glacial ice that made Riverstone shiver at the thought of landing there.

Brrr!

If they could hold out long enough, he hoped they had enough altitude to make it to the middle latitudes of the planet, preferably on the coast. If he was going to crash-land anywhere he wanted it to be someplace warm with sandy beaches and good surf like 42nd Street or #2 near Barnard's Star. Why not enjoy the downtime until Harlowe picked them up in *Millawanda*, he mused?

Man, it's hot! He was sweating bullets. He checked his readouts.

Twenty-nine hundred degrees and holding. Inside temperature, a balmy hundred and four.

He checked the SIBA over the best he could. *Sweet, no leaks!* He guessed that if there was a leak, he would be toast by now. Even a pinhole he would be gonzo, he figured.

The sound of the outside air rushing past was growing louder. No worries. If the sound became too loud, his SIBA would protect his ears from any damage.

But he wondered what the sound meant. Was he starting to break up?

He checked his readouts again. *Twenty-eight hundred! Whoa, gettin' cooler!* It was a step in the right direction. *Twenty-six fifty. Way cool!* His air speed, too, had slowed by ten percent.

At the present, Riverstone and the escape pod were twelve miles above the surface of the planet. As they approached the speed of sound, his SIBA skin temperature was back down to a pleasant 1500 degrees.

After passing the black mountain, Riverstone and the pod crossed a prairie and headed diagonally across a large lake surrounded by a deep green forest. Now the land was moving by quickly. He crossed over another mountain range and a desert before his bugeyes found the ocean again.

Then the escape pod veered off in a sudden course change. Riverstone was caught off guard by the abruptness and tried to raise Leucadia on the com. "Lu! What are you doing?" he asked.

Leucadia's voice was stressed. "We've lost helm, Matthew! We have no way to guide our descent!"

Unable to change his direction without separating his arms from his body, he continued in the same direction and watched helplessly as the escape pod veered away from him. With his arms pressed against his side, he tried to control his direction by using his hands like an airplane rudder to add drag to one side or the other. His effort had little effect. He was still unable to swing around to keep up with the escape pod. His last view of the pod was its diving down into a mass of black clouds.

I can't lose the pod!

He quickly checked his velocity. He was below three hundred miles per hour. His SIBA had cooled to minus fifty, too. A hot afternoon on Mars, he thought. Taking the chance that he had slowed enough to open his wings, he began unfolding them gradually.

Wrong!

The thin film blew open, catching him by surprise. Before he realized what he had done, he was twisting in an uncontrolled frenzy. He tried to correct his path but found himself plummeting into the charged black thunderhead of a violent electrical storm.

17

The Third Problemo

Stepping outside the bridge hatchway, Harlowe and Ian stood on *Millawanda's* upper deck with binoculars, surveying the island on the horizon. The ocean breeze felt like a muggy Southern California summer morning along the coast. The refreshing salt air breeze brought back memories of a time when their lives were simple and carefree. But this was no time for nostalgia. They had a ship to save and friends to find.

Studying the ocean with his binoculars, Harlowe asked for Ian's calculations on where the shuttle escape pods had touched down on the planet.

Ian studied his handheld com and replied, "I got a lock on two of them, Captain."

"How far?" Harlowe asked. He didn't care about the details. He only wanted direction and distance. He would figure out the rest later. Leucadia and Riverstone were his secondary concern; the ship and his crew came first.

Ian pointed back over his shoulder, in the opposite direction of their travel. "Two thousand, three hundred miles and some change that way, Dog."

Harlowe closed his eyes, blaming himself for the miss. "I was hoping we were closer."

"Millie had a nasty ride, Captain. You had to save her first. If you hadn't skipped her across the water like that, we would be two miles underwater by my calculations."

Harlowe grunted. Maybe so, but he still took the blame. He returned to his survey of the island and made a common-sense guess about the escape pods. "That third pod should be close to the other two."

Ian agreed. "Aye, that's a good bet."

Ian's preliminary readouts put *Millawanda* less than nine miles off the island. A long way to pull a 700,000 ton spacecraft, but a great deal closer than the hundreds of miles it would have been if Harlowe hadn't pulled *Millawanda's* nose up in time to skip her like a stone across the ocean. Remarkably, the saucer was still floating on the water when by all accounts she should have already sunk to the bottom. What was keeping her afloat?

To find out why they were suspended above the surface, they walked out to the perimeter edge and peered over the side. The water was clear and green. Far down was a carpet of jagged coral and rocks. Large schools of fish were swimming just beneath the surface. Farther out, dolphin-like creatures were playfully breaking the surface while they fed on the abundant food supply. Through the magnification of the water, the bottom appeared close. In reality they were floating a few hundred feet above the highest reefs.

"Think we can make it to the island without running aground, Wiz?" Harlowe asked, peering down.

Ian pointed at the faint blue light that encircled the perimeter. "She's riding pretty high, Captain. If we can keep her away from the reef, we should be cool."

Harlowe studied the wind direction. "The breeze is with us. That's a plus."

"That could change though. We need to get Millie into shallow waters before she starts taking on water."

Monday came jogging up. "We found three rovers, Captain." Harlowe had earlier sent Monday and Simon to search for anything that might work to tow the saucer across the water. With no power to move herself, *Millawanda* was at the mercy of ocean currents unless they could tow her closer to the island.

Monday pointed at the three rovers swishing out of an opening in the top of the hull with their robob drivers. "This is all we have, Captain."

"Only three? It will take more than that," Ian said.

"They're the only ones with juice, Mr. Wizzixs," Monday replied.

Harlowe saw no need to curse the situation. At this point, with all the bad luck they had thus far, he was grateful for any help he could get. "Understood, Mr. Platter. Nice work."

"It was really Dodger who had found them, Captain." Harlowe and Ian glanced at each other, wondering how Harlowe's little brother could have aided in the discovery of the three rovers.

"Well, sir, the grannywagon was gonzo. Simon and I...I mean, Mr. Bolt, sir...didn't think there were any more. Then Dodger said he knew where a ton of them were. We counted fifty!"

"Fifty?" Harlowe exclaimed.

"That's right, Captain! All lined up in neat little rows, big as life."

"I'm going to have to raise his allowance," Harlowe quipped as he watched the three robobs attach the towlines to the perimeter rim of the ship. "They were the only three working out of the fifty?" he asked, turning to Ian for an explanation as to why so few rovers had juice.

Ian knew the answer. "Millie sucked every ounce of power from whatever source she could find to save us. Once these rovers are out, there's nothing left. My guess is that we'll only have a few clickers, too."

Harlowe watched as the three rovers moved across the choppy water and pulled the hull lines taut. "Sweet," he said and gave the hand signal for the clickers to commence the towing.

Their legs felt the tug on the hull beneath them as *Millawanda* slowly began to move forward.

Harlowe kept his mind occupied, trying to stifle his frustration at everything he had to contend with. He picked up his binoculars and continued his scan of the area. Beyond the island was a long continental landmass he had seen before they skipped across the ocean's surface. Because of the curvature of the planet's surface, the coastline was hidden from view, but he could see the tops of the coastal mountains. They were another twenty miles beyond the island to the east. He figured if the island didn't have what they needed in the way of supplies, he would find something in the utility room to float across to the continental shore. "So what are we going to do, Wiz? Where's the closest gas station on Gazz?"

Ian knew the answer. So did everyone else. It was another one of those questions Harlowe liked to ask that kept the conversation going and the mood light. On a medieval planet with technology about as advanced as 16th-century Earth, there were no cars, airplanes, or In-N-Out burgers. The fastest way to travel was by wind-driven ships. There simply *were* no gas stations!

Harlowe continued to scope out the island. "Nothing but vines." Spaceships from the stars needed power in great concentrations. Vines couldn't fuel a clicker, he thought.

Monday found that odd. "No coconut trees?" he asked Harlowe. "That seems strange, Captain."

Harlowe could care less about the lack of coconut palms on a tropical island. His first priority was to drag his ship safely inside the island's calm, leeward lagoon before the sun went down.

Ian checked his com readouts before pointing at the large moon on the horizon. It was ten times the size of Earth's moon. "We have about five hours before that moon gets high enough for a tide shift. Then we'll be swimming against the tide big time."

"Caution noted, Wiz." Then to Monday he ordered, "Have the clickers step it up a notch, Mr. Platter."

"Aye, Captain."

Harlowe was about to return to the bridge when he caught Ian's long face. "What's the matter, Wiz? You look like you're going to hurl. I've never known you to be seasick."

"I'm not, Captain."

"Millie's got you down? Me too. The possibility of losing Leucadia and Riverstone is bad enough, but we'll find them."

Ian turned his face to the wind. It was as if there was no easy way to say it other than straight out. "There's a second GRB coming, Harlowe."

Whenever Ian shifted to Harlowe's given name from Captain, there was a sense of doom associated with his statement. This time Harlowe didn't convey any reaction. Maybe it was because they had gone through so much that day already and, like Millie, all of his emotional fuel was spent. Harlowe simply had nothing left. "Another burst, huh?" he uttered with all the passion of a limp rope.

Ian's tired face nodded a *yes*.

"How long do we have?"

"Forty-one days."

Harlowe looked up at the blue-green sky as a flock of sea birds flew overhead, away from the island in a hurry. "So we have to gas Millie and find Lu and Riverstone or everything we've done so far is out the door."

Ian had more. "The second GRB will be narly as the first one, maybe worse. I wasn't able to get all the calcs done before we went down. All life on Gazz will be snuffed out, including us, if we don't find Millie some power, and fast."

Harlowe thought for a moment before he asked the next question. "If we find her the power she needs, can we save Gazz again without sucking her dry this time?"

Ian stared at Harlowe for a long moment. "I don't know yet, Captain." He needed more time to work on the problem. He explained to Harlowe that there were too many hurdles for him to give an answer at the moment. "If Lu was here, our chances would improve a ton," he said, straight up.

"We'd better find her quick then."

"Aye."

"We don't have a lot of time, Wiz."

"I'm sorry, Captain. I didn't see it either until the first GRB was almost upon us. The second burst was trailing the first like a big shadow."

"Are you sure there isn't a third, fourth, or fifth one?" Harlowe asked.

"No, this is it."

Harlowe cuffed his hand over his mouth and yelled down the hull to Monday, who was tending the towlines. "FULL SPEED AHEAD, MR. PLATTER!"

18

Rough Landing

Riverstone hung by his dura-line in the driving rain, bouncing and twisting against the rock face of the cliff. It was a wonder he had survived the fall. After being been struck twice by billion-volt lightning bolts and slamming into the side of a cliff, his brains were a chocolate mess. Sheer Gamadin instinct was the only thing keeping him alive. His SIBA saved him from being fried like a chicken, but the jolts tore up his insides. The wings had slowed his descent enough to save him, but the mountain was big and too large to miss. He managed to draw his sidearm, attach a piton, and fired point-blank at the rock before he plunged to a rocky death a half-mile into the gorge below. For most of the day, he remained motionless against the cliff, hanging like a water-drenched spider from his Gama-belt dura-line thread. The rain washed over him in heavy sheets while his SIBA repaired his battered body.

Sometime in the afternoon, a call from Leucadia on his com woke him from his dreamless sleep. At first, he was too disoriented to make a rational reply. No doubt he sounded like he was drugged. It took him several minutes to gather his wits enough to have an intelligent conversation.

"Rough landing, Matthew?" Leucadia asked.

"Yeah...rough," Riverstone replied slowly.

"You okay?"

"I don't feel okay."

"Where are you?" she asked.

He took a moment to check his equipment. He felt his Gama-belt and was relieved to find his sidearm still firmly in place. He then checked his other attachments and found that his nourishment capsules, extra piton clips, and SIBA power units were in good shape. He almost lost it, though, when he couldn't find Alice. The robob cylinder had drifted around to the back of his belt, out of sight. After thanking the clicker gods for her safety, he moved the robob cylinder to its normal place on the left side of his belt.

The storm was still pouring rain, but his bugeyes permitted him to peer through the morass with ease. Above him, the cliff went up another two thousand feet before the face angled away from his view. A mile below him, the deep gorge was filled with a raging river, trees, rocky boulders, and thick brush. Across the gorge was a flat plain of sparse vegetation. According to his nav readouts, it was the right course to follow, but it was not necessarily the fastest route. A tiny blue dot on his screen told him that Leucadia was two hundred twenty-seven miles to the west and slightly north of his location. If he could glide across the canyon, a piece of cake on a normal day, he could make better time running flat out on the plain instead of tripping along rock-filled and flooded canyons.

Leucadia's voice interrupted his calculations. "Matthew...are you there?"

"I'm stuck on a cliff. Probably a two-day run from you," Riverstone finally replied.

"How can I help, Matthew?" she asked worriedly.

"Stay put. I'll be fine once I get going. You?"

"The pod landed off the coast. We're evacuating it now. There appears to be plenty to eat and fresh water. We should be okay until Harlowe finds us."

Riverstone quickly asked, "Have you heard from him yet?"

"No. You?" she asked.

"*Nada*. That's not like Harlowe. If everything was cool, he would have contacted you by now." Suddenly Riverstone noticed something that put him in a panic. Leucadia could feel it from the other end.

"Matthew. You're scaring me," she said.

"Probably nothing, Lu."

"Matthew. Tell me what's wrong."

"It's Millie's transponder light. It's dark. My SIBA took a number of lightning strikes coming down. The light could be funky."

There was a moment of silence before Leucadia answered. "Matthew, my light is out, too. They can't both be bad."

"Okay, worrying won't help. Harlowe will find us," Riverstone assured her.

"My light should be working, Matthew. There's got to be a reason why it's out."

"Millie's tough, Lu. She had to go through plenty, just like us. The GRB could have zapped her instruments. She could be rebooting. There could be a ton of reasons why it's out. You know that."

Leucadia wasn't panicked. She was trying to be practical. "Harlowe would be calling us if he could. He wouldn't wait this long. You agree, don't you? I can hear it in your voice."

Riverstone understood why he often heard Harlowe say, "*Yes dear*", to Leucadia, especially when she wanted an answer that he was trying to keep to himself. Without saying, "yes dear," he simply mouthed it silently to himself before he replied, "Okay, something's whack, but

I don't know what." He then added some reassurance to his reply. "Don't worry. Harlowe's Harlowe. You know that. He's got more lives than a truckload of cats. He'll turn up soon and we'll find out it was just a glitch. You know how that is. Right?"

Riverstone could sense Leucadia's uneasiness on the other end of his com. "I don't feel right, Matthew. I think something happened to Millie."

"Okay, I admit it sounds bad. As soon as I get off this mountain, I'll head your way. Ten-to-one Harlowe picks you up before I get there."

Leucadia didn't sound all that confident when she said, "Hurry, Matthew."

"I will." Then Riverstone asked, "How is everyone?"

"Two pods made it down within a mile of each other. We don't know about the third pod. We lost contact with it," Leucadia replied.

"Sizzle and Sharlon?" Riverstone inquired.

"Sizzle is here, helping me pull everyone out of the water." Then she called out in the background, "Sizzle, where's Sharlon?"

Riverstone could hear the reply. "She's..." Sizzle's voice trailed off and remained silent for a long moment before she spoke again in a panic. "I don't see her, Lu!"

"Oh, my God, Matthew! They think she's still inside the pod. It's underwater. I have to go. Lu out!"

19

Mowgi's Hang-up

The outgoing tide made entering the lagoon a struggle for *Millawanda*, but with all the power that was left in the three rovers and eighty-nine clickers pulling on dura-lines, the Gamadin were finally able to wrestle the giant saucer into the lagoon, where she could rest on the shallow bottom. After making sure *Millawanda* was securely in place, Harlowe swam into the lagoon and touched the side of her hull. "It's okay, girl. Rest easy. We'll find a way to make you right, I promise."

Great jets of air were escaping from around her perimeter. It would take hours for her to settle into her watery nest. She was, after all, a very large ship. Harlowe wanted her at the bottom of the lagoon for several reasons. Aside from the fact that it would take energy to stay afloat—energy she didn't have—he wanted her out of sight. The island appeared deserted, but for how long? He didn't know. Gazz was a populated planet. It was possible ships sailing near the island might see her if she remained above the surface. If a 16th-century ship discovered a 54th-century spaceship, who knows what the unintended consequences might be? As the old saying goes, *out of sight, out of mind.* He had enough problems without having to deal with the inhabitants of a medieval planet, problems like finding Leucadia, Sizzle, and Riverstone before the next GRB hit them in 41 days. He let out a *woe-is-me-how-am-I-going-to-get-out-of-this-pickle* sigh as he emerged from the water. Monday was waiting for him on the beach.

"Is the lagoon deep enough to hide all of her, Captain?" Monday asked, watching the giant bubbles percolate from under Millie's massive hull.

"Deep enough, Squid." Harlowe tapped his sleeve. The dome section wavered for a brief moment before it faded away to nothing. "Wiz calculated all but her dome would be below the surface."

"How long can she stay that way?" Monday asked.

Harlowe tilted his head toward the midday sun. "Millie's on 'E,' Squid. The only thing that's keeping her going is the sun."

"Not enough to get us out of here, huh?"

"Not by a long shot."

Simon was within earshot of the conversation. He approached Harlowe and Monday with a worried expression. "How will we find the girls, Skipper, if Millie's at the bottom of the lagoon?"

Harlowe felt it best to delay telling Simon anything about the second GRB. His crew had enough problems without knowing the world would end in forty-one days if they didn't find a way to revive *Millawanda*. "I'm working on it, Mr. Bolt."

Together the three walked over to a rover lying on its side in the sand. When a rover is parked in its normal state, it remains a foot or so off of whatever surface it hovers over. All three rovers used to pull *Millawanda* into the lagoon were lying in the sand on their sides, drained of power. "We'll need a way off the island first, Rerun," Harlowe commented.

Simon's heart sank. He had already imagined traveling across the Gazzian Sea in a Mach 2 grannywagon and finding his bride-to-be, Sizzle, waiting for him with open arms, whereupon her hero, Captain Starr, would pick her up and hustle them back to the island for a raging beach fire with lobster and vine salad on the menu.

Unable to take Harlowe's word that the rovers were sucked dry of power, Simon ran to the nearest wheelless car lying in the sand and tried to switch it on.

Nothing. The 54th-century vehicle was as dead as the sand it was resting on.

In a panic, he sprinted to the second rover halfway out of the water. The second rover would not power up, either. Kicking its side in disgust, he went for the third. Simon almost ran Mowgi over in the process. Unlike the cats, the undog had his back to the water, focusing his big parabolics and bulging yellow eyes on the vines waving in the breeze. Under normal circumstances, even the cats knew that bothering Mowgi during one of his focus states was a big mistake. Simon was well aware of the undog's temper when disturbed and as a rule would have given him a wide berth. But Simon's bride-to-be was somewhere on the planet, possibly injured or worse, and all he could think about was Sizzle alone in a hostile world, needing his help.

Simon would have been dog meat if Harlowe hadn't made an incredible open field tackle to prevent his First Mate's destruction.

Simon struggled violently to break free of Harlowe's grip. He was out of control. Nothing else mattered.

Harlowe tried his best to calm him but when words didn't work, he picked up Simon and launched him into the lagoon. The struggle continued until Harlowe forced Simon's head underwater and kept it there until he stopped struggling.

Once Simon finally went limp, Harlowe lifted him out of the water and dragged his coughing, puking body out of the lagoon and onto the beach. Simon lay there on his back, shuddering great waves of emotional pain. Harlowe held him down, not because he feared Simon would hurt himself, but because he needed every member of his crew physically and emotionally intact.

"Listen to me, Rerun!" Harlowe swatted Simon's sudden punch away. "Listen to me. We will find her. We'll get Sizzle back alive," he promised as he held Simon's arms down like a straightjacket. "I will not rest until she is with you, Rerun, but I need you with me, Gamadin. I need you by my side or we will fail Sizzle, Lu, Riverstone, and everyone else."

Simon's eyes remained closed. He spat out more salt water, finally nodding that he understood. When he felt the fight drain from Simon's body, Harlowe let go and rolled away, exhaling hard under the noonday sun. He left Simon alone on the sand to think things over.

Not long afterward, Simon found Harlowe and apologized. "Kinda made a toad of myself."

Harlowe had already forgotten the incident. He was focused on the undog. During the entire struggle, Mowgi had stayed put. He was still watching the island of vines with intense curiosity.

"Wonder what's got him so focused?" Harlowe wondered aloud, standing next to Monday. The last time he recalled Mowgi acting in such a odd way, the pursuing Dakadude Humvees were kicking up dust miles away before entering the box canyon in Utah. If the undog hadn't alerted them when he did, they would have been trapped in the canyon and shot full of plas rounds.

Everywhere Harlowe looked, from one end of the island to the other, he saw nothing but long, blood-red vines with broad, pale green leaves. It appeared to be the only form of vegetation on the island.

Ian walked up, glancing at Simon's red face and puffy eyes before he asked, "Problem?"

Harlowe nodded toward the undog and the vines. "Not sure."

Ian followed Harlowe's gaze with a search of his own. "Daks?"

"Vines," Harlowe replied.

"It's not like Mowgi to be bonked out over nothing," Ian observed.

Harlowe agreed. "Have you checked the area with the com? Could be beasties or islanders staring at us and we can't see them."

"It's clear, Dog. Just vines," Ian replied.

The com could detect blue-eyed fleas if it was programmed to, but it could not determine if something was friendly or hostile. That was up to the Gamadin interpretation of the data. Mowgi, on the other hand, made judgment calls on pure instinct. In either case, it took an experienced observer to make the final call, and sometimes it wasn't always clear what that call would be.

"Best to keep the com going until we find out what's bothering him," Harlowe said to Ian. Worried, he glanced down the beach in both directions, wondering where his little brother had wandered off to. "Have you seen Dodger?"

Simon slowly stood and gestured toward the distant point. "He grabbed Prigg and they went looking for pirate treasure that way."

"I told him to stay in sight of the ship," Harlowe growled, taking Ian's binoculars.

A mile away, at the very end of the island, Harlowe found Dodger and Prigg in the direction Simon had indicated. The two of them were kneeling in the sand with their hands tied behind their backs, looking up at a band of renegade beings with long, curved swords and oddly shaped rifles aimed at their heads.

As if it was reading Harlowe's mind, Jewels blinked to the edge of the ship a hundred feet away and tossed Harlowe his holster and sidearm. He snatched the weapons from the air as if he was playing catch. Strapping on his pistols while he, Monday, Simon, Ian, and Mowgi sprinted down the beach, Harlowe wondered momentarily if was he ever going to get a break.

20

Revenge of the Gods

The rain was pouring down hard. Riverstone's internal injuries needed more time to mend, but none of that mattered. After learning Sharlon was still underwater in the escape pod, he had to find a way off the mountain, even if he *was* a sack of broken bones. Lights and sirens were blaring inside his head. Lu, Sizzle, and Sharlon needed his help and he was over two hundred miles away. He had to make it to the coast or die trying.

Riverstone reeled himself another thousand feet up the side of the cliff. When he reached the end of the line, where his first piton head had penetrated the rock face, he looked over his shoulder and focused a couple of miles away on the flat side of the gorge. If his calculations were correct, he was high enough to make the gap with plenty of distance to spare. As an added precaution, he attached another piton head to his pistol in case he came up a little short. When he was ready, Riverstone gave Alice a tap for good luck and pushed off the side of the cliff into the driving rain. Once clear of the cliff, he deployed his wings and gave himself to the mercy of the gale force winds. The unexpectedly powerful gusts forced him farther down the gorge than he expected. At the same time, however, the gusts also gave him the extra lift he needed to fight the turbulence as he made his way down. He didn't have any particular place in mind. Anywhere on the plain would do.

Bad things happen in threes. Riverstone had already been struck by lightning twice during his descent. The Gazzian gods must have thought he still owed them one, because when he was well over the gorge with plenty of altitude left to make it across, a third bolt exploded from the heavens...

21

The Tails

Harlowe counted nine vile humanoids holding Dodger and Prigg at gunpoint. They varied in height, but only two were taller than Dodger. Most were closer to Prigg in height as well as in weight. All wore brightly-colored, thick, muslin-like rags with dark knee-length pants, with scarves of the same material covering their heads. The tallest one wore a "felt" hat that had seen better days. As a group they were unkempt and dirty. They appeared human except that each had a prehensile tail. Two tails were wrapped tightly around Dodger and Prigg's necks.

Harlowe barged into the scene without bothering to introduce himself. "Let them go!" Harlowe said, thankful his language implant worked, even here.

"Or you'll what?"

Harlowe blasted the six ancient blunderbusses from the Gazzians' hands before their simple brains could register another thought.

"Care to guess?" Harlowe stated coldly.

For a moment, no one moved. The delay following Harlowe's demand was more a reaction to his performance than in defiance of him. As soon as Harlowe waved his sidearm like he was going to carry out his threat, however, the tails quickly released from around Dodger's and Prigg's necks.

"Wow, Harlowe that was so cool," Dodger said, running to his brother's side. "Where did you learn to shoot—"

Harlowe handed his little brother off to Ian, who covered the boy's mouth and said sternly in his ear, "Quiet, Dodger."

"Who are you?" the tallest being in the group asked Harlowe.

Harlowe pointed his weapon at the being's head. "I do the talking around here."

The tall Gazzian nodded. He got the point.

"Is this your island?" Harlowe asked.

"Harlowe, you won't believe what we fou—" Dodger tried to say before Ian shushed him to silence again.

A sudden shift in the wind put the tails upwind, subjecting the Gamadin for the first time to their foul stench. Harlowe's first reaction was to tap his SIBA before continuing, but he decided that shocking the Gazzians even further with the bugeyed 54th-century suit would be a bad idea. He would just have to gut it out. He scrunched his nose up and drew a cautious breath before he continued his questioning. "Is this your island?" Harlowe repeated.

"The great hand of Moharr raised our ship out of the sea and carried us here," the Tall Tail explained. He seemed to be the group's spokesman, for everybody else was too frightened to speak. "We are all that is left of our crew," he added, looking over the scraggly lot of survivors.

"Ship?" Harlowe wondered aloud.

Prigg came forward. "Your Majesty. If I may, young Dodger was about to explain. There is indeed a ship that we found not far from here. It appears to have been carried up the side of the island by a giant wave."

Harlowe nodded for Ian to release Dodger so he could carry on with Prigg's story. "It's a ship, Harlowe, like the one Errol Flynn had in the old pirate movies Dad used to like! Prigg and I were running back to tell you when the Tails caught us."

Harlowe and Ian both wanted to hear more. Harlowe returned his weapon to his holster and nodded at the spokesman. "You're up, Tall Tail, show us your ship."

Tall Tail hesitated, finding Mowgi fascinating. "What kind of beast is that?"

Harlowe squatted down and nuzzled the undog's parabolics. "Our watchdog."

"What does he watch?"

"Everything." Harlowe straightened up and added, "Nothing gets by the Mowg."

"Has he been blessed with spirits?" Tall Tail asked.

Harlowe smiled. "Oh yeah, Mowgi is full of spirits."

"Stay on his good side, and he's as gentle as a kitten," Ian warned.

"A kitten?" Tall Tail asked.

At that moment Molly and Rhud came loping along the shore to join the crowd. Harlowe pointed at the two cats. "Our kittens."

Like a flock of frightened geese, the tails took flight down the beach ahead of the cats and didn't stop. They rounded the point and charged to the far end of the cove, where they disappeared behind a cluster of rocks along the shoreline. The Gamadin were puzzled over where the tails had vanished. Then Dodger led them to the narrow canyon where he and Prigg had found the ship earlier in the day. The moment they saw the beached wooden galleon high on the incline, Harlowe felt his luck had turned. The three-masted, primitive Gazzian galleon was lying on its side, far up the steep slope of the island. As Tall Tail tried to explain and Prigg clarified, the galleon had been carried there by a great wave. Amazingly, all the vines where the water had washed up the canyon were dead.

"Is it a pirate ship, Captain Starr?" Dodger asked Simon.

Simon chuckled at the thought. "I think it is, Dodger."

"Wow, that's so cool! A real live pirate ship!"

Ian studied the scene for a moment before he explained, "When Millie hit the water, she created a tidal wave that washed the ship onto the island."

Harlowe saw more. He saw potential. Except for the rigging and broken spars, the galleon's hull appeared intact. A series of Gamadin modifications raced through Harlowe's head. The ship had possibilities! All they had to do was pull it off the mountainside and slip it back into the water.

The galleon was made of heavy slatted black wood and pitch. Before it washed ashore, the galleon carried a single main mast and secondary masts fore and aft. They were all broken and shredded sails were everywhere. Ian had the same idea. He suggested that the robobs pull the vessel off the mountain before the vines rebounded and overtook the ship. "In a tropical climate like this, Captain, it won't take long."

Harlowe agreed.

As they went to inspect the ship, they discovered their first casualty. An unlucky Gazzian sailor had been thrown clear when the tidal wave washed up the canyon, hitting his head against a rock. The vines were already attacking the body with zeal.

"That was our Captain," Tall Tail said to Harlowe, standing atop a boulder.

"Don't worry, Tall Tail, you still have a Captain," Harlowe said.

Tall Tail looked around. "Who would that be?"

Harlowe was unhesitating in his reply. "That would be me, Tall Tail. I will captain this ship."

"You?" the Tall Tail snapped. Harlowe couldn't tell whether the Gazzian was angry or amused. One thing was obvious, though: the tails were unhappy sharing an island with "kittens" or taking orders from a kid. "You may have powerful spirits, but you are too young to master a ship. Your experience of the sea is wanting, boy." He turned to his ship, lying broken on its side. "Even if we believed in your mastery, how could you command a ship that is hopelessly beached?"

Harlowe reared back, gazing over his new acquisition. Mowgi had already climbed to the top of the broken bowsprit, the highest point on the vessel. "You're right, Tall Tail, it's a risky undertaking."

Tall Tail stared at Mowgi in wonder, awed by the undog's scaling ability. Harlowe only laughed. Mowgi was an enigma, even for those who knew him. Harlowe gazed over the fallen rigging, the ripped shrouds, the broken stern wheel, and the long stress cracks along the side of the ship. He proclaimed proudly, as if he were the owner of a new Mercedes, "I love it, Wiz. Let's make it work!"

Ian pulled Harlowe aside with his own assessment. "Tall Tail is right, Captain. You don't know squat about sailing a ship."

Without taking his eyes off of his new possession, Harlowe pointed at Tall Tail and his foul-smelling crew. "You're right, Wiz, but they do."

22

Be Safe, My Love

A southwesterly squall pounded the coast. The high and choppy surf was roaring into the shore, sending the survivors scurrying to higher ground in search of shelter under the palms and bushes behind the beach. Their first concern was for the injured, to keep them warm and comfortable against the elements until the great Gamadin ship picked them up. None of the survivors believed that their stay on the beach would be for very long.

When the injured were settled under makeshift shelters, Sizzle returned to the beach and waited anxiously for Leucadia, who was still at the bottom of the ocean searching for Sharlon. Leucadia finally surfaced, struggling to carry Sharlon's body against the menacing surf. In an instant, Sizzle was swimming through the pounding shore break to assist in the rescue. Together they brought Sharlon onto the beach, where they tried to resuscitate her. She did not respond.

"What can we do?" Sizzle asked, trying to stay calm. "We have no medical supplies to help her!"

Shouting above the thunder and the pelting rain, Leucadia could see only one solution. "I'm giving her my SIBA. It will keep her stabilized."

Sizzle wouldn't allow it. "No, I'll give her mine. She is my mother. You will need yours to communicate with Matthew and Harlowe." She tapped her chest and her SIBA collapsed. As soon as she placed

113

the medallion on Sharlon's chest, the SIBA expanded and encapsulated her, stabilizing her biological functions and putting her into a deeper comatose state. When that was done, they moved her under the trees with the other injured passengers.

*   *   *

It was hours past dark. A giant moon was casting a bright light on the encampment. Sizzle and Leucadia were finally able to rest. The storm had abated somewhat, but the rain stayed constant. Everyone but Leucadia was wet and miserable. She wished she had a SIBA for everyone. Some of the survivors looked at her as if they would steal it if they could. "Where is your Gamadin ship?" they asked her. "When will your mighty Captain Pylott find us?"

"I have not been able to reach him," she told them. From the looks on their faces, she knew they would not accept that answer for long. During times of hardship and famine, the true character of a person comes out. The fight for survival is always a test. She reminded herself often to watch Sizzle's back, as well as her own.

In the morning, once the storm had passed, she would help them make better shelters. If they were warm and comfortable, they would not view her scornfully simply because she was the Gamadin Captain's lady and wore the only protection among the survivors.

Harlowe will come, she reminded herself. She would do whatever she could to help Sizzle and her people. Her gnawing dread, however, remained. Something terrible had happened to Harlowe. Even Matthew was uneasy. Leucadia thanked the stars that he was alive, but *he should have called back by now. Had he fallen from the cliff? Was he injured or lost? It was not like Matthew or Harlowe to go this long without communicating.* She blinked back the tears, praying for their safety.

Suddenly, another dreadful thought occurred to her. *What if they don't come? What if she, Sizzle, and the others are stranded on the planet?*

Stop it, Lu! Harlowe's voice scolded her. *Stay the course. Don't ever give up. I'll find you. You know I will.*

Mentally hearing Harlowe's voice gave her confidence. Of course, he was somewhere *beyond the moon, beyond the rain, somewhere over the rainbow*, she thought to herself, remembering her favorite childhood story. The thought that their souls were together no matter how they were separated comforted her.

She turned to the fire she had made from the small torch in her Gama-belt and put her arms around Sizzle to comfort them both through their misery.

Sizzle looked over her mother's still body in the SIBA cocoon. "Without *Millawanda*, my mother may die," she uttered sadly.

Leucadia took Sizzle's hand. "Harlowe won't let that happen, Sizzle."

Sizzle began to cry. Leucadia marveled at her courage under the circumstances. She had not faltered once since their crash or shown any sign of weakness. Sizzle didn't know if Simon was alive or dead or if her mother would survive. She asked Leucadia, "How can we be sure *Millawanda* saved Gazz? We could be the only ones left on the planet alive."

Leucadia pointed at the trees whipping in the gusts of wind. "Look there! What do you see? And there! What do you see all around us?"

Sizzle took in the palms and sky overhead and listened to the chirps and clicks of the insects. She realized that what she was seeing and hearing was real and that the creatures she saw in the branches were alive. The Gamadin ship had performed a miracle. "Life…" she finally replied. "I feel it, too."

They held each other close. "That's right, Sizzle, life. It still exists on Gazz because of the Gamadin."

Sizzle stared at Leucadia, sensing the dread behind her green eyes that was impossible to hide. "You fear something has happened to your brave Gamadin captain."

Several ideas churned in Leucadia's mind about what might have happened to the Gamadin, all of them bad. She and Sizzle both knew that Harlowe would have called them hours earlier if he was able to. As horrible as she felt, however, she was far from losing hope. Leucadia was determined to keep them all alive as long as it took for help to arrive, and that help would be Harlowe. "Harlowe will find us and your mother will survive," Leucadia said with confidence.

Sizzle traded a glowing glance with Leucadia, each feeling a tribal communication between them. "Then we are on our own for now," Sizzle replied.

Leucadia refused to gloss over her words with false promises. "Yes, for a little while," she answered, then added, "Harlowe will come for us when he is able."

"My sister, Quay, often told me when we were imprisoned on Og that the young Captain would come for us. She was like you. She never doubted for a moment that he would come for her. I asked her how she could be so certain. She simply said, 'He is Harlowe. Harlowe is Gamadin. He will come.'"

Leucadia pushed back her wet hair and sighed. "I worry most about what this will cost Harlowe. There is always a price to pay in the battle against evil." *Harlowe will be okay*, she repeated to herself.

Sizzle held Leucadia closer as the rain continued. "I will help to pay this cost. Together we will help him survive this evil."

"Simon would be proud of you, Sizzle."

Sizzle nodded silently, as if it was too painful to discuss. At the mention of Simon's name, she withdrew just a little, enough for Leucadia to sense her torment.

"What troubles you, Sizzle?" Leucadia finally asked. "Is Simon not treating you well? I have never seen him as happy as he is with you."

"The problem is with me. Simon is the most generous, loving friend a woman could ever have. He is what any Tomarian woman would seek in a mate."

"But not you?"

Sizzle remained motionless, saddened with the inevitable. "I have tried to be someone I am not, Leucadia. I am a Ran. My sister discovered this when she met your Harlowe. Through him she found her destiny. She had to move on or lose the person she must become. I, too, must do the same. I know Simon's love for me is true, but his love is not my fate, Lu. Am I being unfair to us both for wanting something he is unable to give me? It is something I must discover for myself. My place is not Earth, Leucadia. I must follow my sister Quay, for she has shown the way. Can you see this end for me, my sister?"

The conviction in Sizzle's eyes was enough to move Gazz off of its axis.

"Do whatever you need to, Sizzle. After all, it is your life, and yours alone. Make it count, Sizzle, make your life count!"

Sizzle embraced Leucadia, thanking her for her support. "You have my sister's confidence. I know we will survive and that you are the right one, the only one for the Captain."

"What has happened to Quay?" Leucadia asked.

"Quay is somewhere out there, slaying the madness. That is all I know."

"Maybe someday you will tell me more about her," Leucadia said.

Sizzle yawned, barely able to stay awake. "Yes, but now we should rest because we must survive ourselves."

"You are right, Sizzle. We must rest. Tomorrow is another day."

Before she slept, Leucadia searched the horizon one last time with her SIBA oculars on the highest power, looking for any sign of the golden disk floating down from the heavens.

She saw nothing. There was no light, no ship, and no Gamadin warrior within her view.

Good night, my love, she said to him, *be safe and well among the stars...*

23

The Sprint

On the open plain, Riverstone could run flat out toward the coast. The jolt that struck him as he flew across the narrow canyon had knocked him out for only a few hours. When he awoke, the day was already half-over. *Things could have been a lot worse*, he told himself. He had landed in a thorny bush and was happy to see that his momentum had carried him to the plain side of the canyon instead of smashing him against the rocks a mile below in the canyon. A quick body-check confirmed that no bones were broken from the fall. If any animals were around thinking he was an easy meal, the prickly branches probably gave them second thoughts. On the other hand, the sharp needles had no effect on the tough skin of his SIBA. When he climbed out of his thorny bed, however, he found problems. Besides having a major headache and losing precious time, he had no communications with Leucadia. He tried fixing things with a couple of slaps to the helmet, but nothing worked. He had no idea whether the com loss was permanent or just a glitch that would work itself out with a reboot.

After three hours of running, his com was still offline. Fortunately, his nav readouts were functioning flawlessly and he was making good time, sprinting nearly eighty miles in a little over three hours.

He was bookin'!

So far, no land obstacles slowed him down. When he came to a deep gully or gorge, he would either jump down and leap across to the other side, or he'd fire a dura-wire to the other side and reel himself over with the servo pulley he had attached to his Gama-belt. The General would have been proud of his lateral thinking. He grinned proudly as he leaped up and began sprinting again to the next slice in the arid land.

In the distance was his goal: the coastal mountains. His nav displayed a path through a narrow gap that would lead him straight to the shoreline. Once on the other side, all he had to do was run north along the beach for a few more miles until he found where the Tomarian escape pods had crashed. If he was lucky, *Millawanda* would be there, too, her golden body glistening under the Gazzian sun while Harlowe was in the water, streaking across a glassy wave.

He leapt over a twenty-foot dry gulch with ease, his taste buds screaming from imagining all the greasy cheeseburgers, tacos, and fries he had left behind on the *Jo-li Ran*. The loss of that platter would turn this fiasco into a downright tragedy.

He told his stomach to forget the loss and pressed on, running harder, strutting in great leaps in order to make up for lost time.

24

The Millie

Late afternoon on the following day, Harlowe and Ian stood on the poop deck of the galleon, surveying the progress of the pirate ship's renovation. As soon as the captive Gazzian sailors were shuffled off to an isolated part of the island, Harlowe broke out his 54th-century worker bees and proceeded at a blistering pace to pull the beached ship off the mountainside.

No one knew how the Tails would react when 16th-century sailors met 54th-century technology. Even Harlowe and his crew found Gamadin equipment intimidating and often dangerous. *Millawanda* was the prime example. Knowing that this technology was dangerous even to the Gamadin, Harlowe ordered the Tails to another part of the island until the galleon's restoration was finished.

"How are the Tails taking their confinement?" Harlowe asked. Ian looked up to watch a robob swing across a spar to string more line across the main topmast. At eye level, he saw a team of clickers drilling new holes for the anchor bolts that would attach the new bowsprit to the front of the ship. Before the holes for the last bolts were drilled, Mowgi had claimed the forward-most point on the galleon. "The French fries and chocolate shakes are keeping their stomachs occupied, but Tall Tail misses his grog."

"Is that the stuff that smells like gasoline?"

"Yeah, it's like a hundred and ninety proof rum."

"Any left? Maybe Millie could use it," Harlowe joked.

"The vines broke open the barrels and drank their stash."

Harlowe looked at Ian. "They what?"

"They broke open all the food barrels, but left this black sand stuff alone."

Harlowe shot him a *you-gotta-be-kidding* look. "Plants that drink. That's radical." Then he asked, "What's the black sand for?"

"Not sure. They had a bunch of it stacked next to the barrels of gunpowder. I think it has something to do with the cannons."

Harlowe leaned over the poop rail holding his glass of Blue Stuff and admired the robobs' work. The galleon was taking shape. All three masts were repaired and their rigging installed. Simon thought every pirate ship needed a Jolly Roger emblazoned on the foresail to signal death to all who saw it. Harlowe liked the idea, too, and added a Gamadin twist. He ordered a likeness of Mowgi with a maw full of fangs and ball bats in place of the usual skull and crossbones. When Platter asked him why he replaced the bones, Harlowe nodded with satisfaction at Ian's artwork and replied, "I like baseball." Then he added, "Put the Mowg on the mizzen sheet, too." He wanted the undog's ferocity displayed for all to see.

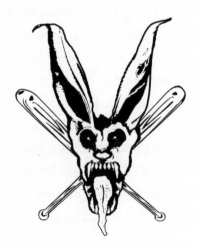

Once the decks were cleared of debris and scrubbed clean, the stress cracks in the hull were shored up and the cannon gunports and hatch covers put in good working order. Except for a few 54th-century additions Ian was fabricating, the pirate galleon was nearly ready to set sail after only three days. The boat looked like a small toy bobbing in a bathtub beside the *Millawanda*.

Harlowe turned to Ian. "Better get the lowdown on what the black sand is from Tall Tail before we go stuffing it in the cannons."

"Aye," Ian replied.

"What else? Any pirate treasure in the holds?

"Zippo. Even Dodger came up empty. What's that tell you?" Ian replied.

"They need Captain Jack Sparrow."

It was Ian's turn to laugh. "They got you."

"Yeah, they got me."

Harlowe twisted around, eyeing the empty gunports along both sides of the ship. Then he looked toward the beach, where a platoon of robobs was cleaning rust and corrosion from the two-thousand-pound cannons. Dodger was barefoot on top of one, stepping along its length like it was a surfboard. "Give 'em a broadside, Mr. Wizzix! Aye, aye, Captain Dodger," he replied, playing both parts.

Harlowe ran his hand along the barrel of a small poop deck cannon that had already been serviced. He marveled at the swirling ornate design around the touchhole and breech. "They cleaned up nice. I'll bet the clickers worked up a few blisters on these."

"They were pretty nasty," Ian admitted.

"Have we added the modifications I wanted?" Harlowe asked, looking down the barrel.

"Aye, Captain, nine-to-one twist, like you ordered."

"Powder and shot?"

"A little ahead of the 16th-century kind. Do you think that's wise, Dog? Maybe we should stick with their powder."

"We have a planet to save, Wiz. A little extra precaution won't hurt." He slapped the cannon's side, giving his approval. "We begin testing as soon as we're on our way."

"Half-load?"

Harlowe thought for a moment. "Good idea. Make sure Rerun gets a how-to from Tall Tail on the finer points of muzzle-loading a pirate cannon."

"Aye, Captain."

They walked forward, to the quarterdeck and down to the main deck, where Harlowe peered down an open hatch. "Are the Tails' quarters ready?"

"Nearly. We had to do a gravity feed for the shower."

"I don't care, as long as it works."

"They've never heard of a shower, Captain."

"They will."

The sun was always a factor. A day on Gazz was an hour longer than Earth. Because the sun was their main source of power, the more daylight, the better. Soon after sunset, the robobs would go dormant until the sun rose again. This frustrated Harlowe, who wanted the clickers working day and night until the work was completed. The robobs were like an army of skilled craftsman. What took weeks for a human, they accomplished in hours. Harlowe was impatient, nevertheless.

Harlowe and Ian watched a robob crew bring in a twenty-foot cylindrical pod loaded with ten thousand pounds of volcanic rock. Holding the pod above their cone-like heads, they marched it below the waterline and attached it to the bottom of the galleon. It was a ballast tank, another piece of magic to the premodern Gazzian mind that would not be used on Gazzian ships for another three hundred years!

"She needs a name, Dog," Ian said.

"All taken care of, Mr. Wizzixs. Come on." Harlowe led Ian aft again. They leaned over the aftcastle and Harlowe pointed at the clickers hanging off the stern plate. One clicker was carving two-foot high letters into the black wood just above the ship's rudder, while a second clicker applied gold paint to the finished letters. Even though there was one more letter left in the name, it was quite clear what the name would be.

"*Millie*," Ian uttered with almost pious reverence. "It's genius, Captain."

"It wasn't my idea," Harlowe admitted. "It was Dodger's."

"Dodger?"

"He came paddling up this morning and asked how the *Millie* was coming along. The little scavenger found a board and paddled down to the point."

Ian searched the ocean out beyond the point with visible alarm. "Why did you let him do that?"

Harlowe stared off down the beach. "It's cool, Wiz. I can see him."

"Did you forget what happened to you on the planet #2?"

Harlowe froze with the memory. He had forgotten about the dangers of alien worlds in his fixation on repairing the galleon. He leaped up, grabbed a dangling mast line, and swung himself out in a long arch. At the top of the arch he let go, plunging into the clear water and swimming toward the beach. When he broke out of the water, Jewels was there again, tossing Harlowe his sidearm as he sprinted down to the point in a dead run. The last time he had forgotten what planet he was on, a giant ichthyosaurus nearly ate him for breakfast!

25

Bruton, Loness and Quil

By the end of the second day, the twelve marooned survivors of the shuttle's escape pods were finally able to work on building shelters and gathering food. The pale yellow sun was bright and warm, the sky cloudless, and the sea a deep green, with only a small chop worked up from the steady onshore breeze from the south. According to Leucadia's SIBA readouts, the survivors had washed up along a continental coast in the middle latitudes of the planet. For the time being, cold weather would not be a problem. But the planet's twenty-degree tilt on its axis meant that the seasonal change would be quite dramatic when winter arrived. "It'll get really cold really fast," Leucadia said to Sizzle. "We should plan accordingly."

Sizzle's long blonde hair was tied back while she worked. Nodding in agreement with Leucadia, she turned toward the other Tomarians, who were erecting a small shack out of tree branches that bore a remarkable resemblance to the large coconut palm leaves found on Earth. The trees here, however, were short and thick, with slender leaves instead of fan-shaped fronds. "My people will need animal furs and plenty of wood to get them through the cold months," Sizzle said.

Leucadia scanned the nearby coastal mountain range. "I will organize a hunting party at first light."

Sizzle pointed to two young Tomarian guards, Loness and Quil, who were working on the shelter along with their superior, Bruton.

The young guards were tall and fit, and appeared quite up to the task of hunting in the wild. "Take them with you."

Leucadia followed Sizzle's gaze toward the soldiers. "I will let them know."

The land away from the beach was like old California, dry and mild, with coastal hills where sage and prickly brushes grew in abundance. There wasn't much water, but they had discovered a nearby stream that had enough water for everyone, at least for the time being. With so much depending on a good supply of water, they knew they had to find more than one source, in case their only supply became contaminated or dried up. Leucadia made mental notes to herself to find more on the next day's hunting foray into the back country.

"I will speak with Bruton before tomorrow," Sizzle said, "and order him to give you permission to take his guards."

Leucadia sized up the big soldier. "I will confront him now."

"He may be difficult."

Leucadia strode off toward the soldiers. "I'm counting on it!"

*　　*　　*

The Tomarian soldiers had no time for Leucadia. They ignored her every time she tried to address them. The tough-minded Bruton saw no reason to respect her. She was an outsider. She was not Tomarian.

Leucadia required every soldier's cooperation if they were going to survive through the winter. She needed them for hunting in the hills, fishing the ocean, and gathering building materials for shelter. It was important that they not think of her as cowardly and gutless. If they did, her leadership status and her value as a functioning member of the group would be lost. Sizzle could order their cooperation, but

Leucadia had a faster solution, one she had once seen her mother, Sook, spring on a group of unruly fans at a Dodgers' game.

Bruton was no small being. As Leucadia approached the Tomarian soldier, he appeared to grow exponentially, reminding her in many ways of Harlowe's android sparring partner, Quincy. He was more than a foot taller than she and easily twice her weight. He was also a respected member of Sharlon's prestigious honor guard. Planted firmly in his thick right hand was a large wooden club that he handled like a Nerf bat.

"What do you want, human —" Bruton started to say. He never finished his sentence. Leucadia's fist shot out like an exploding cannonball. The blow was so hard and well-placed that the big soldier's feet left the ground and his body twisted in the air like a top. When he fell to the ground, he hit the sand with no bounce and without a peep.

Leucadia turned toward Loness and Quil, who stared at her in awed disbelief. "What I want," she said, staring down the two soldiers with her glaring green eyes, "is both of you over there," nodding toward the front of the hut on the beach, "ready to hunt at first light. Do you have a problem with that?"

They both snapped to attention and saluted her crisply. "No, my Lady!" they said in unison.

"First light," Quil confirmed.

Leucadia turned away, dismissing them with her back as she gave Sizzle a discreet wink. Sizzle in turn nodded her approval as if to say, *Nicely done, Lu.*

26

Abduction

It was the following day. Riverstone was twenty-five miles from Leucadia's position when thunder rumbled across the coastal hills. He had run through the night without rest and was near collapse. His SIBA constantly monitored his body's condition, and it would shut down if he didn't stop soon. That was its program. There was no override. The welfare of its occupant was its prime directive. Twice while he was crossing the plains, the suit had halted his run, forcing his body to rest before it would allow him to continue.

Without a SIBA, the roar would have sounded like a distant thunderstorm on the horizon. Riverstone's internal sensors, however, told him the explosion was an unnatural detonation to the north in the same area where the Tomarian pod had put down.

He charged ahead faster, ignoring the limits. He was stopping for no one. Not even his SIBA was going to stall him this time!

Once he made it through the mountain passageway to the coast, the trail heading north turned ugly. The shoreline from there to the water's edge was rocky and filled with numerous arroyos and coastal cliffs two to three thousand feet high. The beaches were not the Southern California sandy highways Riverstone had hoped for. There were not even thin stretches of sand to run on. He was forced to go inland for miles before he could begin heading north again, slowing his leaping sprint to a trot.

When he saw the black smoke rising between two moons on the cloud-less green horizon, his stomach lurched. *Leucadia was in trouble.*

* * *

Leucadia left Loness and Quil with the game they had hunted all day in the canyon. As soon as she heard the explosion from the direction of the encampment, she powered up her SIBA and leapt in twenty-foot strides back to the encampment. She knew only that the blast meant trouble for the survivors.

Back she ran, through the long gully they had followed that morning and along the trail on the side of the canyon. Only when she made it to the top of the trail did she have a panoramic view of the coast. Through her SIBA optics, she zeroed in on a tall-masted galleon dropping anchor off the beach near their encampment. Harlowe and Simon had told her about their Mons Flying Club, and she knew her SIBA was capable of gliding her down to the beach. *But how was it done?* She scanned under her arms and saw no signs of a switch, wings, or any kind of apparatus that looked like it would enable her to fly. Harlowe had tried to tutor her, but she kept putting him off. She was always too busy with her other priorities to learn. Now instead of using this piece of equipment to soar, she had to make her way back through the steep canyons and rough terrain along the coast.

Ugh! She groaned, bolting down the mountainside as the thunder-ing booms of the cannon continued.

* * *

Two more fusillades had roared from the north by the time Riverstone reached the peak of the coastal mountain. He finally looked down on a white sandy beach still miles away. Alice, his faithful clicker, had climbed ahead and gave him a hand up to the ledge, where he clearly saw the thick black clouds billowing high into the clear green sky. A wooden, three-mast warship with its gun ports open was floating in the deep water just beyond the surf. Riverstone stood there, helplessly watching the bright flashes and jettison smoke announce another massive broadside. This one lay waste the palm-covered shacks near the beach. It was at least ten seconds between the flash and the thunderous report of the broadside. In those few seconds, Riverstone activated his SIBA wings and became airborne. Alice leapt outward, collapsed, and attached herself to his Gama-belt. Then Riverstone dove down the side of the mountain, picked up speed and, with wings pulled back, glided like a silent missile toward the fire storm at the encampment.

His descent was so fast and out of control that his legs were unable to match the ground speed when he touched down. He rolled forward, tumbling for many yards along the sand. Then he sprang to his feet and continued running. With his weapon drawn, he charged for the fires, ready to do battle with any enemy that was harming his friends.

At the very edge of the camp he found several bodies, but no living bad guys to shoot. He recognized none of the dead, except for one big Tomarian soldier named Bruton, whom he had met a few times on the Flagship. He had been shot several times.

Continuing his search, Riverstone charged into the fiery camp, turning over still-glowing logs and palm branches. The flames were harmless to him in his SIBA. During his inspection of the burning huts, he found more bodies. None of the dead were Leucadia, Sizzle, or Sharlon.

Seething with anger at himself for being too late, Riverstone turned his attention toward the sea. The man-o'-war's sails had gathered wind. She had lifted anchor and was moving out to sea. With the damage done and its humanoid prizes captured, the galleon had no reason to stay.

Riverstone ran into the surf, charging after the ship. He hit the water in high pounding steps, splashing, kicking up spays of frothy water, and then diving in, stroking for the galleon before it reached cruising speed.

Hurry, Riverstone, hurry! he thought desperately. *SWIM, DUDE! Don't let them get away!*

Powered by his SIBA, he swam though the surf, pushing through, coming out the backsides of waves, heading for the galleon, knowing that if he didn't reach the ship in time, his loved ones would be lost forever.

Suddenly, his SIBA froze. *Not now!* he thought. Without the power it gave his limbs, he was incapable of catching up to the galleon on his own.

But his pleas fell on deaf SIBA ears. The suit could make no decision about when a good time to stop functioning for the well-being of its occupant might be. The power indicators were going dark. There was still plenty of juice left in the suit's power module, but after the three days of falling through the stratosphere, climbing cliffs, running, jumping, and leaping across hundreds of miles of plains, valleys and ditches, Riverstone had used up his own reserve so far that the auto-shutdown kicked in. His legs and arms began turning into lead weights. He was at the mercy of the current and going nowhere fast. Then, for no apparent reason, luck turned his way. The black, beastly flag of a skull with long white fangs turned out of the wind and stopped. The galleon's aft end drifted around, slowly lining up with him.

Sweet!

This was his chance. He started stroking toward the galleon, which remained on its steady course. Exhausted and spent, he gave it all that he had left as he watched the lid of a single gunport fly open with the clanking of rope and tackle, exposing the lethal front end of a black-faced cannon. The muzzle rolled out and zeroed in...on him.

Riverstone poked his head out of the water like a pilot seal and searched the ocean around him. Nothing was near him. It then dawned on him that *he* was the target!

Through the single gunport a match flared, touching the wick at the top of the cannon breech. As Riverstone dove for the bottom, he heard the cannon fire.

27

Surfing the Point

Dodger had never had so much fun! Sliding left on his purple board, he realized that he was the first surfer on Gazz! *How sick is that, dude?* His best friends, Billy Harmatz and Butterball Jones, will be so jealous, he bragged to himself. What stories he would tell them about this planet, a zillion miles away, where the surf was the greatest in the galaxy! He envisioned himself on several front covers of *Surfer Magazine*—all big color photos of him—cutting right, sliding across a glassy face, crouching down, toes to the nose, cutting back, dropping into a tube, while behind him the Gazzian moons looked down on him with happy faces.

He kicked out, dropped off the edge of his board to the sandy bottom, and stood in knee-high water, preparing to take his bow.

Prigg clapped on the beach. "Bravo, Master Dodger! Bravo! Very well done!"

The big cats couldn't have cared less. Molly swiped at something buzzing near her face, and Rhud yawned, rolling on his back in the warm sand. While the work on the *Millie* was being completed, there was little for the cats to do but lie on the beach and soak up the rays. Ian found it strange that the animals preferred the sun over the shade of the vines.

Dodger waved at the little Naruckian, who loved watching His Majesty's little brother perform on his surfboard. The two had hit it off from the start. When Dodger wasn't surfing, he loved listening to Prigg's stories about his big brother's exploits, which by now had become legend across the quadrant. Dodger wanted to teach Prigg how to surf. He was deathly afraid of water, especially water that moved. The Naruckian had never seen an ocean with waves. Naruck was full of polluted seas with no waves at all because there were no moons to push and pull the tides. Prigg was quite content to stay on the beach and clap.

Then abruptly, the quiet afternoon turned tense. Molly and Rhud came alive and were on their paws, ready for action. Both Dodger and Prigg froze in place, wondering why the air had changed until they saw Harlowe with his weapon drawn, running along the beach toward them.

Ignoring his little brother, Harlowe asked Prigg, "How long has he been out, Prigg?"

"He has had five rides, Your Majesty," Prigg replied.

Scanning like a sensor array, Harlowe continued his search out beyond the surf. All seemed peaceful and quiet. To his relief, he saw no immediate danger lurking in the water to harm his little brother or Prigg.

"Whatsa matter, Harlowe?" Dodger asked, becoming worried as he followed Harlowe's anxious gaze across the water.

Harlowe led everyone away from the water, back toward the lagoon. "Precaution, Dodger. We have a rule. No surfing without clickers."

"But there was nothing out there," Dodger argued.

"This isn't Earth. Danger is everywhere you least expect it."

"But you're using all the clickers on the *Millie*," Dodger pointed out.

"When we're gone, Prigg will put sentinels on both sides of the point. Until then, no surfing or venturing away from the lagoon," Harlowe ordered.

"Yes, Your Majesty," Prigg confirmed.

"When are you leaving, Harlowe?" Dodger asked.

"Tomorrow morning."

"Can I come, too?"

Harlowe had promised his mom before leaving Earth that he would keep Dodger safe. "Nothing risky, young man," Tinker had said to Harlowe, more of an order than a request. Taking Dodger along on a high seas voyage was out of the question. The journey would be dangerous. A ship full of Gazzian pirates was no place for an eleven-year-old kid. "We've gone over this before. You're staying here with Prigg and Squid," Harlowe replied, leaving no wiggle room in his voice.

"How long will that be?" Dodger asked.

Fewer than 35 days from now, the second GRB would arrive. Harlowe had slightly more than a month to find his girlfriend and his shipmates before the deadly rays struck the planet again. That was the time he had to work with, and anything longer than that would end in death for everyone and everything, including the planet. "A month," Harlowe replied.

"What if it's longer?"

"It won't be."

There was an unaccustomed hardness in Harlowe's tone. "You sound angry, Harlowe. Don't worry, Lu and Matty will be okay."

Harlowe pulled Dodger close to him, putting a warm arm around his shoulders. "Thanks, Dodge. Yeah, we'll get them back. You'll make sure nothing happens to Millie, right?"

Dodger raised a clenched fist as they rapped knuckles, sealing their solemn vow. "No worries, Harlowe, I'll take good care of Millie for ya!"

A loud beastly cry brought their attention back to the point where Dodger was surfing earlier. A great winged dragon swooped down from the sky and plunged into the surf. A massive white turbulence churned beneath the dragon's wings as its long powerful jaws tore at some movement below the surface.

Dodger's face went slack with confusion. "Mowgi?"

When the water settled, Mowgi flapped his wings and rose from the water with a slithery serpent in his jaws.

Dodger let out a long sigh. There was no need to further explain the need for armed clickers guarding the point.

Harlowe smiled, glancing toward the rocky point where the undog was sharing his freshly-caught feast with the cats as he morphed back into his undog form. Dodger thought that was cool.

28

Spit of Land

From the top of a small bluff above the beach, Leucadia saw that she was too late. There was nothing left of their makeshift shacks. Everything was burned and scattered across the beach. The marauding galleon had weighed anchor and was under full sail, heading north. She zoomed in on the ship with her bugeyes. Among the many dark-haired Gazzians, Sizzle was easy to find. She and the remaining survivors were in shackles on the main deck. She watched curiously as the galleon stalled briefly to fire a cannonball at some poor sea creature in the water. She tried to see what it was but after the blast, the creature was gone. Looking back toward the galleon, the crew was jumping around, laughing at the slaughter of the creature.

Angry and frustrated, she watched the galleon slide over to port, preparing for the next tack that would take it north. The thought of Sizzle and the others shackled inside a rat-infested hold of the galleon was sickening.

Desperate and guilt-ridden, she struggled to think of a way to save them. But without a boat, there was no way of getting to the ship.

As the galleon gathered speed on her new northerly course, Leucadia wondered why the wooden ship stayed close to the coastline. Fear was the likely answer. On Earth, galleons in the comparable time period rarely sailed far from shore for fear of being eaten by giant sea creatures or sailing off the edge of the world.

Looking north again, she saw a point of land jutting out into the ocean. It offered her only shot at catching up to the galleon. She bounced down to the beach and ran north. If she had calculated correctly the direction of the wind and the route she needed to travel, the galleon would need one more course correction to skirt the rocky point, and it would have to tack within a few hundred yards of the point before making its final turn. If she made it to the point in time, she could intercept the galleon as it passed right over her. All she had to do was grab the wooden hull with her claws and climb aboard.

Run, Lu, run!

29

The Gall Moon

Hupp gathered his crew before Gall Moon rose. For a short time, it would be dark and moonless, just the right conditions to carry out his plot to retake their ship from the Croomis. (*Croomis* was the old sailor term used to describe the tailless marauders who came from the southern latitudes to plunder, kill, and enslave the coastal villagers of the north. From the land of the Croomis at the end of the world, no ship had ever returned.)

Hupp deeply hated the Croomis. They had murdered his family when he was a boy. Only the mercy of the gods had saved him. He was hunting small checrats in the hills for his mother when the Croomis raided his village. That evening when he returned, his village was destroyed and the villagers had been killed or taken as slaves.

Three suns ago, Ozma and Noe went back to the ship to retrieve the grog from the wreckage. When they returned without the grog, Hupp was enraged, as was the crew. They wanted their grog. Hupp believed that the sly Croomis Boy Captain had stolen the grog from the ship for himself.

"That is possible, my leader," Noe said, "but our ship has also disappeared."

"The ship was removed from the mountain?" Hupp asked, amazed.

"By the Gall Moon this is true," Ozma confirmed.

Hupp believed that neither Ozma nor Noe had the smarts to conjure up such a story, but the number of slaves that were required to accomplish such a task was beyond calculation. They knew of only six Croomis. Without help from the gods, moving the galleon was impossible.

To confirm Ozma and Noe's reports, Hupp investigated the mountainside himself. To his surprise, the galleon was indeed missing. After much searching, Zim and Pako saw their ship floating in the lagoon, its hull fixed as though it had never been damaged. "We saw the top of the mast with our own eyes, Hupp," Zim reported. "The Croomis have taken our ship and our grog. We tried to see more, but the beast with tall ears turned us back."

"Why didn't you slay the creature?" Hupp asked, who believed his crewmen should be able to slay such a harmless creature.

"The creature is possessed with evil Deeho, Hupp," Zim explained. "We saw its eyes. If we dared harm it, it would have eaten us for sure."

Hupp slapped them away, calling them traa bait for believing such nonsense. Still, the fact that their ship was taken by the Croomis confounded him a great deal. What kind of powerful magic did the Boy Captain possess? If he had not seen for himself his ship floating in the lagoon, he would have believed the spirit of the Croomis had infected them all.

What the Croomis captors intended to do with his crew was unknown. Hupp was the lead master, now that their former Captain was dead. These Croomis were not at all like the ancient plunderers of death, who burned their enemies alive over the white-hot coals of the ximata tree.

The first day they were made to bathe in the sea pool near their camp. They were then given fresh clothes made of a peculiar fabric that did not itch or tear when scraped against a sharp rock. Each day they were given unusual food that was made of layered bread, some strange kind of meat, and stringy plants that no one ate. Everyone liked the crispy straws, however. No one knew what they were. The sorcerer called "Wiz" said it was neither meat nor fowl. The thick, red-colored liquid they put on the straws appeared like blood, but it made the straws even more desirable.

The Croomis also supplied his crew with plenty of fresh water and a vile, dark drink that no one but Ido could swallow. Until they had their grog, the crew would not feel whole, he told the Boy Captain.

The Boy Captain was unsympathetic. "Get over it, Tall Tail. It's Blue Stuff or water. The choice is yours."

"That is no choice," Hupp argued.

The Croomis Boy Captain walked away. "Drink seawater then. That's all there is."

After that, the crew embraced Hupp's plan to overthrow their Croomis captors. None of them could live without grog! Except for the lagoon where the Croomis had taken their ship, the Gazzians were given the freedom to move about the island. The Boy Captain warned them to stay clear of the vines. *They are dangerous*, he told them. The Croomis sorcerer, Wiz, observed that no animals, birds, insects, or even other plants inhabit the part of the island where the vines live. *It is wise to keep your men near the water's edge*, the sorcerer advised, who guessed that the seawater was poisonous to the vines.

Several times over the passing days, one of his crew tried to breach the forbidden boundary and blacked out every time. No one ever saw who brought them back, but when they awoke the following morning, they found themselves resting on the sand with the others as if nothing had happened.

The Croomis had not mistreated his crew, but Hupp distrusted the Croomis Boy Captain anyway. His crew's swords and pistols were taken from them, but they were allowed to keep their knives for hunting or scraping shellfish off the rocks by the sea. If the crew was swift and precise with the plan, there was no reason they couldn't take their ship back easily and sail away with the morning tide.

"Mr. Pitch," a high voice called to him. That was the new name given to Hupp by the Croomis Boy Captain. He said their names were too difficult to pronounce, and since there were nine survivors of his crew, they would each be given a Croomis moniker of great character and distinction.

"Your number two man will be called 'Catch'." The Boy Captain then pointed to Ido, the smallest and youngest of the crew and called him "Shortstop." The others he named were "Twobagger," "Moneyball," "Homerun" and "Zinger." When Ozma and Noe returned from their food gathering, he said, they would be called, "Linedrive" and "Fastball."

The Boy Captain had come alone, accompanied only by his tall-eared pet, who trotted lightly over the sand, making hardly a footprint. The young Croomis wore what appeared to be the Captain's clothes: dark blue pants with a wide black belt held together with a heavy golden buckle. He also wore tall black boots, a loose-fitting linen shirt, and a wide-brimmed hat that was also the Captain's in appearance, yet it wasn't. None of the clothes could be the Captain's, Hupp figured, because the Boy Captain was much larger in size than their leader. Yet, the clothes all fit like they were made for the Boy Captain. Not one garment was torn or showed wear. Every stitch appeared new, as if the garments were sewn together yesterday.

The tall-eared creature's eyes glowed yellow in the night. It made everyone, including Pitch, nervous, for no one had ever seen such a vile creature of the gods. Zim swore he witnessed the small beast kill a traa and then devour the serpent with the white chammels on the rocks. Hupp saw the bones of the traa, but didn't believe such a wild tale was possible. He made a mental note that Zim would receive twenty lashes for his lies, when time allowed.

"Get your ball team together, Mr. Pitch," the Boy Captain ordered.

Pitch and his crew stood their ground, afraid they were being taken to their deaths. The Boy Captain saw the fear on the crew's faces and assured them that no harm would come to them.

"Where are you taking us?" Hupp asked.

"We are leaving the island with the morning tide," the Boy Captain replied.

Hupp snorted. "We have no vessel," he sneered.

"Your ship has been repaired and is seaworthy."

"You are stealing our ship?" Pako asked.

"I am borrowing it for a short time, Mr. Twobagger. For thirty-three days, to be exact. At the end of that time, I will return her to you with my thanks."

"What is our compensation?" Zim asked.

The Boy Captain faced Zim with a pleased grin. "A great treasure, Mr. Twobagger," he stated confidently. "Your ship was a pirate galleon. I have seen your stores. You were not very good at your work."

"Our leader was mostly filled with grog," Pako volunteered.

"That practice will change," the Boy Captain stated.

"You do not drink grog?" the one renamed Homerun asked.

"I'm too young," the Boy Captain answered.

The crew found this amusing. Another Gazzian then asked, "You have other plans, young sir?"

"I do. There will be plenty of bounty for all under my command."

"Jakaa's revenue galleons would make great prizes, young leader," said Zim, grinning while the rest of the crew nodded in agreement.

The Boy Captain smiled. "Then by the next Gall Moon our cargo holds will be filled with Jakaa's wealth."

Hupp was not so sure. "Jakaa's ships are powerful. They have many guns. We are no match for the Emperor's revenue ships."

In a lighting-fast move, Hupp pulled his knife from the back of his trousers and lunged for the Boy Captain, thinking he could catch the young Croomis off guard from an arm's length away. The black crystal blade came within a hair of slitting open the Croomis Boy from one side of his stomach to the other.

Before Hupp was able to bury the black blade into the Boy Captain's gullet, the weapon inexplicably disappeared from his hand.

"This is so cool, Mr. Pitch," the Boy Captain said, holding Hupp's blade up to the light of the newly-risen Gall Moon. "Did you make this? My little brother would love one of these. Do you have any more?"

Hupp said nothing. He trembled inside, unable to fathom the Boy Captain's sorcery. In desperation, he saw the golden blade in the Boy Captain's belt. Hupp was about to lunge for the weapon when he saw the tall-eared creature's eyes and their penetrating yellow glow. He watched its fangs, long as black daggers, drop down from the roof of its mouth. Hupp stopped cold. The Boy Captain's magic was far too powerful under the Gall Moon. He would wait for a weaker moment to challenge him again. A moment when *he* possessed the power.

To Hupp's surprise, the Boy Captain showed no signs of anger when he calmly ordered the Gazzian crew to put their blades on the table rock nearby.

Seeing that their choices were to cooperate or face the wrath of the Boy Captain's creature, the crew wasted no time placing their blades on the rock. The Boy Captain examined the pile of knives. After picking through the assortment, he removed only the black-bladed ones. The other blades seemed of little interest to him. "Thanks. I'll take these," he said while he examined with great interest the black serrated edges with his fingers. When he finished, he ordered, "Meet me at the lagoon by first light, gentlemen, or I'll leave without you."

Hupp knew otherwise. He was a hard-nosed seaman who had more experience sailing the oceans than all of his crew combined. "You will need all hands to sail a galleon."

The Boy Captain's stare met Hupp's without arrogance or ego, but with respect for the leader of his Tails. "Very true, Sir. But mark my word, I will leave you on this island to rot with the vines if you are late. If I require more hands to share in Jakaa's wealth, I'm sure I will find them at the next port, Mr. Pitch!"

Hupp turned to his crew for their reaction. He may have doubted the Boy Captain would follow through with his threat, but his crew of tails believed it. To the last tail, they wanted a share of Jakaa's booty.

Even so, Hupp's plan to retake their ship had not changed. The Croomis boy was no seaman. Of that, he was certain. His face was unmarred and his teeth were intact. His hands were soft and unscarred. His clothes were fresh and lacked odor. He had the look and manners of the royal class. On the high seas, his crew would prevail. There were many ways the Boy Captain could meet his fate.

Hupp's sly nod toward his crew relieved their anxiety as to what would happen next. Another opportunity would come, he told them, when the advantage would be theirs. One day soon, they would once again be the masters of their ship, along with all of Jakaa's riches.

Hupp turned back to the young Croomis, but the Boy Captain was gone. The tails scanned the shoreline and the dense forest of vines on the hillside, but both the Boy Captain and the tall-eared creature had vanished like a puff of smoke. A whirring noise brought his eyes skyward. The moonlight glittered off a twirling object high in the sky as it descended and stuck in the sand.

Ido, now called Shortstop by the Boy Captain, ran to the object and dutifully brought it to Hupp. It was the same finely machined golden blade the Boy Captain had in his belt.

"The Boy Captain has made a trade, Hupp," Zim observed. "A blade for a blade."

A loud cry of death brought everyone's attention to the Gall Moon, now full and bright, covering a full quarter of the visible heavens.

Ido saw the black silhouette first. He pointed to a giant flying beast gliding across the face of the great moon with a headless serpent wiggling in its maw.

30

Let's Boogie

First light was beautiful on the lagoon. Harlowe stood quietly and alone on the beach gazing over his newly restored three-masted galleon. The *Millie's* colorful blue sheets and her black and dark blue hull contrasted like a surreal painting against the pink tints of the drifting clouds, the green sky dome, the horizon of dark purples, and the subtle yellows and oranges the morning cast over the calm blue waters of the bay. The salty air was heavy but not yet warm and muggy. A slight breeze had swung the bow of the *Millie* around on her anchor. She was now pointing out to sea, as if she was eager to fill her sails and glide free on the open water.

All but two of the Gazzian crew arrived before dawn. Fastball and Linedrive were missing. Moneyball said they had gone into the forest of vines in search of grog, but had not returned by the time the other tails left for the lagoon. There was no time to search the island for them. As the Boy Captain promised, the *Millie* would not wait. The remaining tails made no objections to leaving the missing tails behind once Pitch declared their share of Jakaa's booty forfeit.

After they were inspected for hidden weapons, the tails immediately went to work making the final preparations for the *Millie's* maiden voyage. Pitch's loud, baritone voice sounded almost melodic as it resonated off the galleon's sheets. "Watch the spar line there, Mr. Catch! Drop the main sail to full, Mr. Zinger! Now hitch those outer stoppers tight, Mr. Shortstop!" The replies were always the same: "Aye, Mr. Pitch!" to every order.

There was great anticipation among the Gamadin crew. They were all eager to set sail and be on their way, especially Simon. Every day that went by without knowing whether Sizzle was alive or dead was agony to him. At times, he wanted to explode. Harlowe understood the feeling well and kept Simon busy working at his side on the most strenuous chores. Under the circumstances, work was the best medicine for the both of them.

Monday walked up to Harlowe, holding a sheathed broadsword and two flintlock pistols. "As you ordered, Captain."

Harlowe swung the broadsword harness around his neck and placed the sheathed sword at his side. "Thanks, Squid. How do I look?"

"Real pirate-like, Captain."

Next, Monday handed Harlowe a flintlock. "Ammo?" Harlowe asked.

Monday opened the round bottom of the flintlock. "Snap the clip in there. You're good to go for another twenty."

"Sweet." Harlowe stuffed the flintlock in his leather belt. After examining the second flintlock, he placed it in his belt as well. Now Harlowe felt whole again. The 16th-century weapons he found on the galleon lacked the punch required to fight in a hostile ocean. The old *Millie* was a pirate vessel. According to the Gazzian crew, at the time the wave hit them, they were being chased by three of Jakaa's warships. Harlowe wasn't taking any chances. His broadsword may have looked like a 16th-century blade, but it was made of Gamadin dura-metal. Its blade was so hard and sharp it could slice through a foot-thick granite rock without dulling its edge. The two flintlocks had similar 54th-century upgrades. The look may have been medieval, but each twenty-round pistol could shoot a bolt of plasma as accurately as a Gamadin sidearm. Harlowe understood that introducing advanced technology, especially modern weaponry, could have dire consequences in the natural development of a Middle-Age planet. But when it came to saving Gazz and his friends from certain death, tweaking the rules a bit was a precaution he was willing to take to ensure their chances of success.

"We're going to be pirates, Captain?" Monday questioned, while he continued admiring the work that had been done on the *Millie*. He stood next to Harlowe, dressed only in his swim trunks and a Gamadin blue T-shirt.

"Pirates we be," Harlowe replied, feeling the hilt of his new broadsword. "According to my new crew," nodding toward the tails climbing the rigging and scurrying about the deck, "where Lu and Riverstone landed is the heart of Dak country. If we run into Jakaa, I plan to be ready."

"Sounds like trouble, Captain," Monday said. "Should I come along, too?"

Harlowe eyed Prigg and Dodger with concern. The plan was for Monday to remain behind and protect them with 54th-century weaponry. "I need you here, Squid. When those ships that were chasing Mr. Pitch and his crew come up missing, they'll send search parties here. Bank on it." His sad eyes drifted over to *Millawanda*. Her beautiful golden hull sat a little below the water line of the lagoon, just out of sight. She was unable to move, unable to power up, unable to do anything but sit in a watery hole while the Gazzian sun, her only source of energy, kept her on life support. "There's no one I trust more than you to keep an eye on Millie for us, Mr. Platter."

The responsibility of watching over his ship and his little brother was enormous. Monday appreciated Harlowe's confidence in him to do the job. "Thank you, Captain."

Dodger overheard the last part of the conversation and reminded Harlowe that Monday was not alone. He stood straight at attention and saluted, dressed only in his dark blue *No Fear* swim trunks. "Prigg and I will help, too, Captain. We'll protect Millie from any Daks who try to harm her!"

Harlowe knelt beside his little brother. "I know, Dodger. You da man. Mr. Platter will need all the help he can get." He turned to Monday with a wink. "Right, Mr. Platter?"

"Roger that, Captain! Dodger, Mr. Prigg, and I will keep her safe."

After a final hug with Dodger, Harlowe turned to Prigg and said, "I want a report every day, Mr. Prigg."

"Yes, Your Majesty."

"Keep her hidden at all times. If any ship tries to enter the lagoon, you know what to do."

"Yes, Your Majesty. The visuals are programmed," which meant that if any vessel wandered too close to the lagoon, a holograph would display Mowgi in his expanded dragon persona. Mowgi would frighten any medieval galleon away from the island.

Harlowe walked over to the white mounds lying in the sand. He scratched Rhud's belly one last time, then threw his arms around Molly's thick neck. "Take care of my crew, girl."

Molly's raspy tongue licked Harlowe on the side of the face as if to say, "Don't worry, I've got it handled."

He hugged her again, took a deep breath, and turned to say one more goodbye. Harlowe strode to the water and continued until he was waist-deep and able to touch *Millawanda's* golden skin just below the water line. Her familiar, pulsing, blue perimeter beacon was dark and lifeless. "Hang in there, lady. I'll be back with help as soon as

I can. I don't know how or where the help will come from, but I'll find it, I promise. I will find it and you'll be okay again."

Bubbles percolated up from under the hull. For Harlowe, it was a sign. "That's the spirit, Millie, don't give up."

Harlowe wiped his eyes with the white blousy sleeve of his pirate shirt as Monday floated a long blue surfboard over to him.

"Are you okay, Captain?"

Harlowe pressed his lips together and nodded his thanks. The salt air was irritating his eyes. They traded high-fives, then Harlowe took the paddle from Monday, stepped onto the board, and began stroking his way out to the galleon. He reached a line hanging from the main spar, grabbed it, pushed the board away, climbed hand-over-hand up the rope, and swung himself over the quarterdeck rail in one easy motion.

Simon called out, "Captain aboard!"

"Welcome, Captain," Ian said, nodding to let Harlowe know that the ship was ready to weigh anchor. He and Simon were crisply dressed in black trousers, white shirts and wide, dark officer's hats. Not a single Gazzian crew member turned in his direction or offered any greeting whatsoever. Their disrespect did not go unnoticed by Harlowe or the Gamadin. Harlowe expected as much. Unless he earned their loyalty and respect soon, the voyage was doomed. He needed both.

Harlowe was not sure how he would accomplish the task of winning their respect, but he knew it was up to him. Words and commands would be useless. As he often did when faced with a question of leadership, he turned to the ancient Chinese general, Sun Tzu: *Regard your soldiers as your children, and they will follow you into the deepest valleys; look on them as your own beloved sons, and they will stand by you even until death.*

He felt the wood planks solidly under his feet and replied to Ian, "Good to be aboard, Mr. Wizzixs. Water and food processors aboard and working?"

"Limited menu, I'm afraid, Captain," Ian replied. "No taco Tuesdays until we get back."

Harlowe's face suddenly went slack. "Double-doubles?"

"Aye, but no cheese."

Simon jumped up and down like a spoiled kid who didn't get his way. "No cheese? How are we supposed to survive, Skipper?"

"How 'bout shakes?" Harlowe asked.

"All but Strawberry," Ian replied, Simon's favorite.

Simon had lost his girlfriend and now he had no cheese for his hamburgers and no strawberry shakes. "Don't tell me there's no fries, Wiz, or I'm throwing that food generator overboard!"

"We have fries but no ketchup."

Now it was Harlowe's turn to whine. "That's whack, Wiz! Tell me you're kidding, or I'm helping Rerun with the toss!"

Ian was more practical. "No one will starve, Captain."

With a disappointed sigh, Harlowe turned his attention to the main deck. He leaned on the quarterdeck rail and looked over his sluggish Gazzian crew. *The skillful general does not expect perfection of the unskilled soldier,* says Sun Tzu. "Looks like our first command will need a little tune-up along the way, gentlemen."

Ian followed Harlowe's scan of the crew. "We don't have much time to whip them into shape, Captain."

"How 'bout I play General Gunn, Skipper, and knock some heads?" Simon asked. He didn't want anyone delaying his quest to find Sizzle.

The captured soldier should be treated with kindness and respect. This is called using the conquered foe to augment one's own strength, says Sun Tzu. "Negative, Mr. Bolt. We will treat our Gazzian crew like one of our own at all times. Is that clear?"

Simon found that one hard to accept, but he consented to his captain's wishes. "Aye, Skipper. With respect."

"Are we ready, gentlemen?" Harlowe asked.

"Pull the anchor, Skipper. Let's boogie," Simon replied. He had been ready to leave since the first day. Harlowe felt that if he could have found enough suitable wood, Simon would have made a raft and sailed ahead of them.

"Aye, Mr. Bolt, let's boogie," Harlowe repeated. Pitch was holding a forecastle ratline with his tail while he kept an eye on the end of the forward bowsprit, where Mowgi had settled in. "Take her out, Mr. Pitch, if you please," Harlowe ordered.

Pitch looked up at his wind threads. They were barely moving. "I fear there is not enough wind to fill our sails, Captain," he replied, clearly unconcerned as to whether they sailed or not.

On a normal galleon, Pitch would have been correct. There was hardly any wind to push the vessel out of the lagoon. A normal ship like the *Millie* might languish for hours in such a soft breeze. But sails made of 54th-century cloth were quite different from ones made of heavy canvas. They were lighter and more efficient, even in a light wind.

"Point taken, Mr. Pitch, let go the foresail. The *Millie* will grab what she needs."

Pitch believed only dropping the foresail was hardly adequate. In such a small wind, all sails would be necessary. He doubted the Boy Captain's mastery, but he would follow orders anyway for no other reason than to prove him wrong.

"Yes, Captain. As you ask. Foresail it is."

Hanging by their tails from the foreyard, Zinger and Twobagger untied the lines that held the main sheets and let them fall. Down they rippled, gathering air before they unraveled to their full extent. The Gazzians stood open-mouthed as the sails bulged outward and the *Millie* lurched forward.

Before the *Millie* had sailed very far, Harlowe, Wiz, and Simon went aft, to the very end of the galleon, where they waved goodbye to *Millawanda*, Monday, Prigg, Dodger, and the cats on the beach. Harlowe swallowed the lump in his throat, knowing this would be the calmest moment of the voyage. From now on, the seas would become swells of death. The Gazzian crew was unaware of their mission. They had no inkling that the Croomis Boy Captain was leading them into the very depths of Moharr.

Harlowe stepped up to the tiller and asked, "How is she handling, Mr. Catch?"

"Like a gentle lady, Captain."

Harlowe faced the wind and felt the warm, salty mist. Above him, the sails fluttered. Staring at the blue Gamadin symbol of *Millawanda* in front of a bright star emblazoned across the top main sheet, Harlowe answered, "That she is, Mr. Catch, that she is."

31

Kikue

His head rang like it had been slammed against a church bell. He reached out for his pillow to cover his ears, but came up empty. His pillow was gone. He opened his eyes to search for anything that would make the sound go away. His vision was cloudy. He saw nothing familiar. Everywhere he looked were faint soft colors, but nothing to cover his ears. His only working sense was smell. *Hot food! Yeah!* He didn't know what it was, nor did he care. If it were a pot of broccoli – the vegetable he hated the most – he would devour it, pot and all!

With great effort, he rolled off the straw platform and dropped to the floor, knocking the wind out of him. It felt like he had fallen off a cliff. He spat dirt while his head continued to spin. Fighting off the urge to hurl, he tried crawling. Before he had gotten very far, someone grabbed him and placed him back on the bed of straw.

A voice spoke to him, but it was like his vision; none of the words made sense. Desperately he pointed to his mouth, trying to ask for something to eat. Soon a gentle hand brought a cool sip of water to his lips. It was as sweet and refreshing as water from a mountain spring.

"You're a lifesaver, dude," he said to the form hovering over him.

The voice spoke again. This time the tone sounded feminine. If he had to guess, his lifesaver was no dude, but a doe.

He tried rising again, but was quickly stopped when she forced him back down on the straw. He was about to protest when she put a bowl of warm broth under his nose. He grabbed it immediately, downing the liquid in a couple of gulps. Something like a thick rope wrapped around his head and stopped him from swallowing the second bowl too fast. He needed to take his time, the kind voice said.

After five more bowls, he leaned back on the straw and uttered exhaustively, "Where am I?"

The voice spoke but even if he understood, he was gonzo after a bellyful of hot soup.

*   *   *

He didn't know how long he was asleep. He wanted to snooze longer, but an irritating glare kept torturing him awake. Peeking between his fingers, he located the source of the irksome light. It was a loose flap in the doorway that was blowing open and shut in the breeze.

Grumbling with displeasure, he rolled off the straw platform and made his way toward the light. He was on a mission. He grabbed the skin covering the door, but instead of fixing the flap, he stumbled over something and ripped the flap from its ties. His eyes flinched in pain when the full sun blazed in upon him. To escape the glare, he rolled himself into the leather flap like a veggie wrap.

He heard laughing and giggling as he struggled to free himself from the entanglement. He twisted and fought, but like a Chinese finger trap, the more he thrashed about, the tighter the restraints became.

He was close to going ballistic when a gentle hand came to his aid. The now-familiar soft voice calmly spoke as its owner unraveled the skin from around his body. He thanked his savior and remained on the ground, breathing hard and feeling too exhausted to move. All the while, the giggling continued.

"Shoo now. Go away, children," the girl's voice said. "Leave Buntoo-attee alone."

The laughter faded and tiny feet scurried away while Buntoo-attee's breath returned and his eyes adjusted to the sunlight. He rubbed his eyes with the back of his hand to clear them. Though he wasn't quite himself, the ringing in his head had disappeared. He was grateful for that. He was still lying in the dirt with hardly a stitch on, but he forgot about that when he looked up. The face staring down at him had round, dark eyes, olive skin, and hair as black as night, and its beautiful owner smelled like a field of spring flowers. She was a double-double cheese, fries, and a tall blue shake, all rolled into one gorgeous babe. Where he got those images, he had no clue. He knew they were important to him and was confident that in time, the fog in his head would clear. For now, he simply enjoyed the vision.

Buntoo-attee flashed his pearly whites. "Who are you?" he asked, already wondering if she was attached.

"Kikue," she replied.

A loose section of the domed hut's doorway fell to the ground. Riverstone felt embarrassed that his clumsiness had broken it. "Sorry."

"The spirit of Deeho," she said, nodding toward a small moon near the mid-morning sun.

Buntoo-attee squinted to find which moon she was pointing to. There were three moons of various sizes hanging above the ocean in the blue-green sky. He decided it didn't make any difference which moon it was, the explanation worked for him.

"Yeah, Deeho," he replied. Then he waved pathetically at the nearest moon and to his head. "Bad mojo."

Kikue tilted her head, confused. "Mojo?" she asked.

Before he could explain, a long snake drifted through the air and grabbed the skin from off the ground. Buntoo-attee scrambled away, thinking it was going to bite him until he realized the snake was attached to Kikue.

"That's a tail!" Buntoo-attee exclaimed in disbelief. Never in a million years did he see that one coming!

Kikue remained kneeling on the ground with Buntoo-attee as she used her prehensile appendage like a third hand. She calmly brought the skin to her hands and began folding the leather cover on her lap. "Did the pirates of Jakaa torture you, Buntoo-attee?"

"Torture?" Riverstone questioned.

"Where is your attee?" she asked, nodding at his buttocks.

Riverstone looked at his hind end. He had no tail. He looked out the door at other creatures in the coastal village of animal-skinned, domed huts. Not just a few, but everyone in the village had tails. From the looks of things, he was definitely the odd one out.

His mind was confused. Did he once have a tail? Had someone actually maimed him and cut off his attee, as she called it? His mind was a blank. He was at a loss to explain why he had no attee. "Yeah, I guess I was," he concluded.

Kikue then asked for his name and where he came from.

Buntoo-attee thought hard. Both questions eluded him. "I don't know," he said to her.

"Deeho," she said.

Buntoo-attee glanced at the smallest moon. His thinking was a little slow, but he got the joke. "Yes, Deeho," he agreed, then he asked, "Where did you find me?"

Kikue pointed down at the bluff to the ocean. "My father's fishing boat found you drifting in the sea. He believes it is a miracle you survived the traa."

Buntoo-attee had no idea what a traa was, but he was grateful that her father found him.

Kikue stood up and carried the skin back to the hut. "Come, Buntoo-attee. You must eat to fight the Deeho."

"What does Buntoo-attee mean, Kikue?" he asked, still sitting in the dirt.

Kikue turned to him and smiled sheepishly. "Tailless one," she replied.

Buntoo-attee nodded, amused. It was better than no name at all. He tried to stand on his own. At least he tried. The Deeho in his head returned. He reached out to steady himself and found nothing to grab. His legs buckled until Kikue's attee wrapped around his waist and lifted all six-foot-seven inches of his muscular frame off the ground, steadying his balance. The appendage felt warm and snug and not at all uncomfortable. Its strength was amazing, leaving him little doubt that it was more than a third arm. It was also a powerful extension of her body.

32

Sea Legs

On her second morning at sea, the *Millie* was sailing steadily north-ward on a wind from just abaft her beam, slicing through the Gazzian ocean like a 19th century clipper ship. The galleon plowed through swells so fast and heeled over to port so far that her Gazzian crew feared their ship would keel over and sink before the day was done. All of them, green-faced with fear, had wrapped their tails firmly around the main deck rail. They knew nothing about Ian's extended keel and hull reinforcements. The *Millie's* tons of counterbalance gave her the ballast she needed to steer a true course against an aggressive sea.

The sky was gray, like the California coastal sky in May. It made the ocean a dreary blue-green. The spray kicked up by the bow broke over the decks, making everything wet and muggy. The topsails were as tight as bowstrings in the gale; the sheets would have split under the stresses these sails faced if it were not for the lightness and strength of the Gamadin fabric.

Harlowe was late for first watch. Since leaving the island, he had been on deck for only short periods of time. Simon and Ian were concerned. It was unlike Harlowe to be late for any reason. After checking the course with his com, Ian went below to find out why Harlowe was acting so strangely.

By hanging onto the rope and wood handrails, Ian successfully fought the rolling and jarring as he carefully made his way from the aftcastle deck down to the Captain's doorway off the quarterdeck. Before knocking, Ian removed a spiked, old leather glove someone had nailed to the wooden door. Careful about getting stuck by any of the lethal points, he rapped twice. But no one answered. He rapped again and called for Harlowe to answer. Not wanting to disturb his Captain, Ian was about to leave when a loud, guttural sound from within raised the hairs on the back of his neck. Fearing the worst, Ian forced the door open and entered the cabin.

"Captain?" he asked.

Ian saw the problem before Harlowe could answer. Jewels was holding the back of Harlowe's pants while the captain was leaning out the cabin window, unceremoniously hurling his guts out.

"Captain?"

"Whaaaaat?" Harlowe replied from the window.

Harlowe was as white as the *Millie's* sails when he turned to face Ian, wiping his mouth and holding onto Jewel's thin arm. "I'm look-ing for my sea legs," he replied hoarsely.

"You look awful."

"I want to die."

"You'll have to do that later, Captain. We have a few problems."

"Are we making good time? That's all I care about."

Ian smiled with success. "We're booking, Captain. The crew thinks the *Millie* will tear apart any second."

Harlowe spat a sour wad out the window before he came back. "New course laid in?"

"Aye, Rerun had to take over the helm. Pitch and the crew are swallowing shredded wheat without milk over the change. They went bonkers when we lost sight of land."

Harlowe buried his face in the wet towel Jewels offered him and looked for a chair to die in. In the unending pitching and yawing, even the captain had to be tied down.

"The end of the world, huh?"

"Something like that. They fear monsters called traas. They think the *Millie* will be swallowed up by one if they lose sight of land."

Harlowe's eyes peered over the towel. "Those things Mowgi ate for lunch on the island?"

"According to Mr. Pitch, those were babies. The really big ones are in the deep water."

Not long ago, Harlowe would have laughed at such nonsense. On Earth, sailors told stories of giant sea creatures, but not one ever turned out to be as big as the legends portrayed. Hundred-foot squids have been found off the east coast of Maine, and whales longer than galleons were commonly seen. However, it was never proven for certain that sea creatures had ever attacked a ship.

Nevertheless, Harlowe took his Gazzian crew's warning seriously. They may be seamen's tales, but he had been through too many close encounters in his short time away from Earth to know that big creatures really did exist. Gazz was no exception.

"You've been thinking about it. What's your plan for any unwanted guests?" Harlowe asked.

"Mowgi's keeping an eye on things for the present."

"How big are the grown-ups?"

"Big. Zinger says he's seen one swallow a ship."

"The Mowg is tough, but might find one of those a little more than even he can chew," Harlowe said.

Ian agreed with Harlowe. "True. I'll put a clicker in the crow's nest. That should cover our bases."

"Make him look like a hood ornament so the tails don't freak out. Make sure he's got a zapper, too. We're not here to make friends," Harlowe added.

"Aye."

"What else?"

Ian laid the old glove with the spikes on the table in front of Harlowe. "I found this nailed to the door."

Harlowe picked it up and examined it. "Looks wicked. What is it?"

Ian stared at the nasty-looking glove. "I've seen the Gazzians slide these things over the ends of their tails when they're climbing the rigging. Keeps them from slipping."

"With spikes?"

"No. This is the first one I've seen with spikes."

A spike pricked Harlowe's finger. "Ouch!"

"Could be a challenge," Ian speculated.

Harlowe closed his eyes. Searching for his sea legs was taking all of his concentration. His face was pale and his eyes pathetic when he dashed across the room back to the window so he could return more land to the sea.

33

In the Mouth of a Traa

For the first time in two days Buntoo-attee felt alive. He stepped out of the hut and stretched toward the cloudless sky. The bright sun, rising above the hills behind the village, felt soothing. He walked to the edge of the incline and looked down upon a beautiful white sandy beach and a dark green ocean that stretched forever to the horizon. What caught Buntoo-attee's attention, however, were the rolling breakers coming onto shore. They were long and tubular and appeared like glass in the windless morning. Three-to-five foot lines came in from the north and peeled south from a small rocky point until they rumbled quietly upon the flat, open beach in front of the village.

"That's so sick, brah."

It was all Buntoo-attee could do to control himself. He tossed away his animal skin shirt, stepped out of his moccasins, and jogged down to the beach to catch his first ride.

Kikue was returning from their morning collections with the rest of the young women. She saw him trotting down the incline from the village. Putting down her basket of gathered berries, she called to him. "Where are you going, Buntoo-attee?"

"For a swim!" Buntoo-attee replied, waving at her just before he splashed into the temperate water.

She continued watching him in disbelief. Buntoo-attee didn't hesitate at the water's edge. He continued running into the water and didn't stop. *What is he doing? The gods have seized his mind! The sea will swallow him up and he will never come back to me!*

Kikue dropped her basket and ran after Buntoo-attee. "No, Buntoo-attee! You will be killed!" she screamed at him. She was too late. Buntoo-attee didn't hear her panicked calls and dove headfirst into the surf. He was gone.

Kikue was heartbroken. Poor Buntoo-attee! The gods have taken him. She felt helpless and started to sob. If she went any farther into the sea, the gods would devour her too.

Suddenly, she saw Buntoo-attee's head pop out of the water. *Were her eyes deceiving her?* His arms thrashed about as he continued farther out to sea. She had to stop him. A wave crashed over him, and like a giant traa, swallowed him whole again. In reckless disregard for her own life, she bolted into the surf to save Buntoo-attee. She could not let him die. Against all her teachings as a child, she ran after him. The sea would not try to take her Buntoo-attee away from her again.

Kikue dashed into the surf, jumping over one wave after another, escaping the traa's jaws each time she leaped, pushing back the water with her hands, fighting like Buntoo-attee with each leap. Between the waves she saw his head and arms beating the water as if he was unable to escape.

The ocean was over her waist now. When the last wave lifted her off the bottom, she caught a glimpse of Buntoo-attee moving from her at incredible speed.

Then one after another, wave after wave struck her and pushed her back. Each time a wave hit her, she was thrown backward toward the beach. She could make no headway reaching Buntoo-attee. Kikue was becoming tired from the struggle.

Another wave sucked her underwater. She twisted in the chaos, not knowing what was up or down. The traa had her in his maw. Somehow her foot touched the bottom and she pushed upward. She broke the surface and gasped for air, just as another traa was about to swallow her again. Too tired to move, she waited for fate to strike when she was lifted toward the surface. Her nose and mouth filled with water, making her cough violently. Just when she thought all was lost, she was free again, with Buntoo-attee holding her in his arms as they climbed the side of the wave and then down into the trough until she felt the bottom again with her feet.

Buntoo-attee's dripping face grinned at her. "What were you doing, Kikue?" he asked her.

Kikue coughed and spat seawater before she spoke. "The traa…" she tried to say, coughing and spitting, "was going to take you." She pointed behind him with her tail. Another wave was building and becoming more hollow as it prepared to hit them. "We must run, Buntoo-attee, before it eats us!" she cried out in fear for their lives.

Buntoo-attee held her steady with his strong hands around her waist. "It's okay, Kikue. No worries." Just before the wave broke, he lifted her up with a gentle push off the bottom, and they glided smoothly over the top of the wave and settled safely on the backside of the wave. This time it was easy.

Buntoo-attee lifted her over waves several more times until she knew they would not be swallowed by the traa.

"See, it's okay. Waves are fun once you get the hang of it," Buntoo-attee told her.

"They will not eat you and take you away from me?" she asked, her large dark eyes surrounded by her wet, twisted hair.

Buntoo-attee laughed. "No, Kikue. They're cool. Watch me. I will show you how fun they are."

He took her hand and led her back to the beach, where the waves swirled softly around her ankles. "Stay right here and watch me." When her eyes grew alarmed that he was going back in the water, he told her, "What I am doing will not harm me." He wasn't sure why. It just seemed natural to him that whatever he was doing, riding the waves into shore, was something he had done a thousand times before.

He explained that he would go out again, catch a traa for her, and ride it back to her. "You will see, Kikue, the traas here are friendly."

Buntoo-attee turned and trotted back out into the water, where he once again dove into the traas. Kikue waited anxiously. It was only a moment until Buntoo-attee appeared before the traa. He pushed off with a powerful stroke. The traa cradled him in its mouth and carried him all the way into shore, laying him gently at her feet.

By this time, a crowd of villagers had gathered around Kikue to watch the strange, tailless visitor perform his magic.

"You have tamed the mighty traa, Buntoo-attee," the village chief said.

Buntoo-attee thanked the chief and told him it was nothing, really. But Kikue observed how happy the villagers were playing in the surf. "You have given my people a gift they will always remember."

"Why has no one ever played with the waves before?" Buntoo-attee wondered. "Your village is next to an ocean. All your people should know how to swim in the waves."

"You call them waves?"

"Yes, and sometimes we call them other things too, like tubes and swells. You have never heard of such terms before?" Buntoo-attee asked.

Kikue hadn't. "Many of your words are unknown to me, Buntoo-attee. Your village must be far away."

Buntoo-attee thought for a moment. His mind was still a blank. He touched his forehead. "I don't remember my village at all. I don't remember yesterday or why I was in the ocean when your father found me." He turned to her, taking her hand. "Except you, Kikue. I remember you."

Buntoo-attee then kissed her lightly on her mouth.

Kikue had never been kissed before. She looked at him, unsure of its meaning. She stared at his easy smile and straight white teeth with interest. She had never seen such perfect teeth before. She resumed their conversation as if he had never touched her. "Your injuries were severe. In time you will remember."

As they walked along the beach, Buntoo-attee tripped over something in the wet sand. The water covered the object briefly, and then receded again, revealing the end of a tarnished gold cylinder sticking out of the wet sand. The foot-long discovery was lighter than it looked but felt hard and unbreakable. He held it up to the sun. "What is it?"

Kikue didn't know. "I have never seen one like it before."

Buntoo-attee tapped the cylinder with his hand. "It will make a good tool to break shells with."

Kikue took it from his hand. "The gods have given us a treasure. We must not harm it, Buntoo-attee!"

"Give it back! I found it," Buntoo-attee said playfully.

Her tail grabbed the cylinder from her hands and held it away from the both of them.

"That's not fair," Buntoo-attee said, reaching for the object.

"Will you not use it to crack shells?"

Buntoo-attee crossed his heart. "I promise. I'll be as gentle as a lamb with it."

"A lamb?" Kikue asked. "What is a lamb?"

Buntoo-attee put out his hand, waist high. "It's a little farm animal about—" He stopped in mid-sentence and looked at her. "You don't know what a lamb is?"

"No." She transferred the object back to her hand and examined it more closely. "It seems to be made of the same material as your amulet," she observed.

Buntoo-attee stared at her. "My amulet?"

Kikue took Buntoo-attee by the hand. "We will go to my father. He kept it safe for you while you recovered. It was around your neck when you were brought to our village."

34

Tail Overboard

The northwesterly trades continued to blow, turning warmer as the *Millie* sailed north toward a darkening sky. As she cut through the high rolling swells of white-capped peaks and deep troughs, she appeared like a bloated racing yacht headed for the finish line. For two days the *Millie* had been out of sight of land. Her Gazzian crew was terrified. For them this was a dangerous pace that would crack her hull and rip her sails if she didn't reduce her sails soon. When the *Millie* listed as much as twenty-one degrees to starboard under full sail, a brave sailor could reach out over the downside rail and touch the passing sea with ease. Her crew feared that the breakneck speed meant certain death. By now, they'd had enough of the Croomis Boy Captain's perilous quest for Jakaa's treasure, and they had been on the open sea for only two days! They would demand that the *Millie* turn back before the traas destroyed the ship and ate them all. If the Croomis Boy Captain refused, they were prepared to challenge his leadership.

Since dawn, they had huddled together on the main deck to confront the Boy Captain the moment he emerged from his cabin. They outnumbered the Croomis and were well-armed. Moneyball and Twobagger had harpoons with wicked heads fashioned out of the same black volcanic rock Pitch's knife was fashioned from. Simon was at the steerage wheel. Though the movie star was Gamadin, his steering skills were wanting. When Twobagger or Catch was not at the helm, the *Millie's* course was erratic. The galleon often struck the swells head-on. When that happened, she was pushed to the side, causing the three-master to lurch and flop when she should have glided through the humps with relative ease. Ian tried to assist and together they managed to stay the course, but without Gazzian tails to steer in the heavy seas, they were losing speed and would eventually drift off course. Mowgi was the only one keeping the Gazzian crew at bay, his lengthening incisors momentarily preventing the assault on Harlowe's cabin.

Twobagger and Catch were discussing skewering the undog when Harlowe stepped onto the quarterdeck. Simon and Ian were still wrestling with the wheel as Harlowe strode by the helm. Ian half-expected to see Harlowe and his sickly, white face crawl out from his cabin on his hands and knees. Nearly an hour ago, Harlowe looked to be on Death's doorstep, hurling his guts out the backside of the *Millie*. Ian couldn't believe his eyes as Harlowe strutted past them with a spry step. After a confident wink, he faced the Gazzian crew leaning on the quarterdeck rail, appearing as captainly as ever.

How did he do that?

With one hand on the hilt of the black stone knife he had taken from Pitch on the island, Harlowe tossed the tail-glove at the feet of the Gazzian crew huddled below on the main deck. "Who left this at my door?"

Pitch stepped forward, wrapping his tail tight around the main deck rail to keep from sliding across the deck and into the churning sea. The six other Gazzians clutched anything available to keep from falling overboard as well. "I did!" Pitch shouted above the crashing waves, the howling winds, and the fluttering sails.

"I did, Sir!" Harlowe shot back.

Pitch defied Harlowe's rebuttal. He picked up the glove and shook it at Harlowe. "I demand the Right of Challenge."

The undog's small body seemed nailed to the wood deck as his jaws expanded, ready to rip Pitch's arm from its socket.

With his face twisted and determined, Catch lifted his harpoon at the undog. From above, a golden blade with a beautifully carved black-and-green jade hilt smashed into the deck with a solid twang at the feet of the defiant seaman.

"Do that, Mr. Catch, and I'll drop you where you stand!" Harlowe bellowed from the rail, pointing his modified flintlock at Catch's forehead.

"You only have one round, Captain! You can't shoot us all," Pitch sneered.

Harlowe quickly shot five posts from their cleats along the main rail. "Care to rethink your count, Mr. Pitch?"

The *Millie* unexpectedly lurched skyward, blowing off the topside of a tall swell. There was a long moment of silence before she slammed hard down the backside of the trough. Everyone except the undog collapsed onto the deck, losing their footing. It was all Harlowe could do to hold onto his weapon and stay firm to the rail and not find himself tossed from the quarterdeck into the sea. He reholstered his flintlock and climbed back over the rail in time to catch Simon clinging to the wheel upside down, trying to regain control.

Harlowe rushed to the helm and with great effort, turned Simon right side up again.

"Sorry, Captain," Simon apologized, planting his feet on the deck. Together, it was all they could do to swing the bow around to avoid the next hump.

Harlowe pointed at the compass. "Keep her on that five degree mark, Mr. Bolt."

Simon's worried face nodded back. "Aye, Captain. Maybe we should drop a few sails, Skipper."

Harlowe looked up at the jibs with anchor lines taunt like bow-strings. "Steady as she goes, Mr. Bolt. Full sail."

"Aye, sir."

Harlowe searched the quarterdeck for Ian. "Where's Wiz?"

Without taking his focus away from the wheel, Simon replied, "He was right next to me, Skipper."

"Captain!" Ian's voice yelled up from the main deck.

Harlowe fought his way back to the quarterdeck forward rail and found Ian huddled with the Gazzian crew on the main deck, doing what he could to keep them all from being thrown overboard. "We lost Shortstop!" Ian cried out and pointed toward the boiling sea. A hundred yards off the stern, a bobbing head with waving arms was going over a crest.

Harlowe stared at Pitch. "Why didn't anyone throw him a rope?"

Pitch appeared unemotional, as if Shortstop's fate was already sealed. "He is lost. The traas have him now."

The fact that Pitch still refused to help his fellow crewman was disturbing. Harlowe's concern was always his crew first, even if they were Gazzian pirates. He turned back to Simon and called out his order. "Bring her about, Mr. Bolt!"

Simon wrestled with the wheel, but the sea and the wind were against him. The bow would not change course as easily as with *Millawanda*. It wasn't until Harlowe helped out that they were able to turn the *Millie* at all. "What are you going to do, Skipper?"

Harlowe secured the black knife to his belt but removed both flintlocks and gave them to Simon. "We have a crewman overboard, Mr. Bolt."

Having been rescued by Harlowe more than once, Simon understood the situation. "Aye, Skipper."

Harlowe returned to the rail again and untied a mast line from a cleat. Holding onto the loose line, Harlowe shouted to Pitch on the main deck. "Have Mr. Twobagger give Mr. Bolt a hand, on the double, Mr. Pitch!"

Twobagger got a stern look from Pitch to stay put.

Without looking at the undog, Harlowe ordered, "Mowgi! Show Mr. Twobagger the way."

Displaying his six-inch fangs was unnecessary. The undog let out a threatening growl behind Twobagger's back that sounded more like it came from Rhud than a small dog. It was enough. Twobagger scurried up the gangway to the quarterdeck, with Mowgi nipping at his heels.

Now that Twobagger and Simon were at the helm, the *Millie* arrested her forward motion in the rolling sea and turned on a great swing from a starboard tack until she was upright and dropping wind from her sails. When she came around, she gathered wind once again, filling her sails and listing to port as she gathered speed. Harlowe removed his hat and put it in the undog's mouth. "Don't eat my hat, Mowg." Mowgi's bright yellow eyes reflected his distaste, as if he had been given a wet rag to chew on.

When the *Millie* swung from starboard to port, Harlowe took advantage of the ship's momentum to throw himself outward while he still clung to the mast line. Holding the end of the mizzen line, he catapulted as if he was at the end of a long whip into the sky. Partially obscured by the blowing mist from the sea, Harlowe deployed his wings from beneath his 16th-century garments. The Gazzian crew looked on in amazement as Harlowe glided like a seabird and then plunged into the ocean and stroked toward Shortstop's bobbing head.

During the come-about, Zinger had scampered up to the masthead to watch the daring rescue. With his tail wrapped firmly around the mast like a safety line, he leaned out over the main masthead rail, gripping a brace with one hand and pointed his finger toward a monstrous wormlike creature powering through the giant swells on a direct path for Harlowe and Shortstop.

"TRAA!" Zinger screamed at the top of his lungs.

35

Maahoo

It had been a night-long celebration in the village. Kikue and Buntoo-attee had slipped away from the festivities for a long walk along the beach. The light of two Gazzian moons shone low on the glistening, calm ocean, guiding their way. They walked hand-in-hand, while Kikue snaked her tail around Buntoo-attee's waist, holding him in a way she had never held anyone in her life. This warm feeling was a new experience for Kikue. She had watched the young women in the village flirting with the males. They were often silly and unlike their normal selves. Oh, how they carried on with their foolish dance! This childishness would never affect her, she promised…until now. Now she understood their giddiness, their uncharacteristic behavior, and their flushed faces. She understood the joy of the courtship, feeling the warmth inside her and the shortness of breath upon seeing him the first moment of the day. "Maahoo" is what the old females of the village called it. Translated it meant *"the sparkle of the moon within."* When she looked out across the water, there were two lines of *maahoo* pointed their way.

She sighed as she drank in Buntoo-attee's sea-like scent and felt his strength and confidence in the touch of his hand. "What bothers you, Buntoo-attee? Since finding the talisman on the beach, you seem troubled."

Buntoo-attee stopped and brought her closer, kissing her lightly. "It's the amulet, Kik. I feel connected to it and I don't know why. It feels like there is something I must do." He had begun calling her by this shortened name in recent days. He explained that wherever it was that he came from, it was a way of showing affection for someone you care for a great deal.

Kikue cuddled closer, staring amorously up at him with her large eyes. "You must kiss me again."

They kissed but for Buntoo-attee, his thoughts were still troubled. He squeezed his eyes shut, trying desperately to remember. "It's urgent, Kik."

She saw the worry in Buntoo-attee's face and was frightened that she would lose him to the Deeho again. "Do not leave us, Buntoo-attee. You have done so much for our village. The new ways you have shown us to store our water and food mean that our children will not suffer through the time of scarcity. Our nets have never been so bountiful. It is because of you," she said, holding him and wanting him never to leave her, "that our village will be strong again."

Buntoo-attee blinked out of his momentary stupor. "Don't worry, Kik. That's not the plan. I love being here." He pointed at the waves. "Great tubes, great food, and a hot babe. What's not to like?"

She looked at him oddly. "Babe? What is a babe?"

Buntoo-attee's smile returned as he held her at arm's length and wiped the tears from her eyes. "You are, Kik. Anywhere in the galaxy, you're a babe."

"Is galaxy your home?"

Buntoo-attee kissed her again. "I don't know. I wish I could remember." Unable to solve the mystery, he looked to the west. The sun was already rising, pink above the hills. Where had the time gone, he wondered? It was already morning. He took her by the hand and turned toward the village. "We should go back. I'm starving for a half-pounder!"

Kikue shook her head at his odd behavior. "You are always hungry, Buntoo-attee. What is a double-double?"

"A big thick juicy delight."

"It is too early for such a meal."

"There's always time for a double-double, Kik." He grabbed her hand. "Come on. I'll show you." They began loping back toward the village in an easy jog. After a mile, they rounded the point and saw a dhow anchored offshore. Kikue stopped, her face turning fearful.

The words Kikue used to describe the scene were few and troubling. The one word that Buntoo-attee understood, however, was "collector." To him that only meant one thing, and it came from a place in the back of his mind that had one meaning: "tax man."

36

Traa!

The sea was a mass of rolling forty-foot swells. Harlowe swam to the place where Shortstop was last seen, but the little crewman had disappeared. He couldn't be far, Harlowe figured. A quick scan from the top of the swell revealed nothing. If Shortstop wasn't on the surface, there was only one other place he could be.

Under it!

He flicked his eyes, and the sensors inside his bugeyes immediately went radial. There Shortstop was, twenty feet below the surface, his tail searching for something to hold onto in the boundless waters!

Shortstop's heat signature lit up like a beacon. He was sinking fast. There was no telling how long he had been without air. If he was like a human, he had about three to four minutes of breath. *The Guinness record is 17 minutes, but that was after the dude hyperventilated pure oxygen*, Harlowe reminded himself. *That's cheating! Shortstop is small and he's Gazzian. He could die in less time than a human!*

Harlowe kicked harder to swim against the unforgiving current. He knew that every second could mean life or death for his crewman. Harlowe wasn't going to lose him. This wasn't the same as the time he had rescued Lu from Simon's sinking yacht, Harlowe didn't have to worry about air. He had plenty. His SIBA took care of those things. The ocean currents were another matter. They were twisting and pulling him in ten different directions at once.

Never fight nature, his dad Buster had always taught him. *Her power is infinite and you're just a speck of dust. Let the currents be your friend and put them to work for you.*

Stroking to his right, Harlowe found what he was looking for, a current to place him in front of Shortstop. But before he could grab his crewman, an unexpected surge jerked Harlowe sideways. His outreached claw snapped at Shortstop's leg, but the gush was so strong, it ripped the cloth from his grasp. Then, just as unexpectedly, another surge that shot out slammed him back into Shortstop. Now they were sucking face!

That didn't matter to Harlowe. He had found his lost crewman, and not even a forty-foot swell was going to separate them!

Harlowe kicked with all his might and up they went. Twice they were sucked back under before breaking the surface. *Don't fight, let it work for you!* At last they made it to the top of the swell with Shortstop still firmly in his grip. Harlowe saw that Shortstop wasn't breathing. Harlowe pressed Shortstop's stomach and a mass of ocean shot from the little guy's mouth, but it wasn't enough. Shortstop's lungs had stopped working.

"Wiz!" Harlowe shouted in his com over the roar of the roiling ocean and blowing winds. Harlowe knew Ian wouldn't reply, in case one of the Gazzian crewmen was standing nearby. He just gave orders and hoped Ian heard him on the other end. "Reel us in! I've got Shortstop!"

As they rose up the wall of a swell, Harlowe peeled back his bug-eye mask and was about to perform mouth-to-mouth on Shortstop when a giant serpent rose out of the sea.

It was the largest creature Harlowe had ever seen. If there was any doubt about Zinger's tale of a traa big enough to swallow a ship whole, this gargantuan serpent dispelled it. Its maw was so wide it could swallow the *Millie* whole, with room to spare.

Harlowe had only one weapon to defend himself. He unsheathed his black knife, and bravely waved it at the traa. Harlowe and Shortstop rose to the top of the crest, where they came nose-to-nose with the massive creature. The beast's putrid breath blew down on them while its eyes fixated on the knife as if it was in a trance. For whatever reason, the traa then closed its mouth and allowed the swell carrying Harlowe and Shortstop to draw them away.

Harlowe wasn't waiting for any explanation. On the next rise of the swell, Harlowe touched the traa's snout with the tip of his blade and said, "Later, Dude!"

As if his words were a signal, the dura-line attached to Harlowe's Gama-belt went taut, and the two of them pulled away from the traa. The giant serpent didn't seem to notice that it was losing its meal. In front of them, the *Millie* was slicing through the heavy swells and coming up fast. The giant traa slid silently into the sea as the *Millie* came alongside. Harlowe grabbed a bowline and held on as they were lifted onto the main deck. Harlowe paid no attention to the astonished faces around him. He lay Shortstop on the deck and began pumping air into his chest with his mouth.

"Come on, Shortstop, breathe!" Harlowe urged between breaths. The little crewman's face was green. Harlowe had no clue whether it was helping or not. A living human face would be pink, but what did green skin mean on a Gazzian? Was Shortstop already dead?

Harlowe kept working. Twenty minutes later, Ian put a sympathetic hand on Harlowe's shoulder. "He's gone, Captain."

After sucking in a couple of breaths, Harlowe countered, "I'm not losing him, Wiz!"

Almost in tears, Harlowe held the little crewman in his arms and ordered him to breathe. "Wake up, Shortstop! You can't die!"

Waves continued to break over the rail, washing over them all. While the crew searched for steady holds, Harlowe stayed in place, clutching Shortstop with one hand and digging a claw deep into the heavy planks of the deck with the other. A power as mighty as an ocean wouldn't stop Harlowe's effort. On he went, breathing air into Shortstop's lungs. The Gazzians stood, watching in disbelief as the young Croomis captain fought tirelessly for one of their own. They had never heard of such devotion toward a crewman. The laws of the sea are brutal and eternal. To survive Her, one must endure on his own. Even if Shortstop didn't make it, the Gazzians felt a new respect for their Boy Captain, who had altered the law of the sea with this single selfless act.

When the water cleared from the deck, Harlowe felt the spasm of a cough. The green color was draining from Shortstop's face and his normal yellowish tone was returning. Shortstop spat up more water and sat up. He looked around for an understanding as to why everyone was cheering.

Harlowe handed Shortstop off to one of his mates. "Take him below, Mr. Moneyball. Get him some dry clothes and something to eat."

Moneyball didn't look at Mr. Pitch for confirmation. He snapped to attention and followed Harlowe's orders without protest. "Cool, Captain!"

Harlowe wasn't sure if he heard Moneyball correctly. "Cool, Captain?" he wondered under his breath.

Ian filled Harlowe in while they watched Moneyball and Shortstop head below deck. "They've been listening to you and Rerun talk. In another week they'll be speaking SoCal like natives," Ian quipped.

"Next thing you know they'll want hamburgers for breakfast," Harlowe replied.

"Jewels served them that this morning," Ian replied.

Harlowe looked worried. "Fries, too?"

"No, just burgers and shakes."

Harlowe was relieved. "Okay. Save the fries for later."

"Aye." Ian then held up Pitch's glove.

Harlowe took the challenge symbol and tossed it back to Pitch, knowing that if he didn't take care of business now, there would be more problems later. "Did you lose this, Mr. Pitch?"

Pitch grabbed the glove from the air with his prehensile tail and came to stick-straight attention. "That I did, Captain," nodding with a respectful glint in his eye. The challenge was over.

"We have some distance to make up, Mr. Pitch," Harlowe added, putting the incident behind him as well.

Pitch saluted. "Cool, Captain!"

Harlowe did another double take. Gazzians speaking California slang was like Prigg calling him "Your Majesty." This was going to take some getting used to!

Without the slightest protest or demeaning smirk, Pitch began shouting orders to his crew. "Look alive, Dudes! Tighten those mizzen lines, Mr. Zinger!" he shouted above the roar of the crashing waves.

Pitch next twisted around to the quarterdeck. "Bring the *Millie* to her previous heading, if you please, Mr. Catch!" Pitch ordered.

Catch pulled the steerage wheel hard to starboard. "Cool, Mr. Pitch! Resume prior heading!"

Ian followed Harlowe up the quarterdeck ladder, where Simon was helping Catch with the wheel.

"What happened out there, Captain?" Ian asked. "The traa had you."

When they stepped onto the quarterdeck, Harlowe showed the black knife to Ian. "Something about this made him freak out."

Ian took the knife and examined it. "Looks ordinary."

"Any ideas?" Harlowe asked.

"Couldn't be the size," Ian replied.

Harlowe turned to the sea and glanced out in the direction the *Millie* was plowing. The horizon was black with storm clouds. He had conquered a mutiny and saved a crewman and himself from the mouth of a traa. Now, Mother Nature had another challenge for him. Harlowe took the black knife back from Ian. "We'll put the com on it later. For now, it has a more important purpose."

Harlowe placed the knife in Mowgi's mouth. "Stick it in the end of the bowsprit, Mowg."

They watched the undog make his way to the bow of the *Millie* without getting swept out to sea. With incredible deftness the undog jumped down to the main rail, skillfully dodged a breaking wave that broke over the deck, and continued scampering up to the bowsprit like a sticky-footed fly. Every Gazzian sailor wondered how such a feat was possible. Neither Harlowe nor Ian ever worried about the undog falling off the slippery spar. They had watched Mowgi's anti-gravity powers too many times to worry about a four-story wave sweeping the undog out to sea. It just wasn't going to happen.

"I couldn't do that with my SIBA," Harlowe commented as he returned his attention to the black storm ahead.

"Gather what sails you deem appropriate, Mr. Pitch!" Harlowe shouted down to the main deck. "We're in for a Wild Toad's Ride."

Ian grinned, knowing that earlier Harlowe had denied Pitch's suggestion to reduce the sails.

"Things are going to get a little more complicated than I figured," Harlowe admitted.

"No doubt," Ian replied.

"Cool, Captain!" Pitch replied to the command, shouting from the main deck.

37

Master Ogo and His Dakadudes

The collectors, as the villagers called them, were pillaging the huts when Buntoo-attee and Kikue arrived at the village. Large sacks of grain, dried fruit, and fish the villagers had gathered to sustain the village for the coming winter were being hauled away and put onboard the collector's dhow. The idea that there were ten collectors and only one of him, didn't bother Buntoo-attee. He confronted the first collector and grabbed the sack from the collector's hands. The collector tried to fight back, but Buntoo-attee easily disarmed the weapon from the collector before he could use it. The resistance stunned the collector. No villager had ever dared interfere with a high official of the Phagalla kingdom for fear of certain death! Before the situation got out of hand, Kikue rushed to save Buntoo-attee before the collectors killed him.

"No, Buntoo-attee," Kikue cried, stepping between the collector and Buntoo-attee. "They are Jakaa's collectors. We cannot resist. That is the way. They will kill you and our village if we try to stop them!"

"Kill him!" a loud voice bellowed, coming up the incline. The voice belonged to a small, overweight being who waddled his way up from the beach. As he approached in an arrogant huff, villagers and collectors alike parted, giving the pasty-faced toad plenty of room to pass.

As the other collectors drew their swords to carry out the order, Kikue fell to her knees in front of the official. "Please, Master Ogo," she pleaded, "he does not understand our ways." She quickly pointed to his posterior. "Look, he is not one of us. We found him on the beach. He only stopped the collector because he thought he was stealing from our village. He is unaware of your authority that comes from the all-knowing and all-powerful Jakaa." Kikue's head bowed deeper, touching the ground at her knees. "Please, Master Ogo! Spare him, for he is a good Buntoo-attee!"

Ogo stepped defiantly into the parting crowd. His beady yellow and green eyes peered cat-like through vertical slits. Ogo studied the tall muscular being holding one of his collector's weapons. Indeed, he was not from the village, nor was he from Jakaa's empire.

A collector grabbed the weapon from Buntoo-attee's hand and slapped him across the back of the head. "Kneel to Master Ogo or I will cut off your head for your insolence," the officer ordered.

If the blow injured Buntoo-attee, his face displayed no pain. The blow did have an effect on Buntoo-attee, however, that no one saw, not even Kikue.

Buntoo-attee obediently fell to his knees alongside Kikue, bowing his head in the same way as she.

Ogo saw that Buntoo-attee was tailless. "Croomis?"

Buntoo-attee did not answer. The officer kicked Buntoo-attee hard in the side. "Answer Master Ogo or you will taste the sword, Thag!"

Kikue answered for Buntoo-attee. "Many pardons, Master Ogo. He does not know. His memory of his past is lost. When we found him, he was unconscious and without knowledge."

Master Ogo cared only whether Buntoo-attee was Croomis. Anything else about this creature was no concern of his. Master Ogo gave the order to his officer to march Kikue and Buntoo-attee to his dhow. This meant only one thing: Kikue and Buntoo-attee were now slaves of the great and powerful Jakaa. The villagers knew they would never be seen or heard from again.

Kikue's father tried to stop the collectors from taking his daughter, but the moment he began to protest, Master Ogo nodded to his guard. The collector drew his sword and heartlessly cut him down. Kikue screamed in anguish until a collector hit her across her head, knocking her unconscious. Master Ogo did not look back or even care as his collectors marched back to the dhow with their revenues and the new slaves. To him, the villagers owned nothing. All life and property belonged to Jakaa the Emperor. It was the price they paid for protection against the Croomis hordes.

The collectors took Kikue and Bunttoo-attee below deck and bound them like animals. The look in Buntoo-attee's eyes was more than defiant. It was vengeful.

*   *   *

Sometime that night, Kikue felt a hand over her mouth. She tried to scream, but the hand was strong and stifled her scream for help. The bilge of the dhow reeked of rodent droppings and putrid water. From the sway and the rocking of the boat, Kikue knew they were well out at sea and more than likely on the journey back to the Phagallian imperial city of Xu. Jakaa's palace, built on the highest hill in the center of the city, would be visible from miles out at sea. There they would spend the rest of their lives as slaves to the Emperor.

"Kik," the voice of Buntoo-attee whispered calmly. "It's me."

When the fear drained from her eyes, he lifted his hand away from her mouth.

"Stay calm, Kik."

"Buntoo-attee?"

Buntoo-attee carefully removed the rope from her wrists and legs. "Yes, it's me. You're okay."

"But the collectors?"

He helped her to rise and gave her a small container of water to drink. "They are gone," he replied simply.

She sipped the water down. When she was finished, she said, "I don't understand."

He rubbed her legs to get the blood flowing again. "Master Ogo and his dakadudes have left the boat."

Kikue had never heard of the word "dakadudes."

Buntoo-attee explained, "It's just a word my friends and I made up for bad guys."

"Why would the collectors leave their boat? And why would they leave it to you, Buntoo-attee?"

Buntoo-attee smiled sheepishly. "I made them an offer they couldn't refuse," he replied, borrowing a phrase from somewhere in the back of his memory.

Kikue didn't believe it until Buntoo-attee led her from bottom of the boat up to the main deck of the dhow. It was still night. The stars were abundant, and two of Gazz's moons were high and bright in the sky. There was plenty of light to see that Master Ogo and his collectors were no longer onboard. The sacks of loot they had taken from her village were still stacked in rows along the top deck and below in the storage hold.

Kikue was speechless. She still did not know how such an act of providence was possible. Buntoo-attee led her aft to the steerage tiller.

"Do you know how to sail this boat, Kik?" Buntoo-attee asked.

Kikue gazed out across the water. She had sailed many nights like this with her father since she was a little girl. She knew that dhows never ventured too far from the sight of land. Black areas of land along the shoreline were clearly visible on the horizon, along with the bright fluorescent spray of the waves breaking up on the beach. Buntoo-attee wiped the tears from Kikue's eyes as she nodded yes. Yes, she could steer the dhow. She cried, knowing her father's warm smile would not greet her upon their return. More than anything, she would miss his thick warm tail wrapped around her whenever she was troubled, ill, or cold. She swallowed hard, knowing she had to be strong. For whatever reason, Fate had given her this opportunity of freedom. There would be time later for sadness. She took the tiller from Buntoo-attee and directed him to set the main sail as she brought the dhow about, changing course back toward the village.

Buntoo-attee worked the lines to bring the sail taut. Watching his powerful muscles glistening under the moonlit night, she continued to mull over the reasons the collectors had suddenly disappeared. What had happened to Ogo and his collectors? Why did they leave their weapons and personal belongings behind? Where did they go?

38

Nywok Bay

The *Millie* slipped into the bay, dragging torn sheets and sections of her splinted mast with her. She had survived the storm, but she was hurt. A splintered stump was all that was left of her tall center mast. The mizzen and the foremasts had rips in their sheets, but they had enough catch in the sails to float their way into the wide inlet surrounded by a thick evergreen forest of lofty trees and rocky cliffs. It seemed a miracle that they had survived at all. The storm was like nothing the Gamadin had ever experienced. The winds were so violent that even with minimum sail, the three-foot-thick wooden mast base had snapped in two. It was only by the grace of the gods, according to the tails, that the *Millie* wasn't at the bottom of the sea. A crushed section of the starboard rail was a reminder of where the main had fallen. The mast, with its tangled rigging and shredded sail was so heavy that Harlowe had to order the robobs to cut the mast away from the ship lest the weight of the busted mast capsize the *Millie* in the heavy swells. In the presence of the Gazzian crew, clickers wielding dura-metal axes chopped through the splintered wood and heaved the pieces of the mast overboard.

Surprisingly, the Gazzian crew wasn't freaked out by the clickers the way Harlowe and Ian feared they would be. Ian speculated that after seeing Harlowe face off a three-hundred-foot traa and revive

Shortstop from the dead, a clicker popping to life was hardly a surprise. Simon could only laugh. "Don't tell them that dancing with danger is a daily event with Dog. They'll all jump ship!"

Harlowe opened the door of his cabin and nearly tripped over Shortstop, who was lying across the cabin threshold as he stepped out onto the quarterdeck.

"Shortstop, that's not your bunk," Harlowe pointed out.

"Yes, Captain, but this is now where I sleep. I must always be ready for you. My life is yours now," Shortstop explained.

Harlowe looked to his fellow Gamadin for assistance. Ian and Simon, however, figured this was a personal matter between a crewman and his captain. The two Gamadin went on with their duties, leaving Harlowe at the steerage to sort this one out himself. With no help from his Gamadin crew, Harlowe turned to Homerun, who was skillfully guiding the *Millie* into the deep waters of the bay. "That is his faith, Captain. Shortstop comes from a village to the north, where to give one's life back is repaid with servitude until the gods deem the debt settled."

"And if I order him to only serve me as captain?" Harlowe asked.

Homerun shrugged indifference. "His debt to you will have gone unfulfilled, Captain."

Harlowe was beginning to feel the way he felt when at the losing end of an argument with Lu. "Which means?"

"Which means he must return his soul to the mother who bore him," Homerun explained and nodded toward the ocean.

How does a captain quarrel with a crewman's faith, Harlowe wondered. Sun Tzu had nothing to offer him on the subject. Harlowe may have been the absolute ruler of his ship, but he was no god. He sighed, knowing there had to be a compromise somewhere. He gave

Shortstop explicit instructions that his duties aboard the *Millie* came first. He could sleep outside the Captain's door only when the weather permitted, and never in front of the open threshold. Harlowe did not want to trip over his crewman again.

Feeling comfortable that he had saved Shortstop a second time, Harlowe joined Ian and Simon on the port quarterdeck rail, where they were surveying the deserted bay.

The beaches of the bay were all black sand. Typically, that type of sand was made up of tiny fragments of black lava from a nearby volcano.

"No volcanoes around here," Simon noted, looking over the hills.

Ian pointed to a massive mountain far in the distance, so tall that not even the hills around the bay blocked their view of its seven-mile-high peak. Below its majestic snow-covered peak were vast glaciers, even though they were near the equatorial latitudes of the planet. "It's the source of the black sand," Ian explained.

Fifty yards above the beach the forest began. The evergreen forest was thick with tall green trees that were alive with the chatter of Gazzian birds and the high-pitched calls of critters. From their quick survey, it appeared they had come to the right place to find a new center mast for the *Millie*.

However, from his perch on the rail next to the three Gamadin, Mowgi's ears were at full parabolic sensor mode. The undog's low growl was a warning that danger lurked in the trees.

"Something's got him tweaked," Simon said, as he tried to see what the undog saw in the dense forest.

Harlowe turned to Ian and asked, "What's the com say?"

Ian pointed his com at the forest, keeping the device hidden from the tails by facing away from the crew. *Robobs are one thing. Showing*

off too many 54ᵗʰ-century gadgets to a 16ᵗʰ-century crew is irresponsible.
"We're being watched."

"Ya got a number?" Harlowe asked.

"Five hidden in the trees on that side," Ian said, nodding toward the tall cliffs on the port side of the bay.

Harlowe instructed Homerun to keep the *Millie* on her present tack. "Steady as she goes, Mr. Homerun!"

"Cool, Captain!"

As they drifted along, the bay seemed almost too quiet.

"How much time until we're out of here?" Harlowe asked.

"We need a straight tree a hundred feet tall and four feet wide at the base," Ian replied. "Once the clickers strip it and drop it in, we need another few hours to rehang the rigging and then we're outta here." Ian looked up at Harlowe and asked, "How's morning sound?"

Harlowe clearly wanted to keep their stay in the bay as short as possible. "Any way to speed it up?"

"Get me a tree before the sun sets or we will miss the wind, too."

"I'll get you one before lunch."

As the *Millie* pivoted into the wind to drop anchor, a whistling object streaked out of the sky and clanked off a robob's hard metal head. The black stone arrowhead ricocheted off the clicker and fell harmlessly onto the deck. The arrow would have caused injury or death to whomever it struck. As soon as the Gazzians saw the arrow, fear shot through their faces as if they were staring eye-to-eye with a traa.

Harlowe jumped down to the main deck and picked up the arrow. "Do you know who shot this, Mr. Pitch?" he asked, showing his First Mate the arrow.

"A warning, Captain. This is Nywok land. They want us to leave," Pitch replied.

Harlowe touched the broken tip of the arrow with his finger. It felt crystalline and reminded him of the flint arrowheads he had seen in museums. Only this point wasn't glass-like, but of dark black stone.

"Don't worry, Mr. Pitch. We're not staying long," Harlowe said. Without a new mast they couldn't leave, even if they wanted to. Pitch warned them that the seas in this part of the ocean were filled with rocky points and stone islands. Trying to navigate the waters without full sails would be suicide. With twenty-six days left to find Leucadia and Riverstone and save the planet, every moment counted. The *Millie* had no other place to go. Given a forest of tall trees to pick from right off the beach, Harlowe had already made his decision. He turned to the helm. "Put us out of range, if you please, Mr. Homerun."

"Cool, Captain!"

39

Crawlers

Dodger strapped the black knife Harlowe had given him to his leg. It looked so cool around his ankle. He promised Mr. Platter he would be careful and would always slice away from his body whenever he was cutting something. He then grabbed a board from Harlowe's room and headed for the blinker that would transport him to the beach. There wasn't much else to do on the island but surf, which suited Dodger just fine. There were plenty of good spots around the island, and they were all his. All he had to do was pick the one he was in the mood for and keep a few rules in mind at all times: all surfing had to be within sight of the ship with an escort of two fully armed clickers. No exceptions. Harlowe's orders.

His big brother had been gone for a week now, and every day was the same. After a quick breakfast of French toast and eggs (the food processors still functioned, using the residual power from the rovers), Dodger would set out every morning with his two security guards and head for the point, his favorite place to surf. Most of the time, Molly and Rhud kept them company. Also, Dodger and Prigg's friendship continued to grow. When his duties permitted, the little Naruckian was a welcome member of the morning surf brigade.

Prigg enjoyed watching. He was Dodger's greatest fan, clapping and cheering from the beach whenever Dodger made a stunning turn or a cool head-dip inside a glassy tube. When Dodger misjudged a wave and wiped out, Prigg applauded even louder. "Bravo! Master Dodger, you almost made the ride. You will do better next time!"

At night, everyone returned to the ship for low-down. Harlowe's orders. No exceptions. As the Gamadin crew discovered on many occasions, alien planets were no Disneylands or Magic Mountain amusement parks. They were often dangerous. And Vine Island was no exception.

Before they sailed away on the *Millie*, both Harlowe and Ian wondered why there were no animals or trees on the island. The only life form was the vines. Harlowe was uncomfortable about leaving anyone behind, but he had little choice. Sailing a 16th-century galleon on the open seas was many times more dangerous than it appeared to be on the island.

*   *   *

As soon as he and Prigg stepped off the blinker onto the sand, Dodger noticed the ocean had receded a great distance from where he left it yesterday. "That's weird! I've never seen the ocean go out so far."

"Who drained the ocean, Master Dod?" Prigg asked with a straight face. He wasn't trying to be funny. He was genuinely dumbfounded. "Master Dod" was Prigg's name for Dodger. No one knew exactly how he came up with the name, but the name stuck and Dodger didn't mind. He liked it because it made him feel important, like a junior Gamadin.

Dodger laughed as he pointed out over the ocean at the three moons overhead. "No one drained the ocean, Prigg, the moons did it. It happens four times every 24 hours back home. But with so many moons on Gazz, the tide shifts a lot more times." Dodger checked out *Millawanda*. "Look, Millie doesn't have any water around her now. Didn't you have moons and oceans on your planet, Prigg?"

"No, Master Dod, on Naruck we had only small oceans and no moons at all. Only stars."

"That's okay, Prigg. We'll have fun here. I'll teach you how to surf. You'll be the first from your planet to ride a surfboard."

Prigg suddenly looked concerned. "I don't think so, Master Dod. Naruckians don't swim."

Dodger pulled Prigg along. "Everyone needs to know how to swim, Prigg."

Prigg began to turn back toward the blinker. "I believe Mr. Platter needs my help."

Dodger jumped in front of Prigg, blocking him from the blinker. "No, no. You're going with me. It won't hurt at all. We'll find a little pool to learn in. You'll see how easy it is."

Reluctantly, Prigg went along. Several times along the way, Prigg made excuses for returning to the ship, but Dodger was hearing none of it. He was going to turn Prigg into the first surfer on Naruck!

On the way to the point where they hoped to find a pool of water suitable for floating a surfboard, they realized that the vines had over grown the path along the beach and now blocked their way to the point. The clickers didn't care. The robobs stepped over the long, leafy tendrils and continued on up the beach as if the path was clear. Molly stopped short. She wouldn't touch the vines. Instead, she recoiled and sprang over the top of the patch. The leap was an easy one. She landed on the opposite side with plenty of room to spare. A vine, however, had reached up during her leap and wrapped itself around one of her hind legs. She let out an angry roar as she tried to pull her leg free. The robob guard, sensing danger, reacted instantly and shot the plant. Dodger thought he heard a squeal when the round severed the stem.

While that was going down, a heavy crawler shot forth, wrapped itself around Molly's other hind leg and began pulling her toward a mass of vines. More vines joined in, pulling Molly in a coordinated effort to haul the giant cat into the patch. As strong and powerful as Molly was, she could not break free of the plants. The stringy crawlers were as strong as interwoven rope. The more she fought, the more vines latched onto her until all four legs were bound, sending Molly into an angry rage. She began ripping them away with her ten-inch fangs, but when she tore away one of the squealing sections, a new vine slithered around her snout and stopped her from biting more.

Dodger dropped his board and rushed to Molly's aid. He pulled the black knife from his leg and began slashing and cutting at the tenacious crawlers. The knife was incredibly sharp. It cut swiftly through the thickest branches easily, but it wasn't enough. The robobs were doing all that they could, firing into the mass to keep the largest of the stems from advancing. But while the clickers were able to keep the big ones away, smaller vines were snaking along the sand toward Dodger and Molly. Each time a robob fired on a branch, two and three more vines slid in to replace it. Prigg struggled to keep Rhud back. He knew there was nothing the big cat could do to help.

Suddenly, Molly fell on her side. A tendril had bound her chest and cut off her air. Molly screamed in agony as the vines began dragging her from the beach toward the mass.

Dodger kept slashing, knowing that if he didn't get her free, the vines had her. It wasn't long, though, until the crawlers zeroed in on him. As if the plants had eyes, a crawler grabbed hold of Dodger's right arm and tried to rip the knife away. Dodger flipped the black blade to his left hand and chopped through the stem, freeing his arm.

He then dove after Molly and sliced the vine from her chest. At that very moment, two of the heaviest vines yet grabbed them both!

40

It's Complicated

One hour before dawn and the sea was quiet. A slight onshore breeze from the west favored Buntoo-attee and Kikue as they guided Ogo's dhow into a hidden cove, several leagues south of the village. Their plan was to hide the dhow well away from the village before the Emperor's officials discovered the collector's dhow was missing. With such a valuable cargo in the dhow's hold, Jakaa was sure to send a flotilla of galleons in search of the dhow. The village would be destroyed and all the villagers taken as slaves or killed if the boat was found nearby.

Once inside the hidden cove, Buntoo-attee lowered the sails and covered the boat with bushes and branches. Soon, they would transfer the supplies from the dhow to a more secure place inland. Kikue, however, wanted the dhow destroyed before Jakaa's soldiers found it.

Buntoo-attee saw the worry in Kikue and took her into his arms. From the moment he touched her, she knew their maahoo had changed. He was different. He wasn't the Buntoo-attee who had awakened in her hut and tore the flap from her doorway or taught his villagers to swim.

"I need the boat, Kik," Buntoo-attee said to her.

She saw in his eyes that his plan did not include her. Tearful, she asked, "You are leaving me?"

Buntoo-attee held her firmly in his strong arms. "I know who I am now, Kik. I can't stay. I must find my friends. My real name is Matthew Riverstone. I came here from far away to find my friends who were shipwrecked on your land and taken away by one of Jakaa's ships."

"You are not Croomis?" she asked, looking up into his caring eyes.

"No, I am not Croomis, Kik."

Kikue found the concept hard to believe. Only Croomis beings were tailless. "If not Croomis, then what, Buntoo-attee?"

Riverstone wanted her to know the truth, but how far could he go? Was it necessary to put her through the concept of an alien being from another world? "It's complicated."

"What does com-pli-ca mean?" she asked, trying to repeat his word.

"It means I will return for you, Kik, but first I must find my friends. Their lives depend on me."

"They need you as I do?"

"Yes. I must find them before they are killed or lost forever by Jakaa's people."

The worry in his face was frightening. She wrapped her tail around his neck, bringing him to her. They kissed long and passionately and when they separated, they finished concealing the boat. Then they headed to the village for Buntoo-attee to gather the things he would need for his journey.

41

Tide's Out

Dodger heard the sound of Molly's leg bone crack and her helpless, pained roar. She was losing her struggle. She could neither breathe nor do anything to save herself. The vines had her legs and mouth wrapped in an unbreakable grip. Like constricting snakes, they were squeezing the life out of her.

Dodger was Molly's last hope. He slashed and cut and hacked his way through one stem at a time with his black knife. It was the only weapon he had that worked. It was keeping them both alive, but for how long? The vines were relentless and many. Dodger's arm was tiring. The slinking ends were gaining, creeping their way around his legs and arms. Soon his bones would crack under their vice-like stress. He needed something quickly or it was over for him as well.

Dodger's legs were suddenly yanked out from under him, surprising him and causing him to drop his knife. His only defense was gone. He reached for the knife but a crawler grabbed his hand and stopped him. With his other free hand, Dodger tore at a snagged vine that was choking Molly. He managed to pull it away long enough to catch a quick breath before a crawler came up from beneath and wrapped around his free hand. Now Dodger's arms and legs were as useless as Molly's. With both of them unable to move, the vines began dragging them both toward the dense overgrowth of the mass.

Just when all seemed lost, brilliant blue flashes began strafing the mass. The blue light puzzled Dodger until he heard the high-pitched screams of the crawlers. They were the same wailing cries of pain the vines made when he slashed at them with his black knife. Between their broad leaves, Dodger saw more flashes of blue light slice through the thick stems as cleanly as the black knife had. The acrid odor of the burning crawlers irritated his nose, making him sneeze, but he didn't care. The binding vines around his legs and arms started to release. With one arm freed, he reached down and grabbed his knife from the sand. With renewed strength, he hacked his way toward Molly, who was still bound and being dragged up the slope of the island mountain.

"Get away from her!" Dodger yelled at the mass as he sliced and cut like a crazed butcher. "Get away from her!" he shouted again. "Let her go!"

Slash! Cut! Hack, hack, hack!

Finally, Dodger reached the giant cat. He cut the crawlers around her neck first, tossing them aside and turning his attention to the vines wrapped around her chest. Finishing with them, he moved to the vines holding her legs and paws. He didn't stop until every last crawler had been pulled away from her body.

"Molly! Molly! You're free, Molly," Dodger said to her as he moved back to her head.

Molly was lying still and her eyes were closed. She didn't appear to be breathing.

"NO!" Dodger cried out, and lunged with all his might and all of his one hundred twenty pounds onto Molly's massive chest. Almost immediately she began to breathe again on her own in fast, rapid breaths.

Dodger wrapped his arms around her head, kissing her on the side of the face. "That's a good girl. You're okay now."

Dodger was so concerned about Molly, he was unaware of who had saved his life. Monday and a dozen clickers continued blasting the mass of creepers with blue plas cutters, slashing them back and forth like long blue machetes. With great arching swaths they scorched the beach, attacking the crawlers until they were away from the sand and far back up on the hillside.

"Master Dod, Master Dod!" Prigg cried, rushing up to Dodger. "Are you okay?" Two of Prigg's eyes were keeping a keen eye on the vines while the third remained steady on him.

Dodger spat gritty pieces of sand and vine from his mouth. He lay next to Molly, too exhausted to stand. "I'm all right, Prigg, but Molly is hurt bad."

Looking down, Molly's forepaw was bent unnaturally to one side. Monday handed his cutter rifle to a clicker and kneeled beside the big cat to examine her closely. A worried Rhud was at her side, licking Molly's face while Monday made his assessment. "She'll be okay once we get her back to the ship."

With a little help from Dodger and the clickers, Molly rose to her feet, growling with every limping step. Monday instructed a robob to fetch a blinker so she wouldn't have to walk too far. Once the big cat was safely off the beach and in the care of the robob medics, Monday turned to Dodger and asked what happened.

"We were going to the point, Mr. Platter, like we normally do when the vines grabbed us. It was nothing more than that, honest!"

"Harlowe told you not to go near the vines."

"We didn't, Mr. Platter. The crawlies grew across the path," Dodger said defensively. "When we tried to go around, they got Molly." He pointed at the path they normally took to the point. The scattered pieces of vine all around showed that they had indeed overgrown not only the path but the entire beach as well, way past the shoreline.

Now that he had a moment to think, Platter saw for himself the rapid overgrowth of the vines. "Dog had a bad feeling about them because there's no life on the island but the vines."

There was more. Dodger pointed at the ship. "Look, Mr. Platter. Millie's dry."

Monday was amazed. Shifts in the tide were expected, but not two hundred feet!

"What's changed?" Monday asked, more to himself than to Dodger.

Dodger tilted his head toward the sky. He shared an observation he had made earlier in the day. "That big moon is overhead, Mr. Platter."

Gazz's largest moon had been steadily rising since they first saw it the day before Harlowe left. The blue-green mini planet was now directly above their heads and so large that it looked like you could pluck it from the heavens and bounce it like a beach ball. "Yeah, it's pulled all the water out of the lagoon."

The crackling sound of a cutter brought Monday's and Dodger's attention to the hills behind them. It was the clickers. They were blasting away at the vines again. Their slithering ends were already advancing back toward the path.

Monday called the clickers back to the blinker. "We can't stay here, Dodger. I wonder why the vines got this close to the beach? They've never come this far before."

"Maybe the crawlers don't like the ocean," Dodger suggested.

Monday agreed that it was the only explanation that made sense.

However, Dodger only cared about one thing. "Does this mean I can't go surfing, Mr. Platter?"

Monday put a fatherly arm across Dodger's shoulders as he led Harlowe's little brother back to the blinker. "While the tide's out, we'll all stay inside the ship."

42

The Fry Tree

Divine Providence was all Harlowe could come up with to explain how they found a replacement for the mast so quickly. *Sweet!* he thought. After the storms, traas, and broken masts, it was about time some luck trickled his way. It was midday, and the sun was shining brightly. Harlowe had rowed ashore in a dinghy with Mowgi and three robobs, believing he was faced with an all-day task. But no; he was barely used to solid ground again when the tree he was searching for practically found him! He spied it the moment he left the beach. There it was, a short distance up the hillside in the center of a forest clearing. Hauling it out of the forest looked like it would be a no-brainer. The path from the clearing back to the beach was wide enough for a three-lane highway. The tree was calling to him like a hot babe saying, "Take me home, sailor!"

Rather than risk one of his crew being plucked off by an arrow, Harlowe went alone. He patted the SIBA that he wore hidden beneath his clothes, thankful it had been keeping his sea legs strong for the past week. With its supertough dura-skin, his suit was impervious to arrows as well. Once out of visual range from the *Millie*, Harlowe activated his headgear that made him appear like a tall, bug-eyed praying mantis. He also switched on the personal force field on the Gama-belt that Ian insisted he wear as an extra precaution. It was another utility-room discovery his Science Officer made while hunting down a SIBA for Dodger.

Though the undog had already sighted in on the fast-moving Nywoks Ian had identified earlier from the *Millie*, Harlowe took nothing for granted. His sensors confirmed that five life-signatures were making their way to this part of the bay…and fast, too. He estimated that he had a good thirty minutes before arrow tips would be clinking off the back of his SIBA. Even if he worked at light-speed, felling a tree and stripping it would take a lot longer than half an hour.

The last thing Harlowe wanted was trouble. He understood that the Nywoks were only protecting their property. He would be just as tweaked if they had stolen a grannywagon or a blinker. The problem was, he didn't have time to parlay a truce, so he sent the clickers into the forest to welcome the Nywoks. The Nywoks wouldn't feel a thing. A little zap of blue light and they would be in la-la land until morning. It would give him plenty of time to get his tree and drag it back to the *Millie* before anyone was the wiser.

The tree was perfect. It was straight as an arrow. Of course, Mowgi saw things from a different perspective. The instant he made visual contact on the tree, his territorial alarm went off. The undog focused on it with the thought of claiming the new mast tree for himself. Harlowe had to make an open-field tackle to keep the chinneroth from desecrating the new mast.

"Oh, no you don't, butthead," Harlowe said, holding the undog in his arms. "You have a whole forest to nail. This one's mine, dude."

Disappointed, Mowgi turned away. Harlowe felt like a rat, but this was the only tree like it in the forest. It was tall and straight. It looked regal and didn't seem to fit in with the rest of the trees in the forest. To him, it looked like a French Fry Tree. Its needles were long and a tarnished yellow, like In-N-Out fries might look if they were hung on a branch. All he needed was a little ketchup and he could be wolfing down lunch big time!

"I found our mast, Wiz," Harlowe said, speaking into his SIBA com.

Ian was shocked by the quick find. "Already?"

"A little ways up from the beach."

"How tall is it?"

Harlowe leaned back and replied, "Taller than what we had before."

"Cut it down, Captain, and get out of there!"

Harlowe sensed the *hurry-up* in Ian's tone. "No worries. The clickers took care of the Nywoks."

The momentary silence on the com warned Harlowe that Ian had more.

"There's five hundred more coming over the hill, Dog!"

"Five hundred! Where did they come from?"

Harlowe didn't wait for an answer. Five hundred torqued Nywoks would cause a lot more trouble than five. He had at best twenty minutes to cut down the Fry Tree and haul it back to the *Millie*. That was hardly enough time to complete his mission. He needed a diversion.

"Mowgi!" he called into the forest. "I have something for you to do!"

As soon as the robobs returned, Harlowe set them to stripping the branches from the Fry Tree's trunk. Using their blue-powered light cutters, the clickers began slicing through its thick branches as if they were jello. Tree limbs were dropping in great piles to the base of the Fry Tree when the first part of Harlowe's diversionary plan for the Nywoks was put into effect. The shrill of a bloodthirsty beast sent shock waves throughout the forest. The cry was so chilling that goose bumps formed even on Harlowe's neck. He could only imagine how the Nywoks must have felt upon hearing for the first time the undog's heart-stopping screams. Harlowe didn't care what part of the galaxy you were from, a chinneroth's deathly shrill made even the bravest of souls cringe.

The plan was working. The SIBA sensors showed the Nywoks turning away *en masse,* but not for long. When they saw Mowgi flying back to Harlowe, the Nywoks returned in earnest. Getting to Harlowe seemed more important than the fear of being eaten by a wild beast.

Harlowe was fresh out of plans when the first barrage of arrows thudded off his new personal force field. He had to ignore the pesky projectiles and he kept on securing the dura-line cables to the Fry Tree. In the meantime, Mowgi returned to terrorizing the Nywoks, doing his best to slow the main body of the attack.

When the final branch crashed to the ground, Harlowe ran back to the beach and fired a piton-attached line through a small hatch on the side of the ship. The instant Harlowe signaled that the clickers had toppled the trunk of the Fry Tree, Ian was to begin cranking up the winch.

Harlowe waited for the crash of the Fry Tree to tell him it was time to give the signal. But the crash never came. In a panic, he ran back to the still-intact Fry Tree. The robobs were simply milling around the base.

"What happened?" Harlowe cried out. "Cut it down!"

A clicker pointed at the base of the tree in its usual unemotional way. Harlowe knelt down and, sure enough, the clickers had already swiped their cutters through the four-foot base. The Fry Tree sat stubbornly on its base as if it had never been touched. Harlowe looked up, wondering why the tree hadn't toppled over on its own.

What's up with that?

Ignoring the arrows raining down on him, Harlowe grabbed a cutter from a clicker and cut a two-foot wedge out of the trunk. Slowly at first, the giant tree started to lean. The robobs tried to hasten the process by pushing on the tree. They were strong, but the three robobs and Gamadin wearing a fully-charged SIBA could not budge the 30-ton log.

"Captain!" Ian shouted in Harlowe's ear. "Another two thousand Nywoks have just come over the hill!"

"TWO THOU?"

"That's right! Ten minutes!" Ian confirmed.

Suddenly, the Fry Tree began to move on its own. Harlowe looked up when he felt a great wind blowing down from the top of the tree. It was Mowgi, pulling the Fry Tree over from the top. That was the extra *umph* they needed.

Snap!

The tree crashed to the ground, barely missing the clicker standing at its base.

"Now, Wiz! Pull her in!" Harlowe shouted into his com.

The instant the command was given, the dura-line stretched tight. Slowly at first, almost at a snail's pace, the Fry Tree inched toward the bay. Harlowe knew that the winch below the decks of the *Millie* was powerful enough to move ten trees the size of the giant French Fry. With arrows clinking off robobs, Harlowe and the clickers jumped on the moving log as it picked up speed, bulldozing its way down the slope, onto the beach, and into the bay. Mowgi joined them on top of the floating log. His ears stayed at full alert until he, the clickers, and Harlowe were crossing the blue-green water toward the *Millie*.

Zinger tossed Harlowe a mast line. He grabbed it and swung himself up the side and onto Millie's main deck, where he was greeted with a loud cheer. The robobs scampered up the side of the galleon and went below decks while Mowgi appeared at the end of the bowsprit as if he had used a blinker.

Catch and Shortstop looked over the broken railing at the mighty log floating at the side of the ship. Hundreds of arrows stuck in its trunk, making the Fry Tree look like a giant pincushion. Shortstop stared at Harlowe in astonishment. There was not a scratch on his Captain. Shortstop fell to his knees and thanked the Gall Moon for delivering him safely back to the ship.

Standing on the foredeck with Simon, Moneyball asked if indeed the Captain was a god. Simon smiled as he watched Harlowe climb up the quarterdeck ladder to call out orders.

"No, Mr. Moneyball, he's no god, but he does have a few on the payroll."

43

A Secret Little Place

While Kikue returned to the village to gather additional items for his journey, Riverstone re-checked his supplies on the dhow, which was well hidden in the tall reeds of the cove. He didn't need much: water, mainly, some dried fruit, bread, and a special gruel Kikue had prepared for him. It was enough for the three-day journey north to Xu, if the winds were favorable. If he needed more supplies beyond that, his SIBA could take care of all his requirements for weeks.

He could wait no longer. It was time to leave. Two days had passed since the time he and Kikue returned in Ogo's dhow. Each day was one more day lost to him in his search for Leucadia, Sizzle, and the others. Each day was also another day for Jakaa's soldiers to scour the villages along the coast, looking for Master Ogo and his dhow of collections. It was not a question of *whether* the soldiers would come to Kikue's village, but *when*. Knowing the inevitable was near and mindful of the danger he had put the village in earlier, Riverstone hurried to remove all evidence of himself, the tailless Croomis, and sail the dhow for Xu as quickly as possible.

Kikue pleaded to go along to help him sail the dhow. "Two can make faster time, Buntoo-attee," she pleaded.

But Riverstone would not risk her life again. Where he was going was dangerous, even for a Gamadin. She had risked her life and the village for him once. He would not ask more of her.

He touched the SIBA medallion around his neck. The Gamadin device reminded him again of who he was and the life he led before Kikue. He wished he could take Kikue with him after he found his friends. He had dreamed so many times of how life would be with her. Not since Ela had he felt so much warmth and closeness to someone. Their life together might have worked if his memory had remained lost. But now that he was aware of his mission and his duty to a higher calling, how could she be part of that? He had survived in her world, but he couldn't stay there with her either. How long could he keep up the charade, knowing who he was? When would he begin to miss his world, his friends, and his family? How could she even conceive of Gamadin who traveled between the stars?

As he watched Alice clickity-clack over with a tie-line, Riverstone knew the answer to all his questions. He looked up at the late afternoon sky, saddened by the realization that a life with Kikue was a life in La-La Land. Whether they lived on Earth or in a village on Gazz, their *maahoo* was against them. His life was Gamadin, and that was a life full of danger, death, and long stretches away from home. He couldn't wish that kind of life for anyone he loved.

He sighed, feeling the weight of the situation on his shoulders. Leucadia, Sharlon, and Sizzle had to be his only focus. It hurt terribly to realize that Kikue could never be a part of that group of strong, intelligent women.

With his restored memory, using his SIBA and Alice made moving the village supplies from the dhow to the secret cave in the nearby hills a snap. When Jakaa's soldiers returned to the village looking for Ogo and his collectors, they would find nothing. The village had already been swept clean of all their valuables. The soldiers would then look elsewhere for their missing plunder.

That morning, Riverstone had asked Kikue about the flag on the galleon he watched sail away with his friends. Kikue was sure it was a Phagallian warship. She explained that his friends would be transported to Xu and sold in the slave markets there. "Then only the gods would know their fate," she said tearfully. She feared that he would suffer the same fate as his friends. "You are only one against many."

With a boyish smile, Riverstone took her into his arms. "I wish you could come, but this is a mission I must do alone." Though his sailing skills were lacking, Kikue's sailing-for-idiots course gave him a basic understanding of what he needed to do to sail the dhow and navigate the coastline to Xu. Plus, Riverstone had Alice. The robob, who was programmed to transform back to a cylinder when a villager appeared, would become the second crewman he needed on his first sailing experience over the open sea.

"How will you get them back, Buntoo-attee?" she asked him, still calling him by his villager name. "Fate has already taken them. That is the way."

Riverstone looked into her large dark eyes and kissed her before he replied. "I have powerful friends, Kik. Jakaa has never met Harlowe."

"Who is Harlowe?"

"A tough dude."

Kikue did not believe such power existed in all of Phagalla to persuade Jakaa to give up Buntoo-attee's friends.

Riverstone smiled. "Harlowe has a way of persuading people."

"He is as powerful as Jakaa?"

Riverstone laughed. "More power than a million Jakaas," he replied.

"What is a million?"

"A lot. Trust me."

* * *

Riverstone looked out over the bow of the dhow. The yellow sun was flanked by three large moons and sat low on the horizon. The day had gone by so fast! He had to hurry to meet Kikue at the cave just before dark and spend their last night together by a warm fire. He would leave on the morning tide, just after the Gall moon rose.

Riverstone covered his supplies and left Alice to guard the dhow as he set out for the cave. He found that being away from Kikue even for a few hours was depressing. He dreaded the coming morning when he would have to say goodbye for the last time.

The walk to the cave wasn't far. It was well-hidden in the hills by a grove of dense trees. He wondered how Kikue discovered the opening in the first place. From the outside, there seemed to be no entrance at all. The trees were too thick to see more than a few feet into the grove. Kikue laughed when he asked her. She had found it by accident when she was a little girl, and now it was their secret place.

Riverstone kept calling out to Kikue as he squeezed through the narrow spaces between the trees. "Kik, it's me. I'm coming through."

The cave opening reminded him of the crack in the side of the cliff that he and Harlowe had crawled through to find *Millawanda* back on Earth. It had the same characteristic of being practically invisible to anyone walking by. Only here, trees covered the entrance instead of red slabs of rock and sweet-smelling blue flowers.

"Hey, Kik, sorry I'm late. I was... " Riverstone's voice drifted to silence when he saw how dark it was in the cave. If Kikue was there, he would have seen the glow of candles welcoming him into their private little hideaway.

Riverstone figured he had arrived first and she would be along at any moment. He found the striking stones and lit the candles himself. As the light warmed the cave, he saw the blankets neatly spread out on the floor. Nearby, more candles stood up by the small flat rock where they planned to eat dinner. The cups of water were already drawn and the flowers she had gathered that morning were arranged in a wooden bowl on the table. Everything was ready, except for the person who would light up his heart the moment he heard her coming. He had an *ah-ha* moment and smiled. She wasn't late because she was bringing back more supplies for him; she was late because she was preparing a special dinner!

He sighed, his heart aching more than he wanted to admit. In so many ways Kikue was like Ela; innocent, simple, loving. He closed his eyes, basking in the knowledge that he was the luckiest dude in the galaxy for having known two of its most wonderful beings.

With the cave set for their last night and his stomach gurgling for food, he slipped through the trees again and set off down the path toward the beach. He knew she would be coming that way and wanted to surprise her.

He walked fast. The more he thought about stroking her long dark hair and smelling her flowery scent, and tasting her sweet, soft red-brushed lips, the more his excitement grew. All he could think about was sweeping her up in his arms and kissing her. He walked faster still until he was practically running while he jumped and splashed, and played tag with the shore break along the long, flat beach. A half-mile down the beach, there she was! She was tall and hot, her long dark hair blowing to one side in the gentle onshore breeze. So, why was her tail dragging and not held high and bouncy, like it normally was?

He waved at her and shouted her name. "KIK! KIK!"

Tail dragging? What's up with that? It always whips about when she sees me. He thought again. It was their last night. If he had a tail, it would be dragging big time, too.

Then he watched her stumble as though she had tripped over a stone in the sand.

That wasn't right!

He started to run. Something was wrong. Before he reached her, she fell on her knees and rolled onto her side as the shore break swept over her body.

Trembling, he bolted into a full-blown sprint. He rushed to her side and lifted her from the water, feeling her warm, green blood seep through his fingers. When he lifted her to carry her away from the water, he saw the broken shaft of an arrow sticking out of her back.

At that very moment, an arrow swished by his face and splashed into the water behind him. Coming from the direction of the village, three soldiers in leather, breast-plated armor and leggings were running up the beach with crossbows aimed at him. He lifted Kikue into his arms and took off in the opposite direction. Even carrying Kikue, he was much faster than the soldiers. He found a path away from the beach that led through heavy brush.

When he thought it was safe, he lay Kikue down and placed his medallion on her chest. Within moments, the SIBA covered Kikue and began treating her with 54th-century antibiotics and life-sustaining fluids.

Riverstone couldn't wait to make sure the SIBA was functioning properly however. The soldiers he thought he had outrun were right behind them. He could hear their clanking armor as they clamored up the path in hot pursuit.

*   *   *

The Phagallian soldiers stopped, surprised by the tall, tailless boy who waited for them in the middle of the path. The boy was unarmed, except for a small stick. The solders smiled as they lifted their crossbows at him and demanded that he fall to his knees, promising they would be merciful when they cut off his head. The boy stood defiant, challenging the three soldiers to fight. Not wanting to waste their time with such insolence, the soldiers fired their arrows. Using his stick, the boy swatted the arrows aside as easily as he'd slap away a pest. Drawing their swords, the soldiers rushed the boy, threatening to cut him to pieces where he stood. Before they could realize how useless their weapons were, the boy had struck down the charging soldiers, crushing their heads with a force that they would never have dreamed existed.

44

Doldrums

Installing the new mast had gone without a hitch. As Ian had promised, the *Millie* was as good as new and sailing out of the Nywok bay under a full set of patched sails and a good wind by the next morning. For three days, she made good time. Then the stiff breezes suddenly deserted them. After two full days adrift in a windless ocean, they were wandering southwest instead of north. Harlowe was stomping back and forth across the quarterdeck, wishing he could blow against the sails himself to get them moving. On the second windless day, he sent the Gazzian crew out in the ship's dinghy to see if they could row the *Millie* out of the doldrums. For all their efforts, they had managed only to stay even. They had gained nothing and their precious days were slipping away. It was already the middle of the second week and they were still a thousand miles from the debris field of the Tomarian escape pods. Harlowe had expected to be there in under a week to rescue Leucadia and the other survivors, and return to *Millawanda* with plenty of time to spare. Inside *Millawanda* they could all survive the gamma ray burst, but outside they would be sprouting wings.

"What's Wiz doing?" Harlowe asked Simon, who was sitting shirtless next to the wheel, soaking up rays as if he were lying poolside at Harry's Casino. Earlier that morning, Ian had taken a half dozen robobs below deck with strict orders not to be disturbed. For the last nine hours, all anyone heard was constant banging and hammering deep inside the *Millie*. The incessant clatter was driving Harlowe up a wall.

Simon pulled the earbud from his 54th-century Gama-pod on which he'd stored every piece of music ever recorded in its pinhead-size memory. "What was that, Skipper?"

"Forgettaboutit," Harlowe said. Then he leaned over the quarter-deck rail and called for Pitch.

"Yes, Captain."

"Call the crew in, if you please. No more rowing. The sun's nearly down."

Pitch was disappointed. No sailor likes sitting around idle in a calm. He wanted his crew to row more, but Harlowe was right. The ocean was no place to be at night in a small boat. "Cool, Captain!"

* * *

An hour past midnight, when the blue-green and mauve Gall moon was shining bright through Harlowe's cabin window, someone stepped unannounced into his quarters. Harlowe was awake. Most nights he slept little, and this night was no exception. He was always in a constant jumble of worry, calculation, and planning–not for himself, but for the many lives he felt responsible for. Saving Leucadia, Riverstone, Sizzle, his crew—all of them, Gazzians included – was only part of his dilemma. His bigger concern was the survival of his ship and the fate of an entire planet. They were the true focus of his agitation. Until they were safe, nothing else mattered. His friends, the *Millie*, and he were all expendable; the fate of the galaxy depended upon the survival of the Gamadin.

Harlowe knew the intruder was no threat. If there was danger, Jewels would have shot the predator before it entered through the doorway. When Harlowe opened his eyes, it was indeed a familiar face. "What is it, Wiz?" he asked, looking at Ian hovering over him.

Ian appeared exhausted, as if he hadn't slept in days. "It's ready," he replied.

"What's ready? Your secret project?"

"Yeah, it's ready, Dog."

Harlowe yawned. "Will I be impressed?"

Ian smiled like an all-knowing guru. "If it works, you'll kiss me."

As Ian turned to lead the way to the quarterdeck, Harlowe quipped, "I've already kissed one traa too many."

The air was dead still. A slight creaking of the rigging as the ship rolled gently on the glassy smooth ocean was the only sound they could hear. With the heavens full of stars and bright moons, there was enough light to read by. Simon, Mowgi, and the Gall moon were keeping watch while directly above their heads, the two minor moons peered down on them like a pair of Neejian eyes.

Harlowe hadn't bothered to dress. At this late hour, what was the point? He was still in his *No Fear* shorts and bare feet as they walked to the port side of the galleon. He looked over the railing and said to Ian, "Okay, impress me."

Ian pulled out his com and pressed a small blue activator on the side. For a moment, nothing happened. Harlowe started to return to his hammock when Ian held him back. "Give it a second, Dog."

A minute went by. Then the *Millie* began to shudder under their feet. A loud, stiff clank sounded like a heavy bolt dropping into place. A few seconds after that, there was a sound like the creaking of wooden gears when the sprocket teeth engaged. Harlowe jumped down to the main deck and joined the rest of his crew, who had all tumbled out of their hammocks to see what the strange racket was.

Astonished, they watched a hatchway open from the port side of the *Millie* and a bullet-shaped mechanism slid out from within the galleon . On the starboard side an identical mechanism was also playing out. When the mechanisms were fully extended, they opened up like flowers. When Ian tapped his com again, belt drives around the centers of each "flower" began turning the petals in a slow, clockwise manner. Everyone on the main deck braced themselves when, for the first time in days, the *Millie* lurched forward.

Ian turned to Simon, who was also looking at the turning petals. "Do you have the wheel, Mr. Bolt?"

Simon had been so engrossed with Ian's new wind machine that he had forgotten the steerage. "Oh yeah! The wheel," he said and quickly ran back to the steerage wheel. "Got her, Mr. Wizzixs!"

Harlowe grabbed a loose spar line and swung himself up to the quarterdeck, landing beside Ian. He kissed Ian on the forehead with delight. "You da man, Wiz!"

Embarrassed, Ian asked, "Impressed?"

"Big time! I would have never thought of that."

In spite of the festive atmosphere, Harlowe recognized that Ian was still a little too serious. There was something else. "And the downside is?" Harlowe asked, knowing there was always a downer after an upper.

Ian didn't sugarcoat the problem. "There's one clicker pedaling. When it runs out of power, it's history, Dog…" he shrugged, looking hopeless.

"They turn back to cylinders, right?"

"No, they turn to dust. Then the next one takes over and so on. We have seven clickers. You do the math."

"Jewels isn't part of the mix," Harlowe said with finality. He considered his robob servant as human as he was.

"They weren't topped off when we left the island because Millie was out of gas. She's their only recharging station," Ian replied. "No telling how much energy they've already used up playing sailors, Indian scouts, and ship's carpenters."

"How much juice do you think they have left?"

"I haven't a clue. They don't have power gauges. They could be three-quarters full or kissing 'E' right now."

Harlowe pointed at Ian. "Don't tell me they're on 'E' or I'll withdraw my kiss." Harlowe turned and walked to the quarterdeck rail. He felt the wind on his face, watched the slow-moving props that were pulling the *Millie* through the windless water, and wished he had a thousand clickers in the storage bin instead of six.

And Jewels was off limits.

45

The Young Intruder

Tying the leather breastplate around his chest, Commander Gii was discussing the plans for his troops' departure with three of his officers. Suddenly, without warning, a mysterious, young intruder burst into his tent. Outside, soldiers were preparing for the two-day march back to the capital city of Xu with the Emperor's new slaves. Commander Gii had still not found Master Ogo's dhow or the Emperor's valuable cargo that was onboard. The evidence he had suggested the collectors had serviced the village and sailed away. There was no sign of foul play or pirates in the area. The villagers were peaceful seafaring Phagallians. Possessing little more than small fishing spears, nets, hooks, pottery, and baskets, they were incapable of overpowering Master Ogo and his well-armed security force. Commander Gii's conclusion, which he would state in his report to the Emperor, was that the sea, perhaps even a traa, had swallowed the collector's dhow.

Commander Gii knew that returning to Xu without replacements for Ogo's lost goods would reflect unfavorably upon his command. Since Master Ogo's loss left a shortage in the Emperor's accounts, it was necessary to replace the lost revenues, regardless of the circumstances. Even though the village had given their obligatory tithe, ten villagers were taken as "payment." They would be sold in the slave market to balance the Emperor's treasury.

The young intruder was taller than Gii or any of his soldiers. He was also tailless, which heightened the fear of the officers that he might be a Croomis assassin sent to slay Commander Gii, who was known to have many enemies.

Without asking any questions, the officers unsheathed their swords and charged the intruder. The unarmed boy, however, remained calm and unruffled as the officers lashed out at him to keep him from having any chance to slay their Commander. With open hands that possessed the strength of a god, the boy struck down the officers before Commander Gii's eyes.

The intruder stepped casually over the bodies and moved slowly across the room toward the Commander.

Commander Gii was not without his own protection. He snatched a loaded crossbow hanging from a leather rope next to him and fired its arrow at the approaching boy. By some unholy trickery, the boy caught the arrow in flight. He then threw the arrow back, nicking the Commander's ear before it buried itself into the tent pole behind him.

"Are you going to kill me?" Commander Gii asked the boy.

The boy calmly answered, "If you don't cooperate."

"You will never leave this camp alive," Commander Gii warned.

The boy indicated with a slight nod for the Commander to look outside. "I got this far, brah."

Commander Gii went to the small window flap of his tent. What he saw seemed impossible! Outside, covered by the morning mist, his soldiers lay still on the ground as if they were asleep. No guards were at their posts. Campfires were burning unattended. No soldiers were milling about, preparing their morning meals or breaking camp to return to the capital. All life in the camp was at a standstill as if a great blackness had overtaken his command.

Commander Gii replaced the window flap. "What do you want?"

"I'm taking your prisoners back to their village. You will not follow us," the boy said.

"They are Emperor Jakaa's property."

"They're no one's property, Toad," the boy countered. "It will be up to you to make that clear to Jakaa."

"The Emperor owns all that is within the Phagallian land. It is the law."

"The law has been changed," the boy replied with the authority of someone whose power exceeded the emperor's. "You will listen to me."

"If you take the Emperor's property, soldiers will return in greater numbers. They will destroy the village and all life within it. Jakaa will not be denied his revenues," Commander Gii protested.

The boy moved closer until he was looking down at the standing Commander Gii with his deep blue eyes. "Dude, you're not getting it. You nearly killed someone very close to me. I should slam you where you stand."

Commander Gii was unaware of many terms the boy used. Nevertheless, the Commander was a wise officer. He understood the boy's intentions. "I have my orders."

"To kill innocent villagers is no excuse," the boy stated.

"They are villagers."

"Who did no harm to anyone. They are peaceful fishermen. That is all you need to know. If you ever hurt anyone in the village again, Toad, there will be no mercy. I will come after you and every living relative you have. I will wipe you out of existence. It will be as if you had never lived. You've seen what I've done to your soldiers. This is a small example of my power. My authority comes from the great Gall moon above us. Do you understand that, Gomer?"

Angry that this young boy dared to threaten him, a commander of Jakaa's elite troops, Commander Gii reached under his jerkin for the blade he kept hidden there and in the same motion, thrust it forcefully at the boy. The blade penetrated the boy's shirt but went no farther. Again and again, the Commander drove the blade into the young intruder's chest with no effect. The boy's skin was impenetrable.

He was a god!

The young god then grabbed the Commander's hand and with strength Gii had never before felt, forced him to his knees and took the blade away. He lifted the Commander by the jerkin and tossed him like a child out of the tent. Commander Gii watched helplessly as the boy god left the fires of the encampment, taking the emperor's possessions with him. Before the young god left, he took a weapon from his belt and with its unholy blue light, burned the encampment to the ground.

46

Fortress of Daloom

It was late afternoon when the *Millie* sailed into the Straits of Daloom. By using the turbos, Harlowe had hoped to pass through the narrow straits during the quiet of the night, avoiding any conflict with the fortress that guarded the channel. But the trade winds grew strong, and they made better time than they had expected. They had arrived hours ahead of schedule.

Escaping the doldrums had come at a cost. They lost two robobs just getting out of the still seas. Twobagger offhandedly suggested that they make up the lost days by sailing through the Straits of Daloom. He didn't believe for one moment that Harlowe would actually consider such a fatal course.

"Begging your pardon, Captain," Twobagger said, fearing he was sending the *Millie* on a course of death, "I didn't really mean that we should sail through the Straits of Daloom, sir. The passage is the southern end of the Phagallian Empire and it is guarded well. No ship can enter the Empire without the proper privileges of passage."

Harlowe was familiar with the term "privilege of passage." In his battle against Unikala and the Consortium, the Gamadin had defied the Rights of Passage the moment they entered the Omini Prime Quadrant. He had an answer of his own for anyone who tried to stop him or his ship from traveling anywhere. "We're free men, Twobagger. We don't need permission."

Pitch displayed an equal anxiety. "It is the entry to the Sea of Phagalla, Captain. The Emperor Jakaa has built the most formidable fortress to guard the passage. The cannons are the most powerful in the land. A flotilla of warships guards its access. Even if you should get past the cannons, I assure you, great Captain, there is no possible way our grand and magnificent ship will pass the Fortress of Daloom without being destroyed."

Harlowe didn't tell Twobagger or Pitch that he already knew about Daloom. Ian's com had plotted their course even before the doldrums. From the island of the vines, it was the fastest route to the debris field where the shuttle's escape pods rested. He was going through the straits, regardless. This was no time for caution. The next gamma ray burst was coming their way. GRB II didn't care about Harlowe's problems, the Straits of Daloom, his friends, or saving *Millawanda*. Even if their path sent the *Millie* through a school of hundred-foot traas and a dozen strongholds exactly like Daloom, Harlowe was not altering the *Millie's* course.

"Stay cool, Gentlemen. Sails full, Mr. Pitch," Harlowe ordered as he looked up at the sails full of wind. He turned to the steerage wheel and said, "Bring the *Millie* two points to starboard and hold her steady, if you please, Mr. Moneyball."

Looking nervous like the others, Moneyball replied, "Cool, Captain!"

Harlowe tapped Twobagger on the shoulder as the Gazzian stared at the mighty black stone walls of the fortress. "The *Millie* will be okay, Mr. Twobagger."

Twobagger swallowed the tight knot in his throat and wiped his brow with his tail. "I will pray to the Gall moon that you are right, Captain."

"Do that, Mr. Twobagger. A little prayer can help us all. I shall do the same."

The impenetrable Fortress of Daloom was indeed impressive. Its rock-and-mortar battlements were three hundred feet tall, fifty feet thick, and built upon the rocky cliffs that straddled the straits. The ocean-facing side of the fortress was a half-mile wide and lined with more than a hundred cannon that pointed across the straits like a dragon's maw of death. Lookouts on the fortress towers could see the *Millie's* sails hours before she entered the channel. Her presence was no surprise to the garrison that guarded the straits. Three warships were already waiting at the mouth, blocking the narrow passage to the *Millie,* who continued under full sail on an irreversible course.

"Our tour guides, Mr. Wizzixs?" Harlowe asked.

"Appears so, Captain," Ian replied, checking his com.

"How's our range?" Harlowe asked, looking through his telescopic glass with 54th-century optics.

Ian checked his com and replied, "Nearing the flotilla's outer boundary, Captain. Another quarter mile and the *Millie* will be within the fortress' range," he added.

"Let's take care of the ships first."

"Aye, Captain."

Harlowe called to Simon on the main deck. "Lock and load, Mr. Bolt."

Simon smiled approvingly. "Aye, Skipper. Lock and load," he repeated as he headed for the gun deck.

Pitch nervously followed Simon to the lower level. He continued to stare at the Fortress of Daloom through the starboard gun ports, wondering all along if the young Croomis Boy Captain would conjure up enough sorcery to survive straits that no other pirate ship in known history had ever survived.

Simon was whistling the Beatles' *Here Comes the Sun* as he inspected the cannons to ensure that each was properly primed and ready for discharge. Just as Simon got to "…years since it's been here," Pitch interrupted. "Begging your pardon, Mr. Rerun."

*   *   *

The Gazzian crewmen were good listeners. When they called Simon "Mr. Rerun," it was not out of disrespect. The Gazzians' admiration for Harlowe was the reason. Since the rescue of Shortstop, when Harlowe sucked face with a giant traa, their respect for him had transformed beyond his command of the *Millie*. Whenever Harlowe spoke, even the names he used were considered holy. The first time the crew heard Harlowe refer to Simon by his Gamadin moniker, it was ordained to be so. To defy their leader was blasphemy. And so it was "Mr. Rerun," Simon's given title, out of respect for Harlowe. In the same way, Ian and Mowgi were called "Mr. Wiz" and "Mr. Butthead," respectively.

*   *   *

Simon watched the First Mate wrap his tail around the main deck rail as if to squeeze the life from it. "Speak your mind, Mr. Pitch. It's cool," Simon said, as he lined up the muzzle of the Number Three Cannon out the port side of the main deck. Simon's expertise was plas cannons that fired lethal bolts of energy capable of destroying starships a million miles away. He didn't know nearly as much about 16th-century black powder cannons that shot a twenty-pound metal ball a little over a mile. He watched closely while Homerun and Catch began loading the Number One Cannon. They rolled the two-ton cannon back from its port and poured a carefully measured amount of powder down the bore of the barrel. Next, Homerun lifted a golden dura-metal ball to the muzzle while Catch grabbed a ramrod. Together they jammed the ball down the throat so both the powder and ball were packed tight at the bottom of the barrel. The loading was done. They wheeled the cannon back so that the muzzle stuck out of the gunport and waited Simon's further instructions.

Simon had no way of knowing if the charge Homerun and Catch put into each cannon was the right charge for such a long shot. He was too embarrassed to let a 16th-century sailor see a 54th-century soldier who didn't know squat about the medieval weapon. "Let's double up on the powder, Mr. Homerun," Simon ordered.

"Mr. Wiz wanted only a single measurement, Mr. Rerun," Catch reminded the Gamadin.

"I've recalculated the distance, Mr. Catch. Put in two measurements, if you please."

"Cool, Mr. Rerun," Catch replied. He and Homerun followed orders and doubled the measurement of black powder for the remaining nine portside cannons. Simon also wanted more elevation. "Up two notches on this one, Mr. Shortstop, if you please," he said, tapping the breech of the cannon he wanted adjusted.

Pitch's round jade-colored eyes darted from side to side nervously. "Why aren't you frightened, Mr. Rerun? The Fortress of Daloom's cannons could cause great harm to the *Millie*."

"Don't let my pretty face fool ya, Mr. Pitch, I'm plenty scared."

Pitch found the admission surprising. "You are, Mr. Rerun?"

Simon moved on to the next cannon in the line. "I'm always scared. It kinda comes with the territory, Mr. Pitch, if you get my drift."

Pitch "kinda" did. "The Captain always acts like...like..." Pitch couldn't think of the right words to describe Harlowe's actions.

"Like he has a death wish?" Simon replied, helping Pitch along.

Catch, Homerun, and Zinger joined the conversation. "Meaning no disrespect to the Captain, Mr. Rerun, but that would be a proper description of our worry," Pitch replied after careful thought. Catch, Homerun, and Zinger concurred unanimously, each with one frightened eye always on the evil black walls of Daloom.

"Understood, Mr. Pitch. No disrespect taken."

"Will Death be with us the entire voyage, Mr. Rerun?" Homerun asked nervously.

Simon tapped the breech of the fourth cannon. "Raise this one three clicks, Mr. Catch. Let's not fall short." He grinned, "That would be embarrassing."

Simon moved on to Cannon Number Five while he answered Homerun's question about the Captain to the small group of worried sailors. "Well, my Gazzian shipmates, I've known the Captain for quite some time now. What I can tell you, with near absolute certainty, is that the Skipper is just getting started. Every day is a near-death experience. Every day I wake up and find myself alive, I count my lucky stars that I survived another day. That's how it goes when you're under the command of Captain Harlowe Pylott, dudes."

Zinger glanced toward the quarterdeck. Harlowe was peering through his spyglass at the ships threatening their passage through the Straits.

"And the female called 'Lu'. Why does he seek her first instead of Jakaa's treasure?" Zinger wanted to know.

"Once you lay eyes upon her, mate, you'll understand. She's the hottest thing on the planet," Simon replied, as he closed one eye and looked down the barrel.

"She is a treasure?" Catch asked.

Simon chuckled. "A king's ransom, my man."

"One ball each below the waterline, Mr. Bolt," Harlowe ordered from above.

Simon called back, acknowledging the request that he wanted the cannon shot to strike the hull of the ships just below their water line. The result would be to disable the ship by flooding the hull, causing less loss of life. "Aye, Skipper. Below the waterline."

Pitch was near panic. "But the *Millie* is near three cannons short of the Phagallian vessels, Mr. Rerun," which meant that it would take three lengths of a cannon's range to reach the intended targets.

Simon pointed to the second cannon on the line being loaded. "The Skipper knows what he's doing, Mr. Pitch. To your posts, gents," he said to the four shipmates. "Be ready to poke Death in the eye again." Putting a final tap on the fifth cannon, he ordered, "Four clicks up, Mr. Catch."

"That is half-range, Mr. Bolt," Pitch replied, following orders but questioning each step of the operation.

"I'm aware of that, Mr. Pitch. Four clicks up, if you please, sir," Simon commanded a little more sternly this time. If he didn't get the cannons ready by the time Harlowe gave the command to fire, Harlowe would be more than glaring at him from the quarterdeck.

The Gazzian crew hurried to line up the remaining starboard cannon. When they were ready, Simon called up from the gun deck. "Locked and loaded, Skipper!"

"Thank you, Mr. Bolt," Harlowe answered back. Turning to the wheel, he ordered calmly, "Bring her around, Mr. Twobagger."

"Cool, Captain!" Twobagger countered.

The *Millie's* bow swung around and began tacking to port. The Gazzian crew belayed lines, made fast slack sails, reset the mizzen sheets, and reeled in the foresail. Finally, the starboard cannons faced the three Phagallian Men-o'-War. Looming dark and menacing behind them on the black cliffs was the Fortress of Daloom, ready to defend the channel if her galleons needed backup.

A moment later Harlowe gave the command, "GIVE 'EM A BROADSIDE, MR. BOLT!"

Simon waited for the *Millie's* sway and heading to line up with his aiming points, then...

BOOM! BOOM! BOOM!

Three cannons fired, one after another, a split second apart. There was a short delay as the golden dura-metal cannon balls traveled far past their intended targets. Harlowe's jaw dropped when he saw the three cannon balls strike the walls of the Fortress itself!

"Mr. Bolt," Harlowe called down, "our targets were the galleons!"

Simon jumped up to the main deck. He was as surprised as everyone else. With palms up in confusion, he started to defend himself. "I was aiming at the ships, Skipper! I don't know what happened."

Ian ran up to Simon. "How much powder did you put in, Rerun?"

"A little extra."

"How much?"

"Double."

"Double?" Ian cried out, looking skyward. "You could have blown us all up!"

"How was I to know this was a Starbuck's blend?"

"It's a special load, Rerun, you can't—"

Just then, a huge explosion emanated from the walls of the Fortress. A great cloud of fire and black smoke shot a thousand feet in the air. Three seconds later, everyone was blown off their feet from the shock wave, including the *Millie*. The force was strong enough to blow *Millie* violently sideways and tilt her over. The main portside spars dunked themselves, sheets and all, into the water before she swayed back and righted herself. Had she not been equipped with her special ballast, she would certainly have capsized.

Harlowe ordered an immediate account of all the crew. Everyone was shaken but otherwise unhurt; everyone, that is, but Zinger, who had been on the starboard ratline when the shock wave struck the *Millie*. Zinger was nowhere to be found. Harlowe finally spotted the crewman bobbing a short distance astern on the port side of the ship and waving for help. He had been blown overboard by the shock wave. Harlowe found Mowgi back on his perch on the bowsprit and ordered the undog to perform the rescue. "Fetch Mr. Zinger, Mowgi, if you would be so kind."

Mowgi inflated into his dragon-like alter ego, stretched out his thirty-foot wings, and glided across the water toward the distressed crewman. Zinger might have preferred a tossed line, but Harlowe didn't have time to waste turning the *Millie* around. The undog was more efficient.

In spite of Zinger's loud scream of protest, Mowgi was only following orders. He snatched the crewman out of the water as easily as if he were fishing for traa. After a sweeping turn, high in the air over the *Millie's* crow's nest, the undog placed the white-faced crewman on the poop deck and returned to his bowsprit. Harlowe laughed. He doubted Zinger had ever had such a thrilling ride. As scared as he was, Zinger was happy to be back onboard.

"Get below and into some dry clothes, Mr. Zinger," Harlowe ordered.

Zinger climbed down from the poop deck and saluted Harlowe as he squished by in his wet clothes. "Cool, Captain!"

"All accounted for, Captain!" Pitch shouted from the main deck.

"Very well, Mr. Pitch. Damage?" Harlowe added.

"All minor, Captain!" Pitch reported.

"Excellent, Mr. Pitch, belay sails. Let's get our fine Lady moving again, if you please."

"Cool, Captain, belay sails!"

"Course, Captain?" Moneyball asked from the wheel.

Before he could give any kind of course change, he needed to know where the Phagallian warships were. "Steady as she goes, Mr. Moneyball, let's see what we have." Harlowe raised his optics and waited for the smoke to clear. "What happened to the Daloom galleons?" he wondered aloud to himself. All three galleons appeared to have vanished from the ocean.

Harlowe called Ian to the quarterdeck to scan the Straits with the com. Ian's answer was immediate. "They're gone."

"The blast?" Harlowe wondered.

"They were five miles closer than we were," Ian replied, and showed Harlowe the com screen. "See here, here, and here. That's their debris field. They were nuked big time, Captain."

Harlowe whistled his astonishment. He pointed to a large section of superheated debris along the coast. "What's that?"

Ian looked up and turned his eyes toward the Fortress. "Daloom," he replied as he scanned the cliffs where the Fortress should have been.

Thick black clouds of smoke and fire filled the entire sky above the fortress. The indestructible cliff walls of the fortress had fallen to the shoreline in a massive slide of crumbled stone and fiery debris. The great towers they could see from a hundred miles out on the ocean were completely leveled. It seemed that the Fortress of Daloom had simply been blown away. It no longer existed.

Harlowe was upset. He wanted to enter the Phagallian Empire quietly, find Riverstone, Leucadia, and the others, then silently slip back out again. Wiping out the southern part of the country was no way to win friends. "What did you do, Wiz? Nuking the Straits wasn't part of the plan," Harlowe protested.

Ian was beside himself. Simon had overloaded the cannons and overshot the galleons, but the cannonballs were only dura-steel. "The cannonballs wouldn't have wiped out the Fortress like that, Captain."

Harlowe pushed back his wide-brimmed hat and studied the burning fires rising into the evening sky. Simon climbed up to the quarterdeck beside him, looking dismayed.

"Sorry, Skipper," he apologized.

Harlowe and Ian understood that if it wasn't for Simon's mistake of doubling up on the powder, the cannonballs would have fallen much closer to the *Millie*, perhaps too close, and she would be at the bottom of the ocean with the Phagallian galleons. They had been fortunate this time. What had caused such a massive detonation was a mystery. Had the dura-balls struck something inside the fortress walls, or was it something no one had thought of yet? Whatever it was, Simon wasn't the cause. His blunder had actually saved their lives. Simon nearly fell overboard when Harlowe congratulated him and his crew on a job well done.

"Great work, Mr. Bolt! Have Jewels dish up extra fries and shakes for your battery crew tonight," Harlowe ordered, satisfied that the *Millie* would make it through the Straits of Daloom unharmed.

"Cool, Captain!" came the collective cheer from the main deck.

47

The Long Goodbye

It was still dark when Riverstone and Kikue uncovered the dhow and guided it into the shallow lagoon. The wind was steady and warm from the south. The sun would soon rise over the coastal hills, but the stars and moons were bright enough to light his way through the narrow channel and out to sea. When all was ready and the sail let out, Riverstone would set out. Kikue would stay behind. As proficient as she was sailing the dhow—way better than he would ever be—he wouldn't risk her being taken prisoner and sold into slavery. If not for his SIBA, she would have died. Her near-death was too much for him to bear a second time.

Kikue thought he may already be too late to save his friends. It had been nearly two weeks since they were taken, more than enough time to bring them to Xu, where they would be sold as slaves. He prayed she was wrong. Not so long ago, Harlowe had searched an entire quadrant and found him. All he had to do was search a planet. *No one is expendable and no one is left behind* was the motto every Gamadin was taught by the General after the first rimmer. Even if it cost him his life, his mission was to save Lu, Sizzle, Sharlon, and the others before they were lost in Phagallian slave society, and before they were all zapped to nothingness by a storm of gamma rays. He cared so much for Kikue, but the moment he climbed into the dhow and sailed out into the open sea, his only focus had to be on finding his friends. He knew that when he kissed her good-bye, it would be the last time he would ever see her again. He would never forget her.

"Water?" Kikue asked, looking over his store of supplies.

Riverstone tapped the top of the clay pot. "Filled to the brim."

She stared into his eyes, wondering what manner of being would sail into the heart of Death in a boat that was taken from one of Jakaa's chief collectors.

Riverstone smiled. "Don't worry. Long before I enter the harbor, I'll slip off the back and swim to shore."

Kikue was not comforted.

"My present to you. You have it in your hut?"

She nodded. "Yes. I have it hidden."

"Good. Practice using it until you are cool with it."

"I have tried it twice. It is powerful magic."

Riverstone agreed. "Yeah, it's that all right. You may need it only once."

"Yes, Buntoo-attee." Kikue removed a large leather pouch that was tied to her waist and handed it to Riverstone.

Riverstone looked at her cautiously. "What is it?"

"My gift to you," she replied.

Riverstone untied the small leather strap, reached inside, and pulled out what appeared to be a stuffed snake. "Gee, I've never received a tail for a present before."

"If you walk into Xu without it, you will find travel difficult. Jakaa has been at war with the Croomis for many passings. Soldiers will not hesitate to strike you down if they see you without an appendage."

Riverstone curled the tail back into its sack and re tied the leather strap around the neck. "Good idea, Kik. Thanks."

He looked behind the hills and saw the first signs of pink in the morning sky. "I must go now."

While holding the tie line for the dhow, he took her in his arms, dreading that he would have to let her go. They kissed for a long tearful moment. He stroked her hair, climbed into the dhow, lowered the sail, and glided away. Their eyes held each other until the dhow was beyond the point. Once they were beyond the view of anyone from the shore, Alice materialized, shored up the spar lines, and trimmed the sail for his voyage north to Xu.

48

No Survivors

After two days more of sailing from the Straits of Daloom, they arrived where Ian calculated the *Jo-li Ran's* shuttle had put down. The odor of Death still hovered over the beach. Ian scanned the charred remains of the small encampment with his com. His answer confirmed the obvious. "This was their campsite, Captain."

Only the Gamadin and Mowgi were allowed to come ashore. If there was trouble, Harlowe didn't want his Gazzian crew exposed to any danger. Ian's com didn't register any human life forms or other large animals, but a com made no judgments on peril when it came knocking. Harlowe had enough problems already without having to worry about a defenseless crew on an open beach.

It was late morning and the weather was clear and cloudless. The *Millie* was anchored in the calm waters a quarter mile out beyond the gentle surf. The offshore breeze they had come in on was warm and dry. It felt a lot like a SoCal Santa Ana in October. Two large moons above them looked like a couple of smiley cats.

Ian pointed across the ocean. "The debris field extends for miles out that way. The escape pods look intact as well, a hundred feet down just off Millie's port side."

"Tell me Lu and Riverstone aren't here," Harlowe said, kicking aside a charred frond from a cold pile of black remains.

"Not here, Dog," Ian replied.

"What about Sizzle?" Simon asked, fearing that the love of his life might be among the dead.

Harlowe felt bad that he hadn't included Simon's fiancée and apologized. "She's as important as the others, Rerun."

"She's not here either, Simon," Ian said after careful inspection.

Simon wiped his eyes before he asked, "So where are they, Skipper?"

Harlowe turned to Ian, looking for ideas.

Ian bent down near a large open hole in the sand. The encampment had a dozen others just like it spread around the beach and in the palm tree grove. His com blinked, displaying what only he and Leucadia fully understood, Ian concluded, "These were made by cannonballs."

"What's that mean, Skipper?" Simon asked.

"It means there's more to the story that we haven't figured out yet."

"Lu and Riverstone are resourceful," Ian replied, putting a positive spin on what they were looking at. "If they knew an attack was coming, they would have gotten everyone to a safe place."

Harlowe watched as Mowgi sniffed through the debris. "So what happened to them?" he repeated, more to himself than to either Ian or Simon. Harlowe picked up some cut fronds that were stacked in a pile beside a destroyed survival hut. "Looks like they planned to stay a while. They didn't go willingly."

Ian checked his readouts. "They didn't. Riverstone would have used his Gama weapons if—"

Harlowe finished Ian's thought. "If he was here."

"Riverstone was with them. We all heard him on the com when they were in the shuttle," Simon said.

"That's peculiar, all right," Harlowe muttered, wishing he had a crystal ball that wasn't foggy.

Ian had a theory. "Mr. Pitch says we're deep in Phagalla territory. In the old days on Earth, if you were a dude in the wrong place, you were considered hostile. Could it be the Phagallian Daks found them and took them?"

Harlowe stared past Ian. "Any more bad news?" *Where is she?*

"Yeah, if they were taken, they'll probably sell them."

Simon glared at Ian. "Like slaves?"

"We're on a medieval planet, Rerun. Always remember that. That's what people did then. It was common practice to capture people and sell them like cattle."

Suddenly, Mowgi took off like a plas round toward the palm grove behind the encampment. They knew the undog could sense things with his snout that would make a com feel insecure. Without asking why, the three Gamadin tore off after the undog, knowing he had found something important.

They didn't have far to go. Behind a thick clump of bushes Mowgi was digging the way he'd dig a traa bone buried in the dirt. Harlowe and Ian joined in the effort. From the look of things, the ground was soft, like someone had dug a shallow hole and buried something in a hurry.

Less than a foot down they cleared back the sand enough to find the first body part. It was a hand. Even more perplexing was that the body part was enclosed in a SIBA.

49

Fresh Air

Dodger climbed up a fabricated dura-wire ladder to the bridge. The instant his eyes caught the bright sunny day, he couldn't wait to check out the surf. He had been cooped up inside the ship for more than a week, thanks to the recent storms that blew across the island. He needed fresh air and some waves to relieve the funk he was in. The gamma ray burst had sucked *Millawanda* dry of the power she needed to maintain her systems, force field or weapons to protect herself. *Millawanda's* environmentals were shut down. There was no sweet-smelling air anywhere on the ship. Even his jungle hideaway was dark. He had no place to play but outdoors.

The little power *Millawanda* had was hardly detectable. It had been two weeks since Harlowe left the bay in the galleon. Three days ago the blinkers ceased to function. To make their way to the lower levels of the ship or up to the bridge, they had to scavenge dura-wire ladders from the utility room. Sliding doors that normally swished open with ease had to be opened and closed by hand. Worst of all, the food processors were off-line. No one had eaten a double-double cheese, taco, or Dodger Dog for over a week. For Dodger, a day without fries was worse than missing a day of surf. Fortunately, there were enough SIBA energy packs and Blue Stuff containers to last for months. At least they wouldn't starve.

Looking through the massive front windows of the bridge, Dodger was bummed that he was unable to see beyond the perimeter of the ship. He looked up, expecting to see the ocean on *Millawanda's* main viewing screen. The area above the console was empty space.

The screen, like everything else on the ship that required power, had gone dark. How would he know if the tide was back to go surfing if his view of the ocean was blocked? The surf could be cranking, Dodger thought. If he walked to the rim, he could see everything for miles down the beach. Mr. Platter said he couldn't step onto the beach without his permission. But what was the harm in checking out the surf as long as he stayed on the edge of the ship? Geez, he could see everything from there! Harlowe had done it plenty of times.

After the battle with the vines, Monday locked all entryways into the ship and removed all outside blinkers. The hatchways were opened only a couple of hours a day to allow for fresh air when the tide was in or when it was raining. Prigg noticed that when it rained, the vines receded into fetal balls, appearing to protect themselves from the water. When it was sunny and the tide was out, the vines crawled and slithered their way everywhere that was dry around the island. During the dry times, Monday ordered the ship sealed tight, regardless of the tide level. He was taking no chance of anyone getting caught again in their strangling tendrils.

But what was the harm in looking, Dodger wondered. He could make a quick check of the point and be back inside the ship while the ground was still wet outside. He had to hurry though. The tropical sun was already bright and hot. It wouldn't be long before the beach would be as dry as if no rain had ever fallen.

Excited to feel the fresh air on his face and see the waves, Dodger left the bridge and headed through Harlowe's cabin door to the airlock. It was the fastest way to the edge of the ship. Dodger smiled innocently. *Harlowe won't mind, he's my brother!* He released the lock on the first airlock door. He had to pull back the sliding door manually because there was no power for it to slide back automatically. He stepped into the airlock chamber and yanked the second door open as he had done with the first door.

Instantly, a warm fresh breeze engulfed his body. Stepping out into the sun felt like stepping into heaven. He closed his eyes and let the heat from its penetrating rays saturate his skin. After three days of imprisonment, he was free again.

This is awesome!

Thinking he didn't have much time before Monday would be making his way to the bridge, Dodger hurried down the slight, two-football-field-length incline to the ship's perimeter edge to get his visual surf report. All he needed was one short peek and he would be back before Monday knew he was gone.

A strange sound greeted Dodger halfway to the rim. It sounded almost like someone was laughing at him in a low rumbling voice. This sound was like nothing he had ever heard before. He stopped and looked around, half-expecting to hear breaking waves, but there was nothing to see. The hull was smooth and clean from the recent storm. Millawanda's golden surface was already dry and glistening as if she had just been given a bath.

He looked out across the hull and the magnificent view and scolded himself for being such a wimp. He was bummed. The view wasn't what he expected at all. The tide was still out. According Prigg, the tide should have been in and above the perimeter rim. But the ship was still high and dry.

What's up with that, Dodger wondered.

He remembered Prigg's explanation that because there were so many moons, the tides changed in various degrees at least five times a day and sometimes six. The big swing came every fifth day when the Gall moon arrived, setting everything straight again and bringing the ocean with it to flood the lagoon and cover the ship. Today was the fifth day. He should be underwater where he was standing—Dodger was sure of it. Prigg was never wrong, especially when it came to figuring out the tides.

Curious to see where the water in the lagoon had gone to, Dodger continued on to the rim. He hadn't gone far when he stopped in amazement. Holding back the sea was a massive wall of rocks. He couldn't believe his eyes. Who or what could have built it?

How rad is that? Monday and Prigg had to know about this!

Curiosity more than anything else kept Dodger moving forward. He had to see for himself the full extent of the cofferdam before he headed back to the airlock. When he arrived at the perimeter edge, something tickled his leg. He swatted at the insect without looking because the view he saw when he peered over the rim sent his neck hairs straight. The insect was the least of his worries! Everywhere Dodger looked, as far as he could see, vines had grown all around *Millawanda*. The beach was gone. The vines were moving and cackling as they reached upwards, crawling for the top edge of the hull.

Dodger stumbled backwards and the insect returned. He was reaching down to flick the pest away when a tendril grabbed him by the ankle...

50

Cannons from the North

Harlowe was about to retract the SIBA from around the body when Ian grabbed his wrist.

"No, Captain! You can't deactivate the suit right now!"

"I've gotta see who it is," Harlowe said.

"The SIBA is the only thing that's keeping her alive. If we break the seal, she'll die."

"You're sure about that?"

Ian's eyes bore into Harlowe to listen. "I'm sure, Dog!"

Simon's eyes went to light-speed when he heard the body was female. "She?"

Gliding his com along the body, Ian replied. "Female for sure."

"Human?"

"No. Not human." He put a careful hand on Harlowe's arm. "It's not Lu either, Dog. Looks Tomarian. My guess is she's either Sizzle or Sharlon. The readouts would fit."

Simon stared down at the body in shock. "She's alive?"

"Yeah, but she's in a suspended state. That's why we can't retract the SIBA, not even for a moment. She's broken up pretty bad inside. Millie's the only one who can save her now. I'm sure that's why she was put into the SIBA. Whoever did this knew what they were doing. With the suit on low like this, it should keep her alive for weeks."

Harlowe had no doubt as to who it was. "It was Lu. Riverstone wouldn't know that. She's the only one with the brains to figure that out."

"That means she's okay," Ian added.

"Yeah, but where is she now?"

Ian didn't have an answer. Harlowe reached down and was about to pick the woman up when Simon stopped him. "No, Skipper. I have her."

The mixture of fear and dread on Simon's face was so profound that Harlowe gave him the okay without protest. Simon lovingly dusted the body clean, gathered her in his arms, and carried her back to the launch. Before rowing back to the *Millie*, they wrapped her in a canvas blanket to prevent the Gazzian crew from seeing her in the Gamadin suit. The crew had seen enough 54th century technology to thoroughly mess up their heads. *So much for the prime directive!*

Just as they were about to push off, Mowgi became focused again. Harlowe held the departure up while he read the undog's signals. He didn't have long to wait. Thunderous rumblings rolled across the water from the north.

Ian checked his com and reported: "Cannon fire, Dog."

"How far?"

"Twelve point two miles."

Harlowe checked the weapons in his belt, then handed Ian his hat. "Put her in my cabin."

"Think it's Riverstone?" Ian asked, reading his com again as more thunder rolled in from the north.

Harlowe didn't have to think. He knew. "We're deep in Phagallian territory. Something happened here, now something else has them agitated. Something's got them tweaked. Better than even odds on who that is. We'd best check things out before we go in, guns blazing.

You and Rerun return to the *Millie* and sail toward the cannons. Keep her out of sight until I call you in."

"I wanna go with you, Skipper," Simon said.

Harlowe had other plans. "You're staying with Wiz. If the *Millie* runs into problems, I need you at the helm with Homerun."

Simon nodded. When it came to piloting a ship on the high seas, Simon had much more experience than Ian. Besides, he could also protect what might be Sizzle or Sharlon. "Aye, Skipper. I understand."

Ian and Simon began rowing through the flat surf back to the *Millie* while Harlowe and Mowgi headed north along the beach. Once out of sight from the Gazzian crew, Harlowe pulled a Superman-without-a-phone-booth by activating his SIBA, covering his face with the bugeyes and engaging his power assist gravs to propel him in twenty-foot lengths. The undog ran along in easy, loping strides, making it all look natural.

*   *   *

Harlowe sprinted the twelve miles. The world record for a 10,000-meter race on Earth is roughly 26 minutes. Harlowe made the same distance in less than ten. When he encountered the cliffs that stuck out in the ocean and cut off his path, he swam around the rocky points to the other side, where he could resume sprinting along the beach again. Mowgi had it even easier. He took flight and waited patiently on the other side for Harlowe to catch up. When they were within a mile of the cannons, Harlowe and Mowgi veered inland a short distance until Harlowe found a high bluff with a clear view. What he saw was heartbreaking. A fishing village among the palms above the beach was burning. Five Phagallian ships were closing their gunports in the dark grey smoke after finishing the recent broadsides. Troops were now storming the burning debris, searching for survivors. From the way they were hacking away with their long, broad-faced swords, Harlowe could tell exactly what the soldiers were doing. They were putting the final touches on what the gunships had started. The Phagallians were ensuring that no living soul would be left alive in the village.

Harlowe kept Ian informed through the com. Ian asked if there were any survivors. Harlowe's reply was simple. "None." Harlowe zoomed in closer with his bugeye opticals and was surprised to see how few casualties there were on the ground. He saw no prisoners at all, and the number of dead was less than a handful. The village had so many huts that he wondered if any survivors had already been taken away.

By late afternoon the pillage was complete. The Phagallian galleons remained anchored offshore. If they followed what would be normal procedures on earth, the galleons would not attempt to sail along the rocky coastline at night. They would set sail the following morning, which would give the brigades more time to wipe out all traces of the village.

Harlowe could do nothing for the village. From his viewpoint on the bluff, he could see the dead being thrown into raging bonfires on the beach. All of the victims had tails. He was relieved to know that Leucadia and Riverstone were not among them. If they weren't captives of the Phagallians, then where were they? They had to be somewhere nearby. Could they have escaped into the hills? Leucadia and Riverstone had SIBAs. They could escape anyone on the planet if it was just the two of them. And knowing them as well as he did, there was no doubt in his mind they would have tried to save everyone's lives, not just their own.

Too many pieces of the puzzle just didn't fit. Harlowe needed answers. The problem was, he didn't know who to ask or where to go to find the answers. Maybe his Gazzian crew would know something. It was worth a shot anyway.

There was nothing he could do for the village now. He needed to find Leucadia and Riverstone fast. Every second of every day counted. He had fewer than twenty days to find them and return to *Millawanda* before GRB II struck the planet. He had no time for detours, diversions, or sea battles with medieval warships. It was tough for him to leave the village in ruins, but he had to move on.

Before making his way back to the *Millie*, Harlowe paused a moment to appraise the firepower of the Phagallian fleet. All five ships were larger than the *Millie* by a factor of more than two. Four of them were twice her size and carried thirty cannons on each side, while the lead ship was four times bigger and more than two hundred cannons strong.

Harlowe wasn't worried. The *Millie's* cannons were formidable. The nuking of the Fortress of Daloom proved that. With her souped-up firepower, the *Millie* and his crew were more than a match for any Phagallian fleet. Harlowe didn't care how many cannons they had.

He scanned the Phagallian lead ship, he watched a barely-clothed, tortured body being pulled from the hatchway and dragged onto the main deck. The prisoner was tall and muscular with dark short hair. It was the first being he had seen without a tail. Soldiers and officers jeered and struck the prisoner as he was tied to a spar line from the main mast, hoisted up to yardarms, and left to dangle in the hot sun like a piece of freshly cut meat.

That gomer won't last the day, Harlowe thought.

As he watched the body twist in the wind, Harlowe zoomed in on the poor soul's face. His heart stopped.

It was Riverstone.

51

Assault on Millie

Dodger sliced through the vine with one swipe of his black blade, freeing his leg just before dozens of crawlers snaked over the top of the rim. He leaped to his feet and charged back up the incline toward the bridge in a race for his life. More vines began flowing over the top of the rim, crawling and undulating along *Millawanda's* smooth golden hull toward Dodger from all directions.

Dodger had never run so hard in his life and still the crawlers were reaching for his feet.

"MR. PLATTER!" Dodger screamed at the top of his lungs. "MR. PLATTER! MR. PLATTER!"

Dodger felt a vine tap the back of his leg. Every time one tried to latch on, Dodger swiped at it with his blade. Twice a vine wrapped itself around his waist, but each time, he was able to slice it off before it could pull him down.

The open door was a football field away. If he didn't break stride, he could make it. But the crawlers were out-flanking him and closing in on him from three sides. Just when Dodger thought he was vine meal, Monday charged out the door, guns blazing.

The vines squealed in pain as the hot bolts seared through the green mass. Each time a hole opened up, however, new vines closed the gap and resumed the attack. Monday didn't let up. He reloaded his power magazine twice, trying to keep a path open for Dodger. As much firepower as Monday had, it wasn't enough to keep the charging mass of crawlers at bay for very long. "HURRY, DODGER!" Monday shouted above the screeching cries of the vines.

Dodger stumbled but continued tumbling forward, while Monday fried vine after vine that tried to close the path. Dodger dove through the hatchway just as Monday was expending his last rounds on the mass. With hardly a second to spare, Monday leaped back into the chamber and Prigg slammed the hatchway closed.

By the time Dodger, Prigg, and Monday made it, exhausted and out of breath to the bridge, the vines had covered every square inch of the front windows. The vine was so thick that no sunlight penetrated into the ship.

Monday, Prigg, Dodger and the cubs were now prisoners, with no means of escape and no fresh air.

52

On a Phagallian Cruise

Riverstone's body was bloody, bruised, and blistered. Covered with first and second-degree burns, his skin looked the way it would look if it had spent the day under a broiler. He figured he would survive another day or two and then be sliced up and fed to the traas for bait.

He felt stupid. He made a mistake by not telling Alice to wake him when a boat was sighted, especially a Phagallian galleon. But after three days without sleep, he forgot that he had programmed her to collapse into a cylinder the moment she sensed another sentient being nearby. He dozed off at the tiller and when he woke up, the Phagallian galleon had thrown a net over the dhow and captured him without a fight. Alice was not programmed to classify a Phagallian ship as hostile. For all she knew, the galleon was coming to rescue him.

He could hear the General's voice now. *You're an embarrassment to the Gamadin, Jester! A hundred rimmers before sunset, that's an order!* Riverstone tried to salute but couldn't. His hands were bound. "Sir, yes, sir," he muttered weakly.

The Phagallian sailors taunted him as he dangled above the main deck. "You still alive, Croomis? Are you thirsty, Croomis? Would you like some nice cool water? Your odor makes us ill, Croomis. When your skin is fully baked, we will cut you down and feed you to the traas as an offering to the gods for Jakaa, Croomis!" The sailors laughed and threw rotted food at his body so the flies would sting his skin as they fed on him in the heat of the Gazzian sun.

Until night fell, Riverstone made several attempts to banter with his captors in the hope of learning the whereabouts of Leucadia, Sizzle, and Sharlon. Throughout the ordeal, he never gave up hope. He had survived the worst the galaxy had to offer inside the mines of Erati, so hanging from a yardarm was like lying in the sand at 42nd Street. Nothing they could do to him was worse than the hell of Erati.

"Have you seen a tall babe with hair the color of the sun?" Riverstone asked them, his voice raspy and weak.

"Why do you care, Croomis? A female will be of little use to you when you are a traa's dinner!"

"Her father is very wealthy, Toadface. He will make you rich if she is found," Riverstone replied.

"What is a toadface, Croomis?"

"A handsome guy like you, brah, only his breath doesn't smell like the hind end of a traa. Have you seen her, Buttbreath?"

"If she is as beautiful as you say, then she is already Jakaa's slave."

"Where does this Jakaa live, Toad?" Riverstone didn't know how accurate his universal translator repeated his words. From the reaction of the sailors, the personal insults didn't upset them. They spoke to him as if he was quite cordial. Maybe he was, and if so, he was the one being insulted. *Ain't that a hoot?*

The sailors laughed. "You don't know where Jakaa lives?"

"I'm not from around here, Brainiac."

"In the royal palace at Xu, Croomis," another sailor replied.

"Why do you ask, Croom—"

At once, the voice went silent and the laughter stopped. They were replaced by an eerie silence that swept over the decks as if someone had slammed the door on the sailors' fun.

"Well, guys, what do you say? Find Jakaa and I'll make you all rich."

He continued to prod his captors, but no one answered. "Not interested, huh? Stupid Toads!"

Riverstone thought his tormentors had grown bored with him and planned to go below for the night. He felt a tug on his rope and a moment later found himself being lowered, still bound, to the main deck. He felt energized now that he was down and the sun was set. This may be his last opportunity to escape. If he played dead, maybe he could catch them off guard. When the opportunity came along, he would reach out with his powerful legs and slam their faces against the mast. He would cut his bindings with the knife of one of his unconscious tormentors and jump ship. Even in his depleted condition, swimming to shore would take little effort. Once he got to the beach, he would run back to the cave where he and Kikue had stored the food. No one would find him. After he recovered, he would try again to make it north to Xu.

As he was being lowered, a big sailor came within range of his feet. Before touching the deck, Riverstone let fly a massive roundhouse kick that should have crushed the sailor's face easily. To his dismay, his foot stopped cold before his kick could slam into the sailor's body. Riverstone tried again. This time he couldn't move either foot. Both of them were held fast in the big sailor's hands.

"Hold on, pard," the big sailor said to him in a familiar voice.

At first Riverstone thought he was hallucinating, but after a few more calming words, he went limp and let Harlowe ease him down onto the deck.

"What took you so long?" Riverstone groaned.

Harlowe slit the leather bindings from around Riverstone's wrists. Without missing a beat—as lifelong friends in difficult circumstances do—Harlowe replied, "I didn't know you were on a Phagallian cruise." Harlowe lifted Riverstone to his feet, keeping a tight hold on him so he wouldn't fall. "Can you walk?"

"Sure."

But when Harlowe let go, Riverstone immediately fell back into his arms. "Well, maybe not so much," he quipped.

They reached the main deck rail and Riverstone asked, "Where is everybody?"

Harlowe propped Riverstone against the railing and replied, "Sleeping."

Riverstone felt a cold nose beneath the backside of his shorts. "YOW-WEE!"

The undog's yellow eyes glowed with delight in the darkness. Pushing away the nose, he turned and said, "You brought some backup, I see."

"I like having the advantage."

Riverstone searched the night sky. "Where's Millie?"

"Parked down the beach a ways."

"Great. Did you bring some Blue Stuff?"

Harlowe handed him a flask from his Gama-belt. "It's warm."

Riverstone wouldn't have cared if it were boiling. When the blue liquid touched his throat, its revitalizing energy began spreading throughout his body. Three gulps later, the flask was empty. With blue fluid pumping through his veins, Riverstone surveyed the ship's decks. It came as no surprise that the sailors were lying out cold in various positions. Harlowe had been thorough.

Harlowe was about to go over the side and swim to shore. Riverstone held him back. "Can't go yet."

"The cruise is over."

"There's a dude onboard who knows where Lu is," Riverstone replied. "Still want to go?"

That got Harlowe's attention.

53

Dinner with the Admiral

Admiral Radu, the Supreme Commander of the Phagallian fleet, sat at his flagship's dinner table with the captains of the other four galleons. They were celebrating over the vengeance they had taken on the rebellious fishing village that was said to have stolen the Emperor's property from his collectors. Each captain was well dressed in red jackets with gold trim and fringes of sparkly thread that hung from their sleeves just long enough to soak in the food they were eating. The Admiral, by contrast, wore a peach jacket studded with bright green jewels and a red cord that spiraled around his rather rotund figure.

"Let this serve as an example to all who meddle with the Emperor's collectors," Admiral Radu stated, raising his glass in a toast.

They clinked glasses together, sloshing their drinks, and congratulated the Admiral on his victorious attack on the insurgent village. "To the Emperor!" they cheered.

"What is that, Captain Chaan?" Admiral Radu asked, pointing to a golden cylinder.

Captain Chaan picked up the cylinder, displaying it proudly to the table. "One of my crew found it among the Croomis' belongings."

Then the Admiral inspected the medallion hanging from the Captain's neck, noticing it was made of the same golden material. "And was that taken from him as well, Captain?"

263

Captain Chaan smiled as if he had been caught with his hand in the cookie jar. "By the gods, I believe it was, Admiral."

"Is it not therefore our Emperor's property?"

Captain Chaan removed the medallion from around his neck and held it out to Admiral Radu. "May I make a present of this fine Croomis ornament to you, Admiral?"

"You may." As the Captain held out the medallion, the Admiral reached for a pistol hidden in his belt and shot the Captain in the chest. The Admiral held on to the medallion while Captain Chaan collapsed, dead in his chair. In the land of Phagalla, anyone who cheated the Emperor was punished on the spot, no matter how small the infraction.

Servants picked up Captain Chaan's body and carried it to the nearest open portal, where they heaved the dead officer unceremoniously into the water below. After the splash, the festivities and laughter resumed as if the captain had never existed.

Shortly thereafter, the flagship unexpectedly began to sway. "Are we adrift?" Admiral Radu inquired.

The captain on the right of the Admiral answered, "We seem to be, Admiral."

"This is strange. Who ordered my ship to hoist anchor?"

Another captain stood to determine the reason for the unplanned movement. Just then, the door of the cabin crashed inward, snapping off of its heavy iron hinges and crashing loudly to the floor. Lying on top of the door were three of the Admiral's personal bodyguards, out cold.

The startled officers rose from their chairs when two Croomis entered the Admiral's quarters. The officers drew their weapons but before any of them could fire, a Croomis in a light blue shirt and dark breeches shot first. His pistols spit blue flames that blasted each flintlock from the hands of the dinner party. Their shock multiplied when the Admiral's Croomis prisoner entered the room.

"You!" Admiral Radu cried out in a high, outraged voice.

The Croomis prisoner smiled, nodding toward the other Croomis standing next to him. "This is my pard, Captain Harlowe Pylott. He came to rescue me. I would treat him with respect. He doesn't like fat toads who give him bum information."

An officer spoke up. "You will be executed for your—"

A shot from Captain Pylott's pistol blew off the officer's ear.

"He's not here to make friends," the Croomis prisoner said.

The alert Croomis boy saw Admiral Radu's hand make a slight move under the table. Before the admiral could execute his perfidy, he had searing holes through both of his arms. Two small pistols dropped to the floor with a thud.

The Croomis prisoner shook his head in mock disappointment. "Did I mention he has a bad temper?"

Pylott began the questioning. "One of your ships took prisoners from an encampment south of here. Where are they?"

The officers glanced at each other, but did not speak for fear of being shot.

Captain Pylott cocked his pistol and pointed it between Admiral Radu's eyes. "You've got one second, Fatty, or I'm blowing your head off and then I'll go to the next toad for my answer."

Admiral Radu was close to wetting his pants. "Truly, I do not know of the prisoners you speak."

Unseen by all except the other Croomis, Captain Pylott slid a tiny switch on the side of his flintlock. When he squeezed the trigger, the hammer slammed forward, creating a bright spark when it struck the frizzen pan.

Nothing happened. The pistol had purposely misfired.

For the Admiral, though, it might as well have blown a hole through his head. He collapsed, dead, on the floor.

Captain Pylott re-cocked his weapon and pointed it at the next officer's head. "How about you, Toad? Do you feel lucky? Where are the prisoners?"

"The Admiral spoke no false tales. There have been no prisoners taken from the south." The officer looked at the others and they all agreed with his account. The two Croomis appeared to accept the officers' story.

The Croomis prisoner grabbed a young captain's black knife. He pushed food, drink, and tableware onto the floor to clear off a section of the table and carved a symbol into the wood. "That's the flag I saw. Whose ship is that?"

The look on each officer's face betrayed that they all recognized the symbol, but once again, no one was willing to speak. The Croomis captain then let out a low whistle and on that command, a frightening little beast with tall ears and big yellow eyes trotted into the room. The young Captain Pylott patted the beast and welcomed him to what he called "the party." The Croomis prisoner stabbed a large bird the size of a twenty-pound turkey from the table and tossed it to the creature. The creature opened its mouth wide and swallowed the bird whole. Without further persuasion, the first officer stammered nervously, "That is Klagg's ship."

"Klagg, huh? Where can I find him?" Captain Pylott asked.

"Klagg was due back in Xu many days ago."

"So what happened to him?" the Croomis prisoner asked. "He was headed north. I saw his ship headed that way."

With all eyes on the creature, the officers suddenly became very open to all of the Croomis' questions. "Xu is only a three days' sail. We did not pass him coming here. It is very possible that his ship was lost, or by the gods, if the recent storm took his ship too far from the shore, it may have been taken by a traa."

Suddenly the flagship listed violently to one side, throwing everyone to the downside of the room. The captain with the missing ear was killed when the heavy dining table crushed him against the bulkhead. The flagship had run aground along the point of rocks just north of the village. When the officers turned to see how the Croomis had fared, there was nothing to see. They had all disappeared, along with the creature, the cylinder, and the golden medallion from Admiral Radu's hand.

54

On the Same Page

It was the middle of the night. Riverstone had stopped along the beach after he and Harlowe had traveled only a couple of miles in their SIBAs.

Harlowe was impatient. "We have to keep moving, Matt."

"You said there were only a few bodies when they burned the village," Riverstone said.

"That's right. Three or four. It was hard to tell. The rest of the village was cleared out."

"And they weren't on Fatso's ship, either." Matt bit down on his lower lip, thinking out loud. "Unless Kik used the..."

Riverstone didn't complete his sentence. He bolted away, leaving Harlowe and Mowgi to wonder what he meant by "Kik." Harlowe sensed the panic in his flight and didn't try to stop him. Riverstone knew exactly where he was headed. With Mowgi by his side, Harlowe followed Riverstone up the path and into the hills.

* * *

Harlowe had just about caught up when Riverstone veered from the path and into a dense grove of trees. The sudden course change didn't bother Mowgi. The undog followed Riverstone with no problem. Harlowe cautiously followed through the trees, to his surprise into a cave full of tails. Riverstone had already deactivated his SIBA and was stepping quietly among the sleeping bodies. There were over a hundred village men, women, and children huddled together inside the hidden grotto.

Riverstone stopped at one body in particular and woke the young female being. For a moment the girl appeared shocked to see him. After Riverstone hugged her and calmed her with his voice, she reached out and kissed him as if he were the last living being on Gazz. A short time later, Riverstone escorted the girl over to Harlowe and Mowgi, who were patiently waiting to be filled in on the particulars.

"This is Harlowe, Kikue," Riverstone said.

Still holding Riverstone close, Kikue reached out to Harlowe with her tail. "I am honored to meet the great Captain Harlowe, the savior of our world."

By anyone's standards Kikue was easy on the eyes. She was tall and athletic, with long black hair and round dark eyes. She smelled like the sea in a very pleasant way that blended a subtle aroma of salt, seashells, and sand with a fresh and alluring touch of palm. Her manner was gentle. Harlowe understood now why Riverstone was in such a hurry. He wished he could have given Riverstone more time with her.

Harlowe graciously bowed and took her appendage. "Nice to meet you, Kikue." After that, Harlowe excused himself and took Riverstone aside to speak with him alone.

"What's the problem, Dog? You act like we're in a rush," Riverstone said. "Can't it wait until morning?"

Harlowe went right to the point. "There's a second GRB headed for the planet."

Riverstone's expression froze in disbelief. "A second?"

"If we don't find Lu, Sizzle, and the others and get back to Millie, we're all fried."

"How long do we have?"

"Two weeks."

Riverstone breathed a sigh of relief. "Cool. We can get the villagers inside Millie and they'll be okay. She's just down the street, right?"

"Millie is dead in the water. She's a thousand miles from here, washed up on an island. She can't fly, Matt. She has no power. She was sucked dry protecting the planet the first time around. We crashed landed just like you."

Riverstone stared at Harlowe, incredulous. How could anything happen to *Millawanda*?

"It wasn't such a slam-dunk as we thought," Harlowe said.

"Wiz said it would work."

"Well it didn't, and now everyone's burnt bacon if we don't get back to the ship in time."

Riverstone searched for something to say. "Lu would know how to get Millie up and running again."

"Yeah, if we knew where to find her."

"She can't be far, Dog."

"Point me in the right direction and I'll get her back."

"If Millie's down, how did you get here?"

"We found a Gazzian pirate ship that we retroed. We named her *Millie* and sailed her here, looking for you and Lu. Are we on the same page now, pard?"

Riverstone eyed Harlowe skeptically, knowing him the way that only a best friend would. "Who's the captain? Rerun?"

"I am."

If the circumstances weren't so desperate, Riverstone would have laughed. "You? You get seasick just looking at a boat."

"I've made adjustments."

Riverstone returned to Kikue with tears in his eyes. She was walking among her villagers and making sure the children were resting comfortably. A small child was coughing. She held up a clay cup of water for him to drink.

"I gave her a blinker to help save her people..." Riverstone began, his eyes never leaving her.

"You did the right thing, Matt."

"Somehow it doesn't feel that way. If it wasn't for me, the village would have been fine in the first place."

Harlowe wished there was a way to help Riverstone's friend further, but there were no choices left. They had to leave.

"I would ask her to go with me, but I know she'll never leave her people."

Riverstone's pain was all too familiar to Harlowe. The girls in his life were just as committed to their loyalties. Leucadia had risked her life to save not only him but Earth, his ship, and Neeja, while Quay struck out on her own to follow her dedication to bringing freedom to the quadrant. He wished there was another way. The best they could do was follow the original plan and hope they would find a way to save them all, including the planet.

"Who else is with you?" Riverstone asked.

"Wiz and Rerun," Harlowe replied.

Riverstone glanced at him, startled. "Wiz and...Are you joking?"

"We found a crew to help us."

"What did you offer them? Double-doubles?"

Riverstone was kidding but Harlowe wasn't. "Jakaa's treasure ships."

Riverstone's eyes rolled as he shook his head. "Sweet. That leaves Monday and Prigg guarding Millie?"

"And Dodger."

Riverstone eyes shot open with another start. "That's right, you brought Dodger. How's he enjoying the trip so far?"

"I haven't heard from them in three days."

"You worried?"

"A little," which meant to Riverstone that Harlowe was bothered plenty.

Harlowe wanted to give Riverstone more time with Kikue, but Ian was hailing him on the com in a panic. Harlowe went outside the cave to speak. Another ship had entered the bay and the *Millie* was under attack!

55

Last Stand

Monday and Prigg had run out of options. Two days after the vines nearly snagged Dodger, they broke through the outer doorway from Harlowe's quarters. Monday didn't know how they did it, but he guessed that *Millawanda's* normally fail-safe locks malfunctioned from the loss of power. Once the crawlers found their way to the bridge, it didn't take them long to find the shaft down the main corridor and snake their way throughout the ship. The outer doors were the strongest. If they failed, how long would it be before the interior doors failed?

Not long, Monday knew.

Except for the small amount of daylight coming down the shaft from the bridge, there was no light inside the hallways. It was pitch black throughout the ship. Monday found bright Gama-lights inside the utility room, along with plenty of ammo. Inside the ship, the more powerful rifles were useless unless they wanted to blow a hole through *Millawanda's* interior walls. Pistols didn't work, either. There were too many crawlers. Plucking off one crawler at a time was a waste of ammo. When one was shot, another ten took its place. Even a widespread plas round didn't help. The best defense they found was the heat torch they used for melting ice on barren planets. It pushed the horde back some, but in the end, it was only a stopgap. The torch had only so much fuel in its reserve. Unless *Millawanda* was able to refuel their tanks, the torches flamed out after several hours of use.

The robobs had the same limitation. They fought heroically for two days. Then they too ran out of power. Harlowe had taken the fully-charged clickers, thinking there was no sense in taking any of the lower-powered ones that were going to stop working anyway. Since they had no way of getting to the food supply, Monday, Prigg, and Dodger had only their SIBAs to keep them going. And they, too, had only the power cells left in their belts. Once those were depleted, they would starve, suffocate, or both.

By the second day, they were cut off from the utility room and had to retreat deeper into the ship, sealing doors as best they could before moving on to the next room. They waited until the vines found them, and then they shot their way to the next safe zone.

Millawanda was massive, but the number of safe zones was not infinite. They slept when and where they could. Only one of them slept at a time. Two of them always remained awake. Molly and Rhud had stayed with them until, without warning, they headed off down an open corridor that appeared safe. Dodger followed, not wanting to lose sight of the cats in case the vines trapped them. He had his black blade and a pistol Monday had given him for protection. The cats had nothing but teeth and claws, which they discovered on the beach were useless against the horde of crawlers.

Monday and Prigg held the corridor for as long as they could, waiting for Dodger to bring back the cats. If he didn't return before the vines began to overpower them again, Monday and Prigg would have to abandon the corridor for another safe zone and hope that Dodger and the cats found refuge for themselves.

The crisis came when neither Monday nor Prigg could determine which direction was a safe one.

The room they had just retreated into had two doors. Both were shut tight, but behind each door they could hear the telltale scratching and rustling of the vines trying to wedge it open. The only door available to them was the one from which they had come in.

"I think this is where we stand, little buddy," Monday said with a heavy sigh. He checked what was left in his flamethrower. There were about three solid minutes left in the tank and that was it.

Prigg's wayward eyes drooped. He slid against the wall, too exhausted to lift the end of his flamethrower. He was so spent that he could barely keep from collapsing. Monday helped him stand.

Prigg was grateful. "Thank you, Mr. Platter."

Monday patted Prigg's back, proud to be his friend. "You're a good little dude, Mr. Prigg." No one could have fought as valiantly, he thought.

Monday reset the cocking mechanism for Prigg's thrower. Then he strode over to the door they had come through and shut it as well as he could. Now all they had left to do was wait.

Chapter 56

Girlie Captain

Riverstone had no time to say goodbye to Kikue properly. After a quick lip-lock, he was out of the cave entrance. Harlowe was waiting for him, shouting orders to Ian over his SIBA's com. "They're attacking at night? How can they see?"

"Aye, Captain," Ian replied. "It was a perfectly placed shot across the bow, too. I gotta feeling if they wanted to, they could have nailed us. Do you want us to return fire? I can zero in on them using the binos," Ian replied.

Harlowe's first reaction was to protect the *Millie* and return fire, but as he thought about it, why did the attacking ship fire a warning shot in the first place? More importantly, why at night? Phagallians didn't travel at night, and they certainly didn't wage war on something they couldn't see. "How many rounds, Wiz?"

"Just one, Captain," Ian repeated.

He will win who knows when to fight and when not to fight, says Sun Tzu.

"Weigh anchor, Wiz. Get out of there," Harlowe ordered. Something strange was going on. A ship that attacks at night has either a captain who's a loon or one who deserves respect. "Let them have the bay. If they come after you, defend the ship. If not, I want to know who they are."

"What about you?" Ian asked.

"I have Riverstone. We'll meet along the coast somewhere."

"Riverstone?" Ian asked jubilantly.

Riverstone broke in. His com was still on the blink. He leaned close and spoke into Harlowe's SIBA. He was anxious to know more about the attacking ship. "Yeah, I'm alive, Wiz. Do you have your binos handy?"

"Aye, they're around my neck."

With Gamadin optics, Wiz could count the spots on a ladybug's back two miles away and at night, too. "Focus on that ship's banners. Tell me what you see."

Ian described the banners. The top flag was a Phagallian battle flag. The one flying at the top of the aft mast was the one he was interested in. Ian described the open mouthed traa emblazoned on a bright red flag perfectly.

Riverstone turned to Harlowe. "That's the ship, Dog. That's the one that took Lu!" he stated with absolute certainty.

Harlowe returned to Ian. "What's the ship doing now, Wiz?"

"They're waiting, Captain."

"All right. Veg for a while off the north point, out of range of their cannons. We'll swim out to you from the point."

"Aye, Captain," Ian replied.

*   *   *

By the time Harlowe, Riverstone and Mowgi reached the north point of the bay, the attacking ship had dropped anchor. First light was coming over the hills above the beach. The wind was picking up from a storm brewing far out to sea, adding a slight chop to the water. As they stood there, they watched a launch from the ship lower into the water and begin rowing into the shore.

"What are they after?" Riverstone wondered.

"A body," Harlowe replied.

Riverstone stared at Harlowe, dumbfounded. "How do you know?"

"Because I have it." Harlowe went on to explain how Mowgi had led them to the shallow grave in the palm grove. "Who is it?"

"Sharlon. She was slammed in the crash. Lu put her in a SIBA to save her life. She must have figured you would be along in the *Millie* and the clickers would take care of her. Lu must have buried her to protect her from being taken."

Harlowe grabbed Mowgi to settle him down. From the moment the launch left the boat, he'd been jumping around as if he wanted to be released. Four sailors rowed and one steered the tiller in the back. The sailor in the bow directed toward where they were headed. He was tall and slender and tailless. He wore what looked like the finest threads: silky black pants, a light colored shirt with ruffles, a stylish jacket, and a big black hat with plumes of white, pink, and yellow feathers sticking out the top.

"That must be Klagg," Harlowe figured.

Watching the way Klagg strutted from the boat as he led his sailors toward a dense grove of trees, Riverstone made an observation. "Kind of a girlie dude, isn't he? Looks like he stepped out of one of Lu's Fashion Island boutiques."

Harlowe didn't care what Klagg wore. "Let's introduce ourselves."

They removed their SIBA headgear and were transforming into regular-looking beings when Mowgi took off.

*　*　*

The direction Klagg was heading confirmed that the Phagallian captain was on a mission to retrieve Sharlon's body. There could be a million reasons why Klagg wanted the body, but Harlowe didn't care. His only intention was to find Lu and see that she, Sizzle, and everyone else got back inside *Millawanda* before GRB II hit the planet.

The GRB II was the only sure thing Harlowe could count on. Everything else on the trip to Gazz had been one screw-up after another. He would have lost it if he dwelled on how they made it this far. At least Dodger, Monday, Prigg and the cats were safe inside the ship. He didn't have to worry about them.

Right now, Mowgi's taking off without permission was the issue of the moment.

"So what's got the Mowg revved?" Riverstone asked while he and Harlowe made their way through the forest to cut off Klagg and his sailors.

"How would I know?" Harlowe snapped. The thought of showing up to find a bunch of body parts spread all over the forest didn't sit well. He needed to chat with Klagg before Mowgi introduced himself in his usual way.

"He's your pet," Riverstone stated.

"He's no one's pet," Harlowe grunted.

"It would be cool if we found Klagg alive."

"Aye."

"Did you feed him?"

"You know that answer. He feeds himself."

Harlowe was growing irritated by Rivestone's stupid questions until they heard the digging of shovels and picks coming from the grove where Harlowe had found Sharlon. He had expected to hear the sound of the undog wreaking havoc on Klagg and his tails.

When Harlowe and Riverstone peered through the bushes they couldn't believe their eyes. Mowgi was cradled in Klagg's arms, and worse, he was enjoying it!

"Harlowe!" Klagg called out. It wasn't the husky voice of a male being, but a strong feminine one he knew all too well. "Are you here?"

Harlowe wondered if this was a trap like the one back on Og when Unikala had fooled his com by using an exact copy of Quay's DNA makeup. Still, he and Riverstone emerged slowly from the bushes.

The sailors went for their broadswords. "My lady!"

"No, Clann!" Leucadia cried out. "It's okay."

Harlowe walked between the sailors with no regard for their broadswords. "I should have known you wouldn't need rescuing," he said straight out.

"Am I supposed to sit around in a cold, slimy, rat-infested bilge waiting for you to rescue me?"

Harlowe looked into her deep green eyes. They were still bright and full of energy, even in the low morning light. "Yeah, that's exactly what you're supposed to do." He pointed a thumb at his chest. "It makes me look good."

Mowgi slid out of Leucadia's arms. The undog knew enough to leave when sparks were beginning to fly.

Leucadia pushed back her plumes, expecting Harlowe to kiss her. But even though he was relieved she was unharmed, he wasn't in the mood for affection.

"I'm not sucking face with you now," he said, holding her back.

Harlowe faced the two sailors who were prepared to slice him through for being so disrespectful to the Lady Leucadia.

"Don't look so disappointed. We're in a hurry," Harlowe said.

"Do you have—" Leucadia started to say before Harlowe's actions cut her off. The two sailors thrust their swords at Harlowe's midsection. The other two, both with shovels, swung at Riverstone. Before any sailor could understand what was happening, they were all on the ground, eating dirt. Harlowe let fly the blades, sticking them into a nearby tree with a twang. Riverstone simply kept the two shovels to lean on until Harlowe was ready to leave.

Harlowe turned to Leucadia, replying to her question before he led them all back toward the beach. "Yeah, we have Sharlon. She's on the *Millie*."

Lu almost fainted with relief. "Oh, thank God! She'll be all right."

Riverstone helped the sailors to their feet and nodded for them to double-time in behind Harlowe and Leucadia.

"Don't get giddy. It's not what you think." Then from his com, Harlowe ordered, "Wiz, bring the *Millie* back to the bay."

"Is Sharlon alive?" Leucadia asked.

"On life support. Wiz didn't want to risk removing her from the SIBA," Harlowe explained.

Leucadia agreed. "Yes, she must remain that way until *Millawanda* can treat her."

Harlowe was quiet as he stepped up the pace.

Lu could feel the anxiety. "Harlowe, Millie has Sharlon, right?"

"It's not the Millie you know. Sharlon's on the ship you were shooting at coming into the bay."

"That's *Millie*? I don't understand. Where's *Millawanda*?"

Harlowe stopped and faced her. "Millie's down, Lu. Her power was sucked dry by the first gamma burst that was supposed to be a slam-dunk," he said. "She's parked off an island a long way from here, and she's not moving. We've got two weeks to get back to her before the second burst strikes. Do you get the picture?"

"What happens to Gazz?"

Harlowe's face turned grim. "It's not going to make it."

"We can survive inside *Millawanda*?"

"Her hull will protect us even without her shields."

Leucadia's eyes closed sadly. "We can't let Gazz die, Harlowe. We've come this far."

"Look, I'm with you on this, Lu, but Millie's got no power. She's out of gas!"

"No gas?"

"*Nada*. She couldn't jumpstart Baby," Harlowe replied, referring to first car he had before the Daks nuked her in Utah.

Leucadia grabbed his blousy pirate shirt. "There's got to be a way, Harlowe. We can't let that happen!"

Riverstone overheard the discussion and came forward with an idea. "I know where there's a service station."

Harlowe and Leucadia glared at Riverstone. This was no time for jokes.

"It may not mean anything, but when Sharlon and I were on the observation deck looking down at the planet, she was telling me about how she and Anor often went to Gazz to get away from it all."

Harlowe had no interest in vacation stories. "So? What's a Tomarian getaway on a 16th-century planet got to do with gassing up Millie?"

"Sharlon was pointing out a deposit of thermo-grym that Anor had discovered, that's what!" Riverstone continued, "He had big plans to extract the resource, but Sharlon nixed the idea."

Harlowe's eyes rose to the morning sky, as if he was expecting to see one of Anor Ran's cargo ships in the clouds. Riverstone went on. "Sharlon didn't want him screwing up their vacation spot with another business enterprise. She wanted Gazz left alone, and you know who won that argument."

For Harlowe, this information was almost more than he could handle. All of a sudden, the mission had taken on a whole new meaning. "Most people think of a resort for a retreat. That toad thinks of a planet." He turned back to Leucadia. "What do you think? Can it be done?"

"If we have time and enough thermo-grym," Leucadia replied. "But I don't know its properties."

"Wiz does. He used it on Erati to make stuff that blew up," Riverstone replied.

Harlowe was sold. "That works for me."

Leucadia held them up. She had more to say. "You don't understand. *Millawanda* uses a source of power that comes from the Galactic Core, Harlowe. Thermo-grym may be water when she needs nuclear fission just to get her off the ground."

"Fhaal starships use it. They get around pretty well. That's why they slammed Neeja, remember? So did the *Jo-li Ran* and every other ship in the quadrant. They all use thermo-grym to get around."

Leucadia looked to Riverstone for agreement.

"Dog's right, Lu. The quadrant uses it like high-test gas."

Harlowe pointed Leucadia back toward the beach again. "Listen, we've still got a couple of weeks. Between you and Wiz, you'll think of something or..."

Leucadia hustled alongside Harlowe, trying to keep up with his long strides. The feathered plumes on her hat bounced up and down like a bird ready to take flight. "Or what, Harlowe?"

"Or no more vacations," Harlowe replied. Then he added, "At least Simon will be happy to see Sizzle. That will make his day."

When Leucadia did not reply, Harlowe realized that things were not going all that smoothly yet.

"What's happened to Sizzle, Lu?" Harlowe asked.

"It's complicated," Leucadia replied.

Harlowe saw the problem. "She's not onboard your ship, is she?"

"She was taken to Jakaa's palace on Xu. If I don't return with Sharlon, she dies."

They stepped out of the palm grove and onto the beach. Harlowe stated with finality, "Well, she's one of us. We can't leave without her."

*   *   *

The *Millie* was rounding the far southernmost point. She looked grand, gliding across the water in full sail in the morning light. Behind her, on the horizon, the black clouds of a storm were moving toward them. Its fury would not harm them today.

The sailors who came with Leucadia halted as their eyes caught the *Millie's* foresail. The Jolly Roger of the undog's open maw and crossed bats stuck out like a 3-D holograph and made the retroed pirate ship appear like Death coming their way. With hands on her hips, Leucadia looked proudly at her pet's wicked likeness. "If we had seen that, we would have thought twice about firing the warning shot across her bow."

"We haven't made a lot of friends," Harlowe pointed out.

"No doubt," Riverstone said.

Everyone climbed into the launch and began rowing out to meet the *Millie.* Harlowe turned to Riverstone and asked, "Okay, so where's this deposit of thermo-grym, pard?"

There was a long pause as Riverstone's mind appeared to freeze up. Finally, he sighed, "I don't remember."

57

Introductions

Ian and Simon were waiting with joyful hugs for Leucadia, who was back, alive and apparently unharmed. Judging from her white shirt, black trousers, and wide-brimmed hat with fluffy pink feathers, she hadn't suffered at all. Simon had good reason to feel upbeat about Sizzle's fate.

"Where's Sizzle?" He looked over the rail at the launch of Klagg's sailors that was rowing back to their ship. "Where's Sizzle, Lu? Was she with you on the ship?" Simon glanced at Harlowe. "Let's go get her, Captain!"

"Hold on, Rerun," Harlowe said, pushing Simon back by his shoulders. "Let Lu speak."

Leucadia's eyes lost their glow as she told Simon the same story she had recounted with Harlowe. "I'm sorry, Simon, that's all I know. She's been taken to the Emperor's palace at Xu." She took him by the hand. "Rest assured, Sizzle is alive and in good health."

Simon pounded his fist against the main mast as he paced back and forth in an anxious dance. "But for how long? She's a hot babe in the middle of a bunch of medieval thugs, Lu. Where's my *real* pistol? I'll put a plas-round through that Emperor's head tonight!"

Harlowe quickly pulled Simon aside. "Watch your mouth, Mister!" he scolded.

Simon was shaking, he was so angry. "But Skipper—"

"No but's. You keep the planet stuff to yourself." Harlowe looked at all the puzzled faces of his Gazzian crew to see if anything Simon had said about the planet or plas weapons had any effect. The entire crew seemed much more interested in Leucadia than in anything Simon had to say.

Harlowe pointed Simon toward the quarterdeck. "Go to my cabin, Mr. Bolt. We'll talk there." Simon tried to protest. He had a ton of questions to ask Leucadia. "Leave her alone. That's an order."

Simon stood rigid. He wasn't going anywhere until he had answers.

This was no time for revolt. Harlowe stepped between his First Mate and Leucadia and firmly pointed again. "I said that's an order, Mister." His voice was low and unemotional but filled with resolve.

Simon tried to match wills with Harlowe, but it was no contest. Simon's concern was for an individual. Harlowe's was for a planet, a ship, a family, and a crew. Reluctantly, Simon blinked. "Aye, Skipper."

Watching Simon trudge away was difficult. If Leucadia had still been captive, he would have felt the same way. With one problem on hold, Harlowe crossed the main deck to his Gazzian crew, who were standing around Leucadia like she was a movie star.

"You are hot, My Lady," Zinger said, bowing deeply.

"A rather cool babe, wouldn't you say, Mr. Catch?" Homerun said.

"Indeed, Mr. Homerun, very rad indeed," Catch answered.

Harlowe thought Shortstop would never breathe again. "Are you the Captain's doe, My Lady?"

Leucadia looked at Harlowe with a hint of laughter in her eyes. "Speaking SoCal, are we, Captain?"

Harlowe could think of nothing particularly witty for a comeback. "Picked it all up on their own, My Lady," continuing to play the part. He turned to his Gazzian First Mate, knowing how he would answer. "Isn't that right, Mr. Pitch?"

"Cool, Captain," Pitch answered, right on cue.

Leucadia laughed so hard, she snorted.

Harlowe made the proper introductions with all their baseball monikers. Leucadia then leaned over to Harlowe and asked discreetly, "Are they sailors or ballplayers?"

Harlowe turned to his Gazzian crew. They were dressed in fresh sailor's uniforms and had clean faces and playful tails. "They may not look like it, but they can sail circles around an armada of Phagallian ships."

Leucadia could see that Harlowe's captainly pride was genuine and full of love. "You really do care for them."

Harlowe wrinkled his nose. He turned away briefly to wipe his eye. "I wouldn't be standing here with you if it weren't for them."

The Gazzian crew continued to stare at the tall Croomis female with eyes that sparkled like the jewels of the Emperor's crown. Shortstop said, "It is a custom that I must sleep with my savior's lady to protect her."

Harlowe grabbed Shortstop by the belt and scooted him off. "Away with you, Mr. Shortstop. If there's anything My Lady doesn't need, it's protection."

Zinger then saw his opportunity while Harlowe was busy with Shortstop. He took Leucadia's hand, and with his crooked teeth pointing in several directions, grinned. "My Lady. I have never held the hand of a goddess."

"I am honored, sir," Leucadia said, smiling graciously.

Harlowe warned Zinger that Leucadia was no ordinary female. "This female could wrestle a traa, Mr. Zinger, and turn it into a pretzel."

Zinger didn't know what a pretzel was, but he did understand that if My Lady could best a traa, the precaution was well-advised. "Cool, Captain. Your counsel is duly noted." Harlowe could see from Zinger's smirk that his warning had fallen upon deaf ears.

*   *   *

Simon confronted Harlowe as soon as he stepped through the cabin door. "We know where she is, Skipper. She's only a few days sailing from here. We could get her. You know we could!"

"We can't, Rerun," Harlowe began, shutting the door behind him so that no ears but the undog's could hear their conversation. The last thing he wanted to do was pull rank on his First Mate in front of his crew. He preferred the common sense approach in matters of the heart. As much as Harlowe wanted to find Sizzle, saving *Millawanda* had to be everyone's top priority.

"If it was Lu, what would you do?" Simon countered.

"I would be running down the beach to Jakaa's palace right now. But then, I'd hope you or Riverstone would pound some sense into my head."

Simon pleaded for Harlowe's sympathy. "I can't let her die, Skipper, not when she's this close to me."

Jewels brought them two tall glasses of Blue Stuff. Harlowe needed a long swallow before answering. It had been a long day and it didn't appear his Gamadin-to-Gamadin talk with Simon was going as well as he had hoped. Simon needed something besides recycled SIBA water to get his head straight. "She won't die, Rerun."

"Let me go after her alone, then."

Harlowe handed Simon a glass of Blue Stuff.

"No thanks."

Harlowe shoved it in front of his face. "Drink it."

"Is that an order?"

"We both need it." Harlowe held it out a second time and Simon took the glass, but he did not drink. Harlowe continued. "Gazz is our mission, Rerun. You know that. If we go after Sizzle, we might save her from Jakaa, but then what? The planet's toast, and so are we if don't get Millie up and running. Now you tell me, what would Captain Starr do?"

Simon watched the Phagallian ship drift past the open window hatch. The sea had a slight chop from the northeasterly wind. Harlowe's plan was to allow the ship to go free, but only after taking the galleon's sails. After the last storm, the *Millie* had no spare sheets. With another storm on the horizon, sailing without spares would be suicide. The Phagallian galleon had only its upper mizzen sheets. The ship would make it home, just not very quickly. In the meantime, the *Millie* would stay out of sight of land until they decide what to do next to repower *Millawanda*. Harlowe wouldn't say it to his face, but Simon's problem was minor compared to Riverstone's amnesia. His memory had to be jogged somehow, or they would be drifting on a ghost ship forever.

Simon took a short sip of Blue Stuff before he asked, "What do you think our chances are, Dog?"

"Depends on Riverstone. If he remembers where the thermo-grym deposit is, we're better than 50-50. If he doesn't, we're sprouting wings."

"So every living thing on this planet, including us, depends on Riverstone's brain?"

Harlowe took another long drink. "Looks like it."

Relaxed from the calming effects of the Blue Stuff and exhausted from the emotional strain, Simon sat in a nearby chair. "Jester doesn't look so good, Skipper."

"I hear ya, Rerun. As much as we've been through, he's been through more."

"More?"

"The *Jo-li Ran* was blown out from under him. He survived a solo reentry to the planet and was nailed by lightning... TWICE on the way down! He woke up in a thorn bush, ran flat out for a hundred miles to the coast to save Lu, and got nuked trying to rescue her and Sizzle." Harlowe said, making sure he emphasized Sizzle's name for effect. "After that, he was nursed back to life by a hot babe, then he got captured and tossed onto a slave boat. He managed to escape that, but then Jakaa's thugs recaptured him again and tortured him. He was strung up to fry in the hot sun when I found him."

Simon swallowed another gulp. "I didn't realize..."

Harlowe wasn't done. "It gets worse. When we heard the *Millie* was being fired upon, he couldn't even give the hot babe a proper send-off. So give him a break."

Simon met Harlowe's eyes, acknowledging the fact that Riverstone had the edge when it came to bad luck. Nevertheless, the thought of everyone's existence resting on the hope that his memory would kick in soon was discouraging.

Harlowe clinked his glass of Blue Stuff with Simon's and added with a confident wink, "Don't worry, Rerun. Jester's a Gamadin. What he went through since coming to Gazz was a walk in the park compared to Erati. Give him a little time. He'll remember."

Simon nodded. What he saw down in the depths of Erati was the worst hell imaginable and Riverstone had survived it. He finished his drink and put the glass on the table. "Aye. Let's get her done, Captain. I want my girl back!"

"Me too, and my ship."

"Is that all, Skipper?"

"Yeah, we're done."

Watching Simon leave the cabin, Harlowe recognized how much he hurt. He felt like falling on the floor and crying himself on occasion, but he didn't have the time. The only remedy he knew for Simon was staying focused on the mission: save their ship, the planet, and his girl-friend. Now that Leucadia, Sharlon, and Riverstone were back, Sizzle was the only one left. But, the way Leucadia's mood changed when he brought up her name meant something peculiar was going on.

He yawned, making a mental note to ask her about that later. Whatever it was, it could wait until he got some sleep. His eyes drifted lazily toward his hammock hanging on the side of the bulkhead. Wiz could handle the *Millie's* departure. He finished off his Blue Stuff, handed his glass to Jewels, and was about to reintroduce himself to his hammock when Leucadia entered the room.

From the way she leaned against the door as she closed it behind her, threw the latch, and smiled as she turned toward him, Harlowe understood she had not come for conversation. Her glowing green eyes never left him as she removed her pink-plumed hat and placed it on Jewel's triangular-shaped head. She unclipped a jeweled silver barrette from her hair, shook her head, and released her long hair. Even in the muted candlelight of the cabin, it glowed with a soft gold sheen as it tumbled down past her shoulders. Still looking at him, she wet her lips, leaned back against the door, and beckoned for him to come to her. "Miss me?"

"Like a traa," he answered, walking on toward his hammock.

Leucadia stopped him mid-stride, took his arm and turned him toward her. As they drew closer together, she looked up into his tired blue eyes. "Wrong answer, Pylott."

They kissed passionately and fell against the wall. Unable to stand, they fell to the floor, holding each other like they would never let go. Jewels deftly moved away while they rolled across the cabin, oblivious to everything around them.

They slammed against the center table and knocked over chairs. They might have destroyed the cabin entirely had there not come a pounding on the cabin door. "Captain!" Ian voice's cried out.

*   *   *

Ian thought about breaking the door down out of fear that something was wrong—Harlowe's door was always open and now it was locked. Finally, Ian's constant pounding and calling out worked. Harlowe opened the door and stood there. His white shirt was open and its laces torn like ties ripped from their moorings. Leucadia stood slightly behind him, fixing her hair.

Ian felt embarrassed. "Sorry."

"What is it?" Harlowe asked, anticipating that Ian had made a breakthrough with Riverstone's memory.

He knew it was something else as soon as he saw Ian's somber face. "Monday's in trouble, Captain. His com's dead."

Harlowe noticed a gauntlet Ian held in his hand. It wasn't Pitch's. This one was much larger and its spikes were twice as long. "Whose is that?"

Ian held up the gauntlet, careful not to cut himself on the sharp pointed spikes.

"It's Klagg's," Leucadia said, wrapping her hair back above her head.

Ian added. "The Phagallian captain is challenging you for Lu. He won't let you take her without a fight."

The pinkness drained from Lu's overheated cheeks. "He's not what you think."

Harlowe took one last glimpse of his hammock before walking out the door with Ian.

58

Klagg

It was well past noon. All five Gazzian moons were looking down upon Klagg and his crew, who were waiting on the beach. He had arrived with five boats carrying two dozen creepy Phagallian sailors. If Harlowe thought he would dust his opponent quickly and return to his ship to join Leucadia, he had another think coming. The beastly Phagallian captain was enormous. It was going to be a long afternoon.

Harlowe's entourage was less impressive. He arrived on one boat. Shortstop was his second. Pitch and Zinger did the rowing. The undog got a belly laugh from the Phagallians when he jumped out of the launch.

Klagg and his crowd stopped their jeering when Zinger held out his tail for Leucadia, who stepped gracefully onto the beach. There was no doubt in anyone's mind that she was the prize. No one laughed as she walked gently to Harlowe's side while the pink plumes of her hat fluttered in the soft afternoon breeze. Their appreciation of her did not go unnoticed by Harlowe. The way they gazed at her, she was a Gall Moon goddess of the highest order. Klagg, however, had only one thing in mind. She was to be his and his alone. Not even Jakaa's wealth could buy her.

Klagg ignored Harlowe the way he'd ignore an insect. His rage-filled eyes had followed Leucadia all the way from the launch until she stopped beside Harlowe.

"He's bigger than the General," Harlowe said, observing the Phagallian from fifty feet across the sand.

Leucadia spoke softly into Harlowe's ear. "I said Klagg was different."

Klagg was easily seven feet and twice Harlowe's weight. His arms were as thick as Harlowe's legs and his hand could wrap Harlowe's fist, with plenty to spare. To call Klagg a beast was kind. He reminded Harlowe of the pictures he had seen of Big Foot back on Earth. Only on this planet, Big Foot wanted his girl, had a thick leathery tail, and wore boots.

"Is he any good?" Harlowe asked.

Pitch answered for the crew. "He has never been bested, Captain."

Harlowe continued to survey his opponent, looking for a weakness. *The general who wins a battle makes many calculations in his temple before the battle is fought, says Sun Tzu*. Right now, however, Harlowe was too exhausted to find a useful calculation in his brain or anywhere else.

"How did you survive those toads?" Harlowe tried to fight off the stench that drifted over from the pack of filth and wickedness. The sour body odors of the Phagallians made the air of the rodent-infested Horritan City on Gibb smell like a fresh spring day.

"Long story," Leucadia replied.

Harlowe glanced at her. "I want to hear it."

"Now?"

"I might decide to give you back."

Now it was Leucadia's turn to stare at Harlowe. "You're not serious?"

Whether Harlowe was serious or not, his face displayed no tales. "If I'm going to fight for your honor, first I need to know that your reputation hasn't been sullied."

"You have to ask such a stupid question?"

He looked accusingly at her. "Yes, I do! How do I know what happened between you two? Captivitiy does strange things to the head. Look at you. Nice threads, nice hat. Not so bad considering you crash-landed here with nothing. You might have struck some secret deal that I don't know about. It's happened before, you know."

"Harlowe Pylott! Why you—" Leucadia shouted before Klagg interrupted.

"Leave the Lady Mar or die, Croomis!" Klagg cried out as he stepped out in front of his crew.

Harlowe pointed a hot finger at Klagg. "Quiet, butthead, I'm talking to my girlfriend!" He turned back to Leucadia. "Lady Mar, is it? What kind of garbage is that? Lady Maaarrr. Ain't that sweet? Doesn't he know your real name?"

"He didn't want it. He had one all picked out for me," she replied as she smiled at the giant Phagallian captain. "Didn't you, Klaggy?"

Klagg tried to speak, but Harlowe went ballistic over their seemingly cozy relationship. "That does it! Klaggy? I've never heard such a stupid name in my life!" Harlowe looked at Klagg. "You let her call you Klaggy?"

Klagg didn't know what to think. Again, he tried to respond but it was Leucadia's turn to go ballistic.

"You're not my keeper, Pylott! If I want to call him Klaggy, that's my business, not yours. You don't own me and don't try to control me either, or that's it!"

"That's what? Is that a threat?"

"Maybe!"

Harlowe bent down, face-to-face with her, his eyes shooting hot plas rounds through her head and her eyes shooting green daggers back at him. Even Harlowe's own crew was worried. They had come to see a battle between two captains, not two lovers.

"Well, that's sweet! Breaking up with you would save me a ton of problems! It would make my job a lot easier, too, if you went with Klaggy." Harlowe pointed a thumb at himself. "I have a world to save, you know. I don't have time for this nonsense."

Leucadia looked Harlowe in the eye. "So what are we doing here on the beach, then? Let's get going, Pylott."

Harlowe held up Klagg's gauntlet. "Because the dude over there threw this at my ship and I have to fight him or I look like a toad in front of you and my crew." Harlowe looked at Pitch, Zinger, and Shortstop. "Is that right, Mr. Pitch?"

"Cool, Captain, you have been challenged," Pitch agreed.

Harlowe glanced over at Klagg, who seemed dumbfounded by the whole exchange. "See? This is all your fault," Harlowe said to Leucadia.

"You're not laying this one on me, Harlowe!"

"Oh, yes, I am! You're trouble. Now I have to waste my time with that dude over there instead of getting Riverstone's brain straight and looking for thermo-grym."

Leucadia threw her arms around Harlowe's neck. She kissed him, then said in a low, intimate voice, "Enough talk, Pylott. Let's get out of here."

Harlowe's teeth clenched, setting his jaw. "Yes, dear..."

*   *   *

Klagg watched the Croomis captain make his way toward him and his sailors, alone and unarmed. Was the Croomis captain foolish? No one in the empire had ever defeated him on land or sea! With one swath of his tail, he could snap the boy's head from his shoulders without laying a hand on him. This beautiful prize would be his in any case, whether he killed him outright or sliced his body into traa feed. He sighed heavily. Her scent drifted across the sand. It was the most powerful attraction he had ever felt. He was addicted to her. She was like the light of the Gall Moon. Her light had magically transformed him into her slave forever.

Fortunately, the Emperor had eyes for the other Croomis woman Klagg had captured with the Lady Mar. If Klagg returned with the Croomis treasure intact, Jakaa would reward him with the Lady Mar as his prize.

Early in her capture he had tried touching her, believing she was like the other Croomis females. Since he was the master, she must allow him to feel her energy with his or she would suffer the punishment of a hundred whips. That is the way with all captives. But when he approached, wrapping his tail around her body, her eyes became bright as the Gall moon radiating down from the heavens. Without warning, he was abruptly slammed to the planks of his cabin floor and left looking up at an open hatch of stars.

The Gall Moon remained in her eyes as he was exiled from his own cabin, never to return unless he wished to burn in the bowels of Moharr.

Not wishing to soil his own appendage over the Croomis, Klagg would allow his crew the pleasure of killing the Croomis boy as he entered the ring of combat drawn in the sand. To Klagg's great astonishment, however, the Croomis captain disposed of the Phagallian crewmen as if they were mere deckhands.

"Just you and me, Klaggy. No one else," the Croomis boy said, as he continued walking in a straight line toward the center of the ring.

"Die, Croomis!" Klagg roared just before he charged. Klagg snapped his spiked-tipped appendage toward the Croomis' head.

His first assault missed the Croomis boy as if he were made of fog. Harlowe escaped the tail, but Klagg's fist caught the boy's foot as he leaped over Klagg's head and landed hard on the sand. Before the boy could recover, Klagg kicked Harlowe in the side, lifting him high in the air. A normal being should have folded with ribs broken in several places. The boy was as tough as mast wood. He landed on his feet, ready to continue the battle.

Whipping his appendage again at the boy, Klagg tried to snag any part of his body that he could. He found nothing but air.

Klagg bellowed with rage at his failure to land a single spike anywhere on the boy's nimble body. Two, three, four times Harlowe slapped Klagg across the face, then the Croomis boy struck the beastly Captain across the jaw, sending him to his knees. Klagg had never been struck with such power.

The boy backed off and allowed Klagg's crew to help him stand. After a wobbly start, Klagg pushed his crew away. "Get away from me!"

For a moment Klagg's vision lacked direction. Klagg stumbled toward the center of the ring and lashed his tail out wildly at what he thought was the boy. Suddenly, Klagg's tail was caught by an unbelieveable force and held fast. Harlowe yanked Klagg by his tail and said, "Lights out, Klaggy!" They were the last words Klagg heard from the Croomis boy.

59

Riverstone's Brain

It had been a rough three days for Riverstone. The first thing Leucadia did was put him in a warm tub of seawater to soak the crusty grime from his body. Before his rear touched the bottom of the tub, he was sound asleep. Riverstone can sleep later, Harlowe said to Leucadia, as he entered the cabin. He wanted Riverstone up and searching for deposits of thermo-grym now. There would be plenty of time to rest later, when they were all safe. But Leucadia stood guard like a mother hen and wouldn't let Riverstone be disturbed by anyone, not even the Captain.

"Go away, Harlowe," Leucadia said, standing firm outside the sheet that split off the tub from the rest of Harlowe's cabin. She called him "Captain" when they were on the clock or in front of the crew, but in private moments like this, it was always Harlowe. She never called him Dog. She considered that moniker a guy thing. She was *not* one of the guys!

She turned Harlowe around and shooed him out the door. "Matthew must rest, one more night. In the morning, you can wake him." She shut the door behind him, locking him out of his own quarters.

Ian had a belly laugh. "Should I make room in the officers quarters?"

The frustration on Harlowe's face could have stopped a traa. "Say anything more and I'll have you swinging from the yardarms, Mr. Wizzixs!"

Shortstop didn't understand why the Captain was being thrown out of his own quarters, but he did have a solution for his lady's insolence. He handed Harlowe a leather whip with several long strands of braided strips. "For punishing the Croomis Lady, Captain."

Harlowe gratefully took the cat-o'-nine-tails from his helpful crewman. "Thanks, Shortstop, that's exactly what she needs." He slapped the whip against the side of his leg as he strode away toward the main deck. "Next time she steps out of line," he mumbled to himself. "I'll put it to good use."

Then he tossed the whip overboard. Ian was still chuckling.

*   *   *

A wet-headed Riverstone stepped out from behind his makeshift washroom and nearly lost his balance when the ship leaned suddenly to port. The early morning view out the window was of fluffy pink and yellow clouds against a soft blue-green sky. The salt air felt cool and refreshing. Not far off the bow, a fog bank was rolling in, which explained why the *Millie* made the sudden shift in tack. She was changing course to avoid sailing blindly into the grey soup.

Riverstone turned and saw Leucadia sitting at the center table in the room, making adjustments to Ian's com. Millie made another deep turn through low rolling waves, nearly spilling a glass of Blue Stuff on the table. Next to the glass were a half-eaten burger and a full tray of untouched golden fries. The sounds of the ship continued—the creaking wood, the stretching of the rigging, the fluttering of the sheets pulling tight against the gathering wind, and always in the background, the ship's crew calling out orders. "Tighten that mizzen line, Mr. Zinger! Lower away cheerily, Mr. Catch! Look alive there on the forecastle, Mr. Shortstop! Aye, aye, Mr. Pitch!"

Riverstone could barely control himself. "Is this for real?" he asked Leucadia as he stared at the thin strips of yellow potatoes.

Her eyes never leaving the device, Leucadia pushed the tray of food across the table to Riverstone. "It's cold, though."

Riverstone grabbed the burger and fries and stuffed them into his mouth as if he hadn't eaten in a month. For a young man raised on SoCal animal style double-doubles and Alfonso's tacos, the edibles were more valuable than Jakaa's treasures. "I don't care if it's sitting on ice. How does Harlowe do it?"

Riverstone nearly cried when Jewels appeared out of nowhere with a tray of fresh hot double-decker burgers, fries, and a tall glass of chilled Blue Stuff and laid it on the table.

"He never leaves *Millawanda* without him," Leucadia remarked of Jewels. At any other time it might have been a joke. Her concentration on the device left no room for levity.

Riverstone glanced out the window. "What's our course?"

Leucadia looked up. "Away from the fog."

"What then? What's his plan?" Riverstone asked, referring to Harlowe.

The stare of Leucadia's green eyes made him uncomfortable. "He's waiting for you," she replied.

"Me?" Riverstone replied, as he unlocked his jaws and devoured half a hamburger in a single bite.

Right on cue, the heavy wooden door of the cabin opened. Harlowe and Ian came striding in.

"He's up!" Ian said, going to the table to see what Leucadia was doing to his com.

Harlowe glared at Leucadia. "Mind if we talk to him now?"

With a sour smirk, Leucadia gave her blessing. "He's all yours, Captain."

Riverstone was about to down another massive morsel of heaven when Harlowe stopped him. "You can eat later."

Riverstone agonized over the uneaten burger as if denying it was a fate worse than death. "I was just getting started."

"Later." The seriousness in Harlowe's tone left little doubt that Riverstone was back on the clock.

"Yes, sir."

Harlowe turned to Leucadia and Ian, the two brainiacs in the room. "Where do we start?"

Ian went first. "We need to find enough thermo-grym for Millawanda to leave the planet."

"How much is that?" Harlowe questioned.

"A hundred tons should do for a start." Harlowe and Riverstone nearly gagged, but Ian wasn't joking. The amount was so large, it sounded like a prank. He looked toward Leucadia for validation. She nodded her agreement.

Harlowe never dreamed it would take so much thermo-grym to power his ship. "The *Millie* doesn't weigh that much."

Leucadia had a compromise. "It's possible we could use five or six tons to get her off the island. We could then fly her to the deposit to pick up the rest. Kinda like putting an emergency can of gas in the tank until we get to the nearest station."

Ian agreed. "Yeah, that would work."

Harlowe wasn't happy. "So what if the gas station is a thousand miles inland? The clickers couldn't handle that much on a good day. It won't be sitting on the docks ready for us to pick up."

"That will be a problem," Ian admitted. "We need to know where the deposit is first."

All eyes at once went to Riverstone. "I've been trying, Captain," he said.

Harlowe saw his strain. "Nobody's saying you're not, Matt. Somehow we need to figure out how to get that head of yours firing on all cylinders." He turned to Leucadia. "He's your patient. Any ideas?"

Leucadia forced a smile. "A couple."

"How 'bout one that works?"

Leucadia lifted the com she had been working on and put it at the edge of the table. "When Sharlon pointed out the deposit, where were you?" she asked Riverstone.

Whenever he was recalling a moment alone with Sharlon, Riverstone saw the past clearly. "We were orbiting Gazz, standing on the observation deck."

Leucadia touched the com and a holographic image of Gazz appeared above the table. "This is what the planet looks like from a thousand-mile orbit. Anything look familiar?"

Riverstone cocked his head, trying to get the right angle. The view wasn't quite right. With his hands he shrank the globe, turning it around in several directions. Still, he couldn't get a fix on what he had seen when Sharlon pointed out the deposit, mainly because he had his eyes on her instead of the planet.

Leucadia walked over to the globe. "I saw the planet, too." With her fingers, she turned it completely around so the north pole was now the south pole, then turned Gazz on its axis another twenty degrees with a slight touch of her fingers. "How does that look?"

Riverstone's eyes widened. "That's it! That's what it looked like!" He stepped away from the globe to get a better perspective. He pointed to the exact spot where Sharlon had told him the deposit was located, right there on the massive black mountain in the northern hemisphere. "That's it. I'm sure of it. That's the mountain where Anor wanted to dig."

Riverstone turned toward his friends, happy that he finally remembered the location. No one else looked as happy.

"What's the problem? That's it, I tell you. That's the place. Look! There is even a river we can use to transport the yellow stuff back to the *Millie*," Riverstone pointed out.

Harlowe went to the nearest window to take in some fresh air. If he was twenty-one, he might have wished for an adult beverage. "Show him, Wiz."

Ian went to the globe and pointed to the black mountain. "Here's where we need to go." He turned the planet a hundred and thirty degrees around and flipped the globe over. "This is where we are now."

"Where's *Millie*?" Riverstone asked.

Ian retraced 40 degrees and pointed just below the equator. "Here. That island."

"That's a long way in a sailboat," Riverstone admitted.

"We'll never make it before the burst hits," Ian stated. "It would take us a year to make the voyage, even with the turbines and a good wind."

Harlowe remained silent. He stood grimly at the window, his attention focused more on what was going on outside the window than what was being said around the table.

"Would anyone like to hear my second idea?" Leucadia asked the room.

Harlowe returned from the window. He had learned a long time ago that when Leucadia had an idea, it was wise to pay attention. Her brain didn't function like a normal human being's. She was, in fact, only half-human. The alien side of her thoughts raced along at light speed, and not even Wiz could keep up. Harlowe always deferred to her better judgment.

This time, however, it wasn't a question of wanting to hear her second idea or not. The twenty-cannon boom of a ship firing at the *Millie* meant her other idea had to wait.

"BATTLE STATIONS!" Harlowe shouted, as he sprinted for the doorway.

60

Battle on the High Seas

The first broadside caught the *Millie* by surprise. The cannonballs blasted a hole through the fore topgallant and shattered the bow rigging. Mowgi had seen the broadside coming and took flight before the cannonballs hit. They were lucky. Homerun's tail was nearly blown off while he was hanging from the mizzen yard and loosening more sail. They needed speed, and lots of it, if they were going survive the six Phagallian galleons bearing down upon them from out of the fog.

"ALL SAILS ABROAD, MR. PITCH!" Harlowe yelled as he ran out of his cabin. "Clamp those hatchways, Mr. Catch!" he barked, from the quarterdeck.

"Cool, Captain!" his crew shouted back as they scampered up the rigging to the yards to drop sails.

Leucadia joined in as if she was part of the crew. "Bring in that jib line, Mr. Zinger," she ordered from the main deck. "Make it tight!"

There was a slight hesitation on Zinger's part. Taking orders from a female Croomis was not part of his job description. Harlowe quickly resolved the dilemma.

"Do it, Mr. Zinger, or we'll both be sleeping with the traas tonight," Harlowe ordered.

Zinger bolted to action, as did the rest of the crew. It was the last time Harlowe had to give that order.

Harlowe pushed Shortstop away from the steerage wheel to help Homerun roll the *Millie* to port. The *Millie's* bow responded crisply, bringing the ship around for a broadside of her own.

"Mr. Bolt! How are we looking on the starboard cannon? Did you wake the clickers?" Harlowe asked.

"Aye, Captain, awake and ramming in shot and powder. Starboard cannon is locked and loaded, Skipper," Simon shouted back.

"Very well, Mr. Bolt."

Harlowe glanced to his right as the *Millie* made her turn. Her sails filled again, she picked up speed, and ran straight and true, crashing through waves as if she were twice her size. At the same moment, the crew dropped the top mainsail, mizzen and foresail to increase their speed. The *Millie* was now at full sail. Harlowe joined the undog at the bow, where he could watch the first Phagallian galleon coming at them at top speed. The ship was huge, many times the size of the *Millie*. If the galleon struck her, there was no doubt the *Millie* was going to the bottom.

"Ready to starboard, Mr. Bolt!" Harlowe shouted over his shoulder.

"She's ready, Captain!" came Simon's reply.

Leucadia had joined Catch at the steerage wheel when Harlowe went to the bow. She leaned closer to the Gazzian so he could hear her clearly. "Steady now, Mr. Catch. See how the Phagallian lists? She can't fire until her gunports are level. She'll have to right herself for a broadside. When she does, we steer the *Millie* into the wind and give the Phagallians one of our own before she has time to get set."

The silence broke. "Now, Captain!" Leucadia called out. She and Catch forced the wheel over, and the *Millie* righted herself. Diving into the wind broke her forward motion just before the Phagallians heaved to and fired.

"GIVE 'EM A BROADSIDE, MR. BOLT!" Harlowe shouted to the main deck gunports.

BOOM! BOOM! BOOM!

All ten cannons fired in succession.

Exploding balls ripped through the first Phagallian ship. Her masts snapped while her bulkheads and planking exploded into splintered pieces and torn sails toppled onto screaming crewmembers who were running from the debris.

Harlowe grabbed a line and swung over to the quarterdeck. He paused to wave to his gunnery crewmen, who were already cheering loudly at their achievement. "Well done, mates!" he shouted down to them. Turning back to Leucadia, he pointed. "Put our *Millie* on a port tack, if you please, Ms. Mars. Catch that breeze, and when that Phagallian dog is clear, we'll do it again."

"Aye, Captain," Leucadia called back. "To port it is!"

The *Millie* surged forward with her sails full and picked up speed. A second Phallagian ship was behind the burning first ship. There was no clear shot yet. *Millie* had to veer around the first ship and make her pivot.

The unexpected roar of a broadside thundered from behind the first Phagallian ship and echoed across the water. More yards broke and masts fell from the first ship. The second ship didn't spare the first ship. It was using the damaged galleon for cover while it fired on the *Millie*.

Leucadia dove at Harlowe, throwing him down on the deck just before a chain ball whizzed by close enough to tear off his head. The steerage wheel took the impact, when the twisting chain tethered to cannonballs tore through the top spokes and rim.

Harlowe winked his thanks, lifted Leucadia up, and kissed her quickly on the lips. There was little time for more. They checked the wheel for damage. The bow of the *Millie* was heading directly for the first ship, and if they were no longer able to steer, they'd be toast!

They quickly removed the broken pieces. Leucadia tried turning the splintered, half-moon wheel hard about. When the bow of the *Millie* followed, she announced, "We still have steerage, Captain."

"Sweet!"

In the brief minutes it took them to regain control, the *Millie* had drifted off course. Harlowe looked up to see the first Phallagian ship looming dead ahead. A collision seemed unavoidable. With Harlowe's assistance, Leucadia pulled the wheel hard over and not a moment too soon. The *Millie* scraped the first ship's port bow, taking rigging with it from both vessels.

A dozen Phagallian sailors, however, saw the opportunity for revenge. They leaped the narrow gap between the two ships and began swinging their broadswords at the Millie's defenseless crew.

Simon was too busy reloading the starboard cannon to notice the boarders. Ian saw them but was too far away to stop them. Pitch and Fastball had to confront the marauders by themselves. They grabbed cutlasses and hatchets from the deck racks, and greeted the trespassers two-against-twelve. Clearly it was a mismatch, but before they could thrust a single blade into their bellies, Harlowe and Riverstone swung from the yards with pistols drawn. Harlowe cut down four boarders with his modified flintlock before he reached the landing in the midst of the fray. In the ensuing hand-to-hand encounter, the attackers proved no match for the Gamadin. With high-flying kicks and hammer-like fists, they snapped necks with a single blow. Bodies fell as Harlowe and Riverstone cut through the boarders like chainsaws. Pitch and Fastball quickly backed off, stunned by the

ferocity of their Captain and his Croomis friend ripping apart the mob of attackers. They needed no assistance. Mowgi finished the final two boarders when he tore out the chest of one and bit off the head of the other.

Covered with blood of the trespassers, Harlowe turned to Pitch and Fastball. "Get them off my ship."

Still in shock, Pitch and Fastball leapt into action as if Harlowe's orders had been given by the gods themselves.

Riverstone helped with the disposal while Harlowe charged across to the quarterdeck, yelling to Simon as he ran. "Ready to port, Mr. Bolt?"

Simon turned to Harlowe, "Aye, Cap—." Only then, watching Riverstone, Pitch and Fastball heave bodies overboard, did he suddenly realize that he had missed the entire action. Simon didn't need an explanation. He had seen Harlowe's work once before, when he disposed of Sar and his Daks at Og.

No mercy.

"Port cannons ready, Captain!" Simon confirmed.

"Mr. Wizzixs?" Harlowe called out.

"Ready here, Captain." Harlowe bounded up the quarterdeck ladder to rejoin Leucadia and Shortstop.

The second ship was reloading its cannons while she turned to bring her starboard cannons in position for another broadside at the *Millie*. During her gradual turn downwind, however, she exposed her stern to the *Millie's* fire.

"She'll be out of range," Leucadia warned.

Harlowe had to focus not only on the second ship, but also on the third and fourth, which were now coming into range. He could ignore the fifth and sixth for the time being, because both were out of range, even for the *Millie's* enhanced cannons.

"We've made some adjustments," Harlowe said. "Steady as she goes."

Harlowe went to the rail. "We're coming around, mates! Be ready. Mr. Wizzixs! You're up next. I want that second ship nuked on the first broadside."

Ian lifted a thumb's up toward the quarterdeck. "You got it, Captain!" Then he returned to his cannon and finished sighting in on his target.

Harlowe turned to Simon. "Split your broadside, Mr. Bolt. Blow the masts off three and four. Let's see how good a shot you really are."

"A pleasure, Skipper!"

With almost a mile between them, the captain of the second ship could afford to be smug. After all, against a smaller ship like the *Millie*, he knew he had the advantage since, by all measures, they should have been far out of range. Harlowe saw the ship swing its stern around. He dropped his hand and Leucadia turned the wheel. The *Millie* went still, giving Ian a steady plane from which to shoot.

"Show them what it means to mess with our *Millie*, Mr. Wizzixs! FIRE!" Harlowe yelled.

BOOM! BOOM! BOOM!

"Twenty points to starboard, Ms. Mars!" Harlowe directed before the smoke had cleared.

"Twenty points to starboard, Captain!" Leucadia called back.

"Fire when you're ready, Mr. Bolt!"

While Simon jumped from cannon to cannon, making sure they were primed and ready, the second ship exploded. The enormous shock wave knocked Harlowe, Leucadia, and Shortstop off their feet.

Leucadia helped Harlowe up. "What was that?" he asked as they surveyed the damage that was done. Looking out over the water, the second ship had vaporized, and the third and fourth ships were in flames and sinking fast nearly a half-mile away. The other two ships were racing back into the safe invisibility of the fog. The battle was over.

61

The Second Idea

It was near midnight. Leucadia climbed the quarterdeck ladder and joined Harlowe at the wheel. To keep herself warm, she was wearing an animal hair coat she'd found in Harlowe's quarters. She preferred it to her SIBA because it was dark and thick and was oversized like her father's dark blue peacoat that she used to wear for fun when she was a little girl. It was also comfortable and toasty like a couch blanket, and it smelled old like the sea.

She handed Harlowe a hot tin of something close to cocoa to help fight the chilly air. "Want some company?" she asked.

Harlowe gratefully accepted the warm drink. "Sure."

She shifted around next to him and he put his arm around her shoulders. "Better?" he asked.

"Much," she replied, snuggling closer.

She fiddled with the SIBA that Harlowe wore beneath his shirt. "Do you ever take it off?" she asked, looking up at him with her bright green eyes that glowed as if they had absorbed all the light in the heavens.

"Once," Harlowe answered, "and I hurled my guts out."

Leucadia giggled. "My big brave sea captain gets seasick?"

"It's awkward."

"Any word from Monday?"

"*Nada.*"

"That's worrisome, Harlowe. What are you going to do?"

"I'm open to ideas."

The *Millie* was doing a steady three knots in a rolling sea. Three moons were bright and silvery above the western horizon. A fourth minor moon was straight overhead and rather dull, dressed in a drab olive green with burnt orange highlights. It seemed out of place with the others. The Sorcerer's Moons on the planet they called #2 were still the best, Harlowe thought.

"Did you love her?" Leucadia asked, out of the blue.

Harlowe looked down at her as though she had been reading his mind. Perhaps she had been. "You had sprouted wings, remember?" he replied, reminding her that when the whole Gamadin adventure began, she had faked her death in order to help save *Millawanda* and the Earth from Fhaal destruction.

"I can see in your eyes that you still think of her."

Harlowe grinned defensively. "I could be thinking of you."

"But you're not," Leucadia countered, knowing his answer was false. She followed with another question. "Was she beautiful?"

"Why do girls always want to know that?"

"Because we're insecure." She prodded him with a small jab. She wanted an answer. "Was she beautiful, Pylott?" Leucadia persisted.

"You're a lot of things, Ms. Mars, but insecure isn't one of them," Harlowe replied, hoping to avoid the question.

"Answer the question, Pylott."

Harlowe saw a no-win situation developing. "I don't know. She was just a girl. Ask Ian or Rerun. They'll tell you."

"I asked Matt."

"Well, there you go. We all know his taste."

"He said she was a fourteen on a scale of ten."

"She was cute, what can I tell ya?"

"She was gorgeous, wasn't she?" Leucadia insisted.

Harlowe stared up at the ugly moon, wondering where all of this was headed. He stared forward again. "Three beautiful moons, a fair wind at our backs, and you have to spoil the night with nonsense."

"Will you ever see her again?"

Harlowe had enough of the interrogation. He sighed heavily and looked to port, away from her glowing green stare.

"Is that a yes?" she asked.

There seemed to be no escape. He faced her again. "As strange as it may seem, all I could think of was you, even though I thought you were gonzo. I cared for her, sure. I met a lot of hot babes when I was out saving the quadrant from the evil empire. She was one of them."

"And she was beautiful?"

"She was a remarkable girl. You two would have hit it off big together, shopping at the same Rodeo Drive boutiques."

"She had means?"

"Her dad owned a planet and then some."

"A planet?"

"Yeah, a nice one too . . . with waves!"

"And?"

"And you were always there, sticking your nose in my face just when I was about to touch first base, just like you are now."

Leucadia held his arm tighter and smiled. "But was she beautiful?"

Harlowe had no choice. "Yeah, she was hot. You've seen Sizzle and Sharlon. You figure it out. Their gene pool is loaded with hot looks. It's the same with you and your mom. Like mother, like daughter, and all that. The one thing you all have in common is Neeja. It must be something in the water, because every doe I meet from that planet—and I have a good sampling going now—is a babe. Are you down with that? Feel better now that I've spilled my guts out? Can I go back to being captain now?"

"I just wanted to hear it from you. Yes, I do feel better now."

Harlowe shook his head in bewilderment. His dad was right. *If you live to be a million years old, son, you'll never figure out the complexities of a woman.*

Amen, Dad!

Harlowe turned the broken wheel more to starboard and sighed as he stared at the pile of rigging stacked in a mound on the main deck. The *Millie* had not come through the battle unscathed. Necessary repairs would have to be made before they engaged in any more sea battles. No doubt Jakaa had put a high price on the *Millie* and wanted her sunk at all costs. The waters around the Phagallian sea would be infested with warships. If Harlowe was emperor and a pirate galleon was floating around the neighborhood sinking his ships, that's what he would do.

"So what was your second idea," Harlowe asked, hoping to turn the conversation away from Quay to more important matters, like their survival.

Leucadia reached into her coat and withdrew a knife with a short black blade and broken tip. She held it up in the moonlight. "This blade has some unusual properties."

Harlowe remembered touching the traa's snout with it before he almost become a Happy Meal. "Yes, it has." He told her that he had taken a bigger one than that from Pitch, who tried to slice him open with it on the island of vines. "Where did you get yours?"

"From the captain of the Phagallian ship," Leucadia replied.

Harlowe was about to ask her more about her time with Klagg, but decided to let sleeping dogs lie.

"I'll bet it's made of the same black crystal," Leucadia said.

"It looks like the same stuff."

"I need to analyze it to be sure. Where is your knife?"

Harlowe nodded at the undog, sitting in his usual place at the end of the bowsprit. "Hanging from Mowgi's perch."

Leucadia looked at Harlowe like he was missing a few dots. Harlowe explained, "It keeps the traas away."

"Traas?"

"Monsters of the sea."

"Oh, really."

Harlowe scanned the ocean, looking for an example. A subtle florescence on the surface off the starboard bow caught his attention. "Over there. Keep an eye on the water."

As if Harlowe had signaled the serpent, a giant traa nearly a thousand feet long breached the surface to grab a midnight snack it saw flying in the air. The wave it created when it fell back into the ocean rocked the *Millie*. Harlowe and Leucadia watched the traa swoosh gracefully through the water, taking a long moment to disappear beneath the surface.

Leucadia was impressed. "I guess we should leave it there."

"I would."

"Where did Mr. Pitch get his blade?" Leucadia asked.

Harlowe didn't know. He just cared that it saved his life the day when he kissed a traa going after Shortstop. "Why?" he asked.

Leucadia touched the broken tip of the blade. "Because when I broke off the tip and put it inside the cannonball..." She waved her arms open like an explosion. "You saw what happened."

Harlowe's jaw hung open. "That was you? I thought Rerun over-loaded the cannon again."

"It's black thermo-grym. It has a thousand times more energy than the same weight of yellow thermo-grym," Leucadia explained. "Give me two hundred pounds of it and I'll have *Millawanda* flying again."

Harlowe glared at Leucadia. "You've known this for a whole day and you're just now telling me this?"

"We've been busy," was her casual reply.

"We haven't been firing broadsides for hours, Lu!"

"I had to know about Quay."

"Quay? When we're about to be slammed by a burst, every second counts! Millie's the only thing that can save us!"

"I wanted to know," she repeated.

Harlowe had a choice: he could throw her overboard or jump ship himself and go swimming with the traas. Either choice would solve a lot of his problems.

"MR. PITCH!" Harlowe shouted, waking his first mate. *Where did he get that knife?*

62

Rerun's Departure

Harlowe woke up Shortstop and gave him the wheel. His self-proclaimed servant had never steered the Millie, but Harlowe needed Leucadia with him to ask Pitch questions and figured it was a good time for Shortstop to learn. The sea was relatively calm and Shortstop was the nearest crewman.

With shaking hands, Shortstop grabbed a broken wheel spoke. "What if I steer off course, Captain?"

Harlowe pointed to the makeshift compass, a bowl of water with a metal pointer floating in the middle. "Keep the bowsprit on the arrow. You'll be cool."

Leucadia saw the doubt in Shortstop's face while he tried to watch the pointer and bowsprit at the same time. She put her arm around his shoulder and said, "The Captain trusts you, Shortstop. You'll do fine."

"Thank you, Ms. Lu," Shortstop replied humbly. Her words helped, but only a little.

Riverstone and Ian joined Harlowe and Leucadia at the bottom of the quarterdeck ladder. "Got a problemo, Captain?" Riverstone yawned. He was tired like all the others.

"I need to wake Mr. Pitch. Lu will fill you in on the details in my cabin," Harlowe said.

320

Ian saw the small blade in Harlowe's hand. "It's about the black blade, right?"

Harlowe stopped abruptly in mid-stride. "You know about it?"

"I know it's narly."

Harlowe glared at Leucadia for telling Ian, but not him.

"I told him to wait until I talked to you," Leucadia said.

"It doesn't matter. No more games," Harlowe countered. He didn't like being intentionally left out of the loop.

"It wasn't a game," Leucadia said.

Harlowe still frowned at her. "I don't care what you call it. Keep me informed."

"Okay," Leucadia sighed.

"Yes, Captain," Harlowe emphasized.

Leucadia was rankled. The idea that Harlowe was the final and undisputed authority every second of the day was difficult for her to accept. She understood that every ship had its Captain and that while she was part of this crew she had to follow his orders. Still, during the whole time they had been together, she and Harlowe had always been equals. And now...

On Earth, after the Daks killed her parents, she became the ruler of the Mars financial empire. In her world, she was queen bee. Here, this was Harlowe's kingdom. He was king, and survival required everyone to remember that, whether they were on the *Millie* or *Millawanda*. Harlowe was emperor, king, and master of his realm, regardless of their relationship when they were on-the-clock. Leucadia's parents had taught her the importance of loyalty, decipline, and the greater good. She would not disappoint them or Harlowe by letting her ego get in the way.

Still, if Harlowe pushed her too far, she would show him! He was going about this all wrong. The day of reckoning was coming, but

not today. She closed her eyes, swallowed her pride and said dutifully, "Yes, Captain."

Harlowe turned to the both of them. "Do that again and I'll have
you both cleaning the decks with a toothbrush."

"Yes, Captain," they said together.

"Now wake up Rerun. Tell him to pack his things. I want his
SIBA fully charged and ready to go."

"Where's he going?" Ian asked.

Harlowe's mood was short. "Just do it!"

"Aye!" Ian spun around and double-timed it toward the officer's
quarters.

Pitch emerged from the crew's quarters below the main deck and
snapped to attention in front of Harlowe, Leucadia, and Riverstone.
His hair was uncombed, his britches rode not quite right on his hips
and he stood there in bare feet, tucking in his shirt while his prehensile tail helped straighten his hat on his head. "Cool, Captain!"

"Relax, Mr. Pitch. You're not in trouble. I need information,"
Harlowe said, putting the final touches on his hat.

"How may I assist you, Captain?"

Harlowe held up the small blade for Pitch to examine. "Your blade
was made of the same black stone as this, is that right?

Pitch glanced at the blade. "It was, Captain."

"Where did you get it?"

"My blade, Captain?"

"That's right. The one we exchanged back on the island. Where
did you get it?" Harlowe asked.

Pitch looked as confused as Riverstone did when he couldn't
remember one of Farnducky's test questions. "I am truly at a loss,
Captain. It was taken in a raid, I'm positive."

"You're sure?"

"Cool, Captain."

Harlowe turned to Leucadia, holding the black blade. "It might have come from anywhere."

Harlowe patted Pitch on the back. "Thanks, Mr. Pitch. You can return to your hammock. Tell Jewels I said to give you an extra Breakfast Mac for First Meal."

Pitch was ecstatic. "Thank you, Captain! I am sorry I was unable to assist you."

"Me too, Mr. Pitch. Good night."

Pitch tipped his seaman's cap to Leucadia. "Good night, Ms. Lu."

"Sleep well, Mr. Pitch," Leucadia said.

The Gamadin were about to turn back to Harlowe's cabin when Pitch stopped before the crew hatchway.

"Pardon me, Captain. If it's another black blade you're after, they are very common."

"They are, Mr. Pitch?" Harlowe asked.

"They're Nywok blades, sir. They make them," Pitch replied.

Harlowe's eyes widened, surprised. "Nywoks?"

"Yes, Captain. The Nywoks are the only ones who make black blades," Pitch said. "Does that help?"

"Indeed it does, Mr. Pitch! Indeed it does."

Pitch yawned. "Is that all, Captain?"

Harlowe nodded. "Continue on, Mr. Pitch. Good night." The First Mate then ducked into the hold, pulling down the hatch as he went.

Leucadia saw concern in Harlowe's face. "You don't look happy."

Harlowe put his hand on the main mast. "This mast was the Nywoks' sacred tree. They weren't happy about my taking it."

"Why did you take it?" Leucadia asked.

Harlowe stared at the mast, touching its smooth skin like a sacred talisman. He told her how he found the tree in the forest not far from the beach when they needed to replace their broken mast. "We were in a hurry."

Before Harlowe could tell her the rest of the account, Ian and Rerun returned to the main deck and joined Harlowe, Leucadia, and Riverstone. As ordered, Rerun was in a fully-charged SIBA with a few of his things in a small canvas bag. "Good to go, Skipper. What's up?"

"You're going on a flight, Rerun," Harlowe replied.

Everyone but Mowgi and Harlowe looked puzzled. The undog was perched on the front of the quarterdeck rail, appearing as cool as ice.

"I am?" Rerun asked, looking more than happy to fly anywhere off the ship. The question on everyone's mind, however, was why and where was he going?

"Back to the island. Monday hasn't checked in and Wiz can't raise him. I need to know what's going on. I'm worried."

"Understood, Skipper," Simon replied.

"Use your SIBA to call us when you get there. Let's hope something just went wrong with their communications."

Riverstone offered a plausible explanation. "Maybe they were hit by electrical storms, too, Captain."

"I hope you're right, Matt."

"I can't fly with my SIBA wings. I can only glide," Simon pointed out.

Harlowe nodded toward the undog. "Mowgi will give you a lift."

Riverstone let out a low whistle. "That's a long way, even for him, Skipper!"

"A thousand miles, Mr. Bolt," Ian stated confidently.

Harlowe turned to Leucadia. "Can the Mowg do it, Lu?"

Leucadia held out her arms to the chinneroth, who happily skipped down from his perch and jumped into them. She hugged him affectionately. "Can you do it, Mowgi?" The undog panted with his green tongue hanging out his mouth and his big, yellow eyes turned toward Simon. Whether that meant yes or no was uncertain, but when he yipped twice, Harlowe knew it was a go. Ever since Mowgi guided them flawlessly along the back roads of Southern Utah, yipping twice was always a go.

Harlowe picked up a handful of line from the pile of loose rigging. "Did you bring carabineers from the ship, Wiz?"

"Aye, Captain," Ian replied.

"Get Rerun rigged. I want him off the *Millie* before the crew wakes up."

"Aye, Captain."

Simon pulled Harlowe aside and said in a low voice. "Me and Mowgi don't always get along, Skipper. Maybe Jester or..."

Harlowe didn't let him finish. "You're going, Mr. Bolt."

"But Skipper..."

"It's just a ride, Rerun. You don't have to suck face. Just do it."

Simon and Mowgi exchanged stiff glares. The feeling was mutual.

*   *   *

Leucadia chose the top of the taffrail to launch because it was the aftmost part of the ship and the only place where Mowgi could spread his wings without entangling himself or Simon in the *Millie's* rigging. Once the undog was in the air, all Simon would have to do was drop off the stern in his harness and they'd be off. Mowgi didn't need a com. The undog had his own internal guidance system. He knew the way back, regardless of his location on the planet.

"As long as you're with Mowgi, you won't get lost," Leucadia assured Simon.

In his dragon form, the undog had spread his wings far beyond the sides of the ship and hovered in the stiff wind over the sternform. Simon tapped his SIBA headgear and said warily, "If you don't mind, I'll trust my nav-com to get me there."

"Suit yourself."

Ian brought the finished harness to Leucadia. With a simple gesture from her, Mowgi flew close and extended his head over the poop deck rail so Harlowe and Ian could slip the thick collar around his massive neck. Looking like a prisoner en route to the gallows, Simon stepped into his makeshift seat made of sailcloth and dura-thread webbing.

"Will it hold?" Simon asked.

"You could lift the *Millie* with it," Harlowe replied.

Ian attached a small Gamadin device to Simon's Gama-belt.

"What's that?" Simon asked.

"Protection. Don't lose it. It might come in handy," Ian replied.

"Works for me," Simon quipped.

Then, with little fanfare—a safe-trip embrace from Leucadia, a knuckle rap from Riverstone, and a good luck nod from Harlowe – Simon settled into the harness and Mowgi rose into the air.

"See you back at the Ship, Mates!" Simon yelled as he slipped off the stern and floated away from the *Millie*.

"Call me the moment you get there!" Harlowe called after him.

Rising above the swells, Simon gestured back with his thumb and little finger extended in a "hang loose" sign. After one last wave goodbye, he and Mowgi's great dark wings vanished into the low-lying mist of the night.

63

Return to Nywok Bay

After days of hard sailing, the *Millie* quietly reentered Nywok Bay. The ship veered toward the far end of the bay, where they dropped anchor a mile offshore, safely out of range of Nywok arrows and spears.

"Minimal sail, Mr. Pitch," Harlowe ordered in a hushed voice. He stood at the quarterdeck rail with Leucadia, Ian, and Riverstone. The bay was calm and glassy, and the air still. It had been necessary to use the turbos when the wind died on their approach to the bay as if the *Millie* had sailed through a doorway and someone had shut the door to the wind behind them.

Pitch used hand signals to relay Harlowe's commands to his crew. "Stay as quiet as a traa after First Meal, gentlemen."

The crew made itself busy bringing the sails in and carefully stowing the gear. They had sailed for two days straight without being seen, using the turbos for a swift nighttime run through the Straits of Daloom to elude any Phagallian ships that might be waiting in the channel. Half the crew had been up all night, the other half was still sleeping. Only twelve days remained before the second burst, so no one was allowed to rest for long, especially the Gamadin.

"Cool, Captain, minimal sail!" Pitch called back softly.

Harlowe pointed to a tall, cone-shaped mountain on the horizon. "Is that it?" he asked Ian, who was standing next to him at the rail.

Leucadia and Riverstone had turned their eyes with curious interest to the beach cliffs and the forest for the first time. This time the bay was clear of fog. The thick blue-green evergreens stood out tall and pointy along the ridgeline of sharp rocky cliffs. Far in the distance, a great, thirty-thousand-foot, snow-capped cone rose above the clouds from the vast volcanic plain hidden behind the coastal hills surrounding the bay.

"That's totally rad even this far away," Riverstone proclaimed as he admired the mighty black mountain.

"It may look close, but it's far. Over a hundred miles away, Captain," Leucadia added. "We will need to take extra supplies."

Harlowe gave his next order. "It's Riverstone, Wiz and me, Lu. You're staying here." Before Leucadia could protest, Harlowe cut her off. "If things go south, you're the only one who can sail the *Millie* out of trouble using the turbos. More importantly, you're not up to speed in a SIBA. Nywoks are fast. The three of us can outrun them in SIBAs."

"I can run."

"But you can't fly."

"You can show me."

He looked at her with his commanding blue eyes. "Not a chance. You're staying here!"

Leucadia sighed with disappointment. She turned to Ian for support, but all he could give her was a silent nod of understanding. Harlowe's order was final, and he wasn't about to challenge it. Accepting that she had lost the battle, Leucadia winked and grinned her approval. "Hurry back. I'll have dinner waiting, Captain."

Harlowe was surprised by her sudden conformity. He had expected an outrage since she had discovered the black thermo-grym's qualities and wanted to be in on its retrieval. His order had nothing to do with protecting her. It was sound judgment. With Jakaa's ships hunting the ocean for the *Millie*, Leucadia was in at least as much danger at sea as she would be on the mission to find the black thermo-grym. In fact, her years of sailing experience made her the best person to keep the *Millie* safe. He would have ordered her to stay, even if she was as skilled as they were in a SIBA.

Harlowe kissed her on the lips. "Good. We won't be long."

* * *

In full SIBA gear, Harlowe, Riverstone, and Ian slipped off the port side of the *Millie*, away from the land so the Nywok spies that were watching would not see them. They swam a mile under water and surfaced only when they had reached the rocks below the cliffs at the south end of the bay. Slipping between an underwater pile of jagged boulders, they scaled the 500-foot vertical cliffs to the top of the escarpment wall. The color-shifting SIBAs were nearly invisible against the dense gray granite of the cliffs. Anyone up close would need a keen eye to notice any movement against the rock face. To anyone on the *Millie* or along the shore of the bay, they were invisible.

Peering over the top of the cliff, they discovered the forest was anything but deserted. Nywoks were everywhere, hordes of them, in the trees and in the rocky hills above the bay. The trick would be to needle their way up the hill past the Nywok lookouts and then to descend to the plains below. There, they would sprint across the miles of flat grassland to the base of Black Mountain. Ian would locate the deposits of black thermo-grym with his com. If Leucadia's calculations were correct, the three of them would need only this one trip to collect enough black crystal for *Millawanda's* emergency refueling. Once *Millawanda* was airborne, they would return to the mountain and restock her supply with as much black thermo-grym as she needed to top off her tank.

From the top of the cliff, the *Millie* appeared like a small toy boat alone in the water. She was loosing her sails and weighing anchor. As a precaution, Harlowe ordered the *Millie* to the open sea where Phagallian ships were afraid to venture and Nywok raiding parties could not reach them.

"Have you been working out?" Riverstone asked Ian in a whisper. He was surprised at how agile Ian had become since they last saw each other. Ian had kept up with the group the entire way without falling behind even once. Swimming and climbing were two things Ian had stayed away from in the past. Yet, here he was beside them, keeping up with them like it was routine.

Ian nodded a silent "yes." Then he checked his com and pointed in the direction that would lead them around the Nywok sentinels.

64

Gamadin Down

Flying through the storm instead of skirting it was a bad idea. As Simon carried Mowgi's body onto the beach, he was grateful for one thing: the undog's body was back to its small size after being struck by a lightening bolt. If he had stayed his dragon-sized self, they both would have been fish bait at the bottom of the ocean.

Simon had tried to stop the undog from flying them into the storm. "But noooo, you didn't listen to me, did you, Big Ears?"

Simon hadn't stopped scolding Mowgi since the moment he laid the green-blood-splattered undog's body on the sand. How far he had swum with the injured undog, he didn't know. Miles, he figured. The flight had been going so well. They were only a few hours flying time from Vine Island when they were zapped. If he could still get his bearings, he could cover the remaining distance in a day or two. Tops!

Unfortunately, the lightening bolt had wiped out a number of his SIBA functions. Navigation was the first he noticed. The second was communications. When he tried to raise Ian, not even a hum interrupted the dead silence. He could only guess the functions that still worked until he could run a full systems check. His biggest concern was staying alive.

Here he was again, in the middle of something he hadn't signed up for: saving *Millawanda*, Sizzle, and—who would have thought— the undog.

331

"Yeah, but…" he grumbled to himself.

Yeah, but that's only if the Mowg was cool, which he wasn't. He was out. He couldn't fly, walk, or even open his eyes. For how long? Maybe forever? He didn't know. Simon laid his bugeye-covered head across the undog's chest and searched for life with the hypersensitive sensors in his suit.

"Look at you! You're bleeding all over my SIBA," Simon told the unconscious chinner. "That green stuff didn't whack out my SIBA, did it, Mowg? You'd better hope not, or we're in for a whole world of hurt!" Simon made a three-sixty scan of their location. "Where are we, dude!"

Mowgi remained still. Not so much as a whimper came from his snout.

Simon picked up the undog and climbed to higher ground for a look-see. There were no trees to shelter them from the rain, but there were some rocks to lean against. He was tired and wanted some rest. His SIBA was the only thing keeping him going, but who could tell for how long? Before he rested, he had to tend Mowgi's wound. If he didn't sew up the undog's lightning-charred hide, Mowgli would surely die, if he wasn't dead already.

"Don't clock out on me, mutt," Simon commanded as they sloshed along in the wet sand. "You're not done taking me to Millie. I purchased a full ride, and I want my money's worth!"

He found a good spot between the rocks and pulled out the "tent" Ian had given him. It wasn't really a tent in the normal sense; it was more like a personal force field. When you switched it on, the field would form a transparent, protective shield like the ones L.L. Bean sells.

Simon hadn't told Ian that before his Martian experience, camping to him was staying in anything less than a five-star hotel.

Simon switched on the tent and attached it to his Gama-belt. Like magic, the rain stopped drumming on his head and a familiar blue shimmer engulfed both of them. "That's sick!" Simon exclaimed, touching the mushy blue field. In no time, he had broken out his Gama-belt first aid kit and was stitching Mowgi's wounds with dura-wire. Simon cussed out the undog after every stitch, but finally the work was done. Only then did Simon to take the time to lay beside the injured chinner and fall into a deep and dreamless sleep.

65

Insubordination

Harlowe, Riverstone, and Ian made it through the low coastal hills without encountering any Nywoks along the way. Even if a Nywok had seen them in their stealthy SIBAs, their gazelle-like strides were too fast for the fleet-footed natives to catch them on foot or by arrow. As they descended toward the plain, Riverstone and Harlowe continued to marvel at Ian's ability to maintain the fast pace. At the sheer, one-thousand-foot cliff, they looked out across the dry, bush-covered flatlands they would cross to the base of Black Mountain. Harlowe directed Ian and Riverstone to jump first. He would take a couple of final readings and follow them. This was the last leg of the trip. In another eighty miles they'd be at the base of the 30,000-foot mountain.

Riverstone pushed off like it was routine, extending his gossamer wings as he dove away from the cliff.

"Take off, Wiz, I'll meet you below," Harlowe ordered when he saw Ian still standing at the edge of the cliff. "We'll save a ton of time if we jump from here like we did when leapfrogging through *Valles Marineras*."

Ian nodded, but for whatever reason, he continued to hesitate.

"What's with you?" Harlowe asked. "You suddenly got the narlies? This is a baby leap compared to what we did on the Mons, pard."

Ian kept looking down, appearing confused about what to do next. Harlowe didn't know what the holdup was. It was time to

334

go. He reached over and gave Ian a friendly shove to expedite his takeoff. Once he was dropping like a stone, Ian would get over his nervousness and deploy his wings. It was that or suck face with the rocks below.

"HARLOWWWWE!" the voice startled Harlowe. It wasn't Ian's voice; it was Leucadia's. He dropped his com and dove off the cliff. Pinning his arms to his sides, he plunged like a missile after her. Now it all made sense as to why "Ian" was so athletic! Leucadia had experience with the SIBA, but she had no experience flying. She couldn't have known about the suit's wings because no one had shown her how to use them.

Down they went.

"Hold your hands and legs out, Lu!" Harlowe shouted.

She followed directions. The air resistance against her extended limbs slowed her down enough for Harlowe to catch her within five hundred feet of the bottom.

He dove in front of her so she could clamp onto the back of his Gama-belt with her claws.

"Okay!" Leucadia cried out.

Harlowe's wings exploded open without a second to spare. Their landing was anything but smooth. On the way down, Leucadia's foot clipped a rock outcropping, throwing Harlowe off balance. He fought to regain control, only to scrape his arm on the cliff when they were less than a hundred feet from the rock base. He kicked away from the ledge and yawed radically sideways, twisting in a complete somersault just before they touched on a long and fortunately gradual incline.

They lay together motionless in a tangled mess until Riverstone's voice brought them back to their senses.

"HARLOWE!" Riverstone shouted. "Talk to me!"

Leucadia detached herself from Harlowe's belt and rolled away with a groan. Harlowe climbed to his feet slowly and helped Leucadia to hers before he answered Riverstone, "We're okay, Matt. 'Ian' and I have some issues to discuss."

Harlowe retracted his SIBA's bugeye headgear and helped Leucadia do the same. Her long blonde hair tumbled over her shoulders in disarray until she shook her head back and the golden mess fell away from her face.

Leucadia looked up at Harlowe's stern face. "I can explain."

Harlowe was furious. "Nothing to explain. You disobeyed a direct order!"

"Sorry."

"Sorry, Captain!" Harlowe snapped.

"It's just you and me, Harlowe," Leucadia said, trying to reduce the fire to smoke.

"Captain!"

Leucadia could tell by his stone-hard glare that he was serious. Nevertheless, she refused to be treated like one of the crew again. She had reached her limit, and it was time to take a stand. Now was as good a time as any to prove herself as an equal, not a subordinate. With her blindingly fast foot, she took a hard karate kick at Harlowe's head.

Had she known more about Harlowe's training with Quincy and the General, she would never have made such a foolish move. Harlowe slapped the kick away easily. Leucadia was a red belt in martial arts and had been trained by the world's best masters. Yet as hard as she tried, she was no match for his Gamadin-trained reflexes. Finally, Harlowe lowered the boom, knocking her flat on her back.

"Captain," he ordered, hovering over her.

Leucadia gasped for air. "Captain."

"Captain, sir!"

Another gasp. "Captain, sir."

"Mean it!"

"CAPTAIN, SIR!"

Harlowe was angrier than she had ever seen him before. He reached out and pulled her to her feet.

"Ian and I thought—" Leucadia tried to explain before Harlowe cut her off again.

"I don't care what Ian and you thought! There is only room for one captain here, and I'm it!"

She nodded, looking a little frightened at Harlowe's outburst. In all the time she had known him, ever since the day he rescued her from Simon's overturned yacht, he had always been a perfect gentleman to her. They'd had their spats, but this was beyond an argument. It was as if he had just declared war upon her. His fury showed her a side of him she had never seen before.

"You disobeyed my direct order to stay with the *Millie*. I didn't give the order out of concern for you." He leaned into her space even further, spraying spittle as he talked. "Know this, Ms. Mars. I would sacrifice your life and my own to save this planet." She nodded again. She understood it only too well. "Your expertise in sailing is way beyond Wiz's. That's why I needed you there, not here. I don't care how much thermo-puke we find. If anything happens to the *Millie*, we're whacked!"

Leucadia tried to defend her actions, but no excuse was sufficient to counter a captain's direct order.

"Yes, sir."

Harlowe glared at her with cold, insensitive eyes. "This is the second time you've disobeyed my direct orders. There will not be a third, or I promise you, your new quarters will be the lowest, slimiest, rat-infested hole in the ship."

Leucadia felt the steam rising from Harlowe's face. There was no doubt that he meant every word of that threat. "Yes, sir."

Harlowe got in her face again, his spittal splattering her skin. "You WILL say it with conviction!"

Leucadia's jaw set and her muscles tensed while she strained to stay cool. "YES, SIR!"

"When we return to the *Millie*, both you and Wiz will serve whatever disciplinary action I deem appropriate."

"May I speak, Captain?"

"No!" Harlowe looked up the side of the cliff wall.

"I'm not one of your Gamadin."

"You've been drafted! Now, we're going back up there and do it right this time."

"Don't I—"

Harlowe took a deep breath before he shouted in her ear. "MOVE SOLDIER, BEFORE I DROP KICK YOU UP THERE MYSELF!"

Leucadia suddenly snapped to attention and gave him a crisp salute. "YES SIR, CAPTAIN!"

She made one step toward the trail that led them back up the cliff, but Harlowe had other plans. "Not that way, soldier!" he said, pointing straight up the side of the cliff. "THAT WAY!"

66

The Creepies

Simon woke to the grating sound of something rubbing against a hard surface. He rolled over with one eye and looked up at a moving sky. He opened the other eye. The sky was still moving. It made no sense. The sky was undulating in a thousand different directions at once. It wasn't a gray sky or a clear blue sky. It was—

Dude!

His eyes went round. A thousand spiny claws were scratching at the force field dome, trying to get at Mowgi and him through the force field.

Crabs!

He sat up, now fully awake, and stared at these crawling creatures with pinhead eyes and spiny claws and six-inch pincers, eager to devour them both for breakfast.

It's time to blow this place, Simon thought. They had obviously worn out their welcome.

They were okay as long as the force field was between them and the creepy crawlers. He turned to Mowgi and tried to awaken the undog. "Hey, Mowg. Get up!"

Mowgi remained still. His eyes gave no sign that there was life behind them at all. Simon checked the surgery he had performed on the undog's side. It was holding, and the green blood had stopped dripping. Out of the million things that had gone wrong since leaving the *Millie*, at least one thing had gone right.

Simon stared at Mowgi, disgusted. "You don't think I'm going to carry your booty all the way back to the ship, do you?"

Mowgi said nothing.

Shaking his head with a *why-am-I-doing-this*, Simon scooped Mowgi in his arms and stood up. He was relieved that the prickly creatures fell off the sides of the barrier so easily. He was afraid he would have to carry them back the whole way. It made sense, though. The force field had no surface to grab onto. The creepies slid off like dandruff as he climbed from one rock to another. He felt a macabre chill when he thought about what might have happened without Ian's protective tent. Thanking him wouldn't be good enough. He promised himself that he would line the Wiz up with a string of starlets once they returned to Earth.

He stood on top of a boulder and surveyed the beach and the thousands of crawlers all over the sand. Where should they go next? He tried his SIBA nav-com arrays, but they still didn't function. The readouts were dark, just like his communications. He wondered if the problem was temporary or if there was a reboot switch he could press. None of his efforts to fix the problem worked, not even slapping the side of his head.

"For 54th-century, you'd think they would have built them better," he complained to no one in particular.

No one. Not even Mowgi.

Now what?

Disgusted, he turned back toward the beach and tried to get his bearings. But without his nav-com to guide him, Simon was lost. Nothing looked familiar except the ocean and the beach full of creepies.

The undog flies *straight,* he thought to himself. *Yeah, too straight! Why didn't you go around the storm, you green-blooded mutt?* Now it was up to him to get them back to the ship. The only way he could think of to do that was to hoof it and go wherever the road took him.

If there was a road!

Out of frustration, he slapped his head again, hoping his nav-com outtage would fix itself.

Nothing!

His bugeyes were skunk! Not even a snap, crackle, or pop lit up his screens. Two of the essential pieces of equipment he needed to find the way back to Vine Island didn't work!

This is freakin' nuts!

"This wasn't the mission, Big Ears!" he said to Mowgi. "You were supposed to carry me, not the other way around. I'm not liking this one bit! You'd better get well fast, or I'll leave you behind!"

Suddenly, the undog shook and puked a big heave of green slime all over Simon's chest.

"That's disgusting! For all the trouble I went through to save your ugly face!"

Though Simon complained for the next hour about having to carry Mowgi with green puke all over his chest, he was privately happy the undog had shown some signs of life. He was happy, too, that his SIBA didn't disintegrate from Mowgi's hurl the way he had seen his spit corrode metal.

After cleaning himself and Mowgi at a freshwater stream not far from the beach, Simon climbed a nearby hill to get his bearings. He was relieved to discover that his visuals were undamaged. He could see distances easily, and he was able to see small animals in the dark shadows of the trees. Navigation and communications, however, continued to be offline. It would take a full tune-up from *Millawanda* to get them functioning again. That meant he'd have to depend on his own dead reckoning to get back to the saucer.

He looked back toward the ocean. He was a thousand feet above the beach, and he could see for miles. If Simon had anticipated problems on the flight, he would have paid more attention to their course instead of napping. He did remember, however, that Mowgi was heading for the coastal mountain range on the horizon and the v-shaped pass between the two tallest peaks to the south.

"Is that where you were going, Mowg?" he asked the motionless chinneroth.

Mowgi said nothing.

Simon needed answers. He couldn't stay put and wait for someone to find him. He had a mission to accomplish! He realized that he had to become a pet psychiatrist and understand the undog's mind. *When pigs fly, dude! You should become a monk. It would be easier!*

Simson stared at Mowgi and asked, "Why were you headed toward the pass instead of following the coastal route?"

Simon examined the coast again. If the undog took the beach route, he would have veered far to the west, all the way to the horizon. Sooner or later it might get them to a point on the mainland where he could swim to Vine Island. But how long might that take, especially if the coast was not a straight line—and what coast was?

Simon came back to the pass again. *If that was the quickest way, Mowgi would have taken it!*

"He was headed there," he thought out loud.

He didn't have time for wrong guesses. He needed to get to *Millawanda* yesterday. His ride was jacked and he couldn't call Triple-A. He made up his mind to try the v-shaped pass and hope for the best.

Simon glanced down at Mowgi, looking for a yip of confirmation for his wonderful psych work. "That's right, isn't it? You were headed for the pass." Still no yip. "Okay, Mowg, this had better be right, because if it isn't, I'm bringing you back here and feeding you to the creepies."

Yech!

67

Cujos

Leucadia was a natural climber. Reaching the top of the cliff with Harlowe was a piece of cake. Leaping from tall cliffs with frail wings under her arms was another matter. It took a huge leap of faith to visualize her SIBA wings keeping her airborne. She stood at the cliff edge in her best *now-I'm-a-bird pose* and asked Harlowe, "How do I keep from stalling if I hit a head wind?"

"Don't fight it. Go with the flow until you find another wind going the way you want," Harlowe replied.

"What did you do the first time?" she asked.

"Here, I'll show you." Harlowe walked over and once again pushed her off the cliff. "Soar like an eagle, babe," he called out to her as she fell away.

With her wings deployed, Leucadia was ready for flight this time. She let out a tiny yelp, but that was the last of her panic attacks. She was shaky at first, but she hung in there. Harlowe dove alongside her in case she had trouble. She almost stalled once by pulling up too fast, but Harlowe grabbed her Gama-belt and guided her forward. From then on, she glided smoothly. They flew straight and true for twenty miles across the wheat-colored plains until they finally caught up with Riverstone, who had landed and was waiting for them on the ground.

Leucadia touched down as gently as an albatross with Harlowe right behind her.

"What happened?" Riverstone asked.

Harlowe tapped Leucadia's SIBA on the back of her neck, retracting her bugeyes. "I found an imposter."

Riverstone froze in surprise. Pre-empting further discussion, Harlowe set out in twenty-foot strides toward the black mountain. He could explain later. They had lost enough time already.

* * *

They had only gone a few miles when they felt the ground behind them shaking. Leucadia checked her com and found the source of the disturbance. "It's a large mass coming straight for us from the northwest!"

Harlowe and Riverstone climbed a solitary thorn tree nearby to get a better view. They needed only a few seconds to identify the source.

Jumping down from the tree, Harlowe pushed Leucadia forward. "RUN!"

"What is it?" Leucadia cried out, as she ran beside Harlowe.

"Cujos!" Riverstone answered from right behind them.

"Thousands of them!" Harlowe added. "Nywoks are riding them!"

"With black tipped spears!" Riverstone put in.

"Can we outrun them?" Harlowe asked.

Leucadia checked her com on the fly. "They're running at twice our speed!"

"Their rides are bigger and uglier than grogans!" Riverstone noted. What he and Harlowe saw through their bugeyes was a battalion of giant, dog-like creatures with snapping jaws filled with razor-sharp teeth charging straight at them. Riding on thick-harnessed saddles were Nywok warriors in full body armor, with black-tipped spears, bows, and quivers of black-tipped arrows slung across their backs.

Harlowe spotted another cloud of dust on the horizon to their right.

"It's a second unit that will cut us off from the mountain!" Leucadia reported.

Leucadia snapped her com back onto her Gama-belt. Additional readings at this point would be a waste of time. "There's a canyon to our left. If we can make it there, we have a chance. It's steep!"

Faster and faster they ran, but the mighty beasts continued to close in rapidly. They were a half-mile away, but because of their size, they appeared much closer and deadlier. Soon they would be within arrow range. Their SIBAs would protect them from a black-tipped arrow attack, but being trampled by seven-ton beasts the size of elephants was another matter. They would be roadkill afterwards!

With only the length of a football field to go before the edge of the canyon, they watched the fastest Nywoks charge out ahead to cut them off.

Harlowe didn't know if his flintlock would have any effect on the beasts, but before he could find out, Leucadia pulled what looked like two hardball-sized cannonballs from her pack and tossed them at the Nywoks, blocking their way. The explosion dazed the riders and blew a gaping hole in their line. When the smoke had cleared, the three of them were through the pack and leaping off the side of the gorge, flying again toward the black mountain.

"Nice arm!" Riverstone yelled to Leucadia.

Harlowe already had his opticals on the next problem. It wasn't Nywoks. Twenty thousand feet up the mountainside he spied machinery, only these devices weren't 16th-century Gazzian. They had alien symbols written all over them.

68

Dog Trees

What would Captain Starr do? Simon laughed at the thought as he stepped through the tall brush and headed for the mountain pass.

To start, Captain Starr would be munching down on an all-you-can-eat buffet between takes. That's after he spent the morning crash-landing on some deserted planet somewhere in the galaxy. Then in the afternoon, and armed only with his trusty Swiss Army knife, Captain Starr would fight the beast-of-the-day in one take. He wouldn't be trekking through swamps, deserts, and thick forests with a sick mutt in his arms! The great hero of the galaxy would be in a no-win situation, rescuing a babe from a horde of alien cutthroats. The final shoot would be a big lip-lock for his efforts. Yeah, that's what Captain Starr would be doing, and all before dinnertime!

A half step later, Simon stumbled onto a gravel road that led toward the mountain pass.

"Well, nice work, Captain Starr," he said, congratulating himself on his change of luck.

The day was still early. With a good road to follow, he figured he'd make the top of the mountain pass well before dark. *Cool!*

Many miles later, the pockmarked road meandered up a gradual incline toward the pass. Still comatose, Mowgi might have looked like a weird stuffed animal to a casual passerby. It didn't matter. There were no passersby. Simon thought that was strange, but he passed it off as part of being on the road at the wrong time of the year.

Besides the road's obvious disrepair, it had other problems. In several places, he had to leap over huge gaps that had eroded into chasms. Some were thousands of feet deep and more than a quarter-mile wide. At one time, bridges crossed those gaps, but whether through non-use, neglect, or natural disasters, they had all been wiped out, leaving only the stubbly remnants of their once-magnificent structures.

The best workaround was simply to find a takeoff point high enough above the opposite side to glide across with his wings. When he did that, he attached the limp chinneroth to his back with a couple tie-downs and a little Gamadin ingenuity. By the time night rolled around, Simon was at the top of the mountain pass and ready for a well-deserved rest.

He found a soft bed of pine needles beneath a tree just off the side of the road. He lay Mowgi down and prepared to go searching for firewood. With his SIBA continually resupplying his energy needs, all he needed was a short rest and he would be good to go.

After making sure Mowgi was comfortable, Simon scanned the surrounding area for danger. Finding nothing of concern, he tapped the side of his head and peeled his bugeyes down to his shoulders. He took a deep breath of unfiltered air.

His eyes quickly watered as he pinched his nose. "This sucks!"

He turned to gaze at the long valley he had hiked through the entire day. To his right in the far distance, he saw the great Black Mountain that was visible from Nywok Bay. A thick cloud layer covered its extinct caldron and massive glaciers. He turned around and looked at the long descent ahead of him. Like the road, it was devoid of travelers. He was the only one around. He guessed that was a good thing, but a little voice inside warned him to be on his toes. There was always a reason for something. The evergreens were beautiful, tall, and blue-green in color. Nothing threatening seemed to be lurking about in the shadows that would make him feel uneasy. Only the air was disconcerting. It was musty, thick and rancid, nothing at all like the sweet mountain-fresh air he was expecting. It smelled more like the dog park down the street from his home in Beverly Hills.

He reactivated his headgear, much preferring the odorless filtered air of his SIBA to the eyewatering yuckiness around him. Simon didn't worry about the undog. If Mowgi was awake, he would probably be yipping incessantly, thanking him for setting up camp in a forest that smelled like dog.

Simon jokingly told Mowgi to stay out of trouble and not to wander off without a hall pass. "I'm going after some firewood, Mowg. It might get cold now that the sun's going down."

Simon returned with an armful of wood only a few minutes later. When he got back to the tree, Mowgi was covered with spidery-legged creatures the size of his claws.

Simon dropped the wood and ran to Mowgi's aid, screaming and yelling at the top of his lungs to scare the crawlies away. He pulled his flintlock and was about to blast them to sub-atomic dust when the bugs miraculously began dropping dead all around the undog as if they had been gassed.

Camping with crawlies was a downer. Simon grabbed the undog and headed back to the road. All at once, an army of huge crawlies many feet wide—the adults—were jumping out of the trees and chasing him down the road with an evil hunger in their multi-beady eyes and pincer-like jaws.

Simon was unable to deal with the crawlies and hold Mowgi at the same time. In a single mid-air leap, he harnessed the undog to his back and grabbed his flintlock. When he hit the ground again, he had already begun blasting a passage through the crawlies. He used the first twenty-shot clip in a hurry, zapping the line of leggy spiders that was moving to cut him off.

Simon thought Mowgi's puke was the ugliest green he had ever seen until he saw a crawlie explode. That sticky mass of green goo nearly caused him to lose it. Fortunately, his SIBA anticipated his reaction and shot a squirt of Blue Stuff down his throat to calm the urge to blow his wad.

Simon was using up his ammo clips too quickly. He realized he would deplete his supply before running out of crawlies. What other problems might he run into before he reached *Millawanda*...if he reached M*illawanda,*that is? He only had three clips left and many miles to go. *Sheesh! This was only the first day!*

On his next leap, Simon saw his chance. A short distance away was another gap in the road. If he leaped high enough on his next jump, he'd have enough elevation to extend his wings and glide to the other side. If he stalled, though, he would land in the middle of the spider pack. He might survive the bites, but Mowgi was dog meat.

Simon realized he had only one choice. He leaped as high as his legs would take him and spread his wings.

69

Captain Ian

Nothing was more disagreeable to Ian than being the acting captain of the *Millie*. He would rather clean the bilge than command the ship! He preferred to follow orders, not give them, especially now. The fog had returned with a vengeance during the night. Every order he gave had to be the right one or the *Millie* could run aground or slam into hidden rocks beneath the waterline.

Leucadia had taken his com to hunt for black crystals, so he was basically flying blind. More than that, he needed sleep. He'd been at it for two days with no downtime, and he could barely keep his head up. Pitch had stayed with him the whole time. Now he was down, too. Before going to his hammock, the First Mate had put the *Millie* on an easy, five-degree starboard tack, a course he figured was clear of any hazards.

The winds had been light, but in the last hour, the weather had abruptly turned against the *Millie*. Had he been a more experienced sailor, Ian might have anticipated the change by the smell in the air.

An hour before dawn, Ian was alone on deck except for Twobagger and Catch. They helped him correct their course away from the fog bank. If the turbos went bad he was confident he could fix them, but if the *Millie* ran into a storm or even worse, Phagallian galleons, he didn't know what he'd do. Telling himself that nothing would happen while Harlowe was gone, Ian thought he'd steal an hour of sleep before the sun rose.

"The helm's yours, Mr. Twobagger," Ian said with a loud yawn before slumping off to his quarters. "Wake me if there's a problem," he added during the next yawn.

"Cool, Mr. Wiz!" Catch and Twobagger replied together.

"Good rest to you, Mr. Wiz," Twobagger added.

*   *   *

A hard rap on his cabin door woke Ian from a deep sleep.

"Mr. Wiz! Come quick!" Shortstop called to him from outside his quarters.

Ian tapped his SIBA to life, except for his headgear. Harlowe's orders were to keep his Self-contained, Individual Body-armor Array active at all times while he was on duty. His reason came straight from the Boy Scout handbook: *Be prepared.* Harlowe added his own postscript: "Never assume someone won't stab you in the back or a wave couldn't sweep you overboard. With a SIBA you'll survive. Without it, you're dead meat, pard. Use it!"

Ian was already in his breeches and boots. He'd been too tired to undress himself before he lay down. "What is it, Shortstop?" he asked, as he buttoned the top of his white linen pirate shirt.

"The fog has returned, Mr. Wiz," Shortstop replied.

Ian scrambled up to the quarterdeck. Catch and Twobagger were trying to see their way through a fog so thick that Ian could barely see the *Millie's* bowsprit. Catch and Twobagger couldn't see the bow at all.

Ian looked down at the compass. "How long has she been in the soup?"

"Begging your pardon, sir?" Twobagger asked.

"The fog. How long have we been in it?"

"Not long, Mr. Wiz. I sent Shortstop to fetch you as soon as we saw it."

After another quick glance at the compass, Ian pointed slightly to his left. "You did good, Mr. Twobagger. Bring her two points to port and keep her steady."

"Cool, Mr. Wiz," Twobagger replied.

"Should I awaken Mr. Pitch, sir?" Shortstop asked.

Ian glanced at Catch and Twobagger for their opinion. They looked confident and were firmly in control of the ship.

"Let him sleep, Shortstop," Ian replied.

For the next hour they sailed silently through the dense fog. The *Millie* felt like a ghost ship. The only sounds were the gurgling of water under the bow and the gentle flapping of sails in the near-still air. Occasionally, a crewman below deck coughed or sneezed in his sleep. Twice they heard a great splash off to port that rocked the *Millie* from its wake. Unable to see what caused the splash, the three Gazzians became frightened, but Ian assured them it was nothing to worry about. "Probably a traa feeding on the surface," Ian guessed casually, which only widened their eyes even more.

Ian forgot about fatigue. He hoped there were no rocks just below the surface and repeatedly checked the compass. He intended to alter course again back to Nywok Bay soon—that is, if the winds were favorable and the Gall Moon gods were in good spirits. He was beginning to think like a Gazzian, he chuckled to himself. The plan was to swing the *Millie* around back to starboard and sail one more day to the west. That would complete the triangle and bring them back to the bay by three the following afternoon, when Harlowe, Leucadia, and Riverstone should be swimming toward the ship with their stash of black thermo-grym.

The gods, however, had mischief on their minds. Two hours after the sun rose, the *Millie* exited the fog. Two Phagallian men-o'-war were there, waiting for her.

Ian reached for the pocket where his com should have been. It was gone! "ALL HANDS TO BATTLE STATIONS!" Ian shouted.

70

Alien Mine

The morning sun was still a no-show, but its pink-and-green light was peering over the ridgeline. Harlowe, Leucadia, and Riverstone were already studying the mining installation below them from the cliff. They were 27,000 feet up the Black Mountain, where the terrain was barren and covered with snow and ice year-round. Their SIBAs had automatically adapted for them. After a couple of hours of rest, they had ascended to within a few hundred yards of the off-world installation Leucadia identified as a mining operation. "My thermo-grym readings are off the charts, Captain."

Her formality had not gone unnoticed.

Riverstone pointed to a shuttlecraft parked next to a loading ramp. "Maybe we could hitch a ride with that back to Millie," he suggested.

Harlowe thought that was doable. With a stolen shuttle, they could transport enough thermo-grym to fill *Millawanda's* gas tank to the brim. He had another observation. "This is why those ships attacked us when we arrived. They thought we were after their thermo-grym stash."

"We weren't then, but we are now," Riverstone quipped, eager for a little payback after all the trouble they had caused. Harlowe went even further. "Let's put them out of business for good. They don't belong on Gazz."

"Aye," Riverstone agreed, eyeing the steep mountainside above the mine. "A couple of Lu's special cherry bombs should do it."

Harlowe drew his flintlock and removed the casing that gave his Gama-pistol its 16th-century look. He checked the blue light on the back of his grip that told him he was locked and loaded with a full clip of plas rounds.

Riverstone snapped a fresh clip into his pistol and asked, "Ya gotta plan on how we're going in?"

Harlowe nodded straight ahead. "Through the front door." They didn't have time to be tricky. They had to grab the black thermo-grym, nuke the mine, and hustle back down the mountain to Nywok Bay by three.

The assault on the mine seemed easy. Only minimal security guarded the grounds. A secret mine, five miles above sea level at fifty degrees below freezing on a 16th-century planet required perimeter defenses only to keep large animals out of the compound. That could be handled automatically.

The Gamadin silenced the perimeter defenses with a few well-placed shots. Harlowe's plan to march through the front door proved to be more challenging than expected. Taking out the security triggered an automatic backup system that shut and locked the door to the mine.

Harlowe took one of Leucadia's fist-sized cherry bombs and tossed it at the door. The massive explosion covered them all with snow. But when they dug themselves out, they found the door was undamaged. The only result of the blast was a black circle around the grey alien metal. A hundred souped-up 16th-century cherry bombs wouldn't dent it!

That wasn't all. Leucadia's green eyes flared to full bright. "Harlowe!" she cried out. "The mine's reactor is cycling. It's going supercritical!"

"What's that mean?" Riverstone asked.

Harlowe turned away from the door and dashed toward the docking facilities and the shuttle. "They're nuking their mine. They don't want anyone taking their thermo-grym!" Harlowe shouted.

The Gamadin weren't the only ones with survival on their minds. A half-dozen aliens were running for the shuttle's open door. Inside the shuttle, others were firing up the engines. Harlowe and Riverstone cut down the six before they made it to the open hatchway, but the shuttle door began to close. From fifty yards out, Harlowe launched himself at the opening. The gap looked little bigger than a slit, but somehow Harlowe made it through and disappeared behind the now closed door.

Riverstone and Leucadia watched as flashes of blue light flickered behind the forward windows. A yellow mass of alien entrails splattered against the glass and then goo slowly dripped down the sides. A moment later, the shuttle door opened. Leucadia and Riverstone hurried through into a death scene.

No mercy. Harlowe had been thorough.

Leucadia rushed to Harlowe's side on the bridge to assist with the launch sequence, while Riverstone methodically tossed dead aliens to the back of the shuttle. They were not quite done when Leucadia's com sounded again. No one needed a com to understand what it meant: they were out of time.

The reactor blew...

71

Pigpo

Simon glided for miles down the incline of the mountain pass, wishing he had the altitude of the Black Mountain so he could fly all the way to Vine Island without stopping. Where he dropped down, however, was in a patch of dry, prickly bushes far short of his goal. The road had veered off in some other direction two valleys ago. The crawlies were gone, too, obviously preferring the dog trees to the inhospitable bushes.

He ran through the night until he came to the foothills overlooking a vast desert of white sand. Simon tried to see across the rolling dunes with his bugeyes, but even they were now working only intermittently. Like the few systems he had left, his opticals were living on borrowed time.

During one of its brief moments of clarity, he spotted a river to the west that flowed through the desert with a sliver of green lining its banks. If it was indeed a river and not a mirage, sooner or later, it would lead somewhere...hopefully to the ocean, he figured.

Mowgi's condition was unchanged. With the undog still strapped to his back, Simon struck out on foot for the river. To his relief, the river was indeed real. Simon followed the flow away from the mountains for another mile until he found a suitable place to rest. It was a small oasis near the water's edge with a grove of tall, wide-spreading palms that offered some shade. The oasis appeared safe,

358

but he no longer trusted his luck at picking good camping spots. With the crabbies and the crawlies still fresh in his mind, he settled under a palm tree and switched on his protective dome. In no time he was gonzo. He and the undog looked like fraternal twins, their tongues hanging listlessly out the side of their mouths.

*   *   *

Simon snapped awake to the loud crack of a gun. He thought he was under attack and dragged Mowgi with him like a stuffed animal as he dove behind the palm. He had been out long enough for the sun to travel from one side of the river to the other. He heard second, third, and fourth shots before he realized that he wasn't the target of the gunfire. It came from a small regiment of soldiers forging the river toward the oasis. They rode strange animals that looked like a cross between a hippo and a pig. They were big and round like hippos but had short, flat noses, pointy ears, and wide, stumpy legs with pad-like feet.

The soldiers were firing their blunderbusses at something big that moved in the water. Simon couldn't tell what it was until the beast burst out of the river. The beast was so fast and lethal that Simon barely saw the large, saw-toothed creature drag a soldier and his mount bodily, gear and all, back into the river before the other soldiers could do anything to stop it.

Whoa! That was radical, he thought, and made a mental note not to cross the river unless he could fly or walk over it on a bridge. Swimming was a little risky around here!

Put some warning signs out, dude!

While the soldiers were occupied, Simon decided it was a good time to split. He had already worn out his welcome twice in two days, and he didn't look forward to a third. He reattached Mowgi to his back and set out crawling through the underbrush. Using his SIBA invisibility, he slipped past the few soldiers along the river and scurried over one giant dune after another. He almost made it unscathed. Then a soldier riding a pigpo appeared over the top of the dune that he was climbing. To Simon's surprise, the soldier saw him clearly and went for his blunderbuss to kill the odd-looking creature with the big eyes.

Simon couldn't take the chance. He put the soldier out with a stun shot to the head. The soldier fell onto the sand and slid down the dune until Simon put out a foot and stopped his descent. When the soldier stopped sliding, Simon looked at the soldier's face and thought he would have made a good Dak if he was bigger. The soldier would be out for a number of hours, so Simon hustled away before anyone would came looking for him.

Striding up the side of the dune, Simon discovered why the soldier had seen him. His SIBA was losing its stealth properties and was becoming visible. His power was extremely low, so less-critical systems like camoflauge were shutting down. For the time being, his suit would keep him cool and provide him with enough liquid to survive. But for how long? Ian gave him only one power cell because it was supposed to be a quick flight back to *Millawanda*.

Yeah, right!

Simon patted the undog for luck and stared at the top of the mountainous dune. It looked as tall and intimidating as the Black Mountain on the other side of the pass. If this desert was the size of the Sahara, how far he could make it with his crippled SIBA? Not far, he knew.

A loud snort greeted Simon at the top of the dune. The soldier's pigpo had strayed after its rider was shot from his saddle.

Simon accepted the beast's invitation and reached for the animal's reins. "Hey, big guy, what's shakin'?" he said to his new mount. *He's not my regular driver, but who's complaining?*

The beast seemed gentle enough. He didn't run away when Simon approached him and wasn't startled by his off-world appearance. Knowing that walking in the soft sand would get him nowhere fast, Simon tied Mowgi's harness to the side of the saddle and climbed aboard. The saddle felt soft and cushy under him. It was a perfect fit! "All right, Pigpo, giddy-up!"

Simon had found his ride across the desert.

Pigpo

72

Down in the Hold

The shuttle was still on the launch pad when the blast hit. The craft had no shields, but the hangar buffeted the vehicle from the full fury of the blast. However, the avalanche of debris had buried the mine and everything around it, including the shuttle.

The bridge of the shuttle was completely smashed in. Glass and structural beams formed a twisted mass around the protective dome Leucadia put up just in time to save the group. When the chaos had settled, they switched off their personal force fields, pushed aside the rubble, and helped each other out of the tangle of wreckage.

Harlowe's first idea was to blast their way through the broken forward window using one of the miners' weapons. Leucadia consulted her com and threw cold water on that idea. "We would need a Gama-rifle to get us out. There's a hundred feet of snow and debris above us."

Harlowe reached over and removed the small black knife with the thermo-grym blade from Leucadia's Gama-belt. "Can we use this?" he asked.

She smiled. "Maybe, but I'll have to rig it so it will blow outward."

Harlowe handed her knife back. "Do it."

They erected their protective domes again in case the rigged thermo-grym explosive blew away the shuttle as well as the avalanche.

But Leucadia's placement was perfect. The explosion opened a pathway through the forward window large enough to drive an intact shuttle through.

Harlowe and Leucadia waited on the surface while Riverstone stayed behind to look for additional weapons in the shuttle. If anything remained of the mine, it was buried under a million tons of rock and ice.

"So much for the front door." Harlowe looked up and down the mountain, trying to figure out what they were going to do next. Even with their sensor unit, it would take more time than they had to find the thermo-grym inside the mine. He turned to Leucadia and asked, "What's the com say?" Maybe there was a deposit of black stuff close to the surface they could find without digging.

Leucadia clicked the switch on the Gamadin device. "It's not working."

She handed it to Harlowe so he could see it for himself. After a quick once-over, he handed it back. "It's fried."

"The shock wave," she stated, tucking the device back into her pack.

Harlowe stared at the dark smoke rising through the white clouds over the mountain, still wondering how to reach the thermo-grym buried inside the mine. It would take a lot more thermo-grym than a knife blade to blow away the avalanche that covered the mine. "I'm open to ideas," he finally said.

Heavy rumblings below them on the mountain brought them back to the present. Leucadia zoomed in on the disturbance with her long-range opticals. "Harlowe, the Nywoks are still after us with their creatures!"

Harlowe studied the horde of Nywoks coming their way. Thousands of Nywoks riding Cujos were climbing over rocks, plowing through snow banks, and leaping rivers and streams in a manic charge up the mountain after them. "Not us," he told her. "Me!"

Leucadia looked at Harlowe, dumbfounded. "Why you?"

"They have a score to settle."

Harlowe looked down the blast hole toward the shuttle. "What's taking Riverstone so long?"

Harlowe was impatient. The Nywoks were moving fast. In about an hour, the first wave of riders would be here. He wanted to use that time to get as far away as possible. Their SIBAs had survived the blast, but they wouldn't last long without fresh power cells. They would begin feeling the subzero temperatures unless they hurried off the mountain. He was about to shout an order to Riverstone to hurry it up when he got a call from his First Officer down in the hole.

"Dog! Come quick!" Riverstone's voice crackled weakly over their coms.

"What is it, Matt?"

"I think it's black stuff," Riverstone replied. "Lots of it!"

73

Learning to Drive

Riding Pigpo took some getting used to. It was surprisingly fast and nimble for a six-ton beast. Simon fell off of its back the first four times his desert mount burned rubber while ascending straight up a dune. Twice he fell forward over its snout when Simon pulled the reins a little too hard. He wished his saddle came with a seatbelt. With footsteps two feet wide, however, Pigpo was easy to track down. Each time Pigpo took off in the white sand without him, it would exhaust itself within a mile or so and wait for Simon to catch up. Mowgi's harness held fast. He didn't have to suffer the repeated embarrassments Simon did.

"Easy, Pigpo," Simon said, as he gathered the reins and climbed back on.

The basics of riding were simple. The reins were two leather straps clipped to the side of each stubby ear. To go right, Simon tugged right. To go left, he tugged left. To make Pigpo go forward at a normal pace, all he had to do was point the beast's head in the right direction and slap the reins gently on the creature's back.

Easy.

Simon was so tired that it took him four spills to realize he was kicking Pigpo in a sensitive area. Pigpo wasn't a horse. When he giddy-upped him like a horse, even gently, it was full speed ahead, dude!

After his fall, Simon finally got the hang of it. He put his feet forward into the stirrups where they were supposed to go, not down at the side where he might accidentally hit the "go" button.

Moving slowly this time, Simon halted Pigpo at the top of the next dune to survey the land ahead. He was gratefull for his SIBA, without which the hundred-twenty-degree heat would have baked him hours ago. He wondered how Mowg coped with the heat without one. What planet did the undog come from, anyway? Nobody knew, not even Mrs. M when she was alive. Was it hot like this or cold, or somewhere in between? He shrugged. Simon chuckled. What an odd planet it had to have been to produce an oddity like Mowgi!

He rubbed the undog's purplish short hairs with the back of his claw. "You're one man up little dude. I'll say that much, Mowg."

In case Mowgi was suffering from the heat, he covered the undog with a piece of fabric he found in the saddlebag. He didn't know if it made a difference, but Simon hoped it would give him comfort, if only a little bit.

Behind him the mountains were still in view, not much farther away than when he started. Chasing Pigpo all day had slowed him down considerably. It was time to get Pigpo pointed in the right direction and push his pedal to the metal.

Simon aimed Pigpo's snout one-hundred-eighty degrees opposite the pass and mushed on. He was still betting that Mowgi's original course was straight for Vine Island with no side trips.

"Giddy-up, Pigpo," Simon urged, his feet firmly forward. He tugged on the animal's ears gently, trying not to oversteer. "Is this the way to the beach, Pigpo?"

Pigpo replied with a nasally snort.

Simon yawned. He couldn't remember the last time he had a peaceful rest. He stared lazily over Pigpo's head, seeing nothing but dunes clear to the horizon. With the sun descending over his right shoulder, Simon leaned back in his saddle and continued south. He gave the undog a little pat and found another piece of cloth and a stick. He had seen photos of desert nomads using a stick and cloth to fashion a shade tent on their camels. He put the cloth over his head and Mowgi's, located a notch for the stick, and made his tent. He was surprised at how much cooler it made the ride. Impressed with himself, he lay his head down on the saddle and dozed off, rocking and rolling from side to side, like a ship sailing across a calm sea.

74

Scooters

The find was pure luck. If Riverstone hadn't gone snooping around in the shuttle hold for more weapons, they would have left a ton of the refined black thermo-grym behind. Harlowe hadn't noticed the boxes of thermo-grym when he dove through the hatchway the first time.

"Imagine that," Harlowe remarked when he found out that what they were looking for had been right under their noses! Some guardian angel was watching over them. Whether it was his angel, Leucadia's, or Riverstone's didn't matter. One of them was with them.

The refined crystal was packed in shielded, hundred-pound cases. Knocking it around wouldn't set it off, but one single case contained enough black thermo-grym to vaporize the Black Mountain or bust a thousand-mile-wide hole through the atmosphere if a plas round hit it, Leucadia warned.

"We'll be careful," Harlowe said, casually lugging a case up to the top.

"How much can we carry and stay ahead of the Nywoks?" Riverstone asked.

Harlowe wasn't encouraging. "Not much. A hundred pounds each, tops," he replied.

"Will that be enough for Millie?" Riverstone asked as he handed a hundred-pound case to Harlowe.

Harlowe nodded, taking the case and stacking it next to two others. "Lu says it will be enough to jumpstart her. We can come back and pick up the rest later."

"How much time do we have before the burst hits Gazz?"

"Less than six days if Wiz's calculations are right."

"Could he be wrong?"

"You want to bet against Wiz?"

"No. That's always a losing bet," Riverstone replied.

"Smart," Harlowe agreed.

Lecaudia emerged from the hole with an alien apparatus that looked like a large Hoover vacuum.

Harlowe looked at it with interest. Riverstone asked, "What is it?"

"If I'm right, it will help us down the mountain ahead of the Nywoks," Leucadia replied.

Leucadia released two rods and clicked them into place on a center pole, making a T. Next, she pulled out two drive cylinders from a large storage box and snapped them into place. She topped the contraption with a seat. She attached the large storage box to the assembly. "I believe it's a scooter that transports the thermo-grym cases from the mine to the shuttle."

Harlowe grabbed the handlebar, thinking he had come up with a rule Sun Tzu hadn't thought of: *Never leave a broken shuttlecraft behind without first checking its storage hold for goodies.* "Makes sense. Any more?"

"One."

Harlowe pointed back into the hole to Riverstone. "Get it!"

*   *   *

Harlowe and Leucadia were plucking off Nywok riders by the time Riverstone returned with the second scooter.

Harlowe turned to Leucadia. "Help him set it up!"

Leucadia handed Harlowe an alien weapon she had picked up in the shuttle. Another goodie. When he tried it out on an advancing Nywock, Harlowe discovered it lacked the range and power of a Gamadin sidearm, but it shot straight and had a thirty-round clip.

"Hurry up! They're almost here," Harlowe stated. Black-tipped arrows were already whizzing past their heads. A couple of arrows clinked off of his SIBA, reassuring him that not even a black-tipped arrow could penetrate the hide of a 54th-century suit. Still, Harlowe didn't want to get too cocky. The gods gave Achilles an indestructible suit of armor, too, and Paris still nailed him.

Harlowe kept everyone covered while he took care of the Nywoks.

A moment later, Leucadia and Riverstone had both scooters, each loaded with three hundred pounds of refined black thermo-grym crystal. Leucadia hopped onto the first scooter and switched on the power. It rose off the snow without a hitch, in position for her to gun the throttle.

Riverstone jumped onto the second scooter. "Good. This one's got gas, too!"

"This looks like the accelerator," Leucadia said, pointing to a short lever next to his right thumb.

Harlowe nodded at Leucadia. "Get through that pass before they cut you off!"

"Jump on the back, Dog!" Riverstone urged.

Harlowe leaped out from behind his cover and polished off a Nywok beast rider that was moving to block Riverstone and Leucadia's escape.

The beast's foot-long teeth were still snapping while Harlowe continued shooting at approaching riders.

"GO! THAT'S AN ORDER!" Harlowe shouted. He replaced an empty clip and climbed on top of the dead beast for a better firing position.

"Harlowe!" Leucadia shouted. She had no intention of leaving without him.

Harlowe fired five more quick rounds, jumped off the beast, and shoved Leucadia forward. "MOVE! I'LL LEAD THEM AWAY. THEY WANT ME, NOT YOU! I'LL MEET YOU AT THE SHIP!"

Off she went.

Leucadia raced toward the pass, and Harlowe turned to Riverstone while arrows rained down on them like hail. He shouted out, "MATT—DON'T LET HER OUT OF YOUR SIGHT!"

Riverstone slammed what was left of his energy pack into Harlowe's hand and hit the throttle. "DON'T BE LATE!"

There was no time to say thanks. He switched out the power cell in his SIBA and instantly his legs felt the surge of new power. Leucadia and Riverstone were now heading for the pass, so he had no reason to linger. He bounded up the side of the mountain with the entire horde in pursuit. He was right. The Nywoks didn't care about Leucadia or Riverstone. They wanted him.

The Nywoks saw that their arrows had no effect on him and began slinging fist-sized black stones at him instead. The power cell Riverstone had given him read at twenty-percent. Ordinarily, that would be enough to get him back to the *Millie* with plenty to spare, but not at this pace. If he kept it up, it wouldn't even get him off the mountain.

A stone hit his shoulder. The SIBA held up, but the force of the rock caused Harlowe to lose his footing. He rolled over and sprang into the air. When he looked down for solid ground to touch on, he found nothing but air and a bottomless crevasse.

75

Slow Going

The scooters had one flaw. They were slow. Their speed was nowhere near a grannywagon's. They were designed for short hauls back and forth between the mine and the shuttle at school-zone speeds. Leucadia and Riverstone discovered early on that they topped out at no more than thirty miles per hour. It didn't matter whether they were traveling uphill or down. That was the scooter's top speed. In a grannywagon, they would have been at Nywok Bay in less than an hour. On the scooters, it would take the rest of the day, and that's if nothing went wrong. The good news was that they had six hundred pounds of black thermo-grym between them. It was more than enough power crystals to get *Millawanda* up and running before GRB II sterilized the planet, assuming they made it back in time.

Their second worry was the horde of Nywoks chasing Harlowe. With a low-powered SIBA, Harlowe would need to do some fancy footwork to stay ahead of the riders. Even if he did manage to elude them, how would he get back to the *Millie* before they had to sail away? Time was short. They didn't have any left to wait for one individual. Harlowe would have agreed with that assessment.

"I'm worried, Matt. Harlowe's not talking to me," Leucadia said as they drove alongside each other.

"He'll be okay. He's out of range," Riverstone replied.

"He shouldn't be."

Riverstone pointed forward. "There's nothing we can do, Lu. Keep going. We have to make it back to the ship before nightfall."

Leucadia and Riverstone negotiated the pass with no problems. The flat, snow-covered mountainside made driving as easy as buzzing down the sloped sides of the Mons. They only had to avoid the jagged boulders sticking out of the snow every now and then. But at their kid-friendly speed, big rocks were easy to maneuver around. Not once did they have to take their thumbs off the throttle and slow down. They didn't need to worry about pursuit, either. Harlowe had been right. The Nywoks ignored them. They were only interested in him.

Once they were below the snow line, they entered a forest of thick trees, where travel was a little more complicated. They couldn't simply glide over the treetops like they could the snow. The scooters required solid ground for their tiny pulse drives to function properly. This forced them to wind through the trees close to the ground. At times, when fallen trees and dense, impenetrable underbrush made the going too hazardous, they had to find better paths. It took them more than three hours to get off Black Mountain and onto the open plains where they could scoot west with no obstructions.

76

Inner Space

More than a dozen riders on beastly mounts followed Harlowe over the edge of the crevasse. Harlowe had Gama-wings to break his fall. They didn't. With a great whoosh of gossamer material, Harlowe threw out his arms and deployed his wings. He glided gently downward and watched the Nywoks plunge into nothingness. Alone inside the vast emptiness, he continued on, soaring through the silent inner space of the glacier.

Harlowe circled for several minutes while he got his bearings. His nav readouts told him that the only direction available to him was northeast. It was nearly the opposite direction from his destination, but he had no choice. What lay in that direction, he couldn't tell. Something inside the channel was suppressing his SIBA's ability to see anything more than a mile away. He could see only a narrow and crooked passage with no visible way out. He didn't think he had enough lift to make it to the end of the channel, so he had to find an opening somewhere along the way. He saw only tight bends, switchbacks, and false openings. If he made the wrong turn, he would find himself in a dead-end maze and lost forever.

Gliding inside the twenty-seven degree crevasse was unlike anything he had ever done before. The muted blue light was constant, like the twilight just before dawn. The air was still and silent. He felt like he was floating in a dream held up by some magical force that defied gravity. The dream-like quality was amplified by the massive, vertical sheets of glacial ice on both sides of the chasm that went straight down into a bottomless void.

Every now and then he looked up and saw openings in the ice. They must have been as large as the one he fell through, but they were so far away that they seemed no larger than slender slits.

Suddenly, something bumped him. It wasn't a hard thump, but it jarred him slightly off course. He looked around and saw a triangular-shaped creature coming back around for another hit. Harlowe couldn't tell whether the creature thought of him as food or something attacking his domain. But gliding at the mercy of the air, his only choice was to wait and see.

The creature had a blue, iridescent edge to its wings that made up its entire delta-shaped body. It reminded him of an ocean manta ray back on Earth, except this glacial ray had no big pincer-like jaws. The creature had a bottle-shaped mouth and big doe-like eyes for seeing in the muted light of the crevasse. It wasn't large, perhaps ten feet from wingtip to wingtip, but it was fast and agile and quite graceful. It turned on a dime and came gliding back toward him.

On its second pass, the creature flew directly over his head, flipped over, rolled under him, and matched his speed. To Harlowe's relief, the creature seemed playful and curious in its advances and far from aggressive.

"What's shakin', big guy?" Harlowe asked the creature. "You are a guy, aren't you?"

Like a playful puppy, the creature dove, twisted, and flipped over several times, almost inviting Harlowe to join him in the fun. Harlowe wished he had a ball to play fetch.

"Sorry, pard. I'd love to play but I don't have time. I'm trying to save your planet," he said out loud.

The main channel Harlowe was in was turning into four splits in the vertical ice. He needed to decide which channel to take. His nav-com indicated that the far right channel was the correct path. As soon as he turned toward the opening, the com switched and pointed to the third channel to the left instead. But when he veered to make the correction, the com flickered back to the first selection.

Had the nav-com gone schizo, he wondered? It couldn't identify the best way to turn. It had been acting up since he entered the crevasse, and now it was confirming his suspicion that something in the ice was affecting the readouts. Whatever the reason, picking the right channel without the nav-com, was a roll of the dice. He couldn't just hover and circle while he sorted out which channel to enter. The more circles he made, the more altitude he lost. He had to pick one and hope for the best.

TAP!

It was another thump on his back from a second creature, with round pink eyes and a happy snout. Beyond it, a whole pack of happy snouts was headed his way. They were all making a beeline to join the party with the odd-looking visitor with big eyes and frail wings.

What to do? Harlowe thought briefly about shooing them away. He didn't have time to party down with a bunch of kids.

"Hey, does anyone know the way out of here?" he asked them.

When they heard his voice, they flipped and dove and twirled. How they were able to hear him was another mystery. Could they actually hear his voice behind his SIBA or was he communicating with his com? If that was the case, maybe his universal translator was making sense to them.

Whoa, wouldn't that be cool?

Suddenly one of the rays darted into the narrowest channel and the others followed. Harlowe had no clue as to whether that was the right way, but hey, they were the locals! So he joined the pack.

Unlike the kids, he was unable to flap his wings to gain altitude. Here in the crevasse, the air was as still as a tomb. There were no thermals or updrafts to help him gain altitude. Meanwhile, the bottomless floor was growing darker by the second. Soon there would be no light at all below a certain depth. Even with his optics on full zoom, he saw no place to land. There seemed to be no bottom to the crevasse.

He needed to go higher.

As if they understood his worry, several members of the pack split away and flew under him, creating an upward draft that provided lift for his wings. The idea was the right one, but the dance needed some choreography. If the creatures moved too far ahead, he lost altitude. Whenever that happened, the creatures winged back over his head and glided beneath him again. The dance went on two more times before Harlowe understood it was like catching a wave. In order to grab hold of the current, he had to catch the sweet spot inside the airflow.

"Sweet!" If he hadn't needed to be somewhere fast, he would have spent the day riding currents.

The narrow channel the pack guided him into wasn't the one he would have chosen. In places, there was barely enough room for two creatures to fly side-by-side and the channel became very crowded. On more than one occasion it reminded him of the packed hallways at Lakewood High between classes. On several occasions Harlowe had to be careful to avoid slamming into a ray or into a wall of blue ice. But whenever everyone spread out in a long line, they all flew on without a problem.

After a good hour of twisting and turning channels, the pack entered the largest open cavern yet. The walls of blue ice seemed to fall away. It was a vast inner space of blue twilight and no more channels to follow. Except for the bright light above and the darkness below, neither Harlowe nor his SIBA could identify any direction. He had been lost before, but now there was nowhere else to go. All points of reference were gone!

Harlowe had never felt so adrift in his life. If the creatures left him, he'd be toast. Where would he go? His nav-com couldn't tell him any more than Rerun could give directions. He had come to a dead end.

77

Hungry Pride

Leucadia's scooter was the first to fail. She skidded to a stop on the open prairie and that was that. Not only were the scooters slow, but they were good only for short hauls before they had to be recharged. There was no extra room for Leucadia's load of thermo-grym on Riverstone's scooter. So they dragged the scooter to a nearby ditch and covered it with tall grass and brush, with the idea of retrieving the cases when they returned in *Millawanda*. Leucadia climbed onto the back of Riverstone's scooter and they went for another ten miles before his, too, ran out of power.

"What now?" Riverstone asked, knowing the answer.

"We run," Leucadia replied unemotionally.

They each strapped a hundred-pound case to their backs and leaped off toward the afternoon sun. They didn't know if the two hundred pounds they carried would be enough to jumpstart *Millawanda*. Leucadia had no experience with thermo-grym crystals, either black or yellow. She didn't know if even the 600 pounds would have been enough. Nevertheless, one-hundred-pounds each was all the thermo-grym they could carry. It would have to do.

The extra weight on their backs cut their stride down from twenty to twelve feet. They slowed down a little, but on the open flats, they made good time despite the added burden. Good time, that is, until a pride of Gazzian lions spotted them trespassing on their domain.

379

Riverstone saw them first. He and Leucadia changed course, giving the pride a wide berth. This worked for a short time. For the first mile or so, the lions kept pace at a distance, stalking Leucadia and Riverstone the way they'd stalk easy prey.

"Got any ideas?" Riverstone asked. They had only a plas round or two each. That was hardly enough to hold off a pride of twenty lions.

"One," Leucadia answered as they leaped across a wide gully. "Keep going. I'll catch up."

Then she surprised Riverstone by jumping back across the gully, leaving Riverstone to wonder why she was heading straight for the pride. Riverstone thought about running after her. Maybe he could nail a beast or two with his SIBA claws before the beasts tore her apart.

He was astonished when he saw the beasts stop in their tracks, and equally stunned when Leucadia charged them, screaming and flailing her arms up and down like a crazed maniac. What sent them scurrying for the tall brush was her wings. As soon as she spread them out, the beasts took off as if they had seen a land traa.

*   *   *

"How did you know?" Riverstone asked Leucadia, when they were once again running toward the coastal mountains.

"I saw it in a cartoon once," Leaucadia replied. "I thought it was worth a try."

They had gone another mile or two when Riverstone turned to look behind him. The pride had returned, only this time they were running straight at them, looking hungrier than ever.

"Any more loony-toony ideas?" Riverstone asked.

"Get ready to fly!" Leucadia shouted.

The pride was visible over the tall grass when Matt and Leucadia reached the lip of a gorge. Without hesitating at the thousand-foot drop, Leucadia leaped and deployed her wings. Just as Riverstone began his jump, a beast leaped into the air behind him and swatted his leg. The SIBA was too tough for the lion's claws to dig in, but the force of the paw slapping Riverstone's leg twisted him around, spinning him off balance. Out of control, he nose-dived toward the rocky bottom of the gorge, followed by three hungry and panic-stricken lions.

78

Mom and Dad

Harlowe could only guess at how long he had been in the cavern. He should have been halfway across the planet by now. But there still appeared to be no end in sight. The soft blue mist kept him from seeing too far in any direction. The possibility that he was flying in one giant circle occurred to him more than once. He had been relying upon his playful friends for his entire flight. As much as he enjoyed their company, he was beginning to feel that it might be time to part company and strike out on his own.

Just when he was about to perform a wingover and break away, a massive shadow overwhelmed what light there was. Harlowe looked up and his heart sank. It was Mom and Dad coming to check on the children and their new playmate. The two adults had wingspans more than two football fields wide.

They were BIG!

Strangely, Harlowe never feared his life was at risk. If they had wanted to scoop him up in their hundred-foot mouths, he would be sprouting wings by now, even in his SIBA.

The giant creatures glided along, their bodies barely moving. The small-fry fluttered around Mom and Dad's faces like they hadn't seen their parents all day. Harlowe contemplated the miracle that even here, within a vast glacier in a place no one would imagine ever existed, parental love triumphed!

His com registered another drop in altitude. Harlowe had to find a way out of the cavern.

"Sorry, folks. It's been a pleasure meeting you, but I have to find a way out," he said to the family.

Harlowe picked a direction. Whether it was the right way or not didn't matter. Any new course was better than drifting forever in an unknown void. He winged over and drifted away, leaving the family to their happy cavern.

No sooner had he set out than the kids caught up with him, more playful than ever.

Tap! Tap! Tap!

The kids kept nudging him until he was back with the parents.

Harlowe pointed with his head he needed to go. "You don't understand. I can't play with you. I must return to my world."

At that instant, a long thread of light beamed down from an ethereal section of the cavern.

"That's where we're going?" he asked the kids.

The kids danced and twirled and flipped in spiraling somersaults.

"I take it that's a yes," Harlowe replied. The kids continued dancing their aerial boogie. "Sweet!"

As the family and Harlowe flew closer, the thread of light became brighter and more defined. It soon became apparent that the thread of light was, in fact, the way out. The cavern walls were sharp and vertical. Harlowe sailed on, past the great walls of ice, and saw before him a long valley of forests, small hills, and plains.

Harlowe had no idea how, but the creatures must have known all along where he wanted to go. He looked back over his shoulder and nodded goodbye. The creatures were gliding back and forth in front of the opening. They were not going with him.

"Thank you!" he shouted to them. "THANK YOU!"

The father nodded slightly and the mother winked her pink eye as if to say, "Be safe." At least, that's what it looked like to Harlowe. The kids seemed sad as they got only as close to the opening as their parents would let them.

Harlowe waved one last goodbye. "Thanks, little buddies. Take care!" Then he returned to the outside world with a lump in his throat.

As soon as he was away from the glacial opening, the instruments in his SIBA snapped on. He was up and running as normal again. He flew on into the sun that filled his wings with warm air and gave him lift. He put the updrafts to good use and flew west over a glacial river flowing below him in great torrents around rocks and ice blocks the size of houses. A thick forest of blue-green pine trees grew up the steep sides of the valley on both sides of the river. What grabbed his attention, however, was the time. The sun had only advanced a little bit. The SIBA's chronometer confirmed his impression. He had spent only a little less than an hour inside the glacier!

Harlowe reactivated his bugeyes. His SIBA's internal clock remained unchanged. He had only lost fifty-three minutes, not a whole day like he had figured. "Imagine that," he said to himself.

Now that his SIBA was back online, he tried calling Riverstone and Leucadia to see if they were onboard the *Millie* yet with their six hundred pounds of black thermo-grym. No one answered, not even Ian.

That worried him. One of the three should have answered.

He followed the valley and continued until the coastal mountains came into view on the other side of the vast prairie. He was right on course. If his luck held out and the winds held, he would cross the hundred-mile stretch to the base of the mountains without touching a blade of grass.

He tried several more times to raise anyone who would answer, but no one did and no one called back. All he got was dead silence. He ran a systems check, which revealed that if there was a problem, it wasn't at his end. If their coms were working anywhere on the planet, they would have replied if they were able.

The more possibilities he thought of, the more he worried.

Feeling a pit in his stomach, Harlowe flew out over the prairie, where the first black-tipped arrow tinked off his SIBA.

79

The Gorge

Lying spreadeagle on top of a cactus patch, Riverstone stared through thorny barbs at the cliff above, feeling the sensation of déjà-vu. On a planet with far more water than Earth, this was the second time he'd dropped out of the sky and landed on a thorny bed of nails for a cushion.

Go figure!

Finding no bones broken, he pulled himself out of the patch and thought about the old line, "if it wasn't for bad luck, I'd have no luck at all." He carefully unstuck his wings and folded them back into place. Remarkably, the wispy thin material had no slits, rips or tears.

Sheesh!

Riverstone flicked away thorns and twigs from his suit as he looked around, wondering where he was. As far as he could tell, he was at the bottom of the gorge where the lion had knocked him for a loop. The only way out was to climb up the rocky cliffs. He was about to check in with Leucadia when the loud roar of a lion interrupted his concentration. A short distance away, the lion that had followed him into the gorge was miraculously still alive. How had he survived the thousand-foot drop? In any case, the irate beast was still searching for its prey.

Riverstone saw two more less fortunate cats. One's hind end was sticking up, while its tail lay across a rock like a heavy rope. The other was wedged between two bloody rocks. They were both going nowhere.

Riverstone didn't wait around for an introduction to the surviving lion. He ran! He leaped away from the patch and bounced across the boulders like a jackrabbit.

"Lu, where are you?" he shouted into his communicator.

There was crackling and a kind of static spitting noise, but nothing resembling a human voice. For a brief moment, he thought he heard Harlowe's voice calling him, but was undecipherable. One or two words called for "Lu," but that was all. He wanted to take the time to tune it in, but his main priorities were contacting Leucadia and staying a few steps ahead of the lion.

Was she ahead of him or behind? Was she stuck somewhere trying to break free, or had she flown across the gap? He didn't know. She could be almost anywhere, he thought.

"Lu, if you can hear me, just click," Riverstone said again on the fly. He bounced over a boulder, leaped from another, and tapped off the side angle of a third until he hit a narrow trail for a short distance that led him to more fallen boulders.

As rough as the terrain was on him, the lion had it worse. It had no SIBA. It was swift and powerful on the open prairie, but the narrow gorge was an obstacle course. It couldn't always go straight. Yet the giant cat tirelessly pursued him.

Again a burst of static filled his com. This time he knew it was Harlowe calling him. Riverstone replied several times, but Harlowe never acknowledged his calls. Leucadia didn't either, but by then she didn't have to. He could now see her high on the rim of the opposite ledge, waving her arms and pointing down into the gorge.

What are you saying?

He watched her jump ahead, until she disappeared behind the cliff. Riverstone couldn't figure out where she was going until he rounded a bend. There she was again, this time pointing her sidearm down into the gorge.

She was shooting him down a line!

Right on!

Riverstone signaled that he understood her plan. All he had to do was attach the dura-wire to the front of his Gama-belt and he would be flying to the top of the cliff in no time.

Not if the lion had anything to say about it, however! The hungry beast was no more than two leaps behind him. If Riverstone slipped or faltered one time, the beast would be on him.

CRACK!

Leucadia must have read his mind. A blue plas-round from a Gama-pistol exploded at the feet of the prairie lion, causing it to stumble. It quickly recovered from the minor setback and continued its pursuit. The short delay, however, gave Riverstone enough time to grab the dura-wire line and attach it to his belt. Springing from the rock with all of his SIBA might, Riverstone leaped out and up thirty feet as Leucadia began reeling him in like a trophy fish. The lion leaped, too, but its massive paw found nothing but air. As Riverstone rose up the cliff, he turned once to thumb his nose at the giant cat that was feebly trying to climb after him.

*　*　*

"That was close," Leucadia said. Then she noticed his back. "Where's your thermo-grym pack?"

Riverstone reached for the pack that wasn't there. He turned back to the gorge. "It's down there with my pal." In the excitement of trying to stay alive, he had neglected to pick up his pack.

They traded looks. They had started with 600 pounds of thermo-grym. Now they had a single hundred-pound case left.

"Was that Harlowe on the com?" Riverstone asked, still looking down into the gorge for his pack.

"I think so," Leucadia replied.

Riverstone checked his indicators. "My power is on E. I'll be lucky to get back to the *Millie* on what I have left."

"Mine too."

"Harlowe must have escaped the Nywoks," Riverstone said.

Leucadia was also looking into the gorge as if she was planning to go after Riverstone's pack. She took her sidearm out to shoot the cat, but now the entire pride was there. She didn't have enough plas rounds for them all.

With a sigh, she lowered her weapon.

"Will it be enough?" Riverstone asked, looking to Leucadia for hope.

Leucadia reholstered her pistol and began walking toward the coastal hills. The cliff where Harlowe had shown her how to use her SIBA wings was only a few miles away. "It will have to be," she replied.

80

Seed Pods

Simon felt the sway of his yacht, the *Distant Galaxy*, rolling in a gentle rhythm over the swells. The easy and constant movement lulled him into a relaxing, forgetful dream. He heard only the sputtering throaty misfiring of his twin diesels laboring against a strong current.

"Monday!" he called out. "Fix the engines. They're disturbing me!"

A disgustingly foul odor intruded on his dream. *Oh my god! What's that smell?* Something reeked! His cabin smelled like a horse stall.

His eyes flew open and he yelled out again. "Monday! What's happened to my boat? It smells like—"

Simon reached up and tore the ceiling away from his face. To his surprise, it was not the ceiling of his yacht at all, but a small tent shielding his face from the sun. He sat up straight, wondering where his yacht had vanished.

"What the—" he said, twisting around in his saddle. It took a minute to gather his wits. Simon realized that he was not in his cabin. He was riding on top of the mount he had taken from a soldier earlier in the day. His yacht, the *Distant Galaxy*, had sunk nearly two years ago off the coast of Newport, California. This wasn't his yacht he was on, it was…"Pigpo?" he muttered. His desert yacht!

The sun was low on the horizon. Simon had slept through the day. Not once during his sleep did he encounter any crabs, spiders, soldiers, or anything else that would eat or kill him. It had been the most peaceful sleep he had since crashing on the planet.

Mowgi!

He turned, praying that whatever doggy angel was assigned to Mowgi was still looking out for him. His little sides were still. Next he tested his nose. Perhaps the afternoon was getting cooler, but the undog's nose seemed a little cooler and wetter than before. He knew that Mowgi's nose was cold and wet when he was firing on all cylinders.

Mowgi's mouth was dry and had some white crustiness around the edges. The undog was thirsty. He spotted what looked like palm trees a few miles away and pointed Pigpo in that direction.

*   *   *

When they reached the crest of the last dune, Simon was surprised to see the ocean. He didn't expect to see any kind of water for another hundred miles. The palms were not an oasis after all, but a wide stretch of beach lined with an unusual blue-striped variety of Gazzian coconut palms. He saw no fresh water supply nearby, no flowing rivers or creeks, but if the pods were anything like the ones back on Earth, there was plenty of drinkable water inside the coconuts.

Score one for the good guys!

Simon jumped off his saddle and ran to the first coconut he found in the sand. He slid to his knees and wrapped his arms around it like he had found a pot of gold. "Yeah, baby!"

Simon tried lifting the pod to carry back to Mowgi. The seed pod, however, was bigger than a basketball and many times heavier than its earthly counterpart. He proceeded to Plan B and began slicing away the weighty husk with his black knife. He was nearly finished when a heavy thump jolted the sand. He pulled his sidearm and pointed it at the dense ferns under the trees. What was that? He froze in place with his weapon drawn, but he heard nothing but the onshore breeze and the light surf breaking along the beach. Nothing moved in the bushes, either.

"Chill, Rerun," he said to himself.

Then the sand thumped again. It was a seed pod that landed less than a body's length away. He glanced up and saw a dozen more seed bombs clumped together and ready to drop. Not one to temp fate a third time, he dragged the seed a safe distance away to open his treasure.

Simon had spent enough time in the South Seas to become a pro at ripping open a coconut. With a few quick chops with his knife around the top of the nut, he was in. Now the question was whether the water inside was drinkable. If he swallowed bad water from the nut without a fully functioning SIBA, he'd have no way of getting medical help. He decided to give Pigpo the first shot. If his mount liked it, then he and Mowgi would share the rest.

Using the cracked-open part of the shell as a cup, he poured Pigpo a generous amount of the water and placed it in front of his snout in the sand.

Pigpo downed it like it was a chocolate shake.

Simon waited a little longer to see if there was a delayed reaction to the water. Nothing happened. Pigpo rubbed his blubbery cheeks against Simon's shoulder, pleading for more water.

Simon pushed Pigpo's big, snouty head to the side. "Hold on, Pigpo. Mowgi needs some first."

He snuck in a quick sip first before giving Mowgi some of the light green water. It was sweet and refreshing. As soon as it went down his throat, Simon felt his body absorb the fluid like a sponge.

It was almost as good as Blue Stuff in the way it shot life back into his tired limbs.

He spread the cloth like a blanket on the sand and placed Mowgi on it. Then he poured the green liquid over the undog's protruding tongue. Mowgi's tongue instantly absorbed every drop of the water.

"Wow!" Simon said, remarking on the speed of the absorption. He continued filling the empty cup and pouring more water into Mowgi's mouth. After five full cups with no visible side effects, Simon figured Mowgi had gotten enough. He gave the rest to Pigpo, who sucked down every last drop and crunched down the nut as well.

After three more seed pods, everyone was full. Simon hacked up four more nuts for the road. He mounted Pigpo again and put Mowgi safely into his harness. Two Gazzian moons lit their way as he pointed Pigpo south along the beach and said, "Giddy-up!" The only thing left to do was to keep trekking through the night in the hope of seeing Vine Island by morning.

81

Akasumi

Akasumi feared the worse. His wife was dying and the Ozimina Tree that could save her life had been stolen. For nearly four hundred twenty-one passings of the Gall Moon, Ume had been by his side. They met during the storm of Muka when they were young. He had never seen her before. Akasumi's fishing party had come through her village on their way to hunt the great serpents. The villagers told them it was certain death to hunt the mighty traa, but Akasumi was brash and felt immortal. He would kill the beast and bring the village its head so they would never forget Akasumi, the Slayer of Traas.

Akasumi took the water from his servant and put it to Ume's lips. She had not eaten or drunk anything from the day the *dowaa* bit her. "You must drink, Ume, for you will not survive the night," he told her.

He returned the ladle to the servant. Ume would not drink. Her arm and hand were swollen to twice their normal size. The practitioners had tried their traditional cures, their dances, and their medicinal smoke, but none had worked. When Ume's swelling became worse, he sent them away with orders never to return.

He brushed back her long black hair as he dabbed a wet cloth around her face. He smiled when he remembered how beautiful she had looked that day long ago, when he visited her village for the first time. "I am Akasumi. One day I will be king of the Nywoks and lead our people to great power by slaying the great traa."

Young Akasumi heard a villager giggle. It was a young, dark-haired girl with a bow and a quiver of black-tipped arrows. She was tall and striking, like no female he had ever seen before. Around her neck she wore a curious black amulet made of the same dark crystal as her arrows. "You mock your future king?" Akasumi asked her.

"You have never seen a traa, have you, great and future king?" she asked. "If you had, you would share my mirth."

Akasumi's servants prepared to whip the female for her disrespect, but Akasumi found her refreshing, and if the truth be known, *Maahoo* had found his heart. "I have heard only tales, *Doni-tatunni*," which translated meant "girl with bow." Akasumi pointed with his fishing spear toward the coastal hills. "The royal village is on the flatlands, in the shadow of the Black Mountain. I have slain the mighty *jaagoona, the borttas,* and twice killed a *lynics* with my bare hands. Their heads fill my hut. When I am King, a traa will also be displayed amongst my trophies," Akasumi said proudly.

Doni-tatunni laughed again. "Forgive me, great and future king. I have seen a traa. Your royal hut must be very sizeable indeed, for the jaws alone of a traa would swallow our humble village."

Now it was Akasumi and his servants' turn to laugh. "Doni-tatunni, you are as funny as you are insolent. Come with us, then. Show us this village-sized traa you speak of. If it is as big as your village, then indeed, I will order a larger hut for my new prize," he boasted, looking straight at her.

Amusement suddenly drained from Ume's face.

"Hunting for traa frightens you, Doni-tatunni?" Akasumi asked, grinning slyly.

There was no humor in Ume's voice as she replied, "Foolishness always frightens me, future king. For if you pursue such madness, the Nywoks will need a new future king."

Akasumi pointed with his spear at the boats on the beach. "Come then. Bring your bow to protect our party of hunters against your traa."

"Is that an order, great and future king?"

"It is, Doni-tatunni. You will see for yourself how the future king of the Nywoks slays a mighty traa."

*   *   *

A thunderous commotion disturbed the royal village. Akasumi faced his daughter, Shuun, who came hurriedly through the door of the royal bedchamber with the news.

"Father! The warriors are returning!"

"Have they captured the Kilkin?" Akasumi asked. That was all he wanted to know. The Kilkin, or "thief" as translated from Nywok, had stolen the Ozimina Tree from its sacred ground. If Ume died, killing the thief would be his final act before taking his own life. He would not live another day without his beloved Doni-tatunni.

"I don't know, Father, but they travel hastily to the village. It is possible the Kilkin has been captured!"

Akasumi glanced back at Ume. The head servant nodded that it was all right for him to go. The servants would watch over her while he dealt with the Kilkin.

Akasumi and Shuun made their way quickly through the lush gardens of the Royal Compound and down the path that led to the village. The Royal Hut was built on the highest ground above the river. The view was far-reaching. The Royal Compound commanded a sweeping view of the prairie, all the way to the sacred

Nyixx Mountain, otherwise known by the Croomis as Mountain of Night. Racing toward the village were hundreds of Nywok mounts, kicking up vast clouds of red dust. Akasumi and Shuun could feel the thunder of heavy paws beneath their feet. It could mean only one thing: his warriors had found the Kilkin. Akasumi's pace increased in his eagerness to face the one responsible for the impending death of his beloved Ume.

Just ahead of the stampeding mounts was a lone figure. It was leaping in long strides ahead of the pack. Entering the village, the figure slowed and was about to be trampled. At the last moment, it jumped in a single leap like a *neebe* locust, rose high above the treetops, and landed steps away from the startled Akasumi.

The figure turned slowly stood and faced Akasumi and Shuun. Its leathery covering and large eyes were the same red color of the grounds. It carried no spears or weapons, but around its middle it wore a belt with many attachments.

"That was close," the figure said, dusting itself off.

Akasumi and Shuun were taken aback when the figure spoke their language.

Akasumi raised his hands in the air to stop his warriors at the edge of the grounds. The furious mounts clawed angrily to get at the Kilkin they had been chasing throughout the day. But Akasumi did not want the thief killed . . . yet.

When the beastly roars and the chatter of warrior voices settled, Akasumi asked the figure, "Are you the Kilkin we seek?"

The large-eyed figure finished dusting himself off, then he tapped the side of his neck. At once, a mask that surrounded his head retracted, revealing a young Croomis male. For a moment, a wispy blue light around the figure sparkled then faded to almost nothing. This startled almost everyone except Shuun. She found the Croomis intriguing. He had the courage of the Gall Moon to face her father and stand before the Nywoks. He was also her age and strikingly handsome. Apparently, the young girls in the village all noticed the same thing.

Neither the Kilkin's tricks nor his daring frightened Akasumi. He wanted answers. Was he the Kilkin who stole the sacred tree?

"What is a Kilkin?" the young Croomis asked.

"The thief who stole the Ozimina Tree," Akasumi replied accusingly.

The Croomis looked around at the hundreds of warriors and villagers staring at him. All of them wanted to shed his blood. The warriors aimed their bows drawn with black-tipped arrows, ready for Akasumi's nod to kill the one who had wronged the Nywok.

"Yes, I am the Kilkin, then," the Croomis admitted.

Akasumi saw no reason to wait. As king, he was judge, prosecutor, and jury. The Kilkin had been captured and rightly admitted to the crime. His guilt was evident. Akasumi nodded. Death to the Kilkin! Faster than the blink of a *borttas'* eye, a cloud of arrows darkened the sky.

The arrows, however, never touched the Kilkin. The hardened black points tinked off the Croomis boy and fell harmlessly to the ground. More arrows followed, but none could penetrate the young Croomis' armor. After multiple waves of futility, Akasumi raised his hands in disgust. "Enough!" he cried out.

The Croomis kneeled down, examining the pile of broken arrows as he spoke to Akasumi. "I came to apologize, sir," he said. "I was unaware that your tree was sacred."

Akasumi walked to a soldier and took the warrior's sword. "I will slay you myself!"

"It would serve no purpose," the Croomis said, continuing to handle the arrows.

"I am King of the Nywoks. I must right the wrong you have done to my people and my..." He could not say Ume's name out loud.

Sword in hand, Akasumi strode over to the young Croomis. Shuun ran in front of her father to stop his charge. "No, Father!" she said to his face. Shuun was like her mother in many ways. She was beautiful and tall and when she saw folly, she, too, spoke her mind.

"Out of my way, daughter! I command you!" A sharp glance from Akasumi summoned a trio of warriors to assist in carrying out his orders.

Shuun turned on the warriors with her fierce dark eyes. "You dare touch the King's daughter? I will have your heads!"

The warriors froze for a moment. Regardless of the consequences, their first loyalty was to their king. One warrior reached for Shuun. Her punishing foot to the chest sent him to the ground. Dismissing the other two warriors with a wave of her hand, Shuun turned back to her father.

"You told us how Mother saved you from the traa. Your servants were killed by the beast because you thought it did not exist. You were the only one who survived, Father. Mother dragged your dead body to the Ozimina Tree and fed you its golden leaves to bring you life. Like my mother, I must save you today."

"The Kilkin is no traa! He is Croomis. He will bleed from my sword!"

"Listen to me, Father! He is not Croomis. A Croomis would not regret his thievery. He would take the Ozimina Tree's magic for himself and never return." Shuun looked at the Croomis. "He has power beyond the traa. Beyond the Gall Moon!"

"There is no power beyond the Gall Moon," Akasumi countered.

"He has, Father. We know of this warrior." Shuun then addressed the young god. "Your ship destroyed Daloom," she stated.

"Yes. My name is Harlowe. I am Gamadin. I am responsible for taking your tree," he told them.

"Only a god could destroy such a fortress, Father."

Without warning, an angry mount broke from the pack and charged the Gamadin. The Harlowe god held out his arm and bright blue light struck the beast between the eyes. The beast slid forward, coming to a stop before the Harlowe god. It lay still as if it had been shot in the head by a thousand arrows.

The Harlowe felt the side of the beast's head. "He's only stunned. The Cujo will be all right in a few hours."

Shuun looked at her father. His face was tired and drained. He wanted only that his beloved would return to him and restore his royal spirit. She took the black sword from his hand and handed it back to the warrior. "To fight the power of the gods, Father, is the waste of a great king."

The Harlowe god then promised, "I will return your sacred tree before the Gall Moon rises."

Akasumi could not believe the pledge. The Ozimina Tree was the only one of its kind. Its power could never be duplicated or regrown. It was lost forever.

Akasumi would fight neither a god nor his daughter. Fearing that he was about to lose everything dear to his heart, he departed, leaving the fate of his Ume in the hands of Shuun and the young Harlowe god.

82

Broken

They were two hours late. Leucadia and Riverstone made it over the coastal hills with their single pack of thermo-grym without a hitch. But they were two hours behind schedule. It was late afternoon by the time they exited the forest above the cliffs where they had started their mission. The sun was bright in their faces, lying just above the horizon against a yellow, green, and blue sky. They found it odd that during their entire run through the forest, they had seen no Nywoks.

They expected to see the *Millie* lying at anchor in the bay, impatiently waiting for them. But the bay was empty. All the way to the horizon, they saw no sails of the *Millie* or any other ship. Had any of their plans gone right?

With nowhere else to go and no Nywoks to worry about, they made a small campfire and waited at the edge of the cliff. The sun had been down for several hours before Riverstone saw the lights of a ship coming toward them.

Leucadia's bugeyes were the only ones working. "It's the *Millie*," she confirmed. The galleon was moving slowly, even in the good wind. She closed her eyes and held her head.

"What's wrong, Lu?" Riverstone asked.

"She's hurt, Matt," Leucadia replied. "I can see damage like she's been in a battle." She turned to him with tears in her eyes. "I should have stayed with her."

Riverstone silently put his arm around her. Words would have served little purpose.

During the next hour, they saw the extent of her damage. The vaporous light of the Gazzian moons exposed her wounds. Her bowsprit was broken, dangling down and dragging against the bow in the water. Dents and cannonball holes pockmarked the entire vessel. The shattered foremast lay in a splintery mess on the forecastle deck. The mizzen mast below the crow's nest was missing. The only sail they saw was the main. As much as the *Millie* had taken, only the tough Nywok spirit tree remained unblemished.

Leucadia noticed something more alarming. "She's not weighing anchor, Matt! If she stays on her present course, the *Millie* will beach against the rocks!"

Riverstone focused on the quarterdeck steerage wheel. Someone was working desperately to steady the wheel and bring the ship about, but whoever it was kept falling to his knees. The crewman was hurt. He was too weak to turn the heavy wheel. Finally, the steerman fell over and lay motionless on the deck beside the wheel.

Leucadia and Riverstone leaped from the side of the cliff, deploying their wings against the onshore winds in a desperate attempt to reach the galleon before she grounded. They didn't know if they'd make it in time. The winds that buffeted them pushed the *Millie* faster and faster toward the rocks.

"Follow my lead, Matt!" Leucadia cried out. "Use the sail! If we overshoot, we'll never catch her!"

Riverstone only nodded.

The wind made it tough. In the twisting sheers that slammed against the cliffs, they had no sure way to guide themselves to where they wanted. They bounced and weaved from side to side as they fought to line up on their target. They drifted too far in one direction, then over-compensated and drifted back the other way, yet they always kept the main mast as their center guide.

WHAM!

Together they slammed into the main sail and slid down to the main deck. Leucadia nearly lost it when she found herself among the wounded. Robobs were using their 54th-century medicine to keep the seriously injured alive. Pitch had lost an arm, Twobagger was missing a hand, and Shortstop was heavily bandaged where he had lost an eye. They all had bloody, green-stained bandages covering their injuries. Catch and Twobagger were only Gazzians without serious injuries, but they were lying against the foredeck bulkhead, too exhausted to move.

"Where's Wiz?" Riverstone asked.

Leucadia looked toward the bow. Jagged rocks were in their path and coming up fast. "Never mind that now!" She grabbed Riverstone by the shoulders and pushed him aft. "Release the stern anchor, Matt! Once it finds bottom, tie it off good. Keep her line fast. Don't let it play out!"

Riverstone grabbed a loose spar line and swung himself aft, while Leucadia leaped over the quarterdeck rail. She found Ian beside the wheel. He was laid out, but his arms were still trying to grasp the wheel. Leucadia grabbed a broken spoke and pulled with all her SIBA strength to turn the *Millie* starboard.

A section of wheel broke off in her hand. She reached for a broken section of spar and stuck it between broken spindles for leverage. She lifted and grunted with every last bit of her strength. The wheel was slow to respond, but over it went. She looped a rope over the wheel to keep it from falling back, then pulled out the spar and jammed it through another spoke. It wasn't going to be enough. The *Millie* couldn't swing around on a dime to begin with. At this pace, the *Millie* was destined for the rocks.

As if the Gazzian gods took pity, the galleon suddenly heaved over. If not for her special ballast, the ship would have capsized.

"Hard about girl! Hard about!" Leucadia screamed at the top of her lungs. "Hard about, *Millie*! Come on girl! Hard about!"

The motion was so abrupt that Leucadia toppled over the broken steerage wheel. Her SIBA saved her from being impaled on the broken spokes. She pulled herself up and jumped back to the wheel. She resumed leveraging the broken spokes, and slowly, the *Millie* turned. In front of her, tall, black rocks came out of the darkness and loomed over the *Millie* like evil giants preparing to take a bite out of her hull. The *Millie* scraped her sides against their jagged edges, but miraculously she passed them by without damage.

Now that the *Millie* was pointed in a safe direction, they weighed anchor a quarter mile out from the rocky shore.

* * *

Ian's SIBA had saved him from the Phallagian cannon blast, but his shoulder was broken and his face was a roadmap of cuts from iron fragments and splintered wood.

"They came out of the fog," Ian said to Leucadia. "I didn't know what to do." His voice cracked with shame. Leucadia comforted him in her arms.

Riverstone had joined them after surveying the damage to the ship. "You made it back, Wiz. That's what counts."

Ian looked past them both. "Where's Harlowe?"

Leucadia was the first to speak. "We don't know." She looked toward the coastal hills. "He's still out there."

"You got the thermo-grym, right?" Ian asked.

Riverstone removed the bundle from his back and laid the small metal case on the quarterdeck. "A hundred pounds," he said.

Ian's disappointment was clear in his response. "That's not enough, Lu."

Leucadia nodded. "I know."

They all knew that without *a lot more* black thermo-grym, their situation was hopeless. They would need the full six hundred pounds of black thermo-grym just to lift her out of the sea. The hundred pounds would barely keep the lights on. A hundred pounds wouldn't get them off the planet or do anything to save Gazz. All life on the planet was doomed, and everyone on the *Millie* too, if they couldn't get the galleon repaired in time to sail her over a thousand nautical miles in five days with a full supply of thermo-grym. Even if they had the valuable cargo, repairing the damage enough to make her seaworthy again would take weeks. On top of that, where was Harlowe?

Rivestone asked himself, *What would Harlowe do?* Riverstone knew that Harlowe would never give up unless he was...Well, he wasn't dead! Riverstone knew he'd heard the Captain's voice.

Riverstone turned to Leucadia and Ian. "Any suggestions?" In times like this, Harlowe always asked that same question to give himself time to think.

"Have all those who are able to work start clearing the rigging," Leucadia suggested. "We'll need all the sail we can get."

Ian sat down and leaned his back against a broken section of the mizzenmast. Riverstone swapped his SIBA power pack for Ian's.

Riverstone's didn't have much left, but Ian's had zeroed out. The power was enough for Ian's SIBA to repair his broken bones and get him firing on all cylinders again in a few hours.

"The main is the last of our sails, Lu," Riverstone said, pointing to the pieces of sheeting lying in heaps around the decks, "and it's full of holes."

Leucadia surveyed what they had to work with. "There might be enough," she thought aloud. She pointed to the heaps of rigging. "Gather all the sail pieces you can find and pile them there on the main deck. Don't worry about what size they are or their condition. Every piece is important."

Like Harlowe, Ian and Riverstone had learned a long time ago not to question Leucadia's seemingly off-the-wall ideas. They understood why Harlowe often answered her with just a short, "Yes, dear."

*   *   *

It was after midnight. Whatever was left of the sails had been collected into something that looked like a giant pile of dirty underwear. Riverstone stood with his hands on his hips and asked, "What now?"

"While I put the robobs to work, you and Ian clear the foredeck of debris. That includes the bowsprit. I need that whole area clear."

They both saluted. "Yes, ma'am."

"What about Harlowe?" Riverstone wondered again before setting off to work on the bowsprit. "What if he doesn't come?"

Leucadia turned to Ian. "How long do we have, Ian?"

Ian took a deep breath. "By morning, five days. Even with a full sail and a good wind, we'll need a boost from somewhere. Two days south of here we'll hit the doldrums. The turbos can power us through that, but by then the clickers will be out of juice. We need a miracle, Lu. Do you have one?"

Leucadia didn't answer. Catch and Twobagger joined the small group just as Leucadia said, "We leave in the morning with the trades."

Catch and Twobagger looked horrified. "We can't leave the Captain, Ms. Lu!"

"We'll give him until morning," she said.

"If he doesn't make it, I'll go after him," Riverstone stated.

"No, Matt, I need you here," Leucadia countered.

"He would do that for all of us. You know that."

"We're short-handed as it is. If something happens to you, I have no one to turn to but Ian."

"You must not leave the Captain, Ms. Lu!" Twobagger pleaded.

"No more discussion, Mr. Twobagger. The Captain knows how important it is for us to return to Vine Island with the black crystal. That's all you need to know." She then ordered the two Gazzians to the main deck to help with the repairs. Reluctantly, they obeyed. Riverstone understood why Leucadia had been short with the Gazzian sailors. They had no idea what a gamma ray burst was, let alone how it would destroy their planet.

A great yellow and orange glow lit up the horizon in the east. Riverstone glanced at Leucadia. They both knew Harlowe was the cause of it.

Under less troubling circumstances Leucadia would have discussed what Harlowe was up to, but she had a boat to fix before morning. Her only response was short and direct. "He'd better be here by morning."

After she put the clickers to work on repairing the ship, she left the quarterdeck to begin preparation of her own project.

83

Treasure Chest

Acting captain Riverstone's first command decision after taking over in Harlowe's absence was the one he never wanted to make. Wiz thought they should have sailed two hours ago. Catch warned that the moon gods were unpredictable and fickle. They could turn against the *Millie* at any moment and lose their advantage. To temp fate any longer was unwise. The winds were steady and favorable. They must leave now.

The sea beyond the Nywok Bay was as smooth as a highway, and no Phagallian ships were anywhere to be seen. It was the hardest decision Riverstone ever had to make. His best friend was somewhere out there, and they were setting sail without him. How many times had Harlowe risked his life for them? Now Riverstone was nailing the lid on Harlowe's coffin. Even with Leucadia and Ian standing beside him for support, he never felt so alone.

Looking for support, Riverstone turned to Leucadia. He could see in her eyes that she knew his dilemma. "It's time, huh?"

"No choice," she replied.

Riverstone swallowed hard and gave the order. "Do it, My Lady."

Leucadia looked up at the main spars. "Mr. Twobagger!"

"Yes, Ms. Lu!" Twobagger called down.

"Let go the main sheets, if you please."

"Cool. Let go the mains," he called back.

The cannonball holes in the sail had been patched by robobs during the night. The decks had been cleared of debris. The foresail and the mizzen were history. The mains were it! It was all they would have until they reached the doldrums, where they would use the turbos to motor through the windless sea.

"Mr. Riverstone, sir!" Zinger called down from the crow's nest, excited.

"Yes, Mr. Zinger. What is it?" Riverstone asked.

Zinger pointed toward the shore. "Look!"

A mass of bodies was emerging out of the trees to a heavy rhythmic beat and spreading out along the narrow beach. Not hundreds, but thousands were leaping up and down in a rhythmic cadence. "Belay that last order, Mr. Twobagger!" she said. "Loose sails, if you please, sir."

"Hold on, Lu. What's up with that?" Riverstone asked, pointing at the thousands of Nywoks waving their spears and arrows in the air toward the *Millie*.

Ian was anxious to leave, as well. "We shouldn't wait to find out." For him and Riverstone, the message was clear: put to sea before a hail of arrows came flying their way.

Riverstone was about to counter her order to hold their position when Leucadia explained her reasoning. "Their singing is celebration, not war, Matt." She pointed to a lone outrigger carved out of a tree trunk being launched from the shore. It was more than fifty feet long and carved out of a single tree trunk. A dozen or more warriors on both sides of the vessel were in full battle regalia. Each rower held a wide paddle, which he dove into the water in great strokes. The speed of the outrigger was impressive. Riverstone doubted they could outrun the Nywok boat unless they were at full sail. Between the warriors, toward the rear of the craft a regal couple sat together in brightly colored robes upon a single throne. They wore tall, feathery headpieces that waved four feet in the air and arched back over the stern as the boat raced forward. Next to the regal couple stood a tall, dark-haired woman who immediately caught Riverstone's eye.

"Whoa! She's hot!"

A cold eye from Leucadia cooled his jets. At the front of the outrigger stood a tall, tailless human. "That person standing in front looks familiar," Leucadia said.

Ian's enhanced Gamadin eyes saw the human clearly. "It's Harlowe!" he cried out.

Riverstone remained speechless. He had visions of Harlowe tied to a stake full of arrows, not standing in the bow of a Nywok royal yacht!

Ian and Leucadia rushed to the portside gangway to meet the boat coming alongside the *Millie*.

"Swing the lifting boom over the side!" Harlowe ordered while he reached out to grab the tall arching nose of the outrigger's bow.

"Aye Captain!" Ian replied back.

Leucadia and Ian followed Harlowe's directions, untying the boom and swinging it over the side to the center of the outrigger. Harlowe grabbed the rope and called out more orders. "Ready those mains, Mr. Twobagger! Make ready for the open sea, Mr. Catch! Mr. Wizzixs, a fast course back to Vine Island, if you please! No time to waste!"

Harlowe himself took the boom line secured it around a large black chest in the middle of the outrigger. Before he was even finished, he ordered, "Ms. Lu, grab a clicker. It's heavy!"

"Aye, Captain!" she acknowledged.

By the time Leucadia returned with the robob, Harlowe had secured the chest and was saying goodbye to the royalty in the back of the outrigger. He bowed deeply to the two Highnesses, pointed at the *Millie*, the sky, and himself. Then he turned to the young dark-haired woman. He took her hands and held them firmly, as if expressing his thanks. With tears in her eyes and a chin held high, she returned the farewell.

Harlowe turned away and didn't look back. He jumped on top of the chest and gave Leucadia a signal to raise the chest out of the boat. Leucadia swung the boom back around, positioned the chest and rider over the main deck, and set it down. Before she could speak, Harlowe grabbed a spar line and swung up to the steerage wheel. Shortstop was there with a patch over his eye, holding his Captain's hat firmly in hand. Harlowe thanked his young servant and shouted more orders.

"Do we have a heading yet, Mr. Wizzixs?" Harlowe asked.

"Aye, Captain, we do," Ian replied.

"Sheets full, Mr. Catch!" Harlowe called out.

"Cool, Captain! Sheets full, they be!" Catch replied.

From the moment she saw Harlowe on the Nywok boat, Leucadia wanted to leap into his arms and hold him. She wanted to be alone with him, sharing a meal and catching up. But pleasures of the heart would have to wait. Harlowe was the *Millie's* captain again and *she* was his first priority.

Only on a few occasions had Leucadia ever seen Harlowe as tender as when he touched the broken steerage wheel and eyed Shortstop's injury. He sighed deeply and turned to speak with Riverstone, who did all the talking. Harlowe listened. He kept nodding, speaking briefly only to clarify a point or ask a short question while an animated Riverstone described the journey back from Black Mountain.

The mood changed, however, when the subject turned to the *Millie*. She saw tears well up in Harlowe's eyes as Riverstone described what the *Millie* had suffered in his absence. Harlowe continued to listen without interrupting, and when Riverstone was finished, embraced his old friend. Leucadia couldn't hear his words, but she knew Harlowe. He was telling him to hang tough, not to give up, and to trust that they were going to make it through. That was Harlowe. Losing never entered his mind.

Finally Harlowe turned and looked down at her with his big blue eyes. They were stern, focused, and intense. She wouldn't blame him if he threw her off the ship for all the damage she had caused by disobeying his order to stay with the ship. Her self-centered arrogance nearly cost Harlowe the lives of his crew, his colleagues, his galleon, and quite possibly his mighty Gamadin ship. He scurried down the ladder and met her standing next to the chest he brought aboard from the Nywok outrigger.

Eyes straight ahead, heart racing, Leucadia snapped to attention and saluted Harlowe as he walked up to her. "Captain." He was not himself. He appeared shaken and distraught. She had seen him this way only once, when his father died. It was like someone she loved had died, too. She wanted to shoulder all his pain. *Hadn't he suffered enough?*

"Glad to see you…" she started to say, but she was invisible to him. Harlowe walked right by her without the slightest acknowledgement and continued on toward the crew hatchway. With her chin up and her eyes filled with tears, she kept her head pointing straight ahead and did not turn to follow him. Harlowe lifted the hatchway door and disappeared below deck.

His crew *always* came first…

84

The Crew's Touch

It was midday before Harlowe emerged from below deck. Several times Jewels clickity-clacked from Harlowe's cabin to the crew's quarters with a tray stacked with double-doubles, Blue Stuff shakes, and fries. The *Millie* was on a portside tack, heading due south on a direct line back to Vine Island. There was a slight chop on the water and the winds remained steady from the northwest.

Leucadia remained at attention, guarding the chest the entire time Harlowe was below deck. When he finally emerged, he walked slowly to the chest. His eyes conveyed his suffering as he spoke in a low, exhausted voice. "At ease, Lu." She couldn't imagine the pain he must have felt after seeing the injuries his crew had suffered. Knowing him the way she did, he felt every severed arm, every cut, every lost eye, every shattered bone was as if they had been his.

"Any word from Rerun?" Harlowe asked.

"No Captain," Leucadia replied.

"How many days has he been gone?"

"Five now, Captain."

Harlowe stared at the horizon for a moment before he nodded toward the main sail. "Riverstone says you made something that will give us more speed, even in a low wind."

"Yes, Captain," she replied.

"Is it ready?"

"Nearly."

"How many hands do you need?"

"All that are able."

"Very well. Do it. Keep me informed," Harlowe said going to his cabin.

"Yes, Captain."

*   *   *

When Leucadia advised Harlowe that the work was finished, he called all hands who could walk to the forecastle deck. The group that gathered was small: Riverstone, Ian, Catch, Twobagger, and Zinger. Pitch tried to join the party, but he couldn't make it out the hatchway without falling. Harlowe ran over and lifted Pitch to his feet. If the six of them couldn't manage it, a one-armed crewman wouldn't make any difference. "I appreciate your loyalty, Mr. Pitch, but we have enough help."

Feeling hurt and useless, Pitch started back down the companionway to his quarters. Riverstone saw his disappointment and held him back.

"Are you sure, Captain?" he asked with a wink. "Ms. Lu said she needed *all* the available assistance we could muster."

Harlowe caught his mistake and realized that Riverstone was right. Excluding Pitch would injure the morale of his First Mate more than any physical wound. "Aye, right you are, Mr. Riverstone." He turned to Pitch and said, "Not so fast, Mr. Pitch. We certainly could use your help, if you please, sir."

Pitch's face brightened. "Cool, Captain! I would indeed!"

As if the moment had been planned, a clicker opened the crew hatchway and every Gazzian crewman, able or not, dragged himself out of the hold, hobbling, limping, or crawling to get to the forecastle deck.

Harlowe was so proud of his crew that his eyes welled up. Riverstone and Ian assisted the most infirm crewmen up to the deck. To all of the crew, merely being on deck when he needed them the most was their way of showing the deep respect they had for their Boy Captain.

Harlowe had to wipe his eyes while he expressed his heartfelt thanks. Then turning to Leucadia, he said, "It's showtime, Ms. Lu. Let's see what you have."

Leucadia lifted the forecastle hatch and pulled out the end of a patchwork sail the robobs had sewn together per her instructions. She untied a lanyard attached to the top of the main mast and secured it to one end of the cloth. While Leucadia was tying off the lines, Ian queued the crew up on both sides of the hatchway and told them to grasp whatever part of the sheet they were capable of holding. When everything was set, she directed Harlowe to carry the bottom end of the sail to the broken bowsprit.

Harlowe pointed at a carabineer. "That doesn't look like a 16th-century buckle."

"It's not."

Harlowe clicked the carabineer to the bottom sheet and Leucadia gave the final direction. "Hold her up like a kite, Captain. As the crew pulls, let the wind fill her."

"What is it?" Harlowe asked as the crew pulled hand-over-hand, playing out the sheet. On and on the exercise went until it nearly dwarfed the *Millie* in its size. Harlowe began to wonder if the cloth had an end. It was largest sail he had ever seen.

"A spinnaker," Leucadia replied above the cheers of the crew. They watched the two hundred feet of sail gather wind until the

Millie abruptly lurched forward as if someone had just stepped on the gas.

"That's not very 16th-century, Ms. Lu," Harlowe pointed out as he admired the massive sail.

Leucadia smiled. "No, it's not."

The terror he saw on Shortstop's face when the *Millie* raced forward prompted Harlowe to send Riverstone to the wheel. "Better lend Shortstop a hand, Mr. Riverstone, before he runs us aground."

Riverstone smiled. "Aye, Captain. I'll keep her steady." He leaped from the forecastle deck, bounced once on the main deck, and alit on the quarterdeck, where he joined Shortstop at the steerage wheel.

"May I ask what's in the chest, Captain?" Twobagger asked, with a smug grin. "Jakaa's treasure, I hope!"

"Aye, Mr. Twobagger, a treasure it is," Harlowe replied. "We must guard it with our lives."

"Begging my Captain's pardon, sir. May we see what our lives are protecting?" Zinger asked, his yellow-crusted teeth displaying greedily between the gaps of missing teeth.

Since they would be risking death for the contents, Harlowe saw no harm in showing the crew what was in the chest. He ordered Leucadia and Ian to join them all at the Nywok chest on the main deck.

Harlowe stood with Leucadia behind the small group of curious onlookers and instructed Ian to open the chest. "If you please, Mr. Wizzixs."

"Aye, Captain," Ian replied. Bending over the chest, he unlatched the heavy leather strap and opened the lid. Upon seeing the contents, the Gazzian crew slumped in disappointment. For Ian and Leucadia, however, it was the greatest treasure of all—a thousand pounds of black thermo-grym crystal!

85

Stay Safe, Big Guy

For the first time since crashing on the beach, the undog appeared to be on the mend. Though he lacked the normal bounce in his step, he was sitting up, and for short distances, walking beside Pigpo. When he became exhausted, Simon lifted him up and put him back on the saddle. Simon now thought nothing of playing nursemaid to the undog. Seeing Mowgi alive and walking around made all his efforts worthwhile.

Simon followed the coast, nonstop, in a southerly direction. Without his SIBA's nav-com to guide him, it was the only course that made sense. Sooner or later the island would have to turn up. He didn't worry about identifying the island, even if several islands appeared along the way. He was counting on Mowgi to know that answer. Getting to the island would be another problem. He could do it in a fully-charged SIBA. Without one, he would need a way to float across water to the island.

The groves of seed pod trees became more abundant as they continued south. They had plenty to eat and drink along the way. Near the end of the day, they topped a hill and rounded a bend that dropped down into a wide river basin. Simon wondered if the mountain river where he began his trek across the desert would ever turn up again. Now he knew. Fortunately it was not a deep Nile-sized river that emptied into the sea through a wide, fan-like mouth.

From his vantage point overlooking the delta, he saw that the small rivulets snaking through the wide sand bars appeared shallow enough to cross. What would be a problem, though, were all the giant croc creatures that made the delta their home.

Pigpo's sight may have been limited, but his sense of smell was acute. As soon as he caught a whiff of the crocs, he came to a dead stop and would go no further into the delta. Simon didn't blame him. He slid off the saddle and patted the trembling Pigpo to comfort him. "Don't worry, big guy, you don't have to go any farther."

Simon removed the saddle from Pigpo's back and lay it on the ground. He flashed back to his big high school performances, when his mom would give him a cold glass of milk to calm his nerves. Simon cut open a coconut and gave it to Pigpo to take his mind off the crocs. It wasn't cold milk, but it was the next best thing. "There, there, Pigpo. You da man. You'll be okay now."

Mom's remedy worked. When Pigpo had finished, his shakes were gone. Simon turned the mount around so that his big, lumbering body faced north. He wrapped his arms around the big beast's head and squeezed him like a giant teddy bear. "I'll miss you, big dude," he said tearfully.

Simon was surprised at how choked up he was getting about parting with the oversized beast. They had been together for only a couple of days, yet if felt like they had been friends forever. Wow, what was he turning into...an animal lover? He had never kept a pet growing up. His mom said they were too dirty and smelled up the house. Now here he was, playing nursemaid to a mutt and crying over a dumb animal that would forget about him the moment he disappeared around the bend. He would never see Pigpo again, and it hurt.

With his mouth quivering and tears flowing down his cheeks, Simon leaned into Pigpo's thick hindquarter and pushed him away. "Go, Pigpo! Get out of here. Go now! Shoo!"

Pigpo resisted. He wanted to stay with Simon and Mowgi.

Simon was now bawling. "Go on, Pigpo! Hit the road ya big lug!"

It took several hard shoves before Pigpo understood he had to go. The great slothy beast lumbered away and disappeared around the hill. "Stay safe," Simon said, watching until Pigpo was gone. Simon didn't have time to follow Pigpo and see if he continued in the right direction. He just hoped Pigpo had enough sense to stay away from the river. He would never forgive himself if Pigpo became a happy meal for some hungry croc.

Turning back to the undog, Simon sighed. "It's you and me now, Mowg." Mowgi yipped twice as he sat looking across the delta at the slithering crocs swimming in the swampy channels.

"Doesn't look good, does it, Mowg?" Simon asked. He wondered how he was going to make it across the delta. If it was just he, he could wear his SIBA without being seen by the crocs. Mowgi, however, did not have a SIBA. Simon would need to use his personal force field. But its power was so low the blue indicator light appeared out. The delta was miles across. How far would they get before he and Mowgi were croc fodder?

Simon touched his SIBA and powered up his bugeyes to full zoom. The delta was even farther than he thought, and so were the crocs. Just as he was ready to turn bugeyes off, he noticed an island far out in the ocean. *Is that the island where Millawanda is parked?* He turned to look at the mountain gap, which was just a hazy v-shape on the horizon. He tried lining up the gap with the island. With a little imagination, the course Mowgi had been flying seemed to line up perfectly. It was the only hope they had. But to know for sure if it was the right island, he had to get closer. He'd have to cross the delta and travel further south, beyond the crocs. He figured it would take one more day of walking to get close enough for Mowgi to identify the island. If he got a two-yip reply, he could build a raft out of coconut palms and be back on the island that night.

"Cool." He congratulated himself and cracked open his last coconut.

He had a plan.

Feeling hopeful that his journey was almost over, he held out the coconut for the undog to drink and said, "Almost home, little buddy."

Mowgi yipped twice between slurps.

A good sign, Simon thought.

*   *   *

Though Mowgi was able to walk, Simon chose to carry him. From the bluff above the delta, the rivulets looked shallow and easy to cross, but in reality they were many yards across and some had deep and swift currents. Simon didn't know if the undog had recovered enough to swim. They had come this far. He didn't want to lose Mowgi now. More important, however, was the force field. It hid them from the crocs. Without it, the instant they stepped onto the delta, they'd be croc bait!

Simon used parts of Pigpo's saddle to fashion another harness for securing Mowgi to his back again. It fit better than the first harness. The old leather straps were more pliable and softer than the strips of palm leaves.

They were as ready as they would ever be. Simon switched on the barrier and prayed that his plan would work. He didn't have long to wait before the barrier's stealth qualities were tested. Simon pushed back some shoreline reeds and came face-to-face with a giant croc lying right in his path!

"Dude!" Simon gasped. He had never seen crocodile as big as this. The croc appeared to be asleep, basking in the sun. It was twice the size of any croc he had spotted from the hill. If he had seen this Godzilla first, he might have thought twice about crossing the delta at all!

He thought about turning around and following a different path, but a second giant croc slid in behind him, cutting off that option. Three more crocs then joined the party. Simon decided it was time to get moving. With every direction blocked, the only way out was over the top of a half dozen crocs sleeping in the sun.

Simon closed his eyes, prayed for a little luck, and patted Mowgi on his snout. "Get ready to fly little buddy if this doesn't work." Mowgi understood he had to keep silent and stifled a growl.

Simon took two steps back, then leaped up onto Godzilla's back, and hopscotched from here to a second croc, a third, and a fourth until he had hopscotched far enough to land on the sand again. He heard a loud roar behind him. Simon ran until he reached the top of a small knoll. He looked back and laughed silently to himself. The crocs were fighting among themselves.

Simon continued hopping away, laughing. *No one likes disturbing their afternoon nappie!*

86

Happy Anniversary

The bilge was the lowest and most vile place on the *Millie*. No light penetrated its depths at the bottom of the hull. The air was stagnant and reeked of vermin droppings, pitch, human waste, and decay. It was wet and cold in the upper latitudes, and wet and hot like a sweatbox in the tropics. Even the Gazzian rats found it intolerable.

As always, Harlowe kept his promise. For three days, Leucadia and Ian's quarters was the bilge. It was the price they paid for disobeying the Captain's direct orders. They were lucky. If it had been a true 16th-century Earthly punishment, they would have been whipped with a leather cat-o'-nine tails. For more severe defiance, they'd have walked the plank or been hanged. On Gazz, they would have been tossed overboard to a traa.

Riverstone protested, but Leucadia and Ian took their sentence without complaint. Because Harlowe needed either Ian or Leucadia on deck at any time to navigate the ship, they split their time in the bilge in shifts. When one was on deck, the other was below deck. Ian tried to be chivalrous and do twenty hours straight to Leucadia's five. But Leucadia would not accept special treatment. Her time below deck would be equal to Ian's, end of discussion.

The hatch to the bilge cracked open and someone stepped through. Leucadia was expecting no one for another five hours, but Ian must have come through the hatchway to switch places with her.

"It's not time yet, Ian," Leucadia called out.

But was it Ian? Whoever it was shut the hatch and kept moving toward her in silence. She could see better than most humans in the dark, but without her SIBA bugeyes, she could see almost nothing in the murk of the bilge. She readied herself, grabbing a ballast rock from beneath the mucky black seawater in case the form had come to do her harm.

"If you're not Ian, who are you?" she demanded. No answer. She stepped back to give herself more room to maneuver.

The form kept advancing.

"I warn you, I'm armed!"

Something made a minor splash in the water.

The form still did not speak.

Then something clicked and instantly a flame blazed, hurting her dark-accustomed eyes. The flame touched a candle on what looked like a table near the stool that she was sitting on only moments earlier. Another small splash rippled next to the table. In the candlelight, she saw a form sitting in a beach chair. The form placed a large, white paper sack on the table next to the two candles.

"Happy Anniversary," Harlowe's voice said.

Leucadia didn't move. She wondered if she was suffering a hallucination from being down in the bilge so long.

She almost laughed. "You've got to be kidding," she said, with a slight irritation in her voice.

Harlowe pulled his bugeyes from his face. His deep blue eyes gazed at her, defusing her hostility on the spot. "Two years ago today I found you inside Simon's yacht. My life has never been the same since. I'll never forget that day if I live to be as old as *Millawanda*."

Leucadia studied Harlowe, wondering where this was all leading. Was this a joke or was he serious? "How do you know it's our anniversary?"

"I'm guessing," Harlowe admitted.

"Would you have rescued me if you had known where Fate was taking you?" she asked.

Without hesitation, Harlowe replied, "Without a doubt."

It was the most romantic thing she had ever heard from him. "Even here?" she asked, looking around the bilge.

"Especially here."

She sloshed her way over to him and they enclosed each other in their arms, kissing like that first day they met. When they finally paused to breathe, Leucadia pointed at the small tabletop that was just above the water line. "What's in the sack? Filet mignon?" she asked jokingly.

"Better."

Leucadia reached down. After three days of bread and water, she could have eaten the sack. Peering inside she listed the contents: "Two burgers, shakes, and fries."

Harlowe smiled. "How did I do?"

Leucadia gave Harlowe a small kiss before she ripped open the sack and began devouring the contents. It was the most satisfying meal she had ever had, there at the bottom of a bilge with the person she loved.

"You did good, Pylott."

87

The Sacrifice

With Leucadia's massive spinnaker and steady winds, the *Millie* made it to the Straits of Daloom in better time than anyone expected. This time, the Straits were ghostly quiet. Smoke was still rising from the crumbled mass of heated stone that used to be the Fortress. Debris from the shattered Phagallian warships was scattered along the rocky shoreline on both sides of the channel.

Leucadia and Ian had served out their sentences. She was standing next to Harlowe as they sailed past the destruction. "You did this?" she asked.

"It was an accident," Harlowe replied. "Simon used Starbucks in the cannons."

"Starbucks?"

Harlowe bent down and picked up a black cannonball with a blue dot painted on the top. "Wiz made these for special occasions."

Leucadia took it from Harlowe and scrutinized it carefully. "It feels light," she said, tossing the ball in her hand.

"It's dura-steel."

"Why Starbucks?"

"The black powder we found on the *Millie* looks like Starbucks coffee grounds."

Leucadia removed the screw-on cap at the top of the ball and poured the black grains into her hand. She rubbed it between her fingers and said, "This isn't black powder, Harlowe, it's black thermo-grym crystals."

Harlowe stared at her hand and fingered the coffee-like grains himself. "Thermo-grym, huh?"

"Combining the dura-steel with the thermo-grym caused a chain reaction like a low-yield nuclear bomb."

Harlowe took the ball and emptied the contents over the rail. "I'll tell Wiz."

*   *   *

Harlowe hoped for another full day of wind before the gods pulled the plug. A half-day south of the Straits, however, the *Millie* was sitting dead on a glassy sea. She had entered the doldrums a hundred miles sooner than they had expected. Now the prevailing coastal currents were pushing her slowly in the wrong direction. Even in favorable currents, it would be weeks before she regained the wind. A disappointed Harlowe watched his crew gather in the deflated spinnaker and stow it in the fore deck hold. They couldn't wait for a miracle. The *Millie* had to keep moving. Every second lying motionless in the water was time lost for saving the planet Gazz, his Gamadin ship, his crew, Leucadia, Dodger... even himself! It was time for Plan B. "Fire up your turbos, Mr. Wizzixs," he ordered.

"We're down to three clickers, Captain," Ian replied.

That didn't surprise Harlowe. With so many injuries to his Gazzian crew and the accumulated damage to the ship, he had to expend the robobs to keep the *Millie* seaworthy, even though it meant sacrificing robobs to make repairs. He had no alternative. They had to move south.

"We have four, Wiz," Harlowe corrected.

Ian looked troubled. "Jewels? But Captain—"

"Use him."

For reasons unknown, when a clicker lost its power, it did not return to its cylindrical form. It disintegrated. Leucadia speculated that it was a safeguard to protect the Gamadin technology from reverse-engineering.

Ian tried to save Harlowe's beloved servant, but his protests went unheard. In times like this, when everyone's life was on the line, no one, not even a trusted robob servant, was exempt from sacrifice. "Just do it," Harlowe ordered. That was final.

Twobagger and Zinger finished gathering in the mains. The *Millie* needed no sheets to turbo through the windless sea. They would only be a drag on her speed.

"Aye, Captain."

*   *   *

Ian collected the three other robobs before he found Jewels in Harlowe's quarters, putting the finishing touches on straightening the cabin. He didn't need to say a word to Jewels. The servant already knew why he had come so unexpectedly. Ian had no more entered the cabin than Jewels stopped what he was doing and followed Ian out the door. It was a quiet walk below decks, as if Jewels was being led to the gallows in an old movie. Ian wondered if Jewels had sad thoughts, too, or was the robob simply doing what it was programmed to do—follow the wishes of a Gamadin soldier, even if it meant to its end. Remembering the way the robobs had served them selflessly in the past, Ian figured it was their programming.

But Jewels was special. The robob servant acted almost too human in the way it read Harlowe's mind and performed his duties without being told. Before the request was made, Jewels would have laid out the right clothes, prepared the meal, or simply stood by, ready to respond to a problem.

In the hold, Ian raised the outside turbo hatches and cranked the large turbine propellers into position. Two robobs took their places in the twin pedal chairs, looking like spindly cyclists on a stationary bicycle.

When both clickers were in position, Ian gave the command they often used from an old sci-fi movie to start a robob's action. "Nic-toe," and the clickers' legs started churning. With the power of robobs, the turbine blades turned easily, pulling the air in and pushing it aft. Within moments, the *Millie* sprang forward from its dead stop and moved gracefully ahead. Ian could tell from the *Millie's* wake that the turbos were working properly.

He returned to the robobs and saw that Jewels had switched places with the starboard clicker.

"No Jewels! It's not your turn."

He intended to use the other three clickers first. He was saving Jewels until he absolutely was needed.

"That's an order. It's not your turn yet," Ian said to the servant.

Jewels shook his triangle head back and forth, as if to say no. He was taking his turn like the others, and he was taking it now. He wanted no special treatment and ignored Ian's commands to stop pedaling.

Ian stared at Jewels. "You're as stubborn as your boss."

Jewels didn't nod or give any acknowledgment as to what Ian had said. It was almost like he was going to do his duty until he was ordered by Harlowe to stop, or until he also turned to dust.

88

Heat

Simon's tongue was dry and swollen. His lips were cracked and bleeding. If it wasn't for his SIBA, the rest of him would have turned into Gamadin jerky. He and Mowgi had been walking along the beach for two days under a hot tropical sun with no shade and no water. He didn't know how much farther he could go without hydration. One more day, he kept telling himself. If they could make it just one more day, maybe they had a chance to make it back to *Millawanda* before the gamma ray burst struck.

Soon after leaving the crocs behind, his main water source, the coconut palms, had disappeared along with all the freshwater rivulets. The energy he had expended to escape the delta crocs had sucked the last bit of power from his SIBA. His suit stopped replenishing his body with fluids ten hours later.

Water was plentiful a few yards away. There was a whole ocean of it, but it was nothing that he could drink. The salt would have dehydrated him faster if he drank it. Simon did not know if the undog could drink ocean water. Mowgi had made no attempts to drink it so far, which led him to believe that salt water wasn't good for undogs, either.

The General had taught him ways to evaporate fresh water from ocean water, but that would take valuable time he didn't have. If Ian and Leucadia's calculations were correct and he had counted correctly, he had less than a day to find the island and get himself and the undog inside the ship.

Simon shaded his eyes from the burning sun. He had stopped sweating some time ago. That wasn't a good sign, he knew. He wondered if Mowgi felt the effects of the heat as much as he did. "Dude...aren't you hot?"

Mowgi sat with his tall parbolic ears slightly askew. His green tongue panted slightly between his razor-sharp incisors, as if he wanted to answer the question. His eyes were big and yellow, but more normal than mad. All in all, he seemed unaffected by the heat.

"Talk to me, Mowg. Is that why you're so weird? You don't feel things like we humans, do you?"

Simon thought he should at least get a yip or two in response instead of the vacant stare that made Mowgi seem like he was a few dots short. At any rate, Mowgi had no answer for him.

"You know if you could fly, we would be there by now. Wouldn't you rather be sucking down a tall blue one than being here?" he asked.

Silence.

Simon tried to swallow, but he couldn't find enough moisture in his throat to accomplish the task. Fearing that he was wasting his breath, he waved the undog on. "All right, keep movin' then. Can't be too much farther." He looked out across the water for the island again as he had been doing the past two days. The island still looked like it was a thousand miles away. He took one step and tripped on a small shell sticking out of the sand. The ripple of the shore break came around him and he fell into the water. His SIBA kept his body from getting wet, but his head was bare. The seawater felt cool and fresh, arousing him from his delusional heat-induced stupor.

Simon tasted the seawater in his delirium and decided that it was okay to swallow a little bit more. Before his tongue could again touch the salty water, the undog was dragging him away from the shorebreak.

"Okay, okay. I won't drink any," Simon said to the growling chinneroth. Mowgi kept pulling Simon farther and farther away from the waterline. For a moment, Simon lay face-up toward the sun, then, feeling stronger, he climbed to his knees and stood. The undog took Simon's hand in his mouth and began dragging him south again.

Simon, still suffering the effects of sun and dehydration, felt that was wrong. They needed to go the opposite way. North was the right direction. "No, Mowg, this way."

Their tug-o'-war was interrupted by the sound of a beast. Simon looked up. His eyes were blurred and unfocused from the sun. Beyond a few feet, everything was distorted and vague.

What he could distinguish, however, was big, and it was coming their way. He turned. "Hurry Mowgi!" he gutted out, and tried to run. But he tripped on a root and fell again. This time he didn't have the strength to get up. Lying flat on the beach, he felt the beast's pounding footsteps charging toward him.

89

Human Power

In the middle of the night, Leucadia went to Harlowe's cabin with bad news. "The last clicker dusted, Captain."

Harlowe wasn't asleep. He had figured the bad news the moment the cranking sounds of the turbo gears stopped. He was already standing at the window when she came through the doorway.

"How much farther?" Harlowe asked her.

Leucadia stepped to the window, put her arms around him, and nodded toward the south. "There. Just over the horizon," she replied, pointing southwest.

"Time?"

"Nineteen hours, twenty-three minutes before I reached your cabin. Less now."

"We should have hit the southerlies by now."

Leucadia looked down. There was no answer, other than the one they both knew. The *Millie* should have picked up the wind hours ago.

He sighed and kissed her. "Thanks." Harlowe released her and started for the door.

"Where are you going?" she asked.

"Below. The turbos need a pedaler."

"You don't have the power to turn them. You're not a clicker, Harlowe."

"With my SIBA I can turn the pedals."

"You have no power left."

"When I fell into the crevasse, I regained a full charge flying with the Rays."

Leucadia followed him to the turbo hold. She was still worried. "You may need to pedal for hours. Even you can't last more than an hour."

"Riverstone and I will trade off."

"I want to do my part."

"Everyone will get their turn until the SIBA goes dark," Harlowe said.

*   *   *

Harlowe was much taller than a robob. Ian made some quick adjustments to the chair so Harlowe could pedal it. But once he was finished, the turbos came to life. The one thing everyone feared was the fatigue factor. Robobs didn't feel exhaustion. When they lost power, they simply stopped and turned to dust. Harlowe had thought he could pedal for a couple of hours straight before he traded off with Riverstone. But less than an hour into his turn, his legs tired to the point where where he could not turn the turbos fast enough to keep the *Millie* ahead of the opposing currents. Reluctantly, he deactivated his SIBA and let Riverstone take over. Riverstone went on for nearly the same amount of time. Ian took over after that, and then Leucadia, who could pedal for only twenty minutes before she fell out of the chair. Then it was Harlowe's turn again.

The second round was even less fruitful. Harlowe lasted thirty-seven minutes, Riverstone twenty-eight, Ian fifteen, and Leucadia couldn't last more than five.

"We're not going to make it at this rate," Harlowe stated flatly. "Anybody have any ideas?"

"A couple of fast grannywagons would be nice," Riverstone quipped.

"A hurricane," was Ian's short reply.

A light bulb suddenly went on in Harlowe's head. He ordered Ian to come with him topside while Riverstone took his turn with the cycle.

Harlowe took the SIBA medallion from Ian and tossed it to Riverstone.

"Where are you going?" Leucadia asked, hoping she could help. She was feeling guilty standing around the hold while the others cycled.

The quick exchange of taking off the SIBA and reactivating it on the next cyclist was critical. If the *Millie* lost heading for even a short time, the currents would take her backwards and they'd quickly lose all the momentum they had gained.

Riverstone tapped the SIBA. Its power cells registered better than ninety-two percent. As much as they had been pedaling, the SIBAs had taken only a small amount of energy because the pedalists were using only the gravs in the legs and not other power-intensive parts of the suit. Pedaling the remaining distance to the island would be possible if the human cyclist could endure the stress.

"I need to make a call," Harlowe replied. "We won't be long."

*   *   *

Riverstone was nearly finished with his rotation when Harlowe and Ian returned to the turbo hold.

"Was anybody home?" Riverstone asked, sweating heavily as he tried to pass the medallion over to Ian.

Harlowe intercepted the SIBA disk and handed Riverstone a Blue Stuff shake. "I left a message," he replied. He sent Leucadia and Ian topside to check on Catch and Pitch at the steerage wheel. Mistakes could cost them time they didn't have. He then activated the medallion, determined to cycle past his previous effort.

90

What About Me?

Simon was passed out on the beach. His memories of Sizzle kept reminding him that he had to press on. It had been an eternity since he had seen the girl he had given up every starlet in Hollywood to be with. She was the only woman in his life. Once he found Sizzle on Gibb, that was it. He never looked back. If he couldn't have her, he promised himself he would join a monastery. No yachts, no fast cars... no girls. She was an angel, heaven-sent to him. He was committed to her for life, except for his duties as a Gamadin.

Where on Gazz was she? How far away was she? What was she doing this very second? Was she all right? Was she even alive? Sometimes imagining what could happen to a beautiful woman like Sizzle on a 16th-century planet was almost unbearable. The tide had changed. The shore break rippled up and drenched his face, awakening him from his stupor. He opened his eyes, imagining Sizzle was there with her arms out. Instead, he saw Pigpo. The last creature on the planet Simon expected to see!

Simon pushed back Pigpo's sticky wet tongue that was slobbering all over his face.

"Let me breathe, will ya?" his voice rasped to Pigpo.

Pigpo certainly wasn't Sizzle, but at this point in his trek, his old friend was the second most beautiful image on Gazz he could hope to see.

He reached around Pigpo's thick neck and gave him a big hug. "Where did you come from, Pigpo?" Looking down at Pigpo's wide, hairy toes, Simon saw the old saddlebags on the sand. Large teeth marks in the straps showed how Pigpo had carried the satchel.

Simon crawled over on his hands and knees and tore open the flap of the bag. His wish had come true; inside was a large, blue-green coconut! Simon ravenously lopped off the top of the coconut and poured Mowgi and himself a refreshing drink. He had never tasted anything so wonderful in all his life.

Reunited with his friend, Simon climbed onto Pigpo's bare back and urged him forward. He still had a mission to accomplish and he was way behind schedule. Mowgi found his place on Pigpo's rump and they rambled down the sandy beach together, just like old times. Simon was just getting used to riding without a saddle when a squadron of great winged creatures buzzed him overhead. The squad of fast-moving entities was so large and fast, the draft they made blew him off his mount.

"What the..."

He dusted the sand from his SIBA and watched as the squadron of objects continued out over the ocean, en route to some unknown destination. They did not appear to be birds. None of the triangle-shaped creatures had feathers or flapped their wings like birds. They flew straight and silent, soaring like gliders without motors.

Simon stuck out his thumb like a hitchhiker. "How 'bout a lift?" He watched them grow smaller over the ocean. "Thanks for nothing, Toads!" he yelled after them.

Simon turned around to see what the undog thought. Mowgi was gone. Simon looked under Pigpo's round belly. He wasn't there either. That's strange, he thought, as he searched everywhere around the deserted beach. There was no place to hide. *So where did the Mowg go?*

Simon then heard a flapping sound overhead. It was Mowgi, expanding as he took flight and gained altitude. The undog wasn't his usual steady self. He was struggling to stretch himself out to full dragonhood or climb quickly enough to keep his hind legs from splashing through a breaking wave. Simon even lifted up on his heels in a sympathetic effort to keep Mowgi from falling back into the drink.

"What about me?" Simon shouted, all alone with Pigpo on the deserted beach.

91

Harlowe's Rides

When Leucadia rushed down to the turbo hold to inform everyone the *Millie's* main had found wind, it was too late. Harlowe was sweating rivers, having pumped out the last revolutions his legs could churn. Dawn was breaking on the day the gamma ray burst would hit the planet. Even with full sail and Leucadia's jib, they were still a hundred miles short of their goal.

They needed a miracle.

Harlowe climbed to the main deck with Leucadia holding him to support his exhausted body. The sky was cloudless and deep green and the glaring, yellow sun hung low over the water above the eastern horizon. The trade winds from the southeast were blowing steadily. Under other circumstances, he would have felt the warm and soothing air on his face. Harlowe and Riverstone had pedaled through the night. Now neither Gamadin could walk without assistance. Riverstone was still down in the hold, lying next to the turbo cycle exactly where he had collapsed after passing the SIBA back to Harlowe. He lay in an almost catatonic sleep on the wet planks, too exhausted to move or think about the coming doom. After Ian provided him a Blue Stuff shake, Ian brought him to the quarterdeck so they could all be together during their final moments.

Harlowe touched the main mast with his hands, observing the Nywok spiritual tree like it was an old friend. They had been through an embattled history together. Only three weeks had passed since the spiritual tree had replaced their broken main, but to everyone onboard it seemed like a lifetime. Leucadia looked at Harlowe, wondering where his bottomless supply of courage came from. Harlowe would go down with his ship. She knew that when he did, he would be fighting all the way, his cold, dead hands frozen to the steerage wheel.

Leucadia was heartbroken. She could think of nothing more to help him or their situation. Yet, as she studied Harlowe, "hopeless" was not what she thought of. He was not slumping over in defeat or displaying a long face to their inevitable outcome. If they were about to die, no one would know it from his manner. In spite of his enormous physical pain, Harlowe stood tall, holding onto the ancient wood with one arm and Leucadia with the other, while his alert eyes scanned the skies as if he was expecting divine help in the form of a miracle.

She hugged him closer, leaning her head inside the crook of his shoulder. She could smell his sweat and fatigue and feel his radiating warmth. Not one nervous tremor disturbed his muscular frame. She sighed, feeling fortunate at that critical moment just to be with him. In spite of everything, this was where she wanted to be—standing by her young man during his greatest need.

With tearful eyes, she looked up and said, "Thank you."

Harlowe looked down, taking his deep blue eyes from the sky for a moment to focus only on her. "For what?" he asked, wondering what brought on her sudden expression of gratitude.

Leucadia tried to find the appropriate words. She didn't want to say anything that was a downer. This was no time to speak of failure. She had to hang tough no matter what. Wimping out was not an option. "For being you," she whispered.

Harlowe felt her concern. "Don't thank me yet. Not until we're back home, catching a few tubes at 42nd Street."

Smiling, she said, "You're crazy, you know that?"

He grinned, kissed her warmly on the lips, then pointed up to the sky. "Let's be crazy together then." He lifted her up so they were both standing tall. "Come on. We have work to do. Our ride is here."

A large shadow drifted over the ship. When Leucadia looked up, she saw several triangular shapes gliding effortlessly in lazy circles overhead. They were white as snow and glistened in the sun like giant reflectors. "What are they?" she asked.

"Friends," was all Harlowe said as he went to the middle of the main deck and waved to the new arrivals. He ordered Zinger and Catch to follow him forward and gather the heavy, braided ropes used for mooring the ship to the dock.

A ray drifted near the bow, and took the loop end of the mooring rope Harlowe offered into its mouth.

"Amazing," Leucadia said as she watched the giant rays float magically above the water. "They're defying gravity. How do they do it?"

A second ray drifted in and took another loop from Harlowe. "They come from Black Mountain. They live in glaciers laced with thermo-grym. When I came out of the glacier, my suit was good-to-go again."

"They're so beautiful," Leucadia said.

"You should see their home. I'll take you there someday."

Harlowe gave ropes to two more rays. Satisfied finally that he had enough power to pull the ship, he ordered Zinger and Catch to gather in the sheets on the main mast spar.

"All of it, Captain?" Zinger asked.

"All of it, Mr. Zinger," Harlowe replied. "Now up you go, quickly!"

The three Gazzians saluted. "Cool, Captain!" and scampered up the ratlines.

Pitch came to the main deck when he heard the goings-on. Minus an arm, he still wanted to contribute. Harlowe put him to work barking orders to the crewmen, making sure the topmast stays didn't get tangled during the tow. Then he told Leucadia to to fetch Riverstone from the turbo hold. "He's rested long enough. I want him on the quarterdeck in five. Tell him to bring his SIBA."

Leucadia wanted to ask why Riverstone needed his SIBA when it was useless without power. After the confrontation they had on the way to Black Mountain, she had gained so much respect for his command decisions that she let her natural tendency to question his judgment go silent. This was no time to be second-guessing her captain, she thought. Harlowe had a plan he was working on and he didn't need to be bothered by curious subordinates questioning his motives.

"Aye, Captain," Leucadia replied, and went promptly to fetch Riverstone.

Harlowe took a moment to watch her go. She was still the prettiest crewman anywhere in the universe. And the smartest, too, he grinned. Then he climbed to the quarterdeck and took the broken wheel from Moneyball. "Wrap that spar line around you, Mr. Moneyball."

Moneyball grabbed a rope hanging from the main spar and tied it around his waist. "Cool, Captain! Ready!"

Harlowe tapped his SIBA and began communicating with the rays. The moor lines lost their slack, lifting the bow nearly out of the water. The powerful surge of forward motion came so suddenly that even Harlowe had to fight to keep himself planted on the deck. The burst of speed caught Moneyball completely by surprise. The forward motion lifted the crewman into the air like a kite. Only the loose spar line he was holding kept him from crashing against the poop deck bulkhead and falling overboard.

Harlowe grabbed Moneyball's leg before he rose too high and pulled him back down. "Steady, Mr. Moneyball."

"A bit of a surprise that was, Captain," Moneyball said, straightening himself out.

"Can you handle the wheel from here, sir?" Harlowe asked him.

Moneyball took the wheel from Harlowe. "I can, Captain, unless you're planning a few more surprises."

"That's enough for one day." Harlowe pointed to the compass. "Keep her on that bearing, Mr. Moneyball, if you please."

"That I will, Captain!"

"Ms. Lu will give you any change in her course."

"Cool, Captain, on the line she is."

Harlowe heard Riverstone's grumbling before he emerged from the turbo hold. Harlowe leaned over the quarterdeck railing and summoned him to the poop deck. "Double time if you would, Mr. Riverstone. I'm in a hurry."

Riverstone looked around at what was happening, as someone does after waking up without a clue as to where he is or what is going on around him. His eyes nearly popped out of their sockets when he saw the rays out in front, towing the *Millie* like a team of horses. "That's rad!"

Harlowe hoisted Riverstone up the ladder while Leucadia made sure he didn't fall backward.

"Did he bring his SIBA?" Harlowe asked Leucadia.

She had it in her hand. "I didn't want him to lose it."

"Smart," Harlowe said, then added to Leucadia, "Don't let him pass out."

"Aye, Captain," Leucadia replied.

Riverstone smiled down at Leucadia as she carried him along. He was so spent from the cycle his mind was groggy. "I'm in love. Will you run away with me, girl?"

Leucadia paid no attention to Riverstone's babbling and led him up to the poop deck, where they waited for Harlowe to join them. They didn't have to wait long. Before they had finished climbing the ladder, Harlowe was behind her, taking over with her lifting. "I'll take him from here." He held Riverstone's weight in one arm and held out his other hand.

Leucadia passed him the SIBA medallion and asked, "Where are you taking him?"

"To the Ship. Something's wrong. Monday hasn't called in weeks. Rerun should have made it back days ago, and he hasn't called either. I can't wait for the *Millie* to get to the island."

She was about to ask how he was planning to get there, when a traa rose out of the sea. Its head alone was twice the size of the *Millie*.

"Our other ride is here. Gotta go!" Harlowe said to Leucadia. He placed the SIBA medallion around Riverstone's head and activated the suit. The SIBA energized as if it was fully charged. Before she could ask how he did it, Harlowe jumped off the stern with Riverstone onto the back of the traa. Their claws dug into the thick hide of the creature while the traa was sliding below the surface

And then they were gone.

92

A Fortuitous Bump

Pigpo's sudden stop awakened Simon. After Mowgi's desertion, what else was there to do but sleep and dream of Sizzle? It wasn't like he had his Droid along to call up her picture or play games. He awoke to see a fortress a mile down the beach and a flotilla of dhows coming ashore loaded with soldiers. Pigpo had the right idea. The beach wasn't the place for them. If he hurried over the dune, maybe no one would see him.

As they neared the dunes, however, the crack of a musket echoed behind him. The musket ball kicked up sand ten feet to the side of their location. Simon whipped around and saw a lone dhow coming ashore, emptying a squad of loosely clothed soldiers onto the beach. Some carried muskets while others brandished long, curved swords. These soldiers were the first humanoid creatures he'd seen with no tails.

Croomis! He had traveled from the land of the tails and into the land of the tailless.

The single-sailed dhow had come out of nowhere while he was dozing off. It must have been patrolling the coast on its way back to the fortress when someone spotted him.

Now what?

Simon glanced down the beach toward the fortress. The musket report had sounded the alarm. More soldiers with long swords were charging his way. They weren't on foot like the first assault squad. They were on mounts. They wouldn't take long covering the mile on the flat beach. Pigpo could never outrun them all, even if he was fresh.

Simon had only one idea. He jumped off of Pigpo and charged down the dune toward the oncoming soldiers. He switched on his SIBA, hoping he had enough left in his power pack to take care of the first soldiers from the boat.

A fully-armored Gamadin SIBA has a chilling effect on an enemy soldier, especially if he believes what is attacking him is an ungodly entity. Several soldiers did stop, but none ran. Instead, they began firing at the apparition coming toward them. Their musket balls sparked off of the SIBA as if they were striking hard stone. Still, the tailless creature couldn't be stopped. The apparition tore through them, bashing heads and breaking bodies. A soldier or two managed to strike at the ghostly warrior with their broadswords, but they were quickly disposed of. The phantom's skin was impenetrable. The Croomis blades broke into pieces when they struck the phantom's armored hide.

Half the soldiers were lying on the beach and the other half running away. Simon set his sights on the dhow. If he could commandeer the boat, he could use it to make a faster getaway. Less than a mile away, a hundred approaching soldiers were almost within musket range. Grateful that his SIBA had held up well so far, Simon didn't want to test his luck by taking on another hundred musketeers. Even with a SIBA, the numbers seemed pretty risky.

When they saw what the phantom had done to the other soldiers, the crew on the dhow panicked. They jumped overboard and swam to shore, joining the others who were running toward the fortress.

Simon hadn't figured that into his plan. Now he'd have to launch the dhow by himself!

Simon ran over the sand to the beached dhow. He ran into the surf and tried to turn the bow around and put out to sea. Even with his SIBA at full power, he could not push it from the sandy bottom. He jumped onto the deck, swung the mono sail around, went back to the tiller, and prayed there was enough wind for the sail to do the heavy lifting.

The dhow wanted to go, but it wouldn't budge. Simon tried jumping up and down, to no avail. From down the beach, puffs of white smoke alerted him that the soldiers were returning. Musket balls began striking the small sailboat. Then a brigade of mounted soldiers with animals resembling anteaters on hoofs galloped into the water.

Simon rocked the boat, jumped up and down, and wiggled the tiller in a desperate attempt to set the boat free. Just before he ran out of time, the dhow suddenly lurched forward.

Simon held on as the bow of the dhow pushed through the surf, popped out the backside of a wave, and with the sail filled with wind, moved swiftly toward the open sea.

Simon couldn't believe his luck! He thought he was dog meat! Soldiers on mounts angled toward him, splashing through the surf in an attempt to cut off his escape, but they were too late. They had no chance of catching him now. Then he heard the familiar cry of a beast beside the boat.

It was Pigpo!

You idiot! What are you doing? You gotta death wish or something?

Pigpo was behind the dhow, trying to stay with him through the surf. It wasn't luck after all. Pigpo had given the final shove that broke the dhow free.

Simon waved him back to shore. "Go back, Pigpo! You'll drown out here. Turn around! Don't follow me! Go back!"

Pigpo wouldn't listen. His giant head and pink snout kept bobbing through the waves as Pigpo struggled to keep up. The soldiers continued to fire at the dhow, and now some of the balls were striking Pigpo.

Simon saw the copper-colored blood discoloring the water. He knew Pigpo was hit. "No, no!" he cried. He took out his weapon and fired back at the soldiers on the shoreline. But Pigpo was wounded. After each wave he climbed over, he sank deeper into the water. His pink snout was the last Simon saw of Pigpo, who slipped beneath the surface and didn't come up again.

Simon slumped over the tiller. He had never lost such a devoted and dear friend as Pigpo.

93

Starbucks

The Gazzian sun was high overhead when the giant traa breached the surface, lifting five hundred feet toward the sky. The Gamadin detached their grappling claws from the backside of the traa. Before the sea creature could arch downward again and return to the depths, Harlowe and Riverstone had separated from the back of the traa and deployed their wings. With a favorable wind at their backs, they glided on an easterly path toward the island of vines two miles away.

"Where's the ship?" Riverstone asked through their coms.

Even at this distance, with bugeyes at full zoom, they should have been able to spot *Millawanda's* saucer dome. Harlowe spoke aloud, "She has to be there."

"Maybe we jumped off the wrong side of the island," Riverstone offered.

"No. It's this side," Harlowe stated. "There's no way she could have been moved either," he added.

"Well, where is she then?"

Harlowe wouldn't have an answer until they were less than a half-mile out. What he saw was almost unbelievable. The vines had extended out from the beach like a cancer. Harlowe paused. "She's buried under the vines."

Riverstone was impressed. "Cool camouflage, Harlowe. I did that to my boat back at the village. The Phagallians never found it."

"I left her exposed."

"No vines?" Riverstone asked.

"They were a hundred yards from Millie when I left." Harlowe tried to raise Monday on the com. "Platter, come in. This is Harlowe. Talk to me."

He tried to raise both Monday and Prigg, but no one answered. The com was silent, except for Riverstone's.

When they were a hundred yards from the edge of the vines, they noted a strange phenomenon. The ocean stopped.

"What's up with that?" Riverstone asked. They skimmed along the edge of what appeared to be a rock wall built up over a hundred feet above the ocean floor. The wall began at the north peninsula of the bay and bent around in a wide semi-circle until it reconnected again at the southernmost tip of the bay.

"It's a dam," Harlowe concluded.

"Platter's been busy," Riverstone commented. He turned toward the vines and prepared for a two-point landing on top of the vines where *Millawanda's* dome would be.

"MATT!" Harlowe shouted. "Steer clear! Turn around!"

Riverstone heard the urgency in Harlowe's voice and didn't ask why. He banked to the right and headed back toward the wall. A vine end shot up and nearly snagged Riverstone's foot before Harlowe was able to shoot the end with his pistol. It fell, squealing in pain. Other vines tried to grab Riverstone, but Harlowe's aim was deadly. Riverstone glided out of harm's way.

Harlowe landed at the top of the dam, but Riverstone had lost altitude too quickly and ended up short of the wall. Harlowe yelled to Riverstone, "CLIMB!"

Halfway up the side of the rock wall, Riverstone turned and saw a mass of vines coming his way. They looked like they would engulf him in seconds. He sucked in his wings and crawled like a sticky-footed insect up the side of the wall. Harlowe reloaded and tried to stop the vine attack. A thousand rounds wouldn't have stopped the surge of crawling plants however.

Riverstone reached the top of the wall, and Harlowe grabbed his extended arm to pull him up. They had nearly made it when a rogue vine shot out and snagged Harlowe's leg. Together they toppled over the backside of the dam and into the ocean. To their surprise, the vine released its grip from Harlowe's leg when it hit the water and pulled away as if it had been splattered with acid.

While they treaded water away from the dam, they watched the vines slink over the edge of the wall and reach for them. Each time they reached out, Harlowe splashed the crawlers with water and sent them squealing in pain to the dry side of the wall.

Riverstone pointed out the obvious."They don't like water."

To Harlowe, it made all the sense in the world. Early on, he noticed that the vines were the only vegetation on the island. When they first arrived with *Millawanda*, the tides were high enough to keep the vines at bay. While she remained in the bay surrounded by water, she was safe. Later, after they put out to sea, the moons swung around, lowering the tide level. Their combined gravitational pull sucked the water out of the bay long enough for the vines to build a cofferdam across the entrance of the bay.

"The vines built the dam?" Riverstone asked skeptically.

"Who else?"

"That takes smarts, Dog."

Harlowe nodded at the dam. "I know. They built it to keep the water out, leaving Millie high and dry, regardless of the tide change. With the cofferdam in place she is vulnerable. So are Monday, Dodger, Prigg, and the cats."

Riverstone looked over at Harlowe, who hadn't taken his eyes away from the dome of vines. "If they're inside Millie, they're okay, right?"

"Yeah, Monday's smart. He'll keep them safe," Harlowe replied, sounding confident.

"What about Rerun? If he and Mowg didn't know…"

"Mowgi would have known. He knew before we left. He had them nailed all along. We just didn't see it."

"Yeah, but not Rerun. They could have grabbed him just like they did me." Riverstone splashed a big wave at the vines in a fit of anger. A knot of vines squealed as they burned from the water. "How are we going to flush these stupid toads out?"

Harlowe tapped his com. "Lu!"

Leucadia answered immediately. "Here Captain!" Her response was calm and controlled. She could hear in his voice that there was a problem and anticipated his question. "We're ten miles out. The rays have stepped it up. We can be there in twenty. How can we help?"

"I want a broadside ready, loaded with Starbucks," Harlowe ordered.

Leucadia hesitated, hoping Harlowe realized that such explosive power could blow away the entire island.

Harlowe tacked on another directive. "Rig them with a five-second delay."

"That will flood the island."

"Exactly."

"Aye, Captain. Five-second delay," Leucadia replied.

"Riverstone and I will be swimming toward you. Have spar lines in the water about a mile out."

"Aye, Captain. Spar lines a mile out," she replied.

* * *

The Gamadin saw the rays over the horizon as they pulled the sail-less three-master behind them. Leucadia was right. The *Millie* had made good time.

"Lu's the best," Riverstone remarked as the *Millie* came toward them and the bowline was tossed.

"Aye," Harlowe agreed. "The best." He was serious.

He watched Leucadia turning the broken steerage wheel with Moneyball assisting her, masterfully guiding the *Millie* toward their rendezvous point.

They collapsed their SIBAs before they grabbed the lines and climbed hand-over-hand up the side of the ship onto the foredeck. Pitch and Shortstop met them there, with dark seaman's trousers and deck shoes. They tossed their shirts. It was hot and there was no time for a dress code. After tying his pant waist, Harlowe turned to his First Mate and saluted. "Permission to come aboard, Mr. Pitch."

"Cool, Captain! Good to have you back," Pitch replied, saluting with his one arm. "Permission granted."

"Thank you, Mr. Pitch."

Harlowe took his wide-brimmed pirate hat from Shortstop. Then he released the rays. In the way only he knew how, he stood at the point of the bow and thanked them for their help. Harlowe felt empty watching them circle the *Millie*. Their round blue eyes looked sad, wanting to stay. But Harlowe warned them that the coming hours were dangerous and they must return to their home. Harlowe didn't know if they were protected inside the glacier from the gamma ray burst, but he did know that any living thing outside the glacier was toast without protection.

They turned northeast and flew across the water, back to Black Mountain. He and Riverstone made their way to the main deck.

Harlowe pointed to Ian, who was priming and making ready the cannons. "Help Wiz with the Starbucks, Mr. Riverstone. Catch him up on what we're doing."

Riverstone leapt over the downed rigging. "Aye, Captain."

Harlowe made his way up to the steerage wheel, where Leucadia and Moneyball stood at attention awaiting his next command. The first thing Harlowe wanted to do was take her into his arms and lay a big kiss on her sun-red lips for a job well done. As it was on *Millawanda's* bridge, shows of affection were improper etiquette in front of the crew. But etiquette be damned! Harlowe was so emotionally worked up over the days' events, he grabbed her in his arms anyway and laid a big one on her lips. When he broke away, he said, "Ya did good, babe."

Then he turned to Moneyball.

"Job well done, Mr. Moneyball."

Moneyball, with a toothless smile asked, "Do I get a kiss, too, Captain?"

"That will be enough of that, Mr. Moneyball. Go down to the main deck and help Mr. Wiz, if you please."

Moneyball sobered and saluted. "Cool, Captain!"

Harlowe ordered Shortstop and Twobagger up the main ratlines to drop the only sails they had left, the topsails. With the rays gone, the *Millie* needed a small amount of wind power for steerage. While the *Millie* was coming to put her guns in position, Harlowe recounted to Leucadia what took place when he and Riverstone came upon the island.

Leucadia's expression suddenly turned fearful. "Dodger?"

"Yeah."

"Did they answer your call?"

Harlowe bit his upper lip. "No. Nothing from Rerun, either. At least he's with Mowgi."

Leucadia turned Harlowe around and pointed to the stern. Harlowe saw the top half of the undog's parabolic ears as he sat looking out between the railings.

Harlowe felt elated. "Rerun's onboard?"

Sadly, Leucadia shook her head. "Mowgi slammed into the side of the *Millie*. Ian had to dive into the water to pull him out."

Harlowe stared at Mowgi in disbelief. "What happened to him?"

"He's got a long cut on his side," Leucadia explained. "It wasn't a gun wound or an animal. I don't know. Someone sewed him up with dura-wire."

"Rerun."

"Yes."

Harlowe looked toward the mainland, far off on the horizon to the east. "He's still out there, then."

Leucadia nodded. "I think so."

"If he doesn't get inside the ship, he's fried."

Though it was against protocol, Leucadia squeezed Harlowe's arm.

"He'll be okay. He's a Gamadin," she said, trying to help.

Before any more was said, Wiz called up from the gun deck. "Ready here, Captain! Within range."

Harlowe turned to Leucadia. "Do it, Ms. Lu."

Leucadia took the wheel and focused on the island. She swung the bow into the wind and nodded. "Now, Captain!"

Harlowe went to the rail and gave the order. "Give her a broadside, Mr. Wizzixs!"

"FIRE!" Ian's voice cried out.

The *Millie* lurched sideways as the enormous explosion of black smoke and fire blew outward from the side of the ship. A dozen ten-pound cannonballs packed with black thermo-grym flew toward the cofferdam.

94

Up, Up, Up

The Starbucks cannonballs flew straight and true. Leucadia and Moneyball began turning the broken wheel hard to starboard. "Hold on, everyone!" Leucadia shouted forward. The warning was repeated several times until the balls struck the water in front of the wall. Ian had secured every cannon to the deck and sent every crewmen topside. If a two-ton cannon did break free from its moorings, even a glancing blow would crush a body.

The seconds ticked off. Harlowe counted to himself, "Four, three, two, one..." He didn't get to zero before the sea rose in a mountainous swell. A massive wave was rushing toward the *Millie*. Harlowe and Leucadia grabbed each other and clung together to the wheel, waiting for the ocean surge to hit.

The island was completely blocked from view. The *Millie* went up the side of the giant wall. Up, up, up. Climbing, climbing. They steered her bow head-on into the wall and prayed they would make it over the crest before the wave broke over the ship, crushing them all.

Up, up, up...

Climbing...

"Harlowe!" Leucadia gasped. She let go of the wheel and held on to Harlowe for dear life.

The *Millie* angled upward at such a steep incline that only Harlowe managed to hang on. Moneyball lost his grip and slammed against the aft bulkheads. Amid the outcries and shouts of doom, the others held onto whatever they could find.

Up, up…

"It's cresting, Harlowe!" Leucadia shouted over the roar of the wall.

Harlowe held Leucadia fast with one arm and wrapped his other arm around the spokes of the steerage wheel. There was nothing else he could do. They were nearly vertical at the top of the wave. No amount of steerage would make a difference now.

When the wave crested over the top of the forecastle, a wall of white water washed across all decks. Harlowe threw his arms around Leucadia. Together they held against the bone-crushing turbulence of the water. Everywhere it swirled and bubbled, threatening to tear the *Millie* apart. Wood cracked and twisted and screamed from the stress. Moorings broke loose, thick spars snapped. The heavy cannons broke their holddowns and rolled downward, breaking everything in their path.

Then as quickly as the water gushed over them, it subsided. The *Millie* was airborne, floating through time and space as if gravity had left the planet.

Leucadia stared into Harlowe's eyes, knowing the other shoe was about to drop.

BOOM!

The *Millie* hit the backside of the wave, sending bodies crashing to the decks.

For a long disorienting moment, the world was upside down. Harlowe was flat on his back and looking up through the rigging. The masts of shredded sails were swinging from side to side. Water was running down the sides of everything in torrential waterfalls.

Leucadia reached out for Harlowe. He grabbed her hand and said, "I'm here, Lu."

Together they pulled themselves up and assessed the damage. "She's still floating!" Harlowe said, with a mixture of jubilation and relief. He went aft, where Twobagger was tangled in a mess of rigging. Next to him was Moneyball. They were both scratched and bloody, but otherwise intact. They were more dazed than hurt—nothing some Blue Stuff wouldn't cure.

"What's that sound?" Leucadia asked, while she untangled the steerage wheel. The sound resonated across the water. It was like someone in the throes of a painful death.

Harlowe looked toward the island. The cofferdam wall was blown away, no longer keeping the ocean out of the bay. "It's the vines. The Starbucks drenched them. What's left of their line has receded up the mountain." He pointed enthusiastically. "Look! I can see *Millawanda!*"

Her golden hull may have been tarnished and dirty, but her intact dome was clearly visible above the waterline.

Harlowe leaped off the quarterdeck and helped Ian and Riverstone make sure the crew was okay. "All accounted for, Captain," Riverstone reported. "No serious injuries."

That was all Harlowe needed to hear. With his Gamadin crew and his younger brother in doubt, he wasn't about to wait for his Gazzian crew to patch up the galleon enough to bring the *Millie* into the bay. He and Riverstone traded their blunderbuss pistols for fully charged 54th-century sidearms, and dove off the side of the galleon. They deployed their SIBAs even before they hit the water.

95

The Corridors

Harlowe and Riverstone swam the mile and a half to the dome. They emerged from the water with their weapons drawn and stood on the hull in waist-deep water, watching the still-black remains of the vines for the slightest movement. Nothing stirred. Riverstone touched a branch. It remained limp and wilted like overcooked spinach.

"Think they're all that way?" Riverstone asked.

Harlowe only grunted his uncertainty as he walked up the low incline of the ship and out of the water.

Riverstone felt the same way.

Slushing through the dead vines, they walked in front of the massive front windows and around to the outer hatchway that led to Harlowe's quarters. Up close, the damage was disheartening. Dark slime and muck were everywhere. Happily, like the *Millawanda's* hull, the windows were unbroken and intact. Harlowe couldn't imagine a nuclear bomb scratching her. However, the side door from Harlowe's quarters was fully open and filled with dead crawlers.

"They got in that way," Harlowe speculated.

Riverstone felt anger at the desecration of their ship. *Millawanda* was violated and he wanted revenge. He blasted the vines from the doorway and kicked their remains out of the way. Harlowe assisted, tearing burnt strands away from the entrance.

Inside the ship was even more devastation. Harlowe's quarters were ravaged. The large meeting table in the middle of the room was twisted and bent to the floor. His desk was turned over and against a bulkhead. Chairs were broken and their parts spread out over the room. All that had been alive, like his plants, was gone. Pictures were torn off the wall and shattered. He knelt down and picked up his Dodger cap from the floor, handling it like a sacred treasure.

Harlowe tapped his com for inter-ship communication. "Monday? Prigg? Can you hear me? Come in. It's Harlowe. Come in."

No response. Not even a click. Nothing but a foreboding empty silence.

After several more tries, Harlowe concluded that they were either out of power or . . . He wouldn't let himself think about the second alternative.

Riverstone continued kicking and slashing his way through the dead vines until he arrived at the doorway to the bridge. It, too, was packed with foot-thick vines. He blasted the doorway clear and marched onto the bridge. Harlowe was right behind him, covering the rear in case something jumped Riverstone when he wasn't looking.

The bridge was as damaged as Harlowe's quarters. The three command chairs were thrashed and pulled from their foundations. Only one chair was left intact along the console, and that was Simon's weapons station. All the others were missing, twisted, or ripped out from their bases. The back panel of dancing lights that never slept was dark. There was not even a pixel of light.

Harlowe turned off his air recycler to smell the air. "Smell that?"

Riverstone adjusted his breather. "Vine stink."

"Not that. The plas residue."

"Yeah, I smell it."

"Harlowe," Leucadia's voice called, interrupting their conversation. "Are you onboard?"

"We're here. Not good, Lu." A click verified that she got the message, but there was nothing she could add, so she waited for further instructions.

"How close are you?"

"Almost to the bay entrance."

"Beach the *Millie* on the hull and bring the thermo-grym through the bridge doorway. How's our time?"

"Ten hours, twenty-seven minutes."

"Is that enough?"

"It has to be," Leucadia replied.

Harlowe met Riverstone's dour face. They had a little over ten hours to power up *Millawanda* and get her flight-worthy before the gamma ray burst struck the planet. Simply turning on her lights would take more than a miracle. The chance of saving the planet from frying to a crisp seemed astronomical, even to Harlowe. "Aye," he said, clicking off.

"Where would they go?" Riverstone asked, wondering where they would even begin to look for Dodger, Monday, and Prigg in a ship as big as *Millawanda*. It would be like searching through six aircraft carriers from scratch.

"They could be anywhere," Harlowe replied. They looked out the bridge window and watched Leucadia navigate the *Millie* toward *Millawanda's* dome. He didn't worry about the 16th-century galleon denting the Ship's surface. There wasn't a substance on the planet that could mark her flawless skin.

Riverstone had another possibility. "Maybe they made it off the island before the vines overran the ship. They could be on the mainland, Dog."

Harlowe pointed at the scorch marks on the ceiling as they walked to the blinker and looked down the shaft. "Plas marks."

Riverstone studied both directions. "Monday was shooting upward."

"Then they had to be in the corridors because Millie was secured at all times."

"Unless someone let them in."

"Someone blew it," was Harlowe's guess.

"Then they're still here?" Riverstone concluded.

Harlowe looked down the shaft. It was full of dead vines but there was enough room to shimmy down between them. If things got a little tight, they could blast their way through like they had the doorways. "We follow the plas marks."

Riverstone pointed down the shaft with his pistol. "Aye."

Holstering his sidearm, Harlowe grabbed a dead vine like a rope and dropped down into the shaft. Riverstone waited at the top to cover Harlowe's back. When Harlowe reached the bottom, Riverstone joined him while Harlowe covered his descent.

*   *   *

The shaft was a tangled mess. The vines were so thick that when they reached the bottom, the short corridor was black as pitch. Fortunately, they didn't need light. Their bugeyes worked, with or without it. They expended several shots to clear a path to the main corridor. Once they made it, they went directly to the utility room to find a more efficient means to cut through the vines and preserve their plas ammo. So far they had found no living vines, but neither was confident that their luck would last.

What knotted their stomachs the most was the dead silence of the corridors. Now and then, their supersensitive SIBAs picked up the rustling sounds of what might have been something living, but it never lasted long enough for them to identify its source. Harlowe called out several times, hoping it was Monday or Prigg, even Dodger. Only the silence answered his calls.

"There it is," Riverstone said, pointing to the utility room doorway.

"Still open," Harlowe noted.

The way to the utility room was less crowded with vines. Finding nothing alive inside, the vines had apparently ignored the room in their search for food.

Harlowe found the cabinet he wanted. The drawer was already open. Riverstone looked over his shoulder. "Anything missing?'

"A blade and a couple of cutters."

"Only one blade?"

Harlowe lifted two long machete-like blades of dura-metal from the cabinet and handed one to Riverstone. "Yeah, just one. They're too long for Dodger and Prigg."

Riverstone attached the blade to his belt. Then he retrieved a Gama-rifle from another cabinet. It was the same type he had used in Utah that blew off the top of a mountain ten miles away and shot the Dak attack ships in deep space after leaving Earth.

"You'll blow a hole in Millie with that," Harlowe said, remembering their mistakes from the past.

Riverstone led Harlowe into the corridor. "Watch." He pointed the rifle down the long corridor toward the vast center foyer. "I put it on low."

Harlowe gave him the go-ahead. "Do it."

With one pull of the trigger, Riverstone vaporized a five-hundred-foot swath through the vine mass.

Harlowe looked on, amazed. "Sweet."

Riverstone patted the side of the weapon like it was his favorite pet. "This is the only one left in the rack." He checked the blue lights and reset the weapon for its next shot. "I'll bet my dad's Dodger season tickets that Platter has the others."

* * *

The crawlers were only in certain sections of the ship. They were thickest where the scorch marks along the walls were numerous, which meant only one thing to Harlowe: "This is the path they followed."

Far down the main corridor, the trail took a sharp right turn through one room, out another exit to another minor corridor, then doubled back again to a main. They went through so many twists and turns that after a while, neither Harlowe nor Riverstone knew for sure what section of the ship they were in.

"How much longer could Platter keep it up?" Riverstone wondered.

"He had help. Look," Harlowe said, kneeling to observe the floor, "there's more plas fire than before."

"It had to be Prigg."

Harlowe pointed. "Dodger was here, too."

Riverstone searched the charred piles of vines. "How do you know that?"

Harlowe reached into the pile of ash and dusted off a blue baseball hat with big white LA letters on the front. Riverstone knew Dodger wouldn't part with his favorite hat for anything unless...

Their search was interrupted again when Leucadia called. They had safely off-loaded the black thermo-grym chest from the *Millie* and were preparing to bring it aboard *Millawanda*. What were his instructions?

"Stay loose," Harlowe cautioned. "We haven't seen any live crawlers yet, but we've heard noises."

"Aye," Leucadia replied.

Next Harlowe told her to go with Wiz to the lower-level utility room and load up with protection.

"I'm on the bridge, Harlowe. *Millie's* dead," Leucadia said.

"Don't worry about that now. Go to the utility room."

"The others?" she asked hesitantly. The crack in her voice gave away her deep concern for the crew's survival.

"Still looking. Captain out."

Harlowe looked down the large corridor full of vines. "How many rounds do you have left?"

Riverstone patted his ammo clips on his Gama-belt. "I brought extras."

Harlowe motioned again for Riverstone to clear the passageway. "Do your thing."

Once the path was cleared, they knew exactly where they were on the ship. A short distance down the corridor, the vines had made another abrupt turn through the huge double-doorway that led to the pool Dodger discovered that turned out to be everyone's favorite off-duty getaway. There was no doubt about the destination. Harlowe and Riverstone turned to each other and said at the same moment, "Salt water."

Harlowe took the lead, chopping his way through the open doorway with his blade. As he sliced his way into the great poolroom, Riverstone covered him, keeping his Gama-rifle ready for anything that might follow them through the doorway. At the pool's edge, Harlowe sliced through a purplish trunk. A loud squeal cried out as the crawler recoiled in pain. Their worst fears were realized. Crawlers were still alive inside the ship!

Two crawlers blindsided Riverstone, grabbing his legs. When he whirled around to blast them, more crawlers attacked, ripping the rifle away from his hands. More vines came out of nowhere, worming their way along the edge of the pool. Harlowe moved quickly, slicing through their lead branches. The wiggling ends fell into the pool, where they steamed like they'd been dropped into a pot of boiling water. Harlowe pivoted to lop off a vine that had slithered around Riverstone's head. Riverstone was then able to grab his own blade and free his legs.

More crawlers slid through the doorway and were joined by other tangly branches slithering their way toward them from the walls of the poolroom. "Where did they come from?" Riverstone shouted.

Harlowe and Riverstone slashed their way back toward the pool.

"It's a setup. They were here all along," Harlowe shouted back, swinging his dura blade in great arcs.

"That takes smarts," Riverstone surmised.

"Roger that! It's got a brain somewhere like an octopus with tentacles."

Back-to-back, they slashed and cut their way to the pool's edge. The vines seemed endless. When they sliced one end, two more crawlers took its place.

Harlowe got on the com. "Lu!"

She answered promptly. "Here, Harlowe!"

Harlowe couldn't reply. He was too busy chopping tendrils to talk. Riverstone grabbed Harlowe's Gama-belt and yanked them both into the pool. Every time the crawlers reached for them, they screamed the instant they touched the water.

The vines continued to hover over the water's edge like hungry wolves, waiting for any opportunity to grab a head, a leg or an arm.

Each time a vine reached in, Riverstone splashed it with a wave of salty water.

When the two Gamadin finally reached the center island, a pair of happy blue eyes greeted them at the water's edge. Harlowe patted Molly's pink snout. "Hey, girl." She nearly fell into the water, trying to lick him. Behind her, Rhud was turning around like a top, whipping his tail with excitement. Riverstone climbed out of the pool and gave the big cat a bear hug.

Both cats were thin from starvation. Rhud had an old wound across his back and hind leg. Molly had a broken front paw and a large slash that ran across her face and continued over her shoulder and down her side. Harlowe winced when he checked her over. Molly still favored her broken paw, even though it was clear that someone had splinted it together.

The splint was a good sign. Someone was still around to give first aid. Harlowe wasted no time. "Where are they, Molly?"

If she had been well, Molly would have led Harlowe and Riverstone to the others at breakneck speed, but she was weak and injured. Rhud was not much better. Both cats were weak and malnourished. While they limped along through the bushes on the island together, Harlowe resumed his call to Leucadia.

"We're pinned down," Harlowe told her. We're at the pool."

"Have you seen anyone?" she asked quickly.

"No, but Molly and Rhud found us."

"We're coming down."

"No! It's a setup."

"I don't understand."

"The vine attacks are too coordinated. They've got a brain of some sort. We need to find it and nuke it."

"It's on the island," Leucadia stated with certainty.

Harlowe agreed. "It's the only place. Take care of *Millawanda*. Never mind us. Load Millie with the thermo-grym."

"Harlowe..."

"That's an order, Lu. Millie comes first."

Harlowe could hear the worry in her voice. Nevertheless, she kept her cool. "Aye, Captain."

Riverstone tapped Harlowe's shoulder and pointed up at the vines slithering along the ceiling. "They're flanking us."

Harlowe saw the plan. "They're going to drop down on the island."

96

fry the Brain

Leucadia and Ian lowered a two-hundred-pound sack of thermo-grym down the bridge shaft. They didn't need the entire shipment. Two hundred pounds was enough to jumpstart. Before dragging it to the central power core, Leucadia asked Wiz if he could handle the thermo-grym the rest of the way without her.

Ian had listened to the entire communication between Leucadia and Harlowe. He understood the need to search out and destroy the central brain for good. Everyone's life was at stake. EVERYONE'S! "Sure. What are you going to do?"

"I've got a plan. If it works... Well, it's got to work!"

"Harlowe doesn't know."

Leucadia froze Ian in his place with her stare. "You're not going to tell him, either!"

"Lu, he has to know. The last time we didn't tell him—"

"No! You heard Harlowe. Millie's our only concern. She has to live, Ian. Without her we all die."

Once again Ian found himself in another no-win struggle between Harlowe's absolute orders and Leucadia's unauthorized plans. But the first duty for all Gamadin is to protect *Millawanda*, even if it meant disobeying a direct order from the Captain. *Just do the right thing* was all his mind could say. "What are you going to do?" he asked Leucadia.

"Find the Brain. It controls the vines. If I don't find it first, Millie won't launch."

Ian looked for her medallion. "Where's your SIBA?"

"I gave it to Matthew."

Ian closed his eyes. His own SIBA was useless. It was out of power. Whatever she was planning, she would need the SIBA for protection. "Hold on." He was gone only a few moments, but when he returned, he was toting a Gamadin rifle he had retrieved from the utility room. "You'll need this."

Leucadia kissed him on the cheek and turned away.

She slung the weapon over her shoulder as she grabbed the end of a dead vine. She looked back one more time to say, "Save Millie, Ian!" Then she disappeared up the shaft to the bridge.

"Go, girl!" Ian urged after her.

*   *   *

Leucadia first needed something from the *Millie*. She climbed up the rope ladder to the main deck and ran down three companionways to the ship's galley. Finally, she found what she needed: a bowling-ball sized bag of salt.

Twobagger and Shortstop helped strap the bag to her back.

"That's too tight, Ms. Lu. It will be difficult to remove," Twobagger told her.

She headed back up to the main deck. "I can't lose it, Mr. Twobagger."

The two Gazzians struggled to keep up with her as she leaped three steps at a time up the companionway to the main deck. "What are you going to do with it, Ms. Lu?" Shortstop asked.

"Fry the Brain!" she exclaimed. Mowgi was waiting for her on the foredeck, as if he knew he was needed. His eyes still seemed dull. They weren't his normal bright yellow eyeballs with heavy red veins. His coat was lackluster. It was missing the soft, reddish shine it used to have.

She bent down and lifted him up into her arms, hugging him close. "I know there is something troubling you, dear friend, but I need you now."

Mowgi turned his eyes toward her, leaning his head against her shoulder. In his silent way, he was assuring her that he would do what was necessary.

She put him down and said, "My dear Mowgi, we must fly."

As the undog grew, the Gazzian crew looked on in amazement. They had seen him expand into his alternate self before, but each time it was like watching him for the first time. The little creature that dared the giant traa was still a frightening thing to see.

Mowgi expanded so much that it was necessary for him to leave the ship before he was finished. Even before he stopped growing, his great wings lifted him off the stern and out over the saucer dome. He turned back toward the *Millie* with his claws extended and swept low beneath the bow. Leucadia ran across the foredeck, stepped on top of the rail, and leaped onto the undog's back. Together they flew across the bay, rising higher and higher as they headed back toward the island of vines.

97

Purple Haze

Riverstone shot the first vine that dropped from the ceiling. He didn't use the rifle on single tendrils. That was overkill. Pistols were the weapons of choice. They left only scorch marks on the ceiling if they missed, not that Harlowe or Riverstone ever did.

"Why haven't they climbed the ceiling before?" Riverstone asked.

That was a good question. Harlowe didn't know. He cupped his hand over his mouth and called out, "Mr. Platter!"

"Dodger! Prigg!" Riverstone yelled.

The pool was huge. It covered an area the size of a football field. The island was in the center. It was thirty yards long, forty yards wide, and densely packed with tropical trees, arching ferns, and lush bushes. A tall rock cliff in the middle of the island normally dumped a noisy waterfall into the pool. But with no power to run it, it was dry. A loud call could be heard from anywhere in the area.

Riverstone thought he heard something and pointed to their right. "Over there, Dog!"

Molly growled and limped faster in the direction Riverstone had pointed. When they rounded the edge of the waterfall cliff, Harlowe saw a leg sticking out of the brush. "That's Prigg!"

He ran to his little crewman's side and turned him over. He moaned. His middle eyelid lifted slightly, but his eye was unable to focus. He was thin and malnourished like the cats, but he, too, was still alive. Harlowe grabbed his Blue Stuff canteen and gave him a sip. Prigg's orange tongue reached out for more.

Riverstone found Monday close by, in better shape. He grabbed Riverstone's flask and downed the Blue Stuff in three large gulps. He handed the flask back to Riverstone and asked in a raspy voice. "More?"

Harlowe carried Prigg with him, and joined Riverstone and Monday. Searching the area, he asked, "Where's Dodger?"

Monday didn't hear. Harlowe asked him two more times, holding him gently by the shoulders to get his attention. "Where's my brother, Mr. Platter?"

Monday was the only one who could talk. He looked around weakly, searching for Dodger in the blackness. Harlowe wondered how Monday could see anything without his bugeyes. "He was here." A long spray of water shot out from the top of the cliff and struck vines that were hanging down from the ceiling. Their squeals echoed throughout the room and their advance was stopped cold. "It's the water cannon he brought with him. It's the only thing that's kept us alive."

"How did you see that?" Riverstone asked.

No response from Monday.

Harlowe got his attention and pointed at his eyes. "How can you see in the dark?"

"The vines. Take off your bugeyes," Monday replied.

They pulled down their bugeyes from their faces. As their eyes adjusted to the dark, they saw a soft purple haze that filled the room.

Monday reached under a bush and pulled out a vine. "Dead ones don't glow. When we were surrounded we could see clearly, but it's a lot darker now. What happened?"

"We've been using Roundup," Riverstone replied.

Harlowe turned to Riverstone. "Stay with Platter and Prigg."

"Aye."

Monday turned to Harlowe. "Dodger can't hear, either. The squealing. It's made us deaf."

Harlowe gave him a thumbs-up, then he made his way toward the waterjet shooting up at the ceiling.

98

Ding Dong

Vine Island was a small dormant volcano. Flying over the isle took little time, but what Leucadia saw of it from Mowgi's back was a land in constant motion. The Starbucks tidal wave had burned the vines several hundred feet above the waterline. But beyond that point, the purple-green vines were still an undulating mass of living crawlers. The steady wind that blew across the island had no hand in their movement. If she hadn't known how deadly they were, she might have thought they were beautiful. The vines traveled under their own power, guided by the central mind she was looking for.

With a firm grip around Mowgi's neck, she urged the undog lower. Time was growing short.

She watched an ocean bird fly too close to the motion looking for a perch upon which to rest. Several vines shot up from the mass and snagged it out of the air. The bird squawked and struggled, but to no avail. Escape was futile.

Leucadia circled longer to study how the vines squeezed the life from the bird and then passed the poor creature's body up the long hillside of the volcano. Near the top, the body disappeared into a cavern that she had overlooked on her first sweep over the island.

Leaucadia watched as several more prey were brought up the mountainside from different parts of the island to the cave. "That's it, Mowgi! They're feeding the brain."

The undog yipped twice.

As she and Mowgi got closer, she saw that the cave entrance was a secluded opening with a rock overhang that protected it from the salty trade winds from the west. The entire mouth of the cave was choked with vines.

Then the unthinkable happened. Mowgi faltered in flight. Before he could regain his composure, the undog had flown too close to the side of the volcano. Long crawlers shot out, snagged his leg, and began pulling him down. He broke free momentarily by using his lethal claws, but he was immediately attacked by another group of vines. Leucadia brought her rifle around and blasted the thickest sections, but by now they were too low to escape. The intelligence that was guiding the vines was clever. Smaller thread-like vines shot out everywhere, spreading out and grabbing at her face, legs, and arms from all directions. Now vines were wrapping themselves around Mowgi's neck and claws. With one wing still free, he tried to to gain altitude and snap free of the tangling tendrils. But his power to fight had diminished. He lost the battle.

Leucadia could do nothing to help Mowgi. The vines had snared her as well. A thick stem wrapped around her waist and pulled her from Mowgi's back, dragging her up the side of the volcano toward the brain. Mowgi cried out while he struggled to free himself. She whirled around with her rifle and shot blindly. She couldn't see if she helped him or not. The vines were shaking her so violently that her vison was lost.

She fired again at what she thought was the cave entrance. The blast blew away the top of the opening, bringing tons of rock down upon the main branches of the cave. Wild screams echoed throughout the island. She had stung the brain. But now she had to kill it altogether.

She aimed again and shot. This time, the vines jerked her arm and her shot wasn't anywhere close. She took out a mile-long length of crawlers, but it was a wasted shot. As fast as the gap opened, it closed again.

Yanked one way, then the next, she didn't know long it would be before her neck snapped. Then another catastrophe occurred. The bag of salt she was carrying shook loose and dropped to the ground. She tried to grab it but wasn't fast enough. The bag broke against the vines below with little effect. The coarse grains slid harmlessly off the leaves without burning any of the vines. Her plan for the salt would have failed anyway. It wasn't salt but something else in the ocean water that burned the vines!

She thought she had lost the struggle. Then razor-sharp teeth began slicing through the vines holding her, while a claw snatched her waist and yanked her skyward. It seemed that her second shot had found its mark after all. It was enough to let Mowgi break his bonds, and now he was lifting her away from the carnivorous vines.

In spite of all the shaking and jerking, she still held on to her Gamadin rifle. As Mowgi gained altitude, she turned and looked behind. Her vision was dizzy and clouded and she saw only a vague image. But determined to finish the mission, she turned the rifle's setting on high and blasted a new hole deep into the mountain. If she had to blow away the entire mountain, she would! She fired again and again and again until the cone of the caldera was nothing but a molten mass of white-hot rock.

The screams were deafening as the vines howled in pain from the burning fire. Then, as if someone had thrown a switch, the screams suddenly gave way to deathly silence. Mowgi swooped back around toward *Millawanda* and Lu examined the ground below. The entire island had settled into a motionless calm, their life force stilled forever.

Exhausted but relieved, Leucadia could think only of a song from her childhood. *Ding, Dong! The Witch is dead. Ding Dong! The Wicked Witch is dead.*

99

Powering Up

Riverstone called to Harlowe in pain from his com. "What's that noise, Dog?"

Before Harlowe could answer, the purple haze inside the room began to darken. The ear-shattering screams faded into silence.

Riverstone removed his hands from his ears. "What happened?"

Harlowe unwrapped a vine from around his neck. "They're dying, Matt. Their glow is gone." He held up the wilted tendril for Riverstone to see. "Look!"

Riverstone brushed the vines from his SIBA like they were lint. "What happened?"

Without the glow, the pool area was completely dark. Harlowe put on his SIBA headgear and tapped his communicator. "Lu, what's happening out there?"

Ian answered for her. "It was Lu, Captain."

"Lu?"

"Aye. She went outside with a rifle."

Harlowe clicked off his communicator and glared. "I told her to stay with Wiz!"

"Are you going to make her walk the plank?" Riverstone asked.

"I might," Harlowe replied. He returned to Ian. "Where are you?"

"In the power room," Ian replied.

"Is Millie sucking juice? Yet?" Harlowe asked.

"Not yet. I think she needs a jump start, Captain."

"How do you do that?" Harlowe wondered.

"I'm working on it, Captain."

Harlowe checked the time. "Can you do it in less than 19 minutes?"

"Negative. Not even in 19 hours, unless we get a power boost from somewhere."

Riverstone faced Harlowe. "If Lu's outside when it strikes…"

"I know. She's fried. So are Rerun and Sizzle."

"Harlowe," Rivertone said in a panic, "we have to do something! We can't run out of mojo now!"

Harlowe didn't need to be told. They had all been fighting the clock since the moment they crashed-landed on the planet.

Harlowe went to the edge of the cliff, with Riverstone following in his footsteps.

"What about them?" Riverstone asked, pointing back to the pool island where Dodger, Platter, and Prigg were.

"They'll hold out. We need to get to the bridge."

Harlowe and Riverstone dove off the cliff and stroked across the water to the other side. By the time they were out of the pool and headed down one of the long hallways, ambient light inside the corridors had begun to return. Riverstone removed his bugeyes to make sure his mask wasn't defective. "Wiz did it!"

"It's not me," Ian's voice corrected over their communicators. "Millie hasn't started producing power from the thermo-grym yet."

"If not you, then where's she getting the power from?" Harlowe asked.

"I don't know, Captain. The lights just started brightening on their own."

Ian knew that *Millawanda* could not have absorbed the thermogrym on her own. "Something else is providing her power."

Harlowe cared about only one thing. "Will it be enough?"

"I don't know, Captain," Ian replied.

*   *   *

Minutes before impact, Harlowe and Riverstone hacked the vines clear from the console. The lighted wall at the back of the bridge was growing brighter and brighter with each passing moment.

"Come on, Millie! You can do it, girl!" Harlowe stood at the back wall and cheered on the lights that were starting to dance.

Riverstone pointed out the massive front window. "Harlowe, look!"

Harlowe whirled around. He could barely see out the dirty windows but the images were clear. It was the rays. They were lying all over *Millawanda,* transferring power from their bodies into her hull. "Stay with the start-up, Mr. Riverstone. I'll be right back."

Harlowe ran through his quarters and began chopping away at the vines that plugged the door to the outside until he was able to shut the door to the outer hull. "THANK YOU, MY FRIENDS!" he yelled to the rays, who were happily lying over the hull as if they were sunning themselves on the deck of the ship. Harlowe wanted to believe that they were there to help *Millawanda* restore her power, but the way they were horsing around, he wondered if that really was why. They had probably found him to play, hoping he would toss them a ball to fetch. It didn't matter. Just like the incident inside the glacier when he was about to run out of power in his SIBA, they had shown up at the right time.

Harlowe leaped up on the back of the ray and spoke gently to them. "Go home, my friends. You have done more than your share."

With great sadness, the rays lifted in the air, but still they would not leave. "SHOO NOW! GO HOME!"

But like the puppies that they were, they backed away only a short distance. Harlowe, knowing it was the best he could do, turned toward the *Millie,* still listing on her side on top of the saucer's hull.

Harlowe ran to just below the bow of the *Millie.* Anyone who could still walk and crawl was out on the decks, watching the rays in awe.

Harlowe called up to the main deck. "Mr. Pitch!"

"Cool, Captain!" Pitch replied, waving his one arm. "I'm here!"

Harlowe pointed to the saucer dome. "This golden island you see will soon lower to allow the *Millie* to drift free. You have a good wind. Send the men aloft. I want all sails loose and the *Millie* headed for open sea spritely, Mr. Pitch!"

"Cool, Captain, to the open sea she will be! Do you have a heading, Captain?" Pitch asked.

Harlowe pointed east. "There, Mr. Pitch! Sail to that distant shore and find a nice cove for our lady. I will join you there."

"Cool, Captain! A nice cove for the lady," Pitch confirmed, as he summoned his men to climb the rigging and let loose the sheets.

"And Mr. Pitch?"

"Captain?"

"Have you seen Ms. Lu?"

Pitch pointed with his one arm toward the island. "Not since she flew with the great Butthead toward the island. That was last anyone saw of them, Captain."

"Thank you, Mr. Pitch. Carry on."

Harlowe then ran back to the bridge. What else could he do? There was no time to search for her. She and the undog were out there somewhere. How would he find her in time?

* * *

"Millie's sucked it all in, Captain!" Ian called out over the com. "She's good to go!"

"Aye, Wiz. Get your tail up to the bridge, pronto," Harlowe ordered from his center command chair. He turned to his First Officer and asked, "Do the instruments give us a go, Mr. Riverstone?"

Riverstone twisted around and faced Harlowe. "She's not a hundred percent."

"Who is, Mr. Riverstone? Switch on the ignition!"

"Shouldn't we wait for Wiz?"

Harlowe leaned forward. "Do it!"

Riverstone turned back around and ran his hand over the power bars. *Millawanda* sputtered as if she were coughing, trying to clear her throat.

"Come on, Millie. Talk to us," Harlowe urged.

And Millie did. The lights on the console in front of Riverstone reflected off of his face. Harlowe looked over his shoulder. A brilliant glow radiated along the top of the ceiling. The wall of dancing lights was back! Ian crawled over the heap of dead weeds. "Find your chair, Wiz."

Ian looked worriedly around the bridge. "Where's Lu, Captain?"

Harlowe raised *Millawanda's* landing pods and allowed her to sink below the surface just enough for the *Millie* to right herself and drift free. Suddenly the holoscreen above the console switched on, giving them a clear view of the outside world. The *Millie* had loosed her sails and was gathering wind.

Harlowe's face was unemotional. "She's not here, Wiz." He knew the consequences if they didn't reach the radial point in time. They would live, but those left on the planet would fry.

"I need her help with the shields. I can't do it without her, Captain."

Harlowe raised the saucer out of the water and beyond the point where the rays could follow him. "It's all you, Wiz."

At the two-thousand-foot altitude mark, Harlowe shifted her into gear. Within seconds, *Millawanda* was headed for deep space.

"Captain..." Ian pleaded. "We have to find her!"

"I thought you had a new way to zap the burst."

"We do, but it's all her idea. Lu tried to explain it to me in case..." Ian was shaking. "Well, in case one of us didn't make it. I didn't realize it would be her. She knows everything."

"She's half-alien, Captain," Riverstone defended Ian. "Gamma bursts are duck soup for her. You know that. Wiz is Wiz, but he's not Lu."

Harlowe was about to say something close to *he would do it himself*, when they heard more rustling of dead branches from behind the pile of dead vines on the bridge. Harlowe and Riverstone went for their pistols. They knew the only three other beings on board were unconscious and lying incapacitated on the pool island. The wrestling sounds could only mean one thing.

The Gamadin were ready to shoot the first vine that popped up over the top when a tall-eared creature appeared, followed by a voice that said, "Permission to come aboard, Captain." Leucadia slipped past Mowgi and went headfirst into Harlowe's arms.

Ian jumped out of his chair while Riverstone grinned. Harlowe narrowed his eyes. "You're late."

100

Groovin' on a Sunday Afternoon

The rogue wave had come from nowhere. It crushed Simon's dhow like it was made of toothpicks. Every good seaman knows to point the bow toward an oncoming wave. But the wave was too monstrous and fast moving. Even if the bow had been perfectly aligned, the dhow was too small to survive. Simon did the only thing he could to save his life. He tapped his SIBA and dove for the bottom. It still felt like he was inside a giant washing machine. When the wave passed and his head cleared enough to know which way was up, he swam to the surface and found the sea calm again, as if nothing had happened.

The island he found in front of him was the only land in sight. It was a swim, but the distance was doable. He flipped over on his back and started kicking for the island. What else could he do? In an ocean full of traas, you didn't wait around for another boat to pick you up.

As he swam, he wondered about Sizzle. Had she survived captivity? Had she been as resourceful as Leucadia? Was she okay? How he ached to have her by his side again! Did Harlowe make it back to *Millawanda* in time? Were Platter, Prigg, and Dodger okay? He felt like a failure since he had been unable to complete his mission. What about Mowgi? He looked so weak heading out over the ocean. Did he make it?

All those questions and more occupied his mind, as he looked up at the blue-green sky and watched the heavens explode over him. The sky was bright and charged with blue and red energy. He stopped paddling and took in the planet-wide event. This is the beginning of the end, he thought. The burst had arrived and was engulfing Gazz with its lethal radiation. Great shocks of brilliant blue, red, green, pink, and yellow light blazed across the sky. Then horrific explosions of thunder shook the planet.

Simon thought about his death. Would he simply dissolve like a breath mint or fry to a crisp like burnt bacon? If he had his choice, he preferred the breath mint exit. It seemed cleaner and less painful than sizzling to ash. Until it happened, he decided to continue kicking toward the island as if his SIBA protected him. He broke out into an oldies song, *Groovin' on a Sunday Afternoon,* by the Young Rascals. He motored along, having nothing but peaceful thoughts.

He was halfway through the second verse, "We can be anyone we want to be…" when he felt a bump. Simon unsheathed his black knife and waited for the traa to make its second pass.

101

Three, Two, One...ZERO!

Time had run out. Harlowe and his skeleton Gamadin crew had less than a minute to make it all work. Harlowe throttled *Millawanda* for more speed. He had to stay below sub-light or risk blowing past the dispersion point. If he blew past it or if *Millie* was too low over the planet's surface when the burst hit, her force field would be ineffective.

Harlowe watched Leucadia's hands move across the console's lighted bars with masterful skill. The computations streaming from her to the console were mind-boggling. Wiz was right. They would never have survived without her controlling the outward flow of energy to the force field emitters.

Toad, what were you thinking?

"More power, Ian!" Leucadia called out.

"You've got it all, Lu," Ian replied, with his eyes locked onto the readouts in front of him.

Keeping her eyes fixed on her screens, Leucadia called out more instructions without regard to protocol. "Cut the drive, Harlowe! I need that power."

This was no place for bridge etiquette. They addressed each other as if they were all off-the-clock. The chain of command had shifted to Leucadia with no dissent. This was her party. She could have called Harlowe a toadfaced-moron and he would have replied, "Aye, aye, Ms. Lu."

"We're almost there," Harlowe protested, afraid to cut back or risk falling short of the mark.

"It won't matter if we don't get more power. Cut it back!"

Harlowe throttled back, diverting the flow of *Millawanda's* drive to the force-field emitters.

"It's yours, Lu," Riverstone informed her from the chair next to Ian's.

All of their lives rode on their teamwork. There was no weak link. With mere seconds to go before the burst slammed into the planet, no one, not a single Gamadin, choked. If fate took them, they would go down fighting together.

"Ten seconds!" Riverstone said, counting down.

"Ninety percent," Ian added.

"Eight...Seven..." Riverstone continued.

"Throw the switch, Lu," Harlowe said.

"Not yet!" Leucadia replied.

"Four, three, two..."

Harlowe leaned toward her, more than anxious. "Lu..."

Leucadia held her right hand over the glowing yellow activator. "Disbursing..." When it went bright blue, she tapped it. "NOW!"

"ZERO!" Riverstone cried out. The burst struck, rocking the Gamadin ship violently. Blue, pink, and yellow explosions suddenly filled the front windows. They were in the center of an apocalypse, and if they couldn't stop it, no one could.

102

Aftermath

Simon felt the soothing rays of the midday sun on his face. Was he alive or dead? He wondered if heaven was the same on Gazz as it was on Earth. Would he understand their language without his translator? Would Sizzle be there waiting for him? For a moment he stayed put, keeping his dream of lying on a beach of warm white sand undisturbed.

After another moment, he said to himself, *Okay, dude, you can't stay here forever. Open your eyes and get with the program!*

To his surprise, he stared out at an ocean. My gawd, he was on a beach! The shore break was lapping at his feet. The sea appeared unusually calm and the trade winds were blowing as if no catastrophic event had ever taken place. Nature didn't care, he thought. She always survived.

He looked around the island hills behind the beach. The vines that were once thick and lush that covered the entire island were now shriveled and dead. Not one branch or leaf had survived the burst. The thought of his fellow Gamadin horrified him. The heavens had blown up before his eyes. How could anyone have survived that?

He looked down at his legs. The gentle ripple of water touched his feet. How had he survived...really? He should have been toast! He touched the bugeye mask that covered his face and lay back down in the warm sand.

Wow! His SIBA, as powerless as it was, had saved him.

SWEET!

His joy lasted only an instant. He was the only being left alive on the planet. He began to tremble. *What good is that?*

His SIBA had no more power. How long would he last? There was no food on the planet. No plants or animals. Not a single source of food to catch or harvest for him to eat. *What did Wiz say? Nothing organic would survive.*

He was alive, but he felt dead.

He closed his eyes and took deep breaths to calm his sense of doom. He might as well enjoy what few days he had left. Better to go out with a little tan than arrive white and sickly.

Just when he was settling into a nice nap, a shadow drifted over his face. The sun must have moved. He scooted to one side until he was once again in the sun's rays. Something landed on his face and bit him. He swatted it away. "Darn fly." He swatted at it several times before he opened his eyes and went searching for the pesky critter. Death was its only option. He rolled over and ran smack into a hairy stump.

"What the..."

He looked up and the shadow was massive. The stink was pungent but familiar. He looked down at the stump's toes. There was only one thing living with toes like that.

"Pigpo?"

Pigpo bellowed and neighed as he bent his large head down to give Simon a slobbering lick on the side of his face.

Simon jumped up and grabbed Pigpo around his thick neck. "You have more lives than Harlowe, ya big oink!"

Simon didn't care about the slobber. He was so happy to see his loyal beast he would have taken a bath in Pigpo's spittle!

When he calmed down, he realized that it must have been Pigpo who bumped him in the ocean. Without thinking, he must have climbed onto Pigpo's back and let the beast carry him the rest of the way to the island.

Simon hugged his beast again. "You da dude, Pigpo!"

Then Simon paused. "Why are you alive, big guy? You should be fried like the vines over there," he said.

Pigpo grunted. He didn't know. He didn't care. As long as he was with Simon, Pigpo was content.

The fact that he was not the lone life form on the planet gave Simon new hope. Maybe others survived too. Life began to take on a whole new meaning.

*   *   *

When the crew stepped off the blinker onto the beach, Simon was at a loss for words. His legs were so wobbly he fell to his knees because his fellow Gamadin had survived the burst. What puzzled everyone was Mowgi's reaction to Simon. The undog leaped onto the movie star and started licking him all over. Simon wrapped Mowgi in his arms and together they rolled in the sand like they never wanted to let go. Huge tears of joy ran down the sides of Simon's cheeks. "Little dude, you made it!" Then the undog jumped up on the beast's back like he was home again.

Mowgi's joy at seeing Simon and the strange beast perplexed everyone. Harlowe turned to Leucadia, who shrugged an *I-have-no-clue.*

"There's an untold story here," Harlowe remarked.

When all the licking was over, Riverstone handed Simon a tall Blue Stuff canister and asked, nodding at the beast, "What is that?"

Simon looked at his mount and petted his long mane. "I call him Pigpo. Without him, neither Mowgi nor I would be standing here now."

Riverstone smiled. "A new member of the crew, huh?"

Simon turned to Harlowe with pleading eyes. "If the Captain says it's cool?"

All eyes turned to Harlowe, who sensed that if he said "no," he'd have to deal with a mutiny.

"Pigpo, huh?" Harlowe asked with a smirk. "Couldn't you have come up with a better name, Rerun?"

"You mean like Dog, Squid, or Jester?" Simon asked.

"Good point. He fits right in. He is a he, right?" Harlowe asked.

Simon looked at Pigpo. The question of the friendly beast's gender had never occurred to him. "I don't know."

The group forgot the subject entirely the instant a robob in a colorful bowtie clickity-clacked off the blinker with a tray of blue drinks, double-thick hamburgers with extra cheese, extra sauce, and baskets of golden fries with ketchup.

"Hey, Jewels," Simon said, "You da man."

Riverstone looked puzzled. "I thought he was dust."

Ian explained. "You should have seen Harlowe's face when he walked onto the bridge. He nearly did a face plant on the floor."

Harlowe nodded. He straightened Jewel's bowtie and put his arm around his servant's stick and ball shoulders. "Wiz didn't tell me he took Jewels off the turbos before he fully de-energized. He knew it would be against my orders."

Ian laughed. "Yeah, you would have sacrificed him for the cause too."

Harlowe was unamused. Without another word, he returned with his servant back to the blinker. He looked sad just before they blinked back to the ship.

The crew watched him go. Each of them wondered why he was so down when there was so much to be happy about.

Leucadia saw the anguish. "Harlowe hurts because he loves you all so much. Is there anyone here who doesn't believe he would sacrifice his own life to save us? To save Gazz, he had to make sacrifices every day. He nearly lost us all. The fear of losing one of you, even a robob like Jewels, is a burden he carries every day. Would anyone like to take his place?"

No one answered.

103

Jakaa's Challenge

Jakaa's palace stood at the top of the highest hill in the Empire's capital of Xu. It overlooked the ocean and a busy harbor filled with small dhows, tall-masted merchant ships, and the Empire's strength, a fleet of fifty-gun man-o'-war galleons. At the top of the palace was a swimming pool that was fed by cool mountain springs. Like the rest of the palace, the pool was luxurious beyond description. It was the Emperor's favorite place to escape the day-to-day demands on his time. Great stone arches in the front of the pool offered magnificent views for many leagues out to sea and down both sides of the coastline. The floor of the pool was made of the finest white stone brought in from the farthest reaches of the empire. The stone was so pure it reflected green, absorbing the colors of the sky. On certain spring mornings, when the sun rose together with the Gall Moon, the water reflected a kaleidescope of pink, red, and yellow hues. Lining the perimeter were red-jeweled torches that could be seen far out at sea. It was said that one could see the land of Croomis from Jakaa's pool.

For the Emperor's protection, a palace sentry stood inside each of the thirty archways that bordered the pool. They were all hand picked by Jakaa from the finest and most feared soldiers of the empire.

Today Jakaa arrived at his pool earlier than usual. For the past week, his palace had been undergoing a massive renovation. The open-air pavilion of the pool seemed to be the only place to escape the stonemason's dust. The ancient dirty walls of the palace were being scrubbed to prepare for adding a coat of yellow ochre paint over the thousand-year-old exterior. It was rumored that the change was brought about because of the Emperor's new heartthrob, the tailless Croomis witch of the south. To speak such blasphemy of the Emperor's woman out loud was cause for immediate execution.

Jakaa walked to the edge of the pool and handed his robe to a servant. "Is the evening meal ready for My Lady, Adimus?" Jakaa asked.

"Nearly, Sire," Adimus replied. "She wishes more time to prepare herself."

The Emperor was tall, light-haired, powerfully built, and quite young for a leader of such a vast empire. In what was believed to be a Croomis plot, Jakaa had ascended the throne after the assassination of the previous Emperor, Harmatzus the Terrible. At the age of fifteen, Jakaa had eliminated three challengers in the circus with duals to the death. That was eight years ago. Since then, he had survived numerous attempts on his life. On five occasions he had slain the assassins himself.

"A constant ritual, I'm afraid, Adimus," he joked. Though his guards would never laugh out loud at My Lady's expense, the small guffaw in their eyes pleased him.

Every morning, to protect himself against the constant threat on his life, he engaged with his elite guards in strenuous drills with the sword, lance, and bare-fisted, hand-to-hand combat. Many considered him to be the finest soldier in the empire at all three skills. To keep both mind and body resolute and fit through the night, it was his habit to swim a hundred laps in the cold pool before retiring to his private quarters, two floors below.

"Yes, Sire," Adimus replied, the humor in the Emperor's remark still baffling the always dutiful servant. "Shall I give her an appropriate time, Sire?"

Jakaa held his answer. Something wasn't right. His sense of danger had saved him too many times not to recognize its signs. It might have been the breeze that suddenly changed direction or the peculiar scent of tarnished metal his keen sense of smell had picked up. He was uncertain, but whatever it was, it was alien and did not belong.

Jakaa eased away from the pool's edge and searched from arch to arch for the threat. His guards appeared as they should, each standing with their swords and spears ready. An entire division of his troops could not have made him feel more secure.

Still he was not satisfied.

Jakaa stepped under a nearby arch that overlooked the city. Commander Gii, who sensed his unease, joined him. The night flames of street torches were as bright and clear as they should be. Except for a few barking animals and the usual city sounds, all seemed normal. Many levels below the pool and inside the walled compound of the palace, guards walked the ramparts, undisturbed. Guard animals in the courtyard were quiet or sleeping. All was in order there, as well.

"Do you feel it, Gii?" Jakaa asked from the archway.

Gii searched the perimeter along with his Emperor. "Nothing, Sire."

To a soldier standing nearby, Jakaa asked, "Anything, Ton?"

Jakaa knew all of his elite guards by their first names. He also knew their wives, mistresses, and children by name.

The soldier's eyes remained forward, unflinching and ready. "No, Sire. All is as it should be."

Jakaa stepped farther out onto the veranda and tasted the wind. The tarnished metal was more intense than under the pavilion.

Continuing to look out upon the city, Jakaa asked, "That odor, Gii, do you smell it?"

"Sire?"

"Like an ancient blade," Jakaa stated. "Very old and soiled, as if taken from a crypt."

The soldier tested the air. "I do smell it, Sire."

With his appendage, Jakaa quietly removed Ton's sword from its leather sheath and passed it to his sword hand. "Stand ready, Gii."

"Yes, Sire."

The Emperor whirled around toward the pool, where he saw three tall Croomis soldiers standing at the pool's edge. Like mystical demons, they had slipped past his guards without detection. They were so quiet that even Adimus was unaware of their presence behind him.

Jakaa commanded a half-dozen of his guards to dispatch the intruders. The tallest Croomis grabbed the servant and handed him back to the second Croomis. The second Croomis held the servant in place, out of harm's way. When the rest of the Emperor's guards attacked, the Croomis leader dispatched the best of them as if they were small children. Swords were taken from their grips while their spears were broken and batted away. Two spears were thrown across the pool at the intruders' backs. The third Croomis caught the lances in midair and tossed them casually into the pool. Six guards who had stormed the leader were rendered unconscious and allowed to sluff down to the floor.

Jakaa looked on helplessly as the young Croomis leader dropped the sword with a heavy clank against the stone floor. It was the last blade that was taken from his guards.

"You are the pirate of the wind?" Jakaa asked.

"Maybe," the leader replied calmly.

"You destroyed my Fortress of Daloom."

"Among other things."

"Sire!" Gii spoke, pointing straight at the second soldier. "He is the Croomis who stole your property."

The second Croomis stepped forward. "They were no one's property, Butthead. They were innocent villagers."

"You have caused a lot of trouble, Croomis," Jakaa said to the leader.

The Croomis leader did not deny it. "I'm just getting started, Sire. You want an empire to run, you'd best pay attention."

"Have you come to destroy my people?"

The Croomis leader stepped over the bodies and faced Jakaa. He was much taller than the Emperor and younger by several years. This surprised Jakaa even more.

"No, I start from the top," the leader replied. "I destroy leaders who treat their people like pawns."

Jakaa looked down at his fallen guards.

"They are alive," the leader informed him. "They are good men. To kill them would be a waste."

Jakaa stared in confusion at the blue-eyed leader. The sword he held in his hand was within easy striking distance. With a quick flip of his wrist, he could slay the leader. Instead he asked, "If you have not come to kill me, what is it you want? Money? Jewels? I have plenty of both. But you must know that whatever you do take with you, you will not leave the palace with it alive."

"We got this far," the leader stated with such a calm tone that Jakaa felt that he may have been hasty with his threat of death.

The third Croomis suddenly stepped forward. "Where is she, Toadface? Where is Sizzle?"

The leader stopped the third Croomis from charging Jakaa. "At ease, Mr. Bolt. I'll handle this."

"But Skipper—"

The leader kept his arm out straight, preventing his subordinate's advance. "I said, stand down Gamadin."

The anger in the third Croomis' eyes was clear. Jakaa saw the leader's weakness. If one of *his* guards had acted so disrespectfully, he would have been executed where he stood.

The third Croomis eased back and the leader turned to Jakaa. "The female we seek is Croomis. She is our age, tall, with hair the color of new rope. Where is she?"

Jakaa's face turned red. "She is mine!"

"She is not!" the third Croomis shouted back.

"We will not leave your palace without her," the leader replied.

"She is mine!" Jakaa repeated, fuming visibly at the third Croomis.

"Take us to her. We will decide that," the second Croomis stated.

Jakaa was tempted to use his sword on the leader.

As if reading Jakaa's thoughts, the leader warned the Emperor, "Use that, sir, and you will lose your hand."

Jakaa reached behind him. "Gii! Your glove!"

"Sire!" Gii quickly removed his glove from his pocket and handed it to the Emperor.

Jakaa took the glove and tossed the gauntlet at the third Croomis' feet. "I will see you in Moharr before I give up My Lady."

Jakaa then stomped away, slamming his sword to the stone floor.

*   *   *

"What's that mean?" Simon asked as they watched the Emperor storm off, shouting Phagallian profanities. Harlowe knew. Twice, Pitch and Klagg had challenged him with their gauntlets. The Commander walked up to Simon and explained, "The Emperor will meet you in the circus at dawn. The choice of weapons is yours," Gii said.

Simon looked at Harlowe. "Is he for real, Skipper?"

Harlowe shook his head in disgust. He had bigger fish to fry and they were wasting time with Gazzian challenges. "Just dust the toad so we can blow this place. I'm in a hurry."

Riverstone stared at Harlowe, recognizing a look of determination he had seen too many times before. "Tock-hyba?"

Harlowe ran to the end of the balcony and leaped into the air replying. "We owe them a house call."

The three Gamadin spread their wings and glided down to their unseen golden dome floating outside the harbor and waited for dawn.

104

Chivalrous Knight of the Galaxy

The pleasant sound of My Lady's door gong announced that some-one waited to enter. My Lady's chambermaid, Kikue, went to the heavy ornate door made of gold, rubies, and jade inlay and released the latch with her prehensile tail, an operation My Lady still found amusing, for she was tailless.

The Emperor's servant entered the chamber and after a deep bow of respect, announced, "The evening meal is served, My Lady."

"Thank you, Adimus. Inform Jakaa that I will join him when I am ready," Sizzle answered.

Adimus became worried. "My Lady, forgive me, but the Emperor expects you directly."

Sizzle, dressed in a strapless low-cut gown, waved at the servant. "Shoo now, Adimus! The Emperor can wait. I have not finished putting on my colors." In truth, she had been ready for an hour, but she would never be rushed by anyone, not even his Royal Highness, Jakaa the Emperor. "Now go or I will tell the Emperor that you were rude and disrespectful to His Lady."

Horrified at what she might say to the Emperor, Adimus left the chamber, shaking. Kikue closed the door and when the latch was thrown, they both burst into giggles.

"Did you see the look on Adimus's face, My Lady, when you told him the Emperor could wait?" Kikue asked, holding her sides, filled with uncontrollable laughter.

Sizzle fell onto her bed, unable to stand. "I thought he would need a chamber pot," she replied.

A presence entered the room and said, "If this is slavery, where do I sign up?"

The laughter ended. The presence stepped down from the open window and added with a tone of heavy sarcasm, "Cool digs, Sizzle. Movin' on up, I see."

Sizzle stood from her bed, the merriment wiped from her face, and turned to her chambermaid. "Please leave us, Kikue." Kikue hesitated out of fear that My Lady was in danger for her life. "I know this being. He will not harm me."

Kikue bowed, "Yes, My Lady." She gracefully left the two alone in the bedroom chamber.

Simon spoke first. "What's this all about, Sizzle?"

"Does Harlowe know you are here?"

Simon set his jaw. "No."

"You're mad," Sizzle said.

"Mad?" Simon began. "Why should I be mad? I watched you go down in flames. Riverstone saw you taken away in a slave ship. I didn't know if you were alive or dead. I lost sleep thinking of the tortures you could be suffering. Mad, Sizzle? I'll say I'm mad! I'm pissed!"

Simon was so overwhelmed with emotion, he had to pause for a breath before he went on. "I've been shot, blown up and stabbed. I've walked hundreds of miles across lands that would gag a maggot." He stuck a thumb hard into his chest. "I barely escaped being eaten alive by beasts that would frighten Obi Wan Kenobi. I was almost drowned by a tidal wave that would have swamped California. After that, I floated around in an ocean for two days and washed up on an island where I thought was going to die a slow death by a gamma ray burst. Now that I've finally found you, you've traded in your slave outfit for glass slippers and you're the Emperor's babe. No, I'm not mad Sizzle! Why should I be freaking MAD! Everything is as it should be! RIGHT, SIZZLE?"

Emotionally spent, Simon sat down on the edge of the bed, his head cradled in his hands. Sizzle sat beside him, putting her arm around him, holding him next to her.

"I will never stop loving you, Rerun," she said, kissing him on the cheek.

He looked up, his eyes red and glassy. "Oh, that makes me feel better."

"I must stay here, Rerun."

"This is not you, Sizzle! I mean, this place is first cabin but it's still backward. You love chocolate, tacos, popcorn, and movies. Dang, Sizzle, Netflix had to add another portal just for your downloads! This is not your time period. You like modern things. This ain't modern, Sizzle!"

She turned to him and looked with such a deep sincerity that he knew at that moment there would be no discussion about whether she would leave with him or stay. "I can make a difference here, Simon. When Quay and I were on the beach together on Og, I saw the difference Captain Harlowe made in her. His vision of liberty and freedom for our quadrant allowed her to see her destiny. There were things she believed were impossible before she met Harlowe. Now anything is possible to her! She saw her fate. She is a Ran! She is going to change the quadrant. All she could talk about was freedom and the Inde Doc she reads every day. 'This is Omini Prime's future,' she told me. 'I have it right here and I have to take this idea of life to everyone in the quadrant.' I have never seen her so fulfilled, Simon."

"Why didn't you go with her? You would have saved us both a lot of grief," Simon asked.

Sizzle sat up straight and looked at Simon. "It was you, Simon. I didn't want to part with you. For the first time in my life I found someone who was brave and heroic."

"Heroic, huh? I don't feel so heroic."

"You are my hero, Simon. You will always be my hero."

"I'm still that guy, Sizzle. Millie's out there in the ocean, waiting to take us away." He held up a SIBA medallion for her to see. "Look, we can fly out of here, *no problemo*, and be eating tacos and guacamole by the boatload."

Sizzle held onto his arm, soothing his pain. "Your world is notabout us, Simon. The Gamadin are true heroes. Our galaxy depends on you. You are a warrior for freedom."

"Come with me, Sizzle. Be a part of the Gamadin mission. Help us take back the galaxy."

"I must do my part here. I am not my sister or Leucadia. I am needed here. Phagallia can become a place for good. I will make this land free, not from conquest, but from within."

"Phagallia is primitive. They have elitists and servitude. How will you change their way of life?"

"Kikue, my faithful servent, and I have made wonderful plans. And one day when you return, you will see our accomplishments." She turned to him and continued. "When I survived the crash and saw my mother dead, I was alone. Even though I had you, I had no family. I felt I had been given another chance at life. I saw the answer aboard the slave ship with Lu." At the mention of Lu, Sizzle turned solemn. "Lu? Is she all right? A Phagallian captain took her for himself. She is with Klagg."

Simon nodded. "Lu's fine. She is with us now."

Sizzle closed her eyes, thanking her diety. "She is like Quay. A survivor."

"Twins! Harlowe and Lu are still arguing over who found who first. Your mother is okay, too. She pulled out of the induced coma. A few days with the clickers and she'll be good as new."

Sizzle put her hands together and closed her eyes. "Thank the gods they are both safe!"

"A miracle, all right. Everyone is cool. Dodger is bugging Harlowe to go surfing, but the Skipper says it will have to wait. He has unfinished business. Some planet called Tock-hyba."

Sizzle looked worried. "They are powerful. My father has had many transactions with them. He never seemed happy conducting business with Tock-hyba."

"Harlowe has a plan."

Sizzle was still thoughtful about her future. "I know how much this must hurt. I, too, am in great pain. Your strength guided me through those moments when I should have died aboard the slave ship. I survived because of you, Simon."

Simon pretended to listen and be that chivalrous *knight-in-shining-armor* she wanted him to be. Secretly, however, he was a twitch away from sweeping her up in his arms and flying out the window, the way they had flown off her father's mile-high office building together on Gibb. The old Simon would never have thought twice. He would have grabbed her up and made a dive for the window, knowing deep down that's what Sizzle really wanted him to do.

Doesn't every woman want to be rescued by her knight?

But he didn't. With all his might, he resisted. He figured tomorrow would take care of itself. So he remained quiet, never speaking of Jakaa's challenge to him as Sizzle continued telling him why she had to stay on Gazz.

"I saw such suffering that I cannot even describe. Little children cleaning the bilges, climbing rigging, sick with fever. No one gave them treatment or held them while they were sick. They were allowed to die, and then their bodies were thrown overboard as offerings to the traa. From that day on, I swore to myself that if I survived, I would do whatever was necessary to change what I saw on the voyage, even if it meant giving up my life with you, Simon."

"How did you meet Jerk-o?"

"Jakaa," she corrected. "He saw me hanging from a post at the slave market. The final offer had already been accepted, but Jakaa said he would give the merchant ten times the closing price to buy me. The merchant refused at first, but Jakaa would not take no for an answer. He sent Gii to discuss an alternative offer with the merchant. The merchant agreed to Gii's terms almost immediately. As you often say, Simon, it was awkward."

The story reminded Simon of an old gangster movie back on Earth. "Toadface made him an offer he couldn't refuse," Simon suggested.

"Yes, I am sure it was something like that."

Simon stood up. "I should go."

Sizzle took his hand. "Will I see you again?"

"Maybe sooner than you think."

Sizzle smiled. "You are and always will be my chivalrous knight of the galaxy, Captain Starr."

"Yeah, everybody's favorite hero."

Sizzle held onto his arm as they walked together to the open window of her chamber. For a long heartbreaking embrace, they kissed as if it was the first time under the bushes of the Gibbian park. If this would be their last moment together, they wanted it to last forever.

Finally, it was time to let go. Still clasping fingers, Simon stepped up to the ledge. He gave her one last wink. "My Lady." He kissed her hand, then pushed off into the night, never looking back. He was angry, hurt, disillusioned, and unable to feel like that Chivalrous Knight of the Galaxy.

105

The Circus

The Emperor's Circus was impressive. The travertine stone archways and columns of the ampitheater were magnificent. To Harlowe, Leucadia, Riverstone, and Simon, the Circus with its cheering crowd of fifty thousand Phagallians was the last place they wanted to be. They wanted to be on their way home instead of dealing with unfinished business.

The sun was bright and hot, and the sky was clear and blue-green with a few fluffy clouds drifting overhead. A good day for a duel to the death, Harlowe thought.

Harlowe wore his pirate captain's outfit: sword in his wide black belt, flintlocks on his hips, white blousy linen shirt, dark blue trousers, and black boots. Covering his head was his wide-brimmed Morgan hat with the bright red, white, and blue feathers that Millie made just for the occasion. Riverstone wore similar clothes except for the Dodger cap that he turned backward on his head. Leucadia shocked the crowd with a silky blue blouse that was open down the middle and a white hat that would make any Hollywood starlet jealous.

Unlike the others, Simon came to fight. He wore no shirt and had black britches lent to him by Moneyball. He was barefoot and unarmed.

Waiting in the center of the Circus floor were Jakaa and his seconds: Commander Gii, Adimus, and a squad of elite guards. Adimus held two swords in front of him that appeared nearly as tall as he was.

Harlowe leaned over to Simon and spoke softly. "How's your swordplay?"

"Good enough."

"Jakaa practices every day."

"So do I."

"Make it quick, then. I'm in a hurry."

Harlowe turned to Riverstone next. "Things may start to go south when Rerun takes care of the toad. You down with the plan?"

"Don't worry, Dog. Lu and I will find Sizzle and hustle her back to the ship before anyone knows she's gone." Harlowe and Riverstone discussed where she would be in the Circus. "That may take time in his crowd," Riverstone added.

Harlowe looked around. "Yeah, if she's here."

Leucadia pointed to a roped-off area surrounded by guards in the stadium. "Sizzle is in the Emperor's box," she confirmed.

The Emperor's box was walled off from the crowd. It had an opulent red, green, and gold awning over the top that protected its occupants from the heat of the sun. Near the center of the box was a table of assorted fruits, dips, and meats that everyone but Sizzle was enjoying.

"Does she see us?" Harlowe asked, squinting toward the box.

"Yes," Leucadia replied.

Sizzle wore a shiny gold dress that displayed every facet of her youthful body.

"Correct me if I'm wrong, but she doesn't look like slavery has treated her unkindly," Riverstone remarked.

Harlowe turned to Leucadia. "You were the last one to see her. What happened?"

Leucadia was as puzzled as everyone. "She talked about helping the slaves. Perhaps she found a way."

Simon spoke for the first time. "She did. She's staying."

Harlowe faced Simon directly. "How do you know that?"

Simon ignored Harlowe's question and went on to face Jakaa.

Harlowe wasn't sure what was going on. Did Sizzle want to stay or not? If she did, why were they here? If being here was a waste of time, heads would roll. "I'm putting a stop to this," he stated, and was about to march forward to retrieve Simon when Riverstone held him up.

"No, Dog! Let him go," Riverstone said.

"He's going to kill Jakaa and it isn't necessary," Harlowe stated, "even if he is a scumbag."

Riverstone held firm. "He needs closure. Let him go."

Harlowe saw their problems multiplying a thousand fold.

"Trust him, Captain."

Harlowe felt the side of his pant leg where he kept his hidden pistols. He watched Simon take the offered sword from Adimus and begin slicing the air to test its balance. Jakaa did the same. Then the combatants took their distance and faced off.

"I need to trust him, eh?" Harlowe asked.

"Aye," came Riverstone's sure reply.

With both hands firmly gripping their sword hilts, Simon and Jakaa circled each other, looking for an opening to strike the first blow. Neither had helmets nor shields. Simon had been offered one, but he refused. Seeing his opponet refuse protection, Jakaa tossed aside his bejeweled helmet. He would not lose face for this Croomis pig.

At the first clash of metal against metal, a loud ring shook the stadium. Bright sparks flashed everywhere. The crowd came to an instant silence.

Strike again, foil, strike.

Their eyes gleamed with malice as blow after blow rang out their deadly strikes. When they fought close enough in, fists landed bone-shaking hits against face and jawbone. Large red welts on both combatants swelled their eyes, noses, and necks, but no one let go of their hilts.

At one point, Jakaa stumbled. Commander Gii tried to lean in and assist his sire. Harlowe stepped behind him and seized his sword hand. "Big mistake."

Gii found his hand in a vise grip from which he could not break free. Harlowe disarmed the Commander and flung his sword to the far end of the stadium with such force, it split a post in half. The distance the blade traveled was breathtaking. Gii did not make another attempt.

After an hour of heavy blows, slams to the mouth, shoulders, necks, and bodies, the combatants looked like slabs of butchered meat. It reflected well on their courage and character that neither had fallen. When they drew apart, both stumbled backwards, giving themselves time to gather strength. They were not done by any means.

The lull in the combat was short. Jakaa and Simon came at each other with more ferocity than ever. Leucadia looked up at the crowd. She was struck by the silence. Who among them had ever seen a bitter struggle to the death that seemed without end? The crowd was disappointed that one gladiator should live and the other die. The pity was, neither needed to die, but end it must in death.

Then, as if forever had come to an end, Jakaa's sword caught the edge of Simon's hilt and Simon's sword dropped to the ground at

Harlowe's feet. He wanted to reach down and toss it back to Simon, but he could not. It would be the same advantage for which he had stopped Commander Gii. The sword stayed as Jakaa came down on the helpless Simon, running him through with his blade. Simon twisted, appearing to direct the broadsword as it sunk deep. When Jakaa pulled back, the blade was thick with dripping blood. Simon's blood. Simon's eyes rolled back as he fell to the ground, rolled over on his side, and went still.

The crowd cheered, rocking the stadium with their stomping and loud cries of rejoicing for their emperor. "JAKAA THE GREATEST! LONG LIVE JAKAA!" they shouted.

Harlowe rushed to Simon's aid and took his limp head in his arms.

"He is the bravest warrior I have ever fought," Jakaa said, leaning over, sweating rivers off of his face and panting heavily from exhaustion. Adimus was holding him, helping him to stand.

Sizzle ran from the stadium box in tears. "No, no, no! Rerun, my Rerun!" She tried pushing her way through the crowd, but Riverstone held her back. "Let me go to him, Matthew! Please!"

"It's over, Sizzle. He's dead," Riverstone told her. Kikue was there, too, trying to calm her.

Sizzle fell to her knees and crawled toward Simon. She could not let him go to the gods without a goodbye. "One kiss, Matthew! Please, one kiss for my Rerun!" she cried.

Kikue's pleading eyes found Riverstone. Together they lowered her over Simon's bloodied face as she gave him his last kiss. "Goodbye, Rerun."

Harlowe then lifted Simon in his arms and stood before Jakaa. "She is yours, Jakaa. Take care of her or I will return to Xu and level your palace as I did Daloom."

Gii charged Harlowe for his insolence. Before Jakaa's commander could thrust a hidden blade into Harlowe's back, a massive fist dropped Gii in his tracks. Riverstone quickly moved to Harlowe's side and waited for the next attack. Then Sizzle stood like a barrier between Harlowe and Jakaa. Sweat and blood marred her rich golden dress. "Thank you, Captain," she said, "the people of Phagallia will remember this day for all time."

Harlowe's charged blue eyes stared coldly at Jakaa until the Emperor blinked. "You are free to go, Captain. You will have safe passage from our lands," Jakaa ordered.

The Emperor's guard parted and allowed the Croomis and his crew to leave the Circus.

*　　*　　*

Riverstone saw Kikue in an alley across from the docks of Xu. He watched her the whole way. Staying away from the sunlit sections of the buildings and alleys, she tried to move unseen.

He grinned at her innocence. She brushed her long dark hair away from her shoulders as she held her appendage anxiously, peeking around the corner at him with her large dark eyes as he and the others were about to disembark in the dhow.

Kikue had followed him all the way from the Circus. This would be the last time he would ever see her. Harlowe had seen her too. With a slight nod, he sent Riverstone on his way to say a proper goodbye.

*　　*　　*

Suddenly Buntoo-attee was gone. He was not with the others. She tried to find him, but he was nowhere to be seen. Perhaps he went below deck, she thought, to find some rigging. He wouldn't be long in any case. She watched the Captain lay the body of his crewman in the center of the dhow. The female Coomis was sad, wiping her face as she carefully folded the shroud around the body.

"I will miss you, Kik," Buntoo-attee's voice said from behind. He had been as quiet as a shree, apprearing out of nowhere.

He startled her, but only for a moment. When she saw him, she threw her arms around him and never wanted to let go.

They spoke little, and when it was time for him to leave, he wiped her eyes with the end of his white sleeve and turned away. As Buntoo-attee's dhow sailed out of the harbor, Kikue ran along the docks until she could go no farther, watching Buntoo-attee until the sail of his dhow drifted out beyond the far point and was gone.

*   *   *

Harlowe was at the till as he turned the small sailboat south out of the harbor toward the submerged saucer. Simon's body, covered with a bloodstained white sheet, lay in the middle of the boat. When the dhow was far enough to sea where no one from land could see them, Harlowe said to the corpse, "All right, Rerun. You can get up now."

Simon slowly pushed aside the burlap sheet from over his body, exposing the welts, bruises, and cuts he had sustained in his bout with Jakaa. He sat up and removed the bladder of blood he had used to fake his death and tossed it overboard. He said little, preferring to wallow in suffering that ran deeper than any of the physical wounds he sustained. The shroud had given him a place to hide. Harlowe understood that what Simon needed more than sympathy was the strong backing of his fellow Gamadin. Exposing the charade forced Simon to face life again.

"How did you know, Dog?" Riverstone asked.

"We had it choreographed perfectly," Simon said.

"Riverstone's trust me line was over the top," Harlowe replied with a smirk.

Leucadia moved to Harlowe and settled into his arms. She gazed at Simon, knowing the pain of his sacrifice. "You played your part well, Simon. It was a chivalrous act you made today. I am proud of you."

Simon closed his eyes, still heartbroken.

"Could you have defeated Jakaa?" Riverstone asked Simon.

Simon forced a cool grin as he reached for a flask of water on the deck and poured the contents over his head to wash the layers of dirt and blood from his face and bare chest. "It was her choice to stay. I couldn't stop her." He thought for a moment and added, "If anyone can make a difference there, Sizzle can."

"She will, Simon," Leucadia said with confidence.

Simon stared at the wooden planks. "I still lost her."

Leucadia sat down beside Simon and put her arm around his shoulders. "You gave her the greatest gift of all, Rerun. You gave Sizzle her life back. She is free now to make a difference for Gazz. The Phagallians and the Croomis will flourish and one day become a welcome member of the quandrant because of your sacrifice today."

Simon's head lowered, preferring the sight of a wooden deck to the beauty of the planet he had just saved. "Maybe they'll name a park after me. Wouldn't that be a hoot?"""

The conversation ended in a quiet hush. Fate had once again given Simon the shaft. What words could mend his mortal wound? As it has always been, time was the only cure.

Leaving Simon to his thoughts, Leucadia returned to Harlowe's side. She understood the game Fate had in store for them. Talk had no place when the time they all had together was borrowed. From the glances they exchanged, it was only a question as to when the next payment was due. Until then, they remained huddled in each other's company, thankful for the beauty that surrounded them, the planet, and the lives they had saved, the friends and family that were safe, and the time they had with each other.

Riverstone settled into a cushion toward the bow of the dhow with thoughts of Kikue and how a simple life in a fishing village on a beautiful green ocean might have been. If he had never remembered, would he be here now? Lying back, he watched the clouds drift by and felt the sun on his face. Then he closed his eyes and dreamed.

Harlowe's mind was on the future. His mission was not over. He had a score to settle before he considered his task complete. He pulled the tiller toward him, leaning the dhow to port for its final tack around the rocky point. With a full sail and a good wind, they continued south for their rendezvous with *Millawanda*. At their current speed it would be a good hour before they arrived. He nestled his girl closer, getting comfortable against the wooden stern and extending their loan of time a little while longer.

106

Tock-hyba

"The time to strike is now!" roared Rigo-Mesh as he stood before the Tock-hyba High Council assembled for the twelfth deliberation. Declaring interstellar war against the Omini Prime Quadrant was unprecedented. It would require careful strategic planning to overthrow what had been the center of influence for over ten thousand passings. Because of the combined destruction of the Consortium, the Fhaal Empire, and the Tomarian Corporation star fleets by some unknown force, a power vacuum in the quadrant existed. The High Council's ambition was to fill that void before their quadrant rivals did. Using the wealth from its trading history over the passings, Tock-hyba had quietly assembled a fleet of star-class battleships as powerful as any warship known to exist anywhere in the quadrant.

"Tock-hyba should seek out trade agreements, not resources, to sustain such an assault, Rigo," a delegate from the audience suggested.

Rigo-Mesh leaned forward in his stately throne, spotting the delegate in the second row, who was waving an old parchment in his hand to be recognized. "My good friend, Kafrecaa, this talk of freedom and liberty for all has passed. There will be no more discussions of your document."

"Aksu and Sebas have requested that they join us, High Counselor, if our way is peace," Kafrecaa added.

"Your doubts have been noted, Kafrecaa, but there is no going back. Tock-hyba must strike now while Gibb has fallen. Oberna has joined our alliance as well. They have agreed to protect our flank with their starcruisers and attack ships," Rigo-Mesh announced.

The Great Hall of Delegates rumbled with enthusiastic cheers of victory for the High Counselor's plan.

Kafrecaa challenged Rigo-Mesh's scheme again. "With all due respect, High Counselor, since the destruction of the Tomarian Corporation, Tock-hyba's supplies of thermo-grym crystals are limited. We purchase this strategic power source and lack the guarantee of delivery. Erati is still the Tomar Corporation's, but it has been shut down indefinitely. If Tomar discovers our plans, they will cut off our supply. Unless we have an alternate source of thermo-grym for our fleets, an assault upon the Omini Prime and her allies is madness."

The Great Hall rumbled again, this time with the hushed voices of doubt. What Kafrecaa spoke of was truth. Without Erati's thermo-grym, the High Counselor's plans of quadrant domination would go no further than the Great Hall.

Rigo-Mesh raised his hand to quiet the crowd. "We have secured alternative sources, Kafrecaa." An officer and his small group of armed guards marched onto the stage and placed a small box on the table beside the High Counselor. Rigo-Mesh lifted the wooden lid and carefully removed the black crystalline stone from the box. Holding up the black crystal for everyone to see, he exclaimed, "With this, Delegates, we will conquer our enemies! Tock-hyba will dominate the quadrant in perpetuity!"

"What is it, Rigo?" a voice called out.

"Black thermo-grym!" Rigo cried out for all to hear. "It has a thousand times the power of the Erati yellow crystals."

"Does Tock-hyba have control of this valuable resource, Rigo?" Kafrecaa asked.

"Yes, my friend. The source is ours."

The crowd mumbled among themselves as Rigo-Mesh asked, "Are you ready to give your blessing and join Tock-hyba's rightful place as leader of the Omini Prime Quadrant, Kafrecaa? Have your concerns been allayed?"

"I have one other, Rigo. What of the Gamadin?"

Rigo-Mesh waved his hand angrily. "You worry over nothing, Kafrecaa! The Gamadin are ancient children's fables. They do not belong in a serious discussion of conquest!"

"Children's fables do not destroy empires with a single ship, High Counselor! "

Rigo-Mesh faced the crowd of delegates. "Come now, Kafrecaa, does anyone around you believe that the destruction of the Fhaal Empire, the Consortium and the Tomarian fleets was made by a single ship?"

The Great Hall echoed with laughter.

"Then what was it that destroyed their fleets, Rigo? It was no one from this quadrant. We should know this entity before we proceed with a campaign for quadrant domination."

Before Rigo-Mesh could answer, a blue flash of light struck the hundred-foot-high glass wall at the far end of the Great Hall. The massive structure that enclosed the Great Hall was built high on an inaccessible mountainside. Hundreds of plas cannon turrets encircled the mountaintops. In underground hangars nearby, a fleet of heavily-armed aircraft stood ready to launch in the event of an attack. The security surrounding the delegates seemed impregnable. No force had ever threatened this citadel of authority. That all changed, when the glass wall melted before the delegates' eyes.

When the blue light faded, the hole in the glass was large enough for the High Counselor's private airship to easily pass through, with room to spare. An instant later, the blue light struck again. The High Counselor's airship and several others parked on the landing pads outside disintegrated before their eyes. The delegates, who couldn't help but notice, began running for the nearest exits. Where would the lethal blue light strike next? The exit doors, programmed to lock down during emergencies, slammed shut. No one could leave, not even High Counselor Rigo-Mesh.

Outside, thunderous explosions shook the building. The batteries of plas cannons had opened up on the unseen force attacking the Great Hall. Thousands of rounds streaked toward the heavens to bring down the unseen force, but none of the rounds had any effect. A moment later, every plas cannon on the mountaintops was silenced and their long barrels melted to lumps of white-hot metal.

During the breathless silence that followed the destruction, the heavens exploded with charged bolts of blue lightning. From out of the clouds, a golden disk floated between the charged bolts toward the mountain. Its great perimeter of intense blue light nudged the bottom of the newly-formed opening in the wall.

Kafrecaa spoke, fearing that the power of the undeniable supernatural force had come to punish the misbehaved children in the room. "Gamadin…"

During the attack, a dozen armed guards had surrounded Rigo-Mesh to protect him from all threats. Moments later, a small creature with big ears appeared on the floor of the council along with two giant white cats that had blinked into existence at the front edge of the ship's hull. Finally, three soldiers in dark blue uniforms appeared and marched directly toward the High Counselor's throne. The white felines flanked the three soldiers, while the big-eared creature strutted fearlessly in front of the group. Several guards made defensive gestures by drawing their weapons. Although the guards were too far away for their weapons to be effective, the lead soldier took no chances. With blinding speed, he drew his sidearm and, without missing a stride, shot the weapons from the hands of each guard's hand. By now, Kafrecaa was certain of his theory. The soldiers were indeed Gamadin!

When the Gamadin soldiers continued into the Great Hall, the delegates moved to the far ends of the building, giving the soldiers plenty of room. When they reached the middle of the hall, the Gamadin stopped and faced the delegates.

"Who is your leader?" the lead soldier asked, his tone forceful, commanding, and quite impatient.

Rigo-Mesh emerged from behind his guards and spoke with authority. "How dare you come into our Great Hall and demand—"

Crack! Two plas rounds blasted Rigo-Mesh's signature clasps of rank off of his shoulders before he could utter another word. The High Counselor's robe dropped to the floor in a crumpled heap.

"Next one goes between your eyes," the lead soldier warned coldly.

The other two soldiers unholstered their weapons and crossed them in front of their bodies in a disciplined stance. Their eyes were the only parts of their bodies that moved, searching for threats. The felines leaped upon the High Counselor's stage and bared their ten-inch-long incisors. Rigo-Mesh knew that if he didn't do as he was told, the felines would tear his body to shreds.

Rigo-Mesh strode regally down the stairway to the main floor and faced the Gamadin leader. Approaching the soldiers, he was amazed by the apparent youth of the group. They were also strikingly tall, soundly built, and obviously powerful. Their blue eyes betrayed no signs of weakness.

The leader produced a holograph of several starcruisers firing upon a Tomarian starship above the planet Gazz. "Are these your ships?"

Rigo-Mesh held his silence. The soldiers could kill him. If the gods chose, he could become a martyr for Tock-hyba, but he would not divulge his knowledge.

"Mowgi, introduce yourself to this toad," the soldier ordered.

Rigo-Mesh felt an evil breeze behind him. When he looked up, a dragon beast with frightening yellow and red eyes stared down at him. Its thirty-foot wings spread wider than the stage as its maw of long razored teeth drooled over Rigo-Mesh's royal robe, burning holes in the lush red fabric with its saliva. The High Counselor trembled at the thought of being eaten by such a beast if he lied to the soldier. That kind of horrible death was no path to heaven!

"Are these your ships?" the soldier asked again.

"Yes," Rigo-Mesh replied bitterly.

"What were they doing on Gazz?"

"Gazz?"

"You heard me, Toad."

"Gazz is a backward planet. It has no value to us," replied Rigo-Mesh.

The soldier removed a black crystal from a utility pouch attached to his waist. "Does this look familiar?"

Rigo-Mesh stared at the black crystal, afraid to answer.

The soldier suddenly kicked Rigo-Mesh in the chest. He was tired of the non-answers. The High Counselor flew through the air and crashed to the floor, out cold from the blow.

The soldier held up the black crystal. "Listen up! We are Gamadin! The planet Gazz is under our protection. Tock-hyba, Aksu, Sebas, and Oberna, and everyone else in your silly alliance, you are done stripping this planet of its resources. You have been discovered. We know your plans. Your idea of taking the place of the Consortium is a fantasy. Any government that tries to will be destroyed!" The leader pointed at his golden ship. "Look there! Behold *Millawanda*. She is indestructable. She is rad! She is the most powerful weapon in the galaxy and she will destroy every ship in your fleet if you do not heed our warnings. Are we clear?" The mumblings from the crowd conveyed that they were. "Go now! Become free traders. Make peace with your fellow planets. There will be no need to conquer anyone. It is time to be good citizens of this great and wonderful quadrant of yours. I am not asking you. I am telling you. You are free planets; the only freedom you do not have is to take away the freedom of others. Tock-hyba is out of the war business, or the Gamadin will return. There will be no mercy. The choice is yours."

The lead soldier's focused blue eyes captured every delegate as if he was looking at each face in the Great Hall at the same time. No one moved or made a sound. The Gamadin decree was absolute: liberty or death. There was no compromise or appeal. As long as the planets lived peacefully together among the stars, the wrath of the Gamadin was nothing to fear.

With a wave of his hand, the two young Gamadin soldiers who had accompanied the leader returned to their ship, along with their creatures. When they winked out of existence and were gone, the leader noticed the rolled up parchment in Kafrecaa's claws.

"Where did you get that?" the young Gamadin asked.

"It was a gift," Kafrecaa replied.

"May I see it?"

Kafrecaa handed the old document to the young Gamadin leader, who studied the writing as if it were a sacred manuscript of worship.

"Do you know this document, Gamadin?" Kafrecaa asked.

The young leader nodded that he did. "I know it well." He rolled it up carefully and returned the old parchment to Kaffreca and asked, "How did you come by it, Delegate?"

"A girl."

"Tall with dark hair?"

"A remarkable being. She has influenced many. Your decree could have been spoken by her."

The young Gamadin looked around the room. "Is she here on Tock-hyba?"

Kafrecaa remained unemotional. "She was banished by our High Counsel for spreaking dissent against the state."

"She was imprisoned?"

"She escaped before our soldiers found her."

The young leader was relieved at the news. "Escaped, huh?"

"She was never found. Do you know her?" Kafrecaa asked.

"Yes, I know her. You are correct, sir, she is a remarkable being."

"When you see her again, will you tell her Kafrecaa and our people thank her for showing us the way?"

"I would be honored, sir," the young leader replied. Then he turned and casually walked away until he vanished like a flash into the night.

*   *   *

Before the delegates dispersed to their respective districts, they elected Kafrecaa as the new High Counselor. By unanimous decree, he was given strict orders to dismantle the fleet and create a peaceful trading alliance with Gibb, Palcor, and the newest planet in the quadrant to regain its freedom, Neeja.

107

Harlowe's Gift

The *Millie* lay anchored in the calm blue waters of Vine Island Bay. The blue-green sky was cloudless and the sun was bright and tropically warm. The Gall Moon took up a third of the western sky. Three of Gazz's minor moons had also joined the party. Being fashionably late on the horizon, the crest of a fifth moon was coming into view.

The robobs had spent the last several days making the *Millie* whole again. The *Millie's* sails were new and clean. Mowgi's Jolly Roger was replaced by a beautiful purple and green graphic of the Gall Moon. Her rigging was strung with new yellow lines and her decks were freshly scrubbed and oiled. She had a new steerage wheel reconstructed with hard Nywok pine, bright brass fittings, and polished spokes.

The Nywok's sacred Ozimina Tree was returned. In its place the main mast was refitted with a tall, sturdy tree chosen by the Nywoks that was less holy than the Fry Tree. The crew doubted the Fry Tree would ever grow again. The Nywoks, however, had no such belief. They dug the hole and returned the trunk to its holy place in the clearing above the beach. Within hours after replanting, young branches had begun to sprout. Harlowe smiled, watching the branches expand with golden fries right before his eyes. "Now that's a miracle to believe in!"

Back on the island where the vines had once covered the land, lush tropical vegetation was already thriving. Nature, it seemed, had started her own renovation. Simon was especially pleased with the coconut seedlings he brought from the mainland. Little palms were sprouting along the beaches. When the day arrived that he would return to the island, he wanted tall palms spreading their cool shade over his tired body while he, Mowgi, and Pigpo would drink coconut water all day under a relaxing sun.

Onboard the *Millie*, the crew was gathered on the main deck for the transfer ceremonies. By Captain's decree, the galleon that had survived so many perilous adventures over the weeks was being handed back to her Gazzian crew. The Gazzians were lined up at attention as Harlowe and the Gamadin thanked them for their service.

"Mr. Twobagger, steer her true with a fair wind," Harlowe said, shaking his hand.

"Yes, Captain. I will," Twobagger replied.

Next came Shortstop. "Stay clear of the traa's maw, little friend."

Shortstop threw his arms around Harlowe. "Can I go with you, Captain?"

Harlowe knelt down, coming eye-to-eye with the little Gazzian. He shifted Shortstop's new Dodger cap around on his head and said, "I wish that was possible, but you belong here, Shortstop. The *Millie* needs all hands to keep her safe and strong through hostile seas." He turned him back. "Now stand straight and tall, Mr. Shortstop. Be a proud member of the best crew the Gazzian Ocean has ever seen."

Shortstop snapped to attention and saluted, "I will, Captain!" His red cheeks were lined with rivers of tears.

Moneyball, Zinger, Homerun, and Catch were next. Harlowe thanked each one and shook their tails. "I am proud of you, my

Gazzian crew. There was not a moment that I ever doubted your bravery or loyalty to my command. I am forever in your debt, gentlemen. Thank you!"

Finally, there was Pitch. Harlowe slapped the side of his new arm. "How's the new wing, Mr. Pitch?"

Pitch lifted his arm over his head and twisted it around in several directions. "It is like it was never lost, Captain."

"See that it stays that way, Mr. Pitch."

"Cool, Captain, I will!"

Harlowe removed his wide-brimmed hat and straightened its red, white, and blue feathers before he placed the mantle of power upon his First Mate's head. "For you, Captain Pitch. The *Millie* is yours again. Take good care of our Lady."

"Thank you, Captain. A lady she is," Pitch replied, adjusting the hat and standing proudly before his crew.

Harlowe agreed and then gathered the crew around a large chest in the middle of the main deck.

"What is this, Captain?" Captain Pitch asked as he touched the ornate inlaid wood with his new hand.

"Consider it a token of our appreciation," Harlowe replied.

"The trunk has Jakaa's mark," Moneyball noticed.

"The Emperor has made a contribution as well," Harlowe said.

Zinger's eyes were wide with curiosity as he bent down to the latch. "May I, Captain?"

Harlowe patted him on the back. "By all means, Mr. Zinger. You may do the honors."

Zinger lifted the heavy wooden lid. All eyes went round when they saw that the chest was filled to the brim with gold, jewels, and precious treasures.

Simon was touched. For the first time in weeks, a smile crossed his face. "Where did the Skipper get that?"

Riverstone smiled. "From Admiral Radu's storeroom."

When everyone was finished touching their share of the treasure, Harlowe dismissed the crew to the food table. With whooping hollers and cheers, the Gazzians rushed the table. Robobs had stacked it with double-burgers, Dodger dogs, tacos, platters of fries, vanilla, chocolate, Blue Stuff, and pod shakes. Only when the food was gone, however, did Captain Pitch put his face to the winds and give the order to weigh anchor. The Gazzians, too, were eager to leave.

* * *

Leucadia and Ian sat together on the beach and watched the *Millie* lean on a ten-degree starboard tack and clear the bay on her way to the open sea.

"Where are they going?" Ian asked.

Leucadia smiled warmly. "Home."

Ian reached for the com on the towel and pointed it toward the *Millie*. "Where did you put the relay?"

"Inside Captain Pitch's new hat," Leucadia replied. She watched Ian slide his finger across a lighted blue bar. The bar grew bright, then faded back to normal.

His work complete, he laid the com back on the towel. "They'll forget everything?" Ian asked.

"Their short-term memories will fade, but a few things will stay with them."

"It's best this way."

"They've seen too much. Their thoughts need to be of the present instead of the future. Harlowe thought we owed them that much,"

Leucadia explained. "The renovation to the *Millie* was completed?" she asked.

"Last night. The clickers removed the turbos and the keel. She is the way she was in the beginning."

*　*　*

"Come to port ten degrees, Mr. Homerun!" Captain Pitch ordered, standing by the quarterdeck rail, overseeing his busy, clean-clothed crew.

"Cool, Captain! Ten degrees to port!" Homerun replied.

"Make tight those mizzen lines, if you please, Mr. Twobagger! Loose sheets on the foresail, Mr. Shortstop!" Captain Pitch called out, his hands casually locked behind his back.

"Sweet, Captain!" and "Narly!" came the replies, respectively.

*　*　*

Leucadia gazed at Harlowe, who was enjoying the waves out on the point with Riverstone and Dodger. She watched him cut across a glassy face, twisting and turning like he was back at 42nd Street. Down the beach, Simon was giving Prigg and Monday a ride on Pigpo. Mowgi was in his place, perched on top of the big beast's head, looking like the conquering hero. Somewhere not far away in the new jungle, Molly and Rhud were lying in the shade, beating the noonday heat.

Leucadia pondered over another matter. "You've confirmed my calculations?"

"Millie has. You were right. The thermo-grym won't last," Ian replied.

"The amount of thermo-grym she needs was also confirmed?"

"More than Gazz and Erati combined."

Leaucadia faced Ian, already aware of the problem. "Yes. She'll need more thermo-grym than there is available."

"In the quadrant?" Ian wondered.

"It will only be enough to sustain her for a short time," Leucadia stated.

"Can we save her?" Ian asked worriedly.

"If we find her Makers."

Ian's eyes suddenly widened. "They died many eons ago."

"I know. We must find *Millawanda's* origin. That is the only way she will live."

"Where is there enough power to do that?"

Leucadia drew a wide circle in the sand. "This is our galaxy." Next, she pointed to the edge of the circle. "We are here." She then pointed to the center of the circle. "We need to go there."

"The galacatic core?" Ian asked, losing his breath.

"It's her origin. That's where the power she needs exists."

"How far?"

"Farther than we have ever gone before."

"Can she make it?"

"We'll need extra thermo-grym."

"Can she make it, Lu, even with the extra thermo-grym?"

Leaucadia stared at the galaxy in the sand. "Maybe. If we don't find her home or if it takes us too long to locate her origin, we'll need to find another beach with waves."

Ian stared at her in disbelief. "You're talking like we may never come back."

She watched Harlowe all the way to the end of his ride. "I'm sorry, Wiz, but if we fail, *Millawanda* will cease to exist."

"Harlowe will want to know," he said, sadly.

"He'll have to take Dodger home first."

Ian went rigid. "It's six hundred light years, round trip! We may need those miles later."

Leucadia looked at Ian, hard. "It's close in galactic distances, Ian."

"But—"

"You tell Harlowe that he has to take his brother on a one-way trip to the galactic core. What do you think he'll say? How would you tell Tinker?"

Ian tried to imagine what he would say. He could think of nothing. It was all bad news. He looked at Leucadia. "You'll tell him, then?"

She watched Harlowe and Dodger swimming out for another wave, happy and free to frolic together, splash about, and boast how awesome their last ride had been. Riverstone kicked out of his ride and joined them. Together the three headed outside, paddling hard, popping over the tops of waves like playful dolphins.

Leucadia stood. She wanted to be with Harlowe when he finished his next ride. "Yes, I'll tell him." She shielded her eyes with her hand as she watched the fun. "But not today, Ian. Let them be boys a little while longer."

Coming Fall, 2012

Book V

GAMADIN

CORE

Join Harlowe and the Gamadin crew in Book V, *Gamadin: CORE*, coming in the Fall of 2012. After surviving near death on the planet Gazz, *Millawanda* needs a tune-up big time or she will cease working altogether. The only choice left, according to Leucadia and Wiz's calculations, is to return Millie to her makers which, according to the ancient scrolls of Hitt, is a planet somewhere at the heart of the galaxy . . . the Galactic Core. It's a one-way trip if they don't find Millie's origin and the rarest blue crystal of all, which the old ones called "Aara," that *Millawanda* must have to survive. The journey is fraught with peril. Running on only a fraction of her power, Millie must chose her battles carefully. Wiz and the cats had been left behind while crossing the Cartooga-Thatt star desert, when they are attacked by ruthless killers known as "the Mysterians." Millie's course is not totally clear, either. The Gamadin crew must piece together a long forgotten route that no one has traveled for over 17,000 years! Who knows what they will find. . .